W9-COD-519

Crown of Destiny

BERTRICE SMALL

Crown of Destiny

HQN™

ISBN-13: 978-1-61664-434-5

CROWN OF DESTINY

This edition published by arrangement with Harlequin Books S.A.

® and TM are trademarks of the publisher. Trademarks indicated with ® are registered in the United States Patent and Trademark Office, the Canadian Trade Marks Office and in other countries.

Printed in U.S.A.

The World of Hetar now is done.
My faerie tale its course hath run.
Hetar at last will meet its fate.
The magic world hath closed the gate.
But Lara and Kaliq prevail.
For them the light will never fail.

Crown of Destiny

HE HAD KILLED HER WITH HIS BARE HANDS. ACTUALLY he had used only one hand. His long elegant fingers closing about her slim white throat, squeezing, squeezing, until the terror in her dark eyes had faded away to nothingness. She had failed him. He had forgiven her the first time. And the second. But when a third mating season frenzy had come upon him, and she failed yet again, there had been no other choice open to him. Her delicious darkness had attracted him, but she was nothing more than a fertile field in which to plant the seed that would become his son. And after the child was born he had intended killing her anyway.

Now at least he would not have to listen to her foolish ambitions. Or her harping at him to leave the Dark Lands and go out to conquer Hetar. She had never understood that for his conquest to succeed they must be patient, and rebuild his armies. They had time, and this time the darkness would overcome the light. But Ciarda had never accepted the fact that women were for nothing more than pleasures and babies. She wanted to be part of his eventual conquest, foolish creature! Her inability,

however, to give him his heir had been her downfall. He had
thought she was the one. She had believed she was.

And once her body had gone limp in his grasp he had personally carried the lifeless form from her bedchamber halfway
across the bridge leading to his House of Women. Then with
a final look at his half sister's remains he dropped them over the
balustrade of the span into the bottomless ravine. Returning to
his Throne Room, Kolgrim, the Twilight Lord, called Alfrigg,
his chancellor, to him.

"Ciarda is no more," he announced to the dwarf when
Alfrigg stood before him.

"She was not the one," Alfrigg said quietly. "Will you not
now look in the Book of Rule to see what it says to you."

Kolgrim nodded. "Open it," he said.

And going to the stand that held the Book of Rule, the chancellor opened it reverently. Then he stepped back to allow his
young master to see what was written.

Once he had quickly scanned them, Kolgrim beckoned
Alfrigg over to see the words. Very few could read the ancient
tongue so beautifully inscribed upon the pages. Twilight Lords
read them instinctively. Alfrigg had been taught the language
by the former Twilight Lord, Kolgrim's father, because he had
earned his master's trust when no one else had.

The Book of Rule was magical. It was constantly adding clean
pages upon which the words were written by an unseen hand. The
words recorded the reigns of the Twilight Lords past and present.
It offered advice and suggestions to its master. Today it said,

She who was good for naught but pleasures has at long
last been disposed of as was right and proper. Now the wait
begins for She who will produce the next Twilight Lord.
When it is time, the book will advise you on which daughter from the Hetarian House of Ahasferus is to be cho-

sen. Descended from Ulla, her dark womb will bloom for the descendant of Joruun, and your line will be never ending. Now cultivate patience, Kolgrim, son of Kol and Lara. Use this time well so you may be ready.

Alfrigg looked to his master, nodding. "This is good," he said. "Very good."

"Have I spawned any daughters with my women?" Kolgrim asked the dwarf.

"Several," his chancellor replied.

"Kill them, and kill the mothers, too. I want no weeping women seeking revenge or spitting curses at me. And if any are with child, kill them, too. I will use my magic to close the wombs of those remaining, and any new women I take. I will not have my son threatened by a female sibling as my brother and I were threatened. I shall have but one child, a son, by she who is fated to be my mate."

"Excellent, my lord, excellent," Alfrigg approved. "Your father would be so very proud of you."

"But not my mother." Kolgrim chuckled. "That beautiful, impossible creature of blinding light is the only one who can defeat me."

"She will not this time," Alfrigg said with surety.

"How can you be so certain?" Kolgrim demanded to know.

The dwarf shook his grizzled head. "Something deep down within me tells me so, my lord. It is not logical, and I cannot explain it. But you will win this time. I know it! Besides, you are your father's son. There is nothing of Lara in you."

Kolgrim smiled a rare soft smile. "I have her golden hair," he said. "I might have magicked it to be as dark as my father and brother. However it amuses me to keep it light. It reminds me of Lara."

"Why would you want to be reminded of your mother?" Alfrigg asked.

"Is it not wise, Alfrigg, to know your enemy before you attack that enemy?"

The dwarf shook his head in wonder. "There is no sentiment in you, my lord. You are wise beyond your years. Thank Krell your father was imprisoned, for if he had not been I do believe that you and he would have fought over the Dark Lands. That is where the forces of the light have erred in their judgment. They believed by imprisoning your father they stopped what is inevitable. They believed that you and your brother would fight one another for the crown of these lands thus weakening us further for centuries to come. But I hid you both in different places to keep you safe. You knew nothing of your heritage, my lord, until the Darkling Ciarda, your half sister, told you. I never meant for you and your sibling to know one another at all. Those who fostered you both did not know your lineage. I intended to choose one of you to reign when you reached maturity."

"But Ciarda spoiled all your plans with her ambition," Kolgrim said.

Alfrigg nodded. "Aye, she did, and the chaos she caused might have kept the Dark Lands leaderless for years, foolish creature she was."

"Who would you have chosen, Chancellor?" the young Twilight Lord asked candidly. His dark eyes danced with wickedness.

"*My lord!* What a question." Alfrigg chuckled. "Once I came to know you both, there was only one choice possible. You, Kolgrim, son of Kol! Your twin brother was a crude, ignorant bully. Power, wine, pleasures, were all he sought, or wanted. That is why the Darkling Ciarda sought to use him against you, against me. Now she is dead. Your brother is imprisoned with your father, and you, my lord, will triumph eventually."

"You are certain of this?" Kolgrim demanded. "For if you are wrong, Alfrigg, I will slay you without a moment's hesitation before I meet my own fate."

"My instinct for this is what keeps me alive, my lord," the dwarf said.

"I am not a patient creature," Kolgrim said.

"Then you will have to cultivate patience, my lord. Your reward will be worth it. I swear it!" Alfrigg insisted to his master. "You are he who is meant to triumph!"

OVER A HUNDRED YEARS HAD PAST SINCE LARA and Kaliq had triumphed over the dark forces that shared their world. She had reluctantly accepted the cruel fate visited upon magic folk who must watch the mortals they love grow old and die. Dillon, her eldest son, remained young and vital on Belmair, where he ruled as king. His wife, Cinnia, remained by his side, still youthful, too. They had produced a single son, and six daughters, two of whom had shown a talent for their parents' magical abilities.

Anoush, Lara's second born, Vartan's daughter, had lived to be ninety. She had never married, to Lara's sorrow, nor even taken any lovers. Among the Fiacre clan family she had been respected for her healing abilities, but feared because of her talent for prophecy. She had come to suppress that gift for, gentle creature that she was, Anoush did not like distressing others. And as the years had passed, and those who knew her had died that particular talent had been forgotten and she was just considered a healer. She was content to be thought of in that way. Eventually none but a few elderly among the clan families recalled that she was the daughter of Vartan the Great, who had married a faerie woman.

Vartan's exploits were believed nothing more than legend now. In the New Outlands of Terah the clan families had no need to fear for their survival. Separated by a range of high mountains from Terah proper they paid their yearly tribute to the Dominus while growing content with their lives as it was. There were no more great leaders among them. They came to believe their lives had always been as they were now and no longer believed that men like Vartan or the beautiful faerie woman he had wed even existed. They considered the tale of Lara's rescue of the clan families from Hetar's Outlands just a story. Nothing more.

The Devyn sang their songs of the past at the Gathering each Autumn as they had always done. But now the clan families gathered there smiled and nodded, considering most of what they heard fiction, or stories that, while they might have some truth in them, were not quite factual. They could not believe that their people had ever lived lives of such adventure, or known such magic. The names Rendor, Roan and Liam were no more than names to them. They thought of themselves as ordinary agrarian folk. Of late, however, the Taubyl Traders had begun coming over the waters of the Obscura from Hetar to offer the clan families fine goods and slaves for sale. They saw the New Outlands as a fresh new market for their wares, but they also brought with them the foibles of Hetar.

Over the previous twenty years a good-size town had sprung up before the castle of the Dominus. And at the head of each of the seven fiords a smaller town was now in existence. The trading ships from Hetar were sailing directly across the sea of Sagitta into those towns. They came for the fine fabrics, jewelry and crafts that the Terahn artisans created. They brought with them Hetarian vices. At first permission was requested for a single pleasure house in each of the small towns to service Hetarian seamen. But the curious Terahn males allowed to patronize those pleasure houses when there were no Hetarian ships in their own port decided they should have their own pleasure houses, too.

The then Dominus Amhar had requested seven pleasure mistresses from Hetar to come to Terah. They would create a single pleasure house for each of the fiord towns, manage them for three years, chose their own replacement from among their women and then return to Hetar. In return for this favor Amhar sent his youngest daughter, Mahault, named after his sister, as bride to Hetar's Lord High Ruler Palben. Hetar and Terah were bound closer than they had previously been. Lara sighed. How could this be when she had struggled so hard to keep Terah safe from the decadent civilization of Hetar?

Zagiri, her third child had survived her husband, Lord High Ruler Jonah, although Jonah had managed to live into his eighties. Frail of body but astute of mind, he had ruled with an iron hand, bringing Hetar back to its former prosperity. And Zagiri had never stopped loving him or supporting him in all he did. Though almost thirty years younger than Jonah, Zagiri had not lived long after her husband had died. It had always surprised Lara that her beautiful golden child, Magnus Hauk's daughter, had followed Jonah so quickly, so easily. But then Zagiri had never had an ounce of magic in her.

As for Marzina, Lara's youngest child, she had grown into an incredibly beautiful girl. And having spent two years with the Daughters of the Great Creator to learn self-discipline, Marzina had gone to her grandmother, Ilona, queen of the Forest Faeries, again, to learn how to properly use her magic. Then Kaliq had spent two years tutoring her. She was incredibly talented, being the child of two magical creatures, although Marzina had always believed that Magnus Hauk, her mother's second husband, was her father. And thanks to Ilona, no one had ever questioned that Taj's twin sister was so unlike him, being dark-haired while Taj was blond.

Marzina now spent a good deal of time in the forests of Hetar or the mountains of Terah for she and her mother did not always get along. Lara saw in her youngest child what others did not. She saw a ribbon of darkness that frightened her. The black blood of Kol, the former Twilight Lord who had sired her, could not be denied. It ran hot in Marzina's veins along with a streak of faerie cruelty she had inherited from her grandmother. When Marzina had attained sixteen mortal years she had even attempted to seduce Kaliq. He had put her off, but things were never again the same between mother and daughter. Marzina quickly knew she had overstepped herself, and she blamed Kaliq. But Lara knew her lover and life mate far better than Marzina did, and she was not certain she could ever forgive her daughter's lapse, although Kaliq did.

Lara sighed again. Her world was on the edge of something, but she did not know what, nor could she gain any preglimpse of it yet. Rising from the chair where she had been seated, Lara walked out into her gardens. She now lived in the southwest tower of the castle. Praise the Great Creator that it faced the fjord, and she didn't have to gaze down upon Dominum as her grandson had dictated the town be called. It was modeled on The City. But of course few Terahns had ever seen The City. The royal Terahn architect had relied on Ambassador Amren's description of Hetar's capitol. Lara had visited it once, but it was nothing like The City as she remembered it. Dominum was a monument to excess with large building fashioned from marble quarried in the Emerald Mountains.

Both the Ore and Jewel gnomes had objected to this incursion onto their lands. But they were now fewer in number than ever before and could only protest vocally. Lara had spoken to her grandson, the Dominus Amhar reminding him that the precious metals and jewels the gnomes mined were the raw materials Terah's artisans needed for their jewelry and metalwork. If the gnomes refused to go into their mines, Terah would have no work for export to Hetar. She convinced the Artisans and Metalworkers Guilds to support her endeavor. The Dominus Amhar was not pleased to be chastised by the beautiful woman who was his grandmother. But the guild chiefs were another matter entirely. Amhar sent to the gnomes apologizing for intruding upon their lands without first asking, and requesting their permission to quarry for another two months. With his messenger went a dozen barrels of fine wine and six casks of oysters packed in ice. The gnomes grudgingly agreed. The damage was already done to a portion of their mountains.

And so Dominum was raised up with three broad avenues running north to south and three broad avenues that crossed them running east to west. The buildings, however, were mostly empty for the only government was the Dominus and he ruled from his castle. The council formed by Magnus Hauk had been dissolved decades ago by Dominus Taj. How Lara had argued with her son over that, but as Taj had pointed out, there was no need for a council. It had been an experiment and nothing more.

Terahns were used to one form of rule. They wanted no changes made. Their Dominus was good enough for them. It was his duty to make the decisions, not the people. Lara realized that Taj's grandmother, and his three uncles whom she had appointed to be his council had done their job well while she had been off saving their worlds. Her son had been turned into a proper Terahn Dominus from the old school, and she hadn't seen it until it was far too late. And her grandson and great-grandson had followed Taj in maintaining the ancient traditions.

When her mother-in-law had lain dying, she had advised Taj on the sort of wife he should take. A well-brought-up Terahn girl who knew her place, which was in the background, and her duty, which was to give Taj children. And Taj, despite Lara's best efforts, had followed the advice given by Lady Persis. Lara could only silently despair. She considered if Magnus Hauk had listened to his mother Terah would never have been free of the curse of Usi, and it would have probably been conquered by Hetar or the Twilight Lord. But from the moment Magnus had died the Terahns had subtly worked their influence on Lara's son. Perhaps had she been with him more it would not have happened, but there were so many problems that needed to be solved in those days. And it was the magic inhabitants of the world of Hetar who fought to save it.

So Taj had grown up, and married a suitable Terahn wife. Vineeta was pretty enough to keep her son interested long enough to sire the required children. Amhar had been born ten months after the marriage. He was followed by his two sisters, Elvyne and Casperia. Amren, the younger son, had been the fourth, born eight years later, and was followed the next year by Taj's youngest daughter, Mauhault.

But while offering her mother-in-law outward respect, the young Domina Vineeta found it disquieting that her husband's mother looked as though she could be one of her own companions. The daughter of a wealthy widower, she had been chosen by Taj's aunts Anselma and Narda to be Taj's wife. Motherless, she looked to them for advice. As neither of Magnus

Hauk's two older sisters had liked Lara, their opinions drove Vineeta's attitude toward her mother-in-law. Taj's youngest aunt, the Lady Sirvat, Lara's best friend, had attempted to heal the growing breach, but the damage was done.

Anselma and Narda whispered a stream of ignorance and prejudice into Vineeta's small ear. Vineeta had believed it all. She kept her children from their grandmother, clutching them to her dramatically when Lara entered the nursery. The children sensed that something was wrong, and grew to fear the beautiful golden-haired woman who came to see them. Eventually they became so hysterical at the mere sight of Lara that after complaining to her son, Lara had stayed away.

"Children are like that, Mother," the Dominus Taj told her. "They have their shy moments even with their parents."

"I have birthed enough children to know what they are like," Lara had replied sharply. "Those two harpies who are your father's older sisters have taught Vineeta to fear me, and she in turn teaches my grandchildren. Amhar actually hissed at me and made a sign with his hands, which I imagine he has been told is something to ward off evil. I'm afraid I laughed at him, which sent him into a flood of tears and shrieking as he ran from me."

"It is a phase," Taj defended his oldest son.

"It is prejudice," Lara said quietly. "You have no magic in you, Taj, but you are still the son of a faerie woman. Be glad you are an ordinary mortal for if you were not you would face what I now face. It was never so in your father's time. Or perhaps it was, and your father protected me for he loved me. I am your mother, my lord Dominus, and that alone should command respect. But if your wife and aunts are allowed to treat me so shabbily, then your children will, too. Once you stood by my side against those who would mistreat me. You no longer do.

It saddens me, but I will always love you even if I no longer like you," Lara told her son, and by the shocked look upon his face she knew she had made her point.

But she could not, would not stand between Taj and Vineeta. She would not demand that he make a choice between his mother and his wife. That was a mortal way; it was not the faerie way. And so her grandchildren had become virtual strangers to Lara. But when Taj's younger son was to be sent to Hetar as Terah's ambassador, he came to Lara for more knowledge than anyone else could give him.

"Tell me about Hetar," he said.

"Why do you need to know?" Lara asked him.

"I am to represent Terah," Amren said proudly. "You are Hetarian. You know what I need to know."

"I am faerie," Lara told him. "I was born in the forests of Hetar, daughter of Ilona, who is Queen of the Forest Faeries, and a Hetarian named John Swiftsword. Swiftsword was your great-grandfather. His memory is much respected in Hetar, and especially among the Crusader Knights."

"What are they?" Amren inquired.

Lara explained.

"So in Hetar there is a distinct social strata, as there is here in Terah," he said.

"Even more so," Lara told the young man. "In Terah there is the Dominus, his family, and an underclass of merchants, farmers, artisans and the like. In Hetar there is the Lord High Ruler, the High Council made up of representatives from the provinces, as well as a Merchants Guild to which all merchants and shopkeepers belong. There is a Mercenary Guild, the order of the Crusader Knights, the Pleasure Mistresses Guild, the Guild of Pleasure Women. There are farmers and traders, healers and those who perform miscellaneous services."

"It sounds very complicated," Amren noted. "But you must teach me so I know it all, and do not embarrass my father."

"*Must?* How dare you speak to me so, Amren, grandson of Magnus Hauk. In Hetar how one appears is paramount, and good manners are all-important. If you are loud and rude, Hetar will believe that all who live in Terah are the same way. Your first impression will be the most important impression you make. You cannot allow Hetar to continue their foolish fantasy of being the only civilized kingdom in our world. Still I must consider if I will educate you in the ways of Hetar. Is it even possible to do so, considering how you have been raised?"

Amren was a very handsome young man. In many ways he reminded her of Magnus Hauk with his dark blond hair and his blue eyes. But his lips were thin, and his jaw weak. Yet he had a certain charm, Lara thought, and perhaps he could be taught to represent Terah with dignity and elegance. He smiled at Lara now. "Please teach me what I must know, Grandmother," he said.

Lara laughed aloud. "Never since any of you were born have I heard the word *Grandmother* directed toward me," she said. "Come back tomorrow in the second hour after midday. I will have decided by then if I will help you."

"Could you really turn me into a toad?" he asked her half-seriously.

Lara nodded slowly. "If I choose to," she told him.

"The old aunts say you are evil," Amren said.

"Narda and Anselma are a pair of dried-up old biddies. And they were the same in their youth. They know far more of evil than I do. Your aunt Sirvat was the only one among Magnus Hauk's family who befriended me, and she is now gone."

"My mother loves them," Amren said.

"I am glad for them that someone does," Lara remarked

tartly. "Now, go away, boy. When you return tomorrow we shall talk again."

"If I return," he replied.

Lara laughed again and waved him from her. Of course the next afternoon Amren came, and for the next two months he spent time with his grandmother each afternoon learning all about Hetar. When she thought he was near to being ready, she called in the royal tailor and personally oversaw the creation of his wardrobe. The royal tailor, being a clever man, smiled and nodded in agreement with the Domina Vineeta and the Ladies Narda and Anselma when they told him what to do in regard to Amren's clothing. Then, following Lara's careful instructions, the tailor created a magnificent wardrobe of silks, velvets and satins, trimmed in gold and bejeweled with semiprecious stones and crystals. Shoes and boots of the finest leather, some of the shoes burnished with gold or silver. There were capes and cloaks trimmed with fur, some lined in cloth of gold or silver. His sword and the several daggers among his ambassadorial possessions had handles and hilts studded with precious jewels.

When Dominus Taj saw all his mother had done for his younger son, he felt both pleased and sad. Briefly he recalled the childhood before his father had been killed, when she had loved him, and indulged him shamelessly. He remembered warm Autumn days when she would put him before her on her horse, Dasras, and gallop across the plains of Terah into the blue skies above, so he might see their world as others could not. When his father had died she had been his strength, gently but firmly guiding him, putting his interests, and those of Terah, first. Taj now knew by virtue of his years that only his magical faerie-woman mother could have been that bighearted. He realized now that she had saved Terah far more than once, and he was ashamed of his behavior. Looking at her, he said, "I have not the words."

"You do, and I hear them with my heart," Lara replied softly. Then she turned to look at Amren. "He is an intelligent young man, and will serve Terah well, my son."

Domina Vineeta sat nervously nearby with the Ladies Narda and Anselma, watching her husband and his mother.

"Which vessel is to conduct our Amren to Hetar?" Narda asked Vineeta.

"No vessel," was the reply. "He will be accompanied by a Shadow Prince."

Narda and Anselma both hissed their strong disapproval.

"It is practical, and swift," Vineeta dared to say. "And he has been given two personal faerie post creatures to carry his messages back and forth."

"And you allowed the faerie woman to corrupt your son, Vineeta?" Anselma said.

"I am astounded that after all these years of protecting your children from her you would do such a thing. Amren's wardrobe indicates that she has already begun to corrupt him. It is obvious she ensorcelled the tailor into doing her bidding, and not following our most careful instructions. Your younger son looks Hetarian now, not Terahn."

Lara had heard them. It had been years since she had spoken to either of her sisters-in-law, and she was surprised to find they still irritated her. "Amren is most handsome in his new garments. The richness of them gives him more value with the Hetarians with whom he must deal than if he had dressed himself in plain clothing. With Hetar it is always the first impression that is the lasting one. After all these years have you no concept of what Hetar is like?"

They had had no answer for her. Recalling it now, Lara remembered that day as if it were yesterday. Narda and Anselma were long gone of course. Magnus's youngest sister, the Lady Sirvat, Lara's dearest friend, was dead, too. And since her passing Lara had had no friend among the Terahns. Her mother had, some fifty years ago, sent her a serving woman, Cadi, as Lara's longtime serving woman, Mila, had grown old, too.

Cadi was the daughter of a casual encounter between a faerie man and the strong spirit that inhabited an Aspen tree in the domain of the Hetarian Forest Lords. She had been found cradled in the aboveground roots of the tree one May morning by her father, who had been summoned by his former lover. The Aspen told the faerie man that the child was his, and he must take it as she could not raise it. He agreed, bringing the infant to his queen and begging for her aid.

Though he was a faerie of the lower castes, Ilona agreed to raise his daughter, educate her and one day put her in service with Lara. The queen of the Forest Faeries knew her daughter would need one of their own kind by her side eventually. Mortals died off much too soon. And their bodies became infirm, as well. So Cadi had come to serve her mistress when she reached the age of fourteen.

She was a delicate and slender creature with faerie green eyes that she had inherited from her father. But it was her hair that was her most interesting feature. It appeared leaflike. In summer Cadi's head was a bright green that seemed to quiver and quake when the winds blew. In autumn her hair turned bright red and gold. By winter her head seemed nothing more than short brownish twigs that, once the spring came, began to sprout green buds that grew again into odd flat round pointed shapes that so resembled the leaves of the Aspen tree.

Ilona had trained the girl well. Sweet-natured, but intelligent, she served her mistress with loving kindness. And Lara was relieved to have a serving woman who understood her mistress and her magical ways, someone who could be trusted to keep Lara's secrets. Cadi had traveled with Lara to the New Outlands to bid the friend of her youth a final farewell. It had been a poignant and difficult moment for Lara.

Word had come via faerie post that Noss was in her final days. She would not live, her daughter Mildri wrote, to see this year's Gathering. No longer having any official duties in Terah, Lara had called to Cadi, newly come to her then, to join her. Going to the stables, they had mounted Lara's great horse, Dasras, and together they had traveled to the New Outlands.

Seeing Lara again, Noss, now silver-haired and wrinkled, had laughed knowingly. "This journey I will take without you, Lara," she said. "But Liam is waiting for me."

"Do not go just yet," Lara begged her friend. "We are only newly come."

"Who is the girl with the odd hair who accompanies you?" Noss wanted to know.

"Her name is Cadi, and she is my new serving woman," Lara answered.

"Come here, child." Noss beckoned to Cadi, and when the girl knelt next to the old woman Noss chuckled. Her hand reached up to ruffle the faerie girl's head. "She is magic," Noss said. "'Twas past time your mother sent you someone. How difficult it must be to have us all dying about you, dearest Lara. I remember your mother saying 'twas the curse of being a faerie who loved mortals." Noss lay back upon her pillows, and closed her eyes briefly. Then she sighed. "I know my time has come, Lara, and though I am now ancient and crippled I am still loath to leave this world. What lies beyond for us? Do you know?"

Lara shook her head. "I know no more than you, dearest

Noss. They say for those good mortals, and you are surely one of them, there is another, but different world of joy, where you will be united with those you love who have gone before you. And for those wicked mortals an entirely different place of punishment exists. 'Tis all I know."

"Will you live forever?" Noss asked.

"I don't know," Lara said. "My grandmother Maeve died after many hundreds of years in this world, but where she went, or if her essence disappeared entirely forever I do not know, Noss."

"Does Ethne?" Noss wondered, referring to Lara's spirit guardian, who lived in a crystal Lara wore about her neck.

"I never asked her," Lara replied. "And I am not certain I am ready to, or to know the answer she might give me." The crystal at the end of the chain about her neck glowed briefly, and Lara was certain that she heard Ethne's tinkling laughter.

Noss gasped, for she had heard the light laughter, too. "I heard her!" she said excitedly. "I heard Ethne laugh! I did!" Noss sat up.

That and the words I now speak to you, Noss of the Fiacre, are my parting gift to you. You have loved my mistress well for lo these many years. Your friendship has been a faithful and true friendship. When you are ready, go into the light unafraid, Noss of the Fiacre, for your mate is eagerly awaiting your arrival. Have no fear of the door now opening for you. Step bravely across it, knowing you have done well in this life, and you go forth carrying many faerie blessings with you.

And Noss felt just the lightest of kisses upon her cheek. Her faded brown eyes filled with tears. "Thank you, Ethne," she managed to say. Then she turned her head to look at Lara. "My time has come," she told her oldest and dearest friend with a sigh. "Will you remain by my side until I am gone, dearest Lara?" The old woman closed her eyes and lay back again upon her pillows.

"I will, dearest Noss," Lara responded, taking Noss's hand in hers. "I will not leave until you have." And the faerie woman sat by the side of the only mortal friend remaining to her as the day waned. Finally, as the sun sank away in a blaze of reds, oranges and golds edged in pale green, a deepening blue sky above it filled with small gilt-edged purple clouds, Noss of the Fiacre, widow of Liam, lord of the clan family, stepped bravely through the open door to leave this life for the next. And as she did, Lara heard the joyous cries of welcome for Noss from those beyond that door. She smiled, and looking to Noss's daughter, Mildri, said softly, "Your mother has left us."

Mildri wept quietly for some minutes, and then, her mother's daughter, she arose, saying to Lara, "You will remain for the Farewell Ceremony, of course."

And Lara had. She and Noss had been friends since they were mere girls. They had shared slavery together. Had been reunited by the Shadow Princes. Had traveled across the plains of the old Outlands together encountering adventures Lara would never forget. She had protected Noss, who had been three years younger than Lara. And when Lara's first husband's cousin had fallen in love with Noss, and Noss with him, it had been Lara who had arranged their marriage. And it had been a happy marriage, producing several sons and a daughter. Noss's destiny had been to be a wife, a mother, a Fiacre clanswoman. And while Lara's fate had been a far different one, their friendship had never wavered. But now Noss was gone.

Remembering that day so many years ago, Lara wept again briefly. How many mortals had she lost? And now she found herself in a world that did not remember who she was, or her many accomplishments that had helped the mortals inhabiting the world of Hetar to survive and stay within the light. But something was about to happen. Something was going to change. The uneasiness she felt did not bode well. She needed to go to the oasis of Zeroun to think. To escape all the mortal emotions that surrounded her and could divert her thoughts.

"Cadi!" she called to her servant.

"We are going to Zeroun," Cadi said as she came forward to join her mistress.

Lara laughed. "Is it that you read my thoughts now?" she said.

"Nay, I should not presume, my lady. But I know that when you get that certain look upon your face, we are going to Zeroun," Cadi answered with a smile.

"I would ride Dasras," Lara said. "But I will send you now to prepare my dwelling ahead of time." With a wave of her hand Lara opened the magical golden passage saying but one word, *"Zeroun!"* And without another word Cadi stepped into the tunnel and hurried down the shimmering passage. The tunnel closed. Taking a white silk cape lined in soft natural-colored wool from her wardrobe, Lara draped it about her and with another wave of her hand transported herself to the stable where Dasras was housed.

The great white stallion looked up, nodding a greeting to her as Lara magicked his blanket, his saddle and bridle on. "In a hurry, are we?" Dasras asked drily as the cinch magically tightened itself about his belly. "Where are we going?"

"Zeroun," Lara told the horse. "Your stall is dirty. Has it not been cleaned?"

"The grooms are careless now," Dasras said. "Ever since Jason's grandson died I have not had a personal servant." He stamped a hoof and shook his head. "My mane has not been combed recently," he said. "The time draws near, mistress, for us to leave this place. Terah is no longer a home to us."

"I know," Lara half whispered, and felt the tears springing to her eyes. Taking up a currycomb she ran it through the stallion's thick mane, tears now falling softly. "That is why we go to Zeroun. I must think on what to do."

"We should go to Shunnar," Dasras responded. "You know the prince has wanted you there. He was even willing to raise up a palace for you so you might maintain your cherished independence."

"Perhaps I should go to the Forest Kingdom of my mother," Lara suggested.

The big stallion snorted derisively. "Nonsense," he told her. "Besides I cannot run free in the forest with all those trees. Climb upon my back now, mistress, and let us be off to Zeroun. I am eager to take to the sky today."

Lara did as Dasras bid her, pointing at the stable doors, which flew open allowing them to exit. The stallion burst forth from the stables into the open courtyard, gaining a certain satisfaction as the stablemen and grooms scattered, making a path for him. They were afraid of him, he knew, feeding and watering him grudgingly because they were more afraid of Lara. But his stall was not cleaned as often as it once had been, nor was he curried and combed. His great wing extended, and Dasras took to the skies.

"Do you think he'll come back this time?" one of the stablemen asked another.

"Who knows with that wicked lot," his companion said. "I hope they're gone for good. But we had best clean the beast's stall while we have the opportunity."

Above them Dasras turned in the blue sky, setting his direction toward the Emerald Mountains.

IN HIS LIBRARY the Dominus Cadarn happened to gaze out the large window in his library and saw Dasras as he gained altitude. He squinted, then grabbed for his peering tube, setting it to his eye. As he guessed, Cadarn thought with a frown. The faerie woman who was his great-grandmother was upon the stallion's back leaning low over the beast's neck urging him onward. Where did she go when she disappeared from the castle? He was actually afraid to ask her, but each time she went he half hoped she would not return.

Cadarn turned away from the disquieting sight. He was expecting his uncle Amren, who had just returned from Hetar. There was a new trade agreement to be discussed. He had already seen the paperwork, and was not pleased with it. Hetar could no longer continue to take advantage of Terah as they had been doing. And it was going to be up to Amren to tell that to Hetar. The young Dominus considered it might be time to retire his uncle. Amren was elderly now. He had lived most of his life in Hetar. Of late Cadarn had begun to consider his uncle's loyalties lay more with Hetar than with Terah. The Dominus had placed a spy in his uncle's household. His spy believed that Terah's ambassador was taking large bribes from the Merchants Guild and possibly from the Coastal Kings. And his uncle's wife was a Hetarian woman from the important noble house of Ahasferus. Oddly, he could understand Amren's duplicity, but if he could gain confirmation of it, his uncle would be replaced. He would not embarrass Terah or their family by exposing Amren's sins, of course. As Dominus, he would simply say that his uncle was entitled to a comfortable retirement, and thank him publicly for his long and faithful service. But of course the difficulty would lie in finding another to serve who would not be corrupted too soon. He considered his own younger brother, Cadoc. Cadoc already had a wife, and his loyalties would not be torn, although eventually, Cadarn thought cynically, he could be bribed.

A knock sounded upon the library door.

"Come!" the Dominus barked, and the door opened to reveal Amren. "Ahh, uncle, come in, come in," Cadarn invited the older man. "We have a great deal to discuss today. I do not like the new trade agreement, and so it must be renegotiated." He smiled toothily at Amren's obvious distress even as he waved him to a chair. "We must do better for Terah, uncle. For Terah is our first priority, isn't it?"

Ambassador Amren smiled weakly. "Of course, of course!" he agreed.

Dominus Cadarn restrained his laughter. Aye! It was past time to replace the old fool. With or without further proof of his dishonesty, it was time for a change.

DASRAS FLEW OVER THE EMERALD MOUNTAINS, and as Lara looked down, she could see that the marble quarries gouged from the steep land were beginning to fill in again with new green growth. That was something to the good, she thought, and her spirits lifted. Clearing the mountains where the Jewel and Ore gnomes still worked their mines, they crossed the great plains of the New Outlands. Nothing had changed here. The clan families lived as they had always lived, tending their herds, their flocks and their fields. Each Autumn the clan families would all attend the Gathering, reuniting with one another briefly before returning to their own lands. There were a few more villages than before, but little else had changed. They lived by the same laws as ever.

On the edge of their lands an ocean stretched. It was called the Obscura. Until a hundred or more years ago, few had known of its existence. Now the Taubyl Traders crossed this sea to trade with the clan families. On the far side of the Obscura, the desert realm of the Shadow Princes lay. Only from the skies above were their palaces and great green valley visible. Beyond them lay Lara's destination, the oasis of Zeroun, with its graceful palms, beautiful waterfall and crystal clear pool. Dasras's delicate hooves touched down upon the warm golden sands, and he slowly came to a halt, his wings folding themselves away as he danced to a stop. Lara slid easily from his back.

"Send Cadi to lift the saddle from my back, mistress," Dasras said. "I see my shelter is already waiting for me." A striped awning was set near the water, a stall and feed boxes beneath it. The stall had fresh sweet hay within it. One of the boxes was filled with oats, the other with the mixture of green vegetables, carrots and apples that Dasras favored.

"I brought the combs and brushes," Lara told him, pulling them from her pocket. "I will ask her to groom you, as I saw you had not been attended to in many days before we departed the castle. I will speak with the head groom about that when we return."

"Then we are returning," Dasras said. He did not sound pleased.

"This time, aye. Something of import is about to happen, my old friend, and instinct tells me that I need to be in Terah when it does."

The stallion nodded his head, and then turning, trotted off to his shelter.

Cadi came forth from Lara's beautiful turquoise-blue silk tent, standing beneath the blue-and-coral-striped awning. "You did not dally, mistress," she said with a smile.

"Nay, I did not." She sighed. "I needed to come to Zeroun quickly." Turning so she might see the entire oasis, she cast a protective spell about it, making her refuge invisible to the human eye. Few ever came this way, but it was foolish to take chances. "I will swim before the prince comes," she told Cadi, shedding her cloak and her robe. Then, walking to the clear pool, she stepped into it, smiling as the cool water rose up about her. There was something cleansing about this particular pool. Swimming to the little waterfall, she let the flowing waters pour over her head. Swimming back into the pool itself, she was amused to find Kaliq was suddenly there.

He was grinning, obviously pleased with himself, and swam to her.

Lara laughed, filled with happiness. "You always know," she said.

"I always do," he agreed, and taking her into his arms, kissed her a long deep kiss.

"Ahh, Kaliq, my love," Lara said as she broke off their embrace, "the very sight of you makes me joyful, my lord." She brushed a lock of his dark hair from his forehead.

Catching the hand she used, he brought it to his lips, and kissed the palm softly. "If I make you so happy, Lara, my love, then come and live with me in Shunnar."

"Soon," she promised. "I will soon, Kaliq," Lara told him.

He was surprised by her answer, for she had always insisted her place was in Terah. "What has happened?" he asked, and taking her hand, led her from the water across the soft sand into the tent.

Cadi immediately came forward with soft white robes. She tossed the first one in Lara's direction, and it immediately enfolded itself about her beautiful mistress. She did the same with the garment she held for Kaliq. "There are refreshments on the table, mistress, master," she said to them. "Dasras needs my attention if you do not require my services any further." Then with a smile she hurried from their presence.

Lara flung herself among the multicolored pillows surrounding the low ebony table. Reaching for the decanter of frine she poured them each a goblet, handing her companion one. The brass bowl that always sat upon the table was filled with fresh fruits, and Cadi had added a small plate of tiny crisp honey cakes. Lara reached for one.

"What is the matter?" Kaliq repeated the question.

"I don't know," Lara told him. "But I am filled with a sudden awareness that something of great portent is about to happen. I have not felt like this at all in the last century. I suppose I have grown complacent like an ordinary mortal."

"Have you sought for an answer?" he asked her. He, too, had been afflicted the same way as she had. Something was changing, and not necessarily for the better.

Lara shook her golden head. "Nay, my thoughts have been too confused, Kaliq. I very much needed to come here to Zeroun to clear my head and contemplate what I must do. Even Ethne has been strangely silent, my lord." She touched the crystal star pendant that hung about her neck, and it glowed but briefly as her fingers caressed it.

"Your thoughts, I suspect, have been deliberately confounded, and until you realized it, you remained in Terah. Fortunately, you are a strong being, and came to understand that something was not right. Lara, you must not dwell among the mortals any longer. I say this not just for my sake, for our sake, but for yours," Kaliq said. "You must be clearheaded and strong for what is coming."

"What is coming?" she asked him.

He shook his dark head, and his blue eyes were concerned. "Even I cannot answer that, my love, but it is past time we began to look again more closely at Hetar's world. Their inability to learn from their mistakes has been discouraging. Both you and I have avoided looking too closely in recent decades because if these mortals cannot learn from their own errors, what is to become of them? But now I suspect the time is coming for us to involve ourselves with them once more."

"I seem to have no more influence with either the Terahns or the Hetarians," Lara told him regretfully. "As the years have passed my appearance has disconcerted them more and more, for they grow old, and I do not. They seem to have lost their belief in magical beings and our world. They have rewritten the history of Hetar to suit themselves. And the New Outlands is no better. Vartan and his faerie wife have been relegated to fiction. And once Noss and my daughter were gone, there was no one who remembered me among them. They think they have always lived in Terah, and as their way of life has changed little over the centuries, who is to nay-say them? It is as if everything we have done was for naught, Kaliq. I have made a grave error in remaining among the mortals. I should have disappeared years ago, appearing only when I was needed. Now I have become little more to them than an oddity. They attempt to ignore me as much as they can for my very presence disturbs them. But, Kaliq, my love, I could not leave while Magnus's son lived. That small part of me that is mortal would have felt it a betrayal."

"Yet Taj has been dead lo these four years," Kaliq said. "You had no real affinity with your grandson, Amren, and even less with your great-grandson, Dominus Cadarn. Yet you remain in Terah. You do not belong in Terah. You belong with me in Shunnar."

"In Shunnar I do not hear the voices on the wind that I need to hear to know that all is right with our world," Lara told him. She sipped at her goblet thoughtfully.

"And what have those voices told you of late?" he asked her.

"They are suddenly silent, Kaliq," Lara answered him. "That is why I have come to Zeroun. To regain my equilibrium, to sharpen my senses. They have grown dull with boredom, and complacent with the unchanging pattern of my life."

"Something is amiss in the magical worlds," Kaliq replied. "The winds blow in Shunnar as they have never blown before. There is a chill to them, and my fellow Shadow Princes grow restless of late, for none of us can find answers to all the questions that are whispering about us."

"It is the darkness," Lara said suddenly and with perfect clarity, and she shivered.

"Then certainly your son is preparing an assault against the light once more," Kaliq said, nodding.

Lara no longer denied her maternity where Kolgrim, the Twilight Lord, was concerned. Her mortal children had never known, of course, nor did Marzina. But the son she and Kaliq shared knew of his half brother. Lara was glad that Dillon ruled the kingdom of Belmair, that bright distant star that shone down on the world of Hetar.

She need only worry about her youngest child, her daughter Marzina.

Kolgrim's father had forced his seed upon Lara while she was visiting the Dream Plain. For this outrage he had been imprisoned for all eternity in a windowless dungeon deep within his own castle. No one knew he was there now except his successor—who had entrapped his twin brother with their father—Lara, Kaliq and several other members of the magical community. Lara had been pregnant at the time with Magnus Hauk's son.

When Lara birthed twins, a son and a daughter, her mother had remarked how like a faerie ancestress the infant girl looked. Marzina was pale of skin, with black hair and eyes that eventually became the color of violets, while her brother was a golden child like their father, and his older sister, Zagiri. Everyone had accepted the word of the Queen of the Forest Faeries, and nothing was ever thought of how different Marzina looked from all of her other siblings. And Lara had never told her daughter the truth of her birth.

"What wickedness is he now up to," Lara wondered aloud. "Has he not enough to do ruling his own turbulent kingdom? Certainly Ciarda gave him his son, and he is kept busy teaching the little devil all manner of wickedness."

"Ciarda failed. She was not the chosen bride," Kaliq said. "He killed her."

"*What?* Why did you not tell me, Kaliq?" Lara wanted to know.

"I did not consider it important," he replied.

"Oh, but it is! It is very important," Lara exclaimed. "Kolgrim is preparing to take his chosen bride, my love. That is the change I have felt. He has consulted the Book of Rule and learned where to find the girl. If we can find her first, prevent him from mating with her, there will be no new Twilight Lord. We can defeat the darkness for good! If I had known that Ciarda was dead, I should have thought of this sooner."

"We cannot defeat the darkness entirely," Kaliq said. "There must always be a balance between the light and the dark, Lara."

"*Why?*" she asked.

"Because there has always been a balance," he replied.

"That is not an answer, my lord. Would not a world without avarice and cruelty be good? A world whose inhabitants actually cared for each other rather than were jealous of one another, and sought to do harm to each other."

"Mortals have not yet reached that strata, nor have those of us in the magic kingdoms, though we are much further along," Kaliq said. "If there were no temptations, no reasons for striving or improvement, what would be the point of it all,

Lara? Even the magical kingdoms must have a balance of dark and light."

"Are you saying we shouldn't prevent Kolgrim from siring a son?" she asked him.

"Your son has kept the peace for more than a century, Lara, and yet do you see an improvement in either Hetar or Terah?" Kaliq queried cleverly. "Have the mortals inhabiting those kingdoms grown kinder or more thoughtful of each other?"

Lara shook her head in the negative. "I despair," she said.

He laughed, wrapping an arm about her. "You are too serious, my love," Kaliq told her, and then he pulled her close, his mouth taking hers in a soft and sensuous kiss. He smiled against her lips as his kiss drew the tension from her body, and with a sigh she relaxed against him. Pressing her back against the colorful pillows the Shadow Prince undid the row of tiny pearl buttons that held her caftan closed. His lips wandered down her slender pale throat to bury themselves in the valley between her breasts. His tongue plunged between the twin orbs, licking slowly as he inhaled the fragrance of freesia, which she now favored. He adored her. He always had.

Lara actually purred with delight as he began to make love to her. She had not been with him in several months, and she could not now remember why that was. Reaching out, she caressed his neck with her fingers, encouraging his rising passions. She had loved other men in her lifetime both physically and emotionally, but none was like the great Shadow Prince. Kaliq's love for her was pure, and burned with an unquenchable fire as did her love for him.

He lifted his head, and his clear bright blue eyes starred into her green ones. "I could be with you like this forever and a day," Kaliq told her.

Lara smiled. "I wish it also, but it seems we have mortals to look after, and the darkness is seeking to escape the bounds of Kol's kingdom."

"There is time," he told her, smiling back.

"No, there isn't," she said. Then adding, "Well, perhaps a little time. Cadi?"

"Is quite busy grooming Dasras, and afterward will fall asleep by the waterfall, my love," Kaliq murmured as his dark head bent to find the tempting nipple he wished to nuzzle and savor. He began to suckle upon her, and as he did Lara realized that they were both quite naked for he had divested them of their garments. She stretched herself to her full length beneath him. The tug of his lips on her nipple was translating itself into a ripple of excitement that spread down her torso, culminating in a tingling deep between her nether lips. His teeth nipped at the very sensitive tip of the nipple, and Lara shuddered with relish, anticipating more delights to come.

A hand kneaded her other breast strongly, pinching its nipple hard, and she squirmed slightly beneath him as the action sent a jolt of enjoyment through her. Her fingers insinuated themselves into the thick dark thatch of his black hair, digging into his scalp. His mouth found hers again, kissing her deeply, their tongues fencing with one another until she sucked hard on the fleshy organ. Pulling away, he began to trail a path of kisses down her torso while her fingers traced a delicate pattern across the warm flesh of his smooth back with gentle nails.

He shivered when her finger sensuously stroked the dimple that lay above the crease separating his buttocks. His tongue encircled her navel, dipping into it briefly. Then Kaliq's dark head moved lower, positioning itself between her milky-white thighs. His tongue ran slowly again and again along the shadowed slash between her plump nether lips. She hissed softly when it poked between the soft flesh, now glistening with new moisture, to find the tempting nucleus of her sex. Slowly he encircled it, then his tongue flicked it back and forth until she was squirming with her excitement. He held her hips in an iron grip until she was whimpering with her need for him.

Raising his head he knelt between her legs. Taking his massive love rod in his hand he ran up and down her wet slit, pushing it between the flesh to touch her already-quivering and swollen love bud. He pressed the tip of his cock against it hard, watching the fierce desire filling her beautiful face. *Beg!* he commanded her in the silent magic language. *You have kept me waiting for months, my faerie witch. I have a need to punish you for it, Lara, my love.*

You might have eased your lust on another, she told him.

Never! he swore to her. *From the moment I pledged myself to you, I have not given any part of myself to another. There is no pleasure without you, my darling faerie wife,* he declared passionately.

She was surprised. Nay, she was astounded by his use of the word *wife*. Aye, they had pledged themselves to each other a century ago, but Shadow Princes rarely gave the title of *wife* to a lover. "Oh, Kaliq!" she exclaimed aloud to him. "Yes! Yes! Love me, my dearest lord, my magical husband and mate! *Love me!*"

He withdrew his cock from her flesh replacing it with his lips, sucking hard on the swollen bud until she cried out. When she did, he mounted her and drove himself deep into the wet heat of her tight sheath. He groaned with delight, and her cries told him all he needed to know. He thrust deep and hard until Lara was screaming softly, the tears slipping down her face as he gave her the intense pleasure that only Kaliq could offer.

They clung to each other, their fierce need rising, rising with each wild thrust of his mighty cock. Neither of them, it seemed, could quite get enough of the other. But slowly, slowly, their passions came to a sharp peak. Lara cried out as she reached the culmination of her desire. The world erupted before her eyes. She shuddered so hard she wondered that she did not explode. And Kaliq cried her name aloud as his juices burst forth to flood her hidden garden. *"Lara! Lara, my love!"* Then the pleasures receded slowly, leaving them both weak, their skin damp with their exertions, but content beyond all measure.

They slept for an hour, and when they awakened, stretching lazily, the ebony table which they had somehow in their hungry lust managed not to tip over, filled itself with a beautiful meal. Upon it were icy-cold raw oysters, a juicy capon that sliced itself at their command, fresh green asparagus with a tart sauce, a warm round loaf of bread and a dish of butter. Kaliq gobbled most of the oysters, although Lara did manage to eat a few. They ate thin slices of capon. She teased him with the asparagus, dipping the vegetable in the piquant sauce, then licking the tip of the stem suggestively, sucking the stem slowly until, seeing his manhood begin to burgeon, Lara giggled wickedly. Then she fed him some asparagus, too, lapping the sauce when it drizzled from the corners of his mouth.

The food disappeared when they were finished, replaced with a bowl of strawberries and a pitcher of thick cream. Kaliq amused himself putting a berry upon each breast, and lining several down her torso. Next he poured the cream on her breasts, plucked each berry off with his teeth and licked up the cream, sucking her breasts. Then he drizzled the cream down the line of berries upon her torso, and one by one nibbled the strawberries off her quivering flesh, licking the cream away, as well.

When he had finished, Lara made him stand up. Then, kneeling before him she dipped his swelling cock into the pitcher, which had magically refilled itself. The cream was quite thick and clung to his dense length. Like a cat, Lara slowly, daintily, licked the manhood before her. Pushing his legs farther apart, she pushed the pitcher up between them to cover his jewels in the cream. Setting the pitcher aside, now she positioned her head so she might lick the cream from his sac.

When she had finished, sitting back upon her heels, he fell to his knees and turned her about so that she knelt before him, her buttocks raised and facing him. Kaliq took Lara's hips between his hands, guiding his throbbing cock into her female channel. Her submissive position allowed him to delve deep. He pumped her hard until she was yearning with her need, pleading with him to give her pleasures. As filled with lust as she herself was, he complied. Lara screamed with her delight, and he howled like a beast as this time they met with perfect timing upon passion's plain. Finally exhausted with their mutual satisfaction, they fell into a deep sleep amid the colorful pillows wrapped within each other's arms.

Lara woke to find Kaliq staring down at her. His blue eyes shone with such love she felt humbled by him. Outside the sky was light, but they instinctively knew it was not quite yet dawn. Without a word they arose and walked from the tent into the warm waters of the pool. The pale gray sky morphed slowly into a light blue, and then a richer blue. On the horizon, tendrils of color began to reach out. Pink, rose, peach and gold oozed out, staining the blue background. Kaliq and Lara watched as a ruby-red sun burst forth briefly, staining the rippling sand dunes of the desert bloodred.

"I have never seen the sand crimson before," Lara said softly to him.

"It is a recent, and not particularly welcome phenomenon," he replied. "We do not know what it means."

She was surprised. "But the Shadow Princes know everything," Lara said.

Kaliq laughed. "I misspoke, my love. We know it portends some evil, but we do not know what evil."

"The evil is my son Kolgrim," Lara answered him. "Of that I am certain, my lord. I must return to Terah and learn what my grandson Amren knows. If something is amiss, or of import within Hetar, Amren will know."

"Unless he heard of it before he departed The City, he will not," Kaliq said. "And we have learned from our own sources that Cadarn means to replace his uncle with his own brother, Cadoc."

"Why? Amren has served Terah well," Lara said.

"He has, but of late, at the urging of his Hetarian wife, he has begun accepting bribes in order to feather his own nest. Cadarn has not been particularly respectful of his aging uncle. He mistrusts him, and rightly so. But Amren is intelligent, for a mortal, and senses that something is amiss with the Dominus. He would remain in Hetar given the opportunity," Kaliq told her. "He has become friends over the years with Prince Nasim, and confides in him. Your grandson trusts few, but he trusts Nasim, who keeps nothing from his Shadow Prince brothers."

Lara nodded. "He was at the castle when I left. If he is still there I will speak with him, my lord. Though he was kept from me as a child, he has sought my advice over the years in dealing with Hetar in Terah's best interests."

Kaliq nodded. "He respects you, or so Nasim says. But he also fears you and your magic, my love. Nasim has allowed that fear to remain, believing it best that it did."

Lara chuckled. "Aye, he was right to do so, my lord." The sand beneath her feet was soft. Pushing off, she swam to the waterfall and let the cooler water flow over her. Joining her, Kaliq was unable to resist taking her into his arms and kissing her. Briefly she melted into his embrace, her lips welcoming him, but then she drew away and swam back into shallower water, walking from it up onto the beach and letting the morning sun dry her off.

Kaliq followed her. "You are going back," he said.

She nodded. "Aye, I am. But I promise you that when I have learned what I must, I will come to Shunnar. It will be my home as it should have been all these years past."

"Shall I raise you up a palace of your own, my love?" he asked her.

"You love me, my lord, and if you think you can live with me, I shall be content to have the bedchamber that is mine, and nothing more. But if you would prefer we live together but apart then do what you will," Lara told him. "I will bow to your will in this one matter."

"But no other." Kaliq chuckled. "I am satisfied to have you in your old chamber, Lara, my love," he told her. "And Cadi has her own quarters, as well."

"Take Dasras with you to Shunnar," Lara said. "Since his longtime groom died, he has been neglected by the Dominus's servants. I return to Terah to gain what knowledge I can, but then I am gone. There is nothing left for me there now. I was foolish not to realize it years ago. My mortal children are gone. Kemina outlived Arik, but now both of these religious houses have been corrupted. There is nothing for me at the Temple of the Daughters of the Great Creator. Oh, Kaliq!" Lara turned to look at him. "Why did I not realize sooner that my time in Terah was finished? I behaved like a mortal who cannot accept change, and clung to a past long gone."

"But you needed to let go by yourself, Lara," he said.

"But now I fear I may have given Kolgrim an advantage," she answered.

The Shadow Prince shook his dark head. "Nay, my love. Everything is as it should be. With this decision you have finally shed that last bit of your mortal skin. Once you make the magic world your home you will become entirely magic. But that is a decision that was yours alone to decide. I am pleased that you have finally made it."

They walked back to the pavilion where Cadi awaited them, smiling. "I have your breakfast, mistress, master," she said. Then she magicked white silk robes with necklines and cuffs trimmed in delicate gold threads and miniature transmutes, smiling when the little jewels glowed crystal clear with a faint golden cast. Transmutes, mined by the Jewel gnomes in the Emerald Mountains, were gemstones that changed color according to the wearer's mood. Their color showed Cadi that both her mistress and the Shadow Prince were happy.

Lara and Kaliq sat down again among the pillows to eat. Their meal consisted of creamy yogurt, apricots, melon and green grapes, warm new bread, butter and a sweet hot tea, pale purple in color, brewed from the tiny new leaves of the Umbra trees that grew at Shunnar. Only the Shadow Princes had access to this tea for the Umbra trees were rare. Their fruits made a purple dye used for painting the nipples. The sweet flesh was coveted, for it also possessed an aphrodisiac quality.

"I am returning to the castle today," Lara told Cadi. "When I have done what I must, I will leave Terah behind. We shall live in Shunnar. You may come with me or go with Prince Kaliq now. I am sending Dasras with my lord and will travel by magic."

"I'll come with you," Cadi said. "I don't even want to think what your mother would do to me if I left your side."

Lara didn't bother to argue the point. She was glad her serving woman would be with her. Terah was lonely enough now as it was. "We will not linger, Cadi. I promise." When she had finished her meal, Lara left the pavilion and went to where Dasras stood shaded by the palms beneath his own silk awning.

The great white stallion looked up at her from his bin of oats. "Good morning," he greeted her. "Less than a day, and you already look relaxed once again."

"The time has come for me to depart Terah for good," Lara began.

"All praise to the Great Creator!" Dasras said with a nod of his head.

Lara laughed. "But first I must return there to conclude one final bit of business. Then I shall collect Andraste and Verica and make Shunnar my home. I want you to go with the prince. Cadi and I shall travel by simple magic this day."

"As you will, mistress," Dasras responded. "As always, you have made a wise decision. There is, however, a boon I would ask of you."

"Whatever you desire," Lara told him.

"The great-grandson of my original groom, Jason, is called Leof. He is only a boy. He attempted to care for me when my former groom died. The older men were jealous and drove him away, yet none of them wanted to take responsibility for my care for they feared me because I am magic. Leof has managed to sneak into the stables now and again to bring me apples and carrots, but the last time the head groom caught him and beat him badly. I promised the boy that if I ever left Terah for good I would take him with me, mistress. Will you bring him with you when you return to Shunnar?"

"You have my word on it, Dasras. And he will take care of you. Og will teach him all he needs to know. His mortal kin are grown, and prefer the nomadic life of the desert dwellers. His wife is long dead. Leof will make a good companion for Og, as well. What of the boy's family? Do they need him?"

"He was the youngest of his generation. Jason was quite old when he was born, but he lived until the boy turned five. I remember him bringing Leof to the stables with him. Of course he was no longer caring for me, but he oversaw those who did. And he began to teach the boy. But once Jason was gone it all changed. The boy was driven away. His family is large. They will not miss him."

"Then I see no impediment to his coming. Has he learned, like all the others at the castle, to fear me?" Lara asked Dasras.

"Nay, his grandfather told him how kind you were, and I have reassured him the same," the stallion said.

"I'll have Cadi find him and bring him to me. The choice to come must be his, Dasras. You do understand that, don't you?" Lara said.

"I do, but he will come," Dasras responded in positive tones.

"Then I will leave you in Prince Kaliq's hands, my faithful friend," Lara said, patting the beast and giving his velvety nose a rub. She then hurried to find Cadi.

Her serving woman was clearing away the dishes. She looked up, smiling. "Are we ready?" she asked. Cadi waggled her fingers and the dirty dishes disappeared.

Lara nodded, then she called, "Kaliq, we are going now."

He was immediately at her side, his arm about her supple waist, drawing her close. "Do not linger long, my love," he said, brushing her lips softly with his own.

Reaching up, Lara caressed his strong jaw. "I won't," she promised.

Smiling into her faerie green eyes, the Shadow Prince released her.

With a wave of her hand Lara opened the Golden tunnel that magic folk often used to transport themselves from one place to another. Then she and Cadi hurried through into the swirl.

It closed behind them as they moved along, shutting entirely as they exited into the small windowless room that Lara had always used for her magic. Lara looked about her then turned to Cadi. "Pack this room up and send it to Shunnar. Then join me in my apartments," she instructed her serving woman.

As she departed the little chamber, she heard Cadi already murmuring the spells that would render the space empty as it had not been in over one hundred and twenty years. She realized that she felt no sadness in this at all and smiled a small smile. Encountering a guardsman on her way to her apartments, she asked him, "Is Prince Amren still in the castle?"

"He is, my lady."

"Tell him his grandmother would see him in her apartments," Lara told the man.

To his credit the man-at-arms bowed politely. "At once, my lady," he replied.

Lara gave him a smile and moved quickly by him, finally reaching her apartments. They were empty, for only Cadi served Lara now. The faerie woman looked about her. Everything was in order, neat and clean, but the sensation of love, of life, was no longer there. She shook her head. Aye. 'Twas past time she left Terah. The memories here had long ago faded, leaving in their place a melancholy. Why hadn't she noticed it until now?

Then she sensed an approach and turned quickly, even as the door to her apartments opened, and her grandson Prince Amren entered. "Come in, my lord," she invited him pleasantly. "Sit down. We must speak on matters that concern you." Going to a painted sideboard Lara poured a goblet of dark red wine for her grandson and another for herself. Handing it to him, she sat down opposite Amren.

"What matters?" he asked her, taking the goblet with a nod of thanks.

"The Dominus Cadarn plans to dismiss you, and replace you with his brother, Prince Cadoc," Lara said bluntly.

"How can you know this?" Amren demanded, surprised.

Lara raised a delicate dark eyebrow. "Really, my lord, how can you even ask such a question of me?" she replied. "Do you think because you have been raised to fear me and ignore what I am that my powers are lessened to any degree? When something concerns me, I make it my business to know what I must."

"You must be mistaken, Grandmother," he said, but he did not sound very sure. "I have served Terah well since my youth."

"Aye, Amren, you have. Both your father and your grandfather would be most proud of your devotion to your duty to Terah." He was still a handsome man, Lara thought. How old was he now? Seventy? Aye, seventy.

Her words pleased him well, she could see, but then he asked her, "And are you proud of me, Grandmother?"

Lara laughed. "I suppose I am in my own way, Amren," she told him.

"What do you want then of me?" he asked her candidly.

Lara laughed again. "How Hetarian you have become," she said, "but of course you are right. A favor for a favor, eh, Amren?"

And now he chuckled. "'Tis the Hetarian way," he agreed, "and the truth is I have spent most of my life in Hetar. My wife is Hetarian, and our children."

"Will you remain in Hetar when the Dominus dismisses you?" she wanted to know. "You have a home in The City, and one in the province of the Outlands. I doubt your wife would enjoy living in Terah."

"I had not considered being cashiered from my position," Amren said slowly. "You know how important one's position is in Hetar. An ex-ambassador has not the status of an ambassador, but Clarinda would indeed be unhappy here in Terah. And we should not have the enjoyment of our grandchildren."

"The Dominus does not want to hear anything I have to say," Lara told her grandson, "but I shall put the thought into his head to create a new position for you. You shall be Terah's Trade Commissioner. There will certainly be opportunity for you to extract some goodly bribes in such a position, Amren."

His face grew red, and she saw him preparing to vehemently protest her words.

Lara smiled a wicked smile. "Do not bother to deny it, grandson," she told him. "Have I not said that I learn what I choose to learn? Know what I wish to know? I am more than well versed in Hetar's foibles and vices for I was born there, and lived my early years in The City. Did you know that your great-grandfather Swiftsword gained the regalia he needed to compete in the tournament that earned him his place in the Crusader Knights by selling me into slavery?

"Gaius Prospero, who later ruled as Hetar's emperor, bought me. He planned a private auction with the owners of the Pleasure Houses for he expected to earn a great profit from me. But alas, I was considered too beautiful, and the Guilds feared I would cause more trouble than I was worth. So instead I was sent with a caravan of Taubyl Traders to be sold outside The City. It was from there I began to follow my destiny, and learned who and what I am, Amren. Oh yes, I know Hetar well. Very well."

"I did not know any of this," Amren said slowly. He was surprised by her revelations. "You did tell me of Swiftsword before I first went to Hetar. And his memory is still honored. He died in some battle, didn't he?"

"Aye, it was a great battle," Lara said. "I fought in it myself."

Amren's mouth fell open in shock. "But you are a woman," he gasped.

Lara smiled a brief smile. *Andraste! To my hand!* She called to her sword in the silent language. The sword leapt from its place over her tall stone hearth, and into her grasp. It was a beautiful weapon. Its broad blade a smooth polished steel. The gold hilt of the broadsword had a woman's head at its tip. The head possessed ruby eyes.

"I am Andraste, and I sing of victory," the sword said. "Greetings, grandson of the Great Magnus Hauk."

"It speaks!" Amren said. "What trickery is this?"

"Surely you knew my sword spoke, grandson," Lara said, amused.

"It was but a child's tale," he said slowly.

"Most children's tales such as this one come from fact, my lord," Lara told him. "Certainly you believe I am magic. Can you deny the evidence of your own eyes?"

Amren shook his head. "Nay, I cannot. Is it all truth, Grandmother?"

"I do not know all you have heard, but probably it is," Lara said. "But let me tell you about the Battle of The City before I reveal to you what I want. The Twilight Lord Kol, who ruled the Dark Lands in those days, brought together a great army made up mostly of Wolfyn, but other dark entities, as well. They sought to conquer Hetar and had already ravaged the Midlands. Now they stood before The City. Their battering rams could not even dent the great gates nor could their fire machines pierce the protection that the Shadow Princes had put about The City. Hetar's soldiers stood upon The City's walls and laughed the Wolfyn to scorn. And then, when we were ready, we opened the gates ourselves. As our army had marched forth to face the enemy's, a platform moved to fill the gate. It was from there that the Emperor Gaius Prospero and Hetar's dignitaries watched the ensuing battle. I personally killed the Wolfyn high commander of Kol's armies, Hrolleif. And when the other Wolfyn saw it they howled their grief, but then the battle resumed. The ground before The City was awash with blood. And when our mutual enemies had all been slain the skies opened up and a heavy rain poured down, cleansing the earth. When it had ceased, all evidence of the battle was gone, for both blood and bodies had disappeared. As many, if not more, Terahns were killed that day, and so Hetar was considered to owe us a great debt. Remember that, Amren. Terah helped to save Hetar once long ago. I will wager such a thing is not taught to the youth of Hetar, but then neither is that same history taught in Terah any longer.

"And once again over a hundred years ago, soon after your grandfather, Magnus Hauk, was killed in an accident, the magic world saved Hetar once more from its own folly when one of Kol's daughters attempted to subvert a mortal man to her own purposes, and bring both Hetar and Terah into the Darkness. Your father was but a child then, and I ruled as a shadow queen until he was old enough to take the reins of power himself. Both kingdoms have been involved with one another for decades.

"But now what is it I want from you, my lord? In return for what I have told you this day, I would have you be my eyes and ears to the court of the Lord High Ruler. The new position I will see you gain in order to keep your status in Hetar will still allow you entrée to that court. I would know all the gossip you hear even if you believe it to be inconsequential. I will make that decision, Amren."

"Will not the fact that the Lord High Ruler of Hetar is my blood kin allow me entry to the court no matter my position," Amren asked. Then he answered his own question. "Of course not. How foolish of me to think it. You ask little for what you give, Grandmother. Why is that?"

Lara laughed once more. "I am magic, Amren."

"I do not understand magic," he said candidly.

"Nay, I suppose you do not," she sighed. "Can you not believe the evidence of your own eyes, grandson?" Lara asked him. "My sword speaks for there is a powerful battle spirit within it. Verica, to me," she called aloud, and her staff flew to her outstretched hand. She turned it so her grandson might see the ancient bearded face carved within it. "Verica, please greet my grandson, Prince Amren of Terah."

"I know who he is," Verica said. "He is the only one among Dominus Taj's children to speak at any length with you, and then only because he needs your knowledge." Verica's sharp eyes glared at Amren. "Is that not so, Terahn prince?"

Amren nodded, a little less startled now than when Andraste had spoken in her deep, forbidding voice. Then he looked to Lara. "The sword speaks, the staff speaks, but this magic was in them. It is not yours."

"You must see to believe then." Lara chuckled. "Aral change!" And suddenly a small bright bird was flying about the chamber. "Do you believe now?"

Amren ignored the bird. "Where are you?" he demanded of her. He swatted lightly at the quick avian who dived at his head.

"Aral change!" He heard her voice again, and suddenly a large golden cat sat before him. Amren jumped back, genuinely terrified, his eyes wide as the cat raised a massive paw and placed it on his shoulder. He could not move and considered himself already dead. He struggled to speak but could push no words forth from his tight throat. Then in his fear he saw that the cat had green eyes. Faerie green eyes! He gasped with a mixture of both surprise and shock.

"Lara change," he heard his grandmother's voice again, and

she was suddenly before him, her hand still resting upon his shoulder. "Now do you believe, Amren?"

"You can shape-shift," he said, his voice returning. "I had heard of it."

"Come!" Lara said, taking his hand while with her other she opened a Golden tunnel for them and led him into it.

"Where are we going?" he asked her nervously. "What is this place?"

"It's a passageway to wherever we magic beings choose to go," she said as they exited the tunnel onto the oasis. "This is Zeroun. Within a day's ride are the palaces of the Shadow Princes, Amren. Have you ever been to the desert kingdom."

"Nay, just to The City, the Midlands and the New Outlands," he said slowly. "How can I be certain this isn't all a hoax you have designed?" Amren queried.

"Shall I return you home to The City, grandson? Are you ready to return?"

"You can't. I have yet to see the Dominus." Then a sly look came into his eye.

"But if I do not see him he cannot dismiss me, can he?"

"Of course he can," Lara said. "He will simply send word to you with your replacement, Amren. But if I return you to The City now, you will have time to prepare your wife, Clarinda, for the changes to come. Tell her only what you need tell her. Trust no one but the Shadow Princes who are there to aid you, and me. But do not attempt to betray me, Amren. I can, and I will turn your life into a horrific disorder if you do."

He nodded. "I understand, Grandmother. I will keep faith with you for you have always been more than fair with me despite my…" He hesitated.

"Your ignorance?" Lara suggested.

Amren chuckled. "Aye, my ignorance."

"Then you shall go now," Lara said.

"Wait! How will I contact you?" he asked her.

"Commit these words to memory, Amren. *Grandmother, Grandmother, heed my plea. Cease all else and come to me.* Say these words, and I will come to you."

"I will remember them," he said.

"Very well then. Farewell, my lord Amren," Lara said. Then she magicked him away with these words. *Amren, return to The City from whence you came. I'll call when you must come again.*

Terah's ambassador suddenly found himself standing in his privy chamber within his own house in The City's Golden District. He was astounded, and to be certain he was not dreaming he pinched himself hard. "Ouch!" he exclaimed. He was not dreaming! What an amazing thing had just happened to him. He had actually seen magic. He could no longer deny that it existed, but he would never admit such a thing aloud. He would be considered a fool, and his stature diminished if he did. But magic was real. Who knew what rewards it could bring him from his grandmother if he cooperated with her. And she asked little. Report on the gossip within the court and The City itself. And Ambassador Amren of Terah always heard the gossip first.

3

LARA RETURNED TO THE CASTLE OF THE DOMINUS.
Cadi was waiting for her.

"What do you want to take, mistress?" she asked.

Lara looked about her. "Just my personal possessions," she said.

"The portrait of Magnus Hauk?" Cadi inquired.

Lara shook her head. "Nay. I have his face painted within a small oval. I shall give the large portrait in my day room to Dominus Cadarn. Find me some guardsmen to carry it to him."

The serving woman sought out two strong young men-at-arms, bringing them to her mistress. "You will carry a large portrait of the Dominus Magnus Hauk to Dominus Cadarn," she told them.

Lara pointed at the big painting upon the wall. She motioned her hand up, and the picture in its ornate, carved gold wood frame rose off the wall. She beckoned the image forward with a single finger until it hung in the air directly in front of her. Then, turning her hand over, she signaled the painting down. "There," she said to the two openmouthed guards. "You may take it now to the Dominus with my compliments."

"Well, don't stand there slack-jawed," Cadi said. "Do as you are bid."

Almost bemused, the two men-at-arms picked up the portrait between them and removed it from Lara's apartments.

"You might have just placed it on the wall you wanted instead of letting those two clods struggle through the castle with it," Cadi said.

"You saw how those two young men reacted when I removed the picture from the wall. They have grown up believing there is no magic. Imagine if I had simply magicked the portrait onto another wall. It's unlikely anyone would have noticed it. I wanted those two to see my magic. Now I will seek out my great-grandson and set the painting on a wall of his choice so he may be forced to acknowledge magic," Lara told her servant.

Cadi laughed. "This generation of mortal Terahns has really rankled you, mistress, haven't they?"

Lara smiled ruefully. "Their refusal to believe in magic is very irritating," she admitted. "After Taj came of age and began to rule himself, I seemed to lose interest for a while in everything. I spent time with my mother, with Kaliq, at Zeroun, even back in The City for a brief time when Zagiri needed me. I became complacent, and when I did, Magnus's family managed to bring Terah back into its past. They did not shun me for they were too afraid of me. They simply included me as little as possible, and my travels made it all the more easy for them." She sighed. "I let the magic die here, and they are the worse for it. I cannot change what is past, but before I leave I shall give my great-grandson a good dose of magic so that even if he chooses to ignore magic in the future, he knows that it exists whether he acknowledges it or not." She looked about her apartments. "Nay, there is nothing to take but that which I have instructed you. Magick it all to Shunnar, Cadi. Then follow it. I shall come after I have spoken with the Dominus."

"Very good, mistress, but one thing before I go," Cadi said. She gestured with her hand and suddenly Lara was clothed all in gold and silver. "Mortals believe that first impressions are important, but I believe the last impression is equally important. The Dominus has not rendered you the respect that you deserve, my lady. Today he will." Lara walked across the chamber to the long glass mirror she possessed. She viewed her servant's handiwork. The gown was a mixture of both silver and gold, hammered as fine as the best watered silk. The bodice was sleeveless and bejeweled with multicolored small stones in red, blue, green, yellow, lavender, pink and some that were clear. Its V neckline allowed for Lara's gold chain with the crystal housing her guardian spirit, Ethne, to be well and fully displayed. Below her breasts a skirt of tiny, narrow pleats hung gracefully. A cape of pure gold was fastened to each of her shoulders by delicate gold epaulets studded with emeralds. It would trail behind her when she walked. Her long golden hair hung loose, held by a gold circlet with a large emerald directly in its center. Upon her feet were silver slippers.

Lara smiled, well pleased by what she saw. Her own image seemed to give her new strength. It had been many years since she had allowed herself to be the faerie woman she really was. She nodded her thanks to Cadi then said, "The mirror." With a final look about these rooms in which she had spent so many years, Lara walked through the doors into the corridor. It was unlikely she would ever return here.

She closed her eyes briefly so she might see where the Dominus was. She smiled. He was in his Throne Room at this moment, surrounded by his small court, his wife, the Domina Paulina by his side. Lara decided as she walked toward the Throne Room to make a simple entry. "Announce me," she said to the dignified, elderly majordomo at the door. "The Domina Lara."

The majordomo walked silently forward. He pounded the silver-knobbed staff of his office upon the floor of the chamber. "The Domina Lara, widow of Dominus Magnus Hauk, daughter of a queen, enters this chamber now," the majordomo said in stentorian tones. Then he murmured in a voice only she could hear, "I am the grandson of Ampyx, great lady. I remember what others choose not to recall." With a small courtly bow he stepped aside so Lara might enter the great chamber.

His words almost brought her to tears. "Faerie blessings on you, grandson of Ampyx," she murmured as she passed him by. Ampyx had been Taj's personal secretary. The crowded throne room parted to let Lara pass through. Her cape shimmered as it moved behind her. She saw the stares and heard the whispers as she moved by these Terahn mortals. Finally reaching the foot of the throne, she bowed low to her great-grandson. "Greetings, Dominus Cadarn, son of Amhar, grandson of Taj, great-grandson of Magnus Hauk," Lara said in her beautiful voice.

"Greetings, Great-grandmother," he replied. He was uncomfortable addressing her in this manner, for she was so young and so beautiful that she appeared to be no more than in her late twenties. His great-grandmother should be ancient and bent. Nay! She should be long dead.

"I have come to congratulate you, my lord Cadarn," she responded.

"Congratulate me?" Cadarn Hauk looked genuinely puzzled. "What have I done to deserve your praise, my lady?"

"Why your decision to send your younger brother, Cadoc, to Hetar as its new ambassador is brilliant, as is your determination to elevate your uncle, the lord prince Amren, to the new position of Lord High Trade Commissioner for Terah. Your cleverness has brought great status to Terah within Hetar, my lord. And so I hope you will accept my congratulations. I feel comfortable now at long last in my own decision to leave Terah." She smiled up at him.

He was astounded. Looking out over his court, he saw that they were all frozen in place. "What have you done?" he asked her nervously.

"Given us an opportunity to speak privately. No one will hear us, and when we are through none of them will even realize this small interlude happened," Lara told Cadarn Hauk quietly.

The Dominus sat down heavily upon his throne. "I told no one of my decision to send Cadoc to Hetar," he said. "How could you know?"

"You have never believed in me, my powers or my world, Cadarn. But that does not mean we, it, do not exist. We do. You are right to replace Amren. He has lived in Hetar for most of his life and is more Hetarian than Terahn. He has reached an age where he would garner some wealth, for wealth is all-important in Hetar. Nonetheless he has served you faithfully and honestly. That is why you will give him this new position. He maintains his status in Hetar, brings more stature to Terah and can do no harm as a trade emissary."

"And he can collect his bribes," Cadarn said with a small smile. Then the smile was gone. "I do not like being told what to do, my lady. I do not like a mere female making my decisions for me. But you are damnably clever. You have gained your own way while making it all appear as if I have done this. Very well, I agree."

"Thank you," Lara said softly.

"You say you are leaving Terah? Why? And where will you go?" the Dominus Cadarn asked her. "I know that you and I have no close relationship, but you are my blood. For the sake of Magnus Hauk I need to know you are safe and cared for, my lady." Turquoise-blue eyes, so like her late husband's, looked directly at her.

"I am going to Shunnar, the palace of the Shadow Prince Kaliq. I should have departed Terah years ago, but I could not seem to make myself go despite all the changes that I despised happening about me. Kaliq is my life mate, and I have always had a home at Shunnar. I will be more than safe in my own magical world, Cadarn. But I am touched that you would consider my welfare."

"I have heard you speak of this Shadow Prince before, my lady, but Shadow Princes are but legend. They do not exist now, indeed if they ever did," Cadarn said.

Lara shook her head in amazement. "Cadarn, look about you. Your court stands frozen. I have stopped time. You stand in the presence of magic, and yet you do not believe. Do your eyes not see, my most mortal descendant? How do you explain to yourself the great-grandmother who looks like a young woman? How do you justify any of this? Do you think you dream, Dominus of Terah?"

He had the grace to look briefly confused, but then he said, "I do not have to account for any of this, my lady. Perhaps I do dream. And if you truly mean to go, it will make it easier, for then there shall be no one whispering about your unseemly appearance, or the superstitious murmuring about something that is not like magic. No one here really knows you. The wife of Magnus Hauk is more legend than truth."

Lara shook her head. "You are a fool, Cadarn. Your great-grandfather was unique in that his mind was more open than any Terahn before him, and since him. While Magnus Hauk ruled, Terah existed in a golden age. But those who could not, would not, tolerate change have destroyed all he and I worked for, Cadarn. There is nothing left of our world, and I weep. Once Terah was a shining light. Now you have allowed Hetar to bring world-weariness and corruption into it. You believe in nothing. I pity you."

"Lady," he said, "I think you are ill. Return to your apartments, and I will send the physician to care for you."

Lara laughed. "Nay." She turned toward the court, and with a small motion of her hand, restored all as it had been. "Lords and ladies of Terah," she said to them, and curious, they looked at her. The men admired her beauty. The women her rich garb. "Your Dominus does not believe the witness of his own eyes. He claims there is no magic in your world, that there are no Shadow Princes. He is wrong. Now behold the truth! *Prince Kaliq, heed my call, and come to me from out yon wall!*"

The great Shadow Prince stepped forth from the chamber's wall and walked to where Lara stood. "Is it time, my love?" he asked her.

It is time. Let me depart first, and then you will make your exit. These fools will not believe in magic, and so I would leave them with something their own eyes cannot deny, my lord.

The men and women in the chamber were buzzing with astonishment. They stared at the tall dark-haired man with the bright blue eyes who was so richly, yet simply garbed. They had all seen him step from the wall. How had that happened? Was it some Hetarian conjurer's trick?

Lara turned again to look at her great-grandson. "I will leave you now, my lord Dominus," she told him. "I will not desert Terah, but you may not see me again, Cadarn Hauk. Explain away the magic you have viewed today. *But it does exist.*" She looked to Cadarn's wife. "Faerie blessings upon you, Domina Paulina," Lara said in a gentle and kind voice. "Now farewell!" There was a clap of thunder. A thick puff of lavender smoke rose about her. When it cleared, Lara was gone from the castle's Throne Room.

The Terahns gasped aloud collectively, looking about for her.

"Farewell, Dominus," Kaliq said. Then with a dramatic swirl of his cloak, he, too, was gone.

Cadarn Hauk called out to the servants in the chamber, "Open the windows at once! We have been poisoned by some bad air, and seen that which does not exist." He turned to his wife. "Are you all right, Paulina?" he inquired solicitously.

The Domina nodded silently. Her husband might deny what they had just seen, but she could not. Being a proper Terahn wife, she kept her thoughts to herself.

WATCHING WITH KALIQ from the ether, Lara heard the Domina's thoughts and smiled to herself. Then they reappeared in Shunnar together.

"Welcome home, my love," he said to her as he gathered her into his arms and kissed her tenderly. "My brothers have planned a banquet tonight to welcome you."

"Will it be like the first banquet I attended here," she teased him mischievously.

"If it would please you, aye," he said.

"I am world-weary, Kaliq. I need to regain that level of trust I once had," Lara told him. "Mortals are most tiresome, and yet I still have hope for them."

"You are younger than I, my love, but it is good you can still have faith," he said. "I promise not to be jealous tonight as long as you end the evening in my arms."

"I swear it!" Lara told him. "Now I must go and rest, Kaliq." She left him, walking across the enclosed garden that separated his apartments from hers. The day was warm, and the fragrance of flowers perfumed the air. Cadi was awaiting her.

"You look tired," the serving woman said.

"I am. I shall rest in the heat of the afternoon, then bathe.

The Shadow Princes have planned a banquet tonight to welcome me back. We shall all take pleasures after the meal. Come and join in with us. They are incredible lovers."

"I will," Cadi said. "I have never had a Shadow Prince for a lover. If their reputations are truth then it should be a most enjoyable time, mistress. I have put some iced berry frine by your bedside. What will you wear this evening?"

"Just a simple white silk gown," Lara said. She poured some frine into the cup next to the decanter and sipped at it. Shedding away her elegant garments and setting the cup aside, she lay down upon her bed, and immediately fell asleep. Awakening several hours later, Lara saw through the open colonnade that evening was falling. Stretching lazily, she called to Cadi, and her faerie serving woman was immediately by her side.

"The bath attendants are awaiting you, mistress," Cadi told her.

Lara stood up. She was entirely naked, but neither she nor Cadi were embarrassed by her unclothed state. "I have not slept so well since I was last in Shunnar," she remarked with a smile. "It is the deep silence I think." Then Lara walked to her private bathing room, greeting the familiar bath attendants. "It is good to be home," she said.

And to her own surprise she realized that Shunnar was indeed home to her.

The head bath woman came smiling forward. "It is about time you came home, my lady Lara," she scolded gently. "It is past time, for that matter." She pinned Lara's hair atop her head. Then leading her to a shell-like indentation in the marble floor, she picked up her soapy sponge and began to scrub. When Lara was thoroughly soaped she took up her strigil, which was a thin scraper, and scraped the soap and dirt away. "Did they not bathe you properly in Terah?" the head bath woman asked.

"There are no baths in Terah or Hetar like here in Shunnar," Lara said.

"How they can call themselves civilized I don't know," was the pithy reply as the head bath woman turned a gold faucet and sprayed her charge with warm water. Then she soaped Lara once more and plied her scraper again. This time however she seemed satisfied with her results and hummed beneath her breath as the rinse water sluiced down the beautiful woman's body. Then she led Lara to a warm scented bathing pool to relax.

Lara leaned back against the marble sides of the pool and closed her eyes. From long habit she lifted a hand from the water so that another bath woman might manicure her nails. When the first hand was done she lifted the second to be attended to, sighing with contentment. About her the warm scented water lapped at her breasts and shoulders. Rose petals floated on the slightly oily surface.

A serving woman came with a basin and unbound and gently washed and rinsed her hair as she luxuriated within the pool. When she finally stepped out of the water, she was patted dry with a slightly moistened cloth, then wrapped in a warm towel and led to a chair, where the nails on her feet were carefully pared as her hair was dried with a silken cloth and brushed. Then she was taken to a padded table where her body was massaged with sweet oils. Lara sighed contentedly as the strong fingers worked the flesh of her shoulders, her legs, her breasts and her belly. Lastly the massage woman attended to her mound, her nether lips and her sheath.

"You will be tight for each of your lovers this evening, my lady," she said, her fingers covered with a special cream as she pushed into Lara's sheath, massaging it. "You will give each who mounts you great pleasure. Prince Kaliq asked me to especially attend to you for this very reason."

Lara smiled to herself. Aye, tonight she would regain her trust, her equilibrium, her balance by joining with the Shadow Princes at the end of their banquet as she once had as a very young girl. The experience had left her strong. She wondered what the same intimacy would do tonight. Lara found she was eagerly looking forward to it. That Kaliq wanted her to relive this moment made her love him even more. He understood her as no other did. And he would sublimate his own jealousy to help her regain what she had lost by remaining too long in Terah. He was a truly incredible man.

She thanked the massage woman and, rising from the table, returned to her bedchamber where Cadi was waiting to help her dress. The gown she held out was just what Lara had wanted. White, gossamer sheer, with an iridescent sheen it seemed to float over her head, the delicate silk caressing her as it fell to her ankles. It was sleeveless, the bodice fitted to display her beautiful round breasts, its neckline draped gracefully to expose her collarbone. The skirt was neither fitted nor full, falling in an elegant line. She wore no jewelry but her gold chain with its crystal star, and a narrow circlet of gold with a single emerald in its center restrained her gilt-colored hair.

Lara waved away the gold bejeweled sandals Cadi held out to her. "Nay, I do not need them," she said. "We are ready."

"Thank you for inviting me," Cadi said. The pretty faerie was naked but for a dainty chain of gold that was fastened about her waist, and settled upon her full hips. She had painted the nipples of her breasts with Umbra dye, and tonight she allowed her small, delicate iridescent wings to display themselves. The wings had been a gift from Queen Ilona, for not all faeries were allowed to possess wings.

The two women walked across the garden to the main corridor, which was a colonnaded walkway. Lara could not resist looking over the baluster into the green valley below, where the herds of horses belonging to the Shadow Princes ran free. They were as magnificent as ever, and she immediately picked out Dasras surrounded by a group of admiring young mares. Cadi saw him too, and when their eyes met the two giggled.

Kaliq came to greet his beautiful life mate and her companion. "How lovely you both look," he said, taking Lara's hand in his, his bright blue eyes devouring her. "My brothers will be honored by your company this evening." He smiled at Cadi. "I am pleased you have consented to join us." His brothers would enjoy sharing pleasures with the lovely faerie, but he would not lay a hand upon her for she was Lara's companion.

"Thank you, my lord," Cadi replied, and then as they entered the great banquet hall she was surrounded by several Shadow Princes eager to have her for a supper companion. She would not lack for lovers this evening.

The banquet hall of Kaliq's palace was filled tonight with his handsome brothers. Some of the Shadow Princes had beautiful companions sharing their broad dining couches with them and Lara recognized many of them. There was her sword master, Lothair. He nodded to her, and from the twinkle in his blue eyes she knew he would take pleasures with her later. She saw Princes Eskil, Nasim, Coilen and Baram among others. She acknowledged them with a polite tip of her head as Kaliq led her to the dais where they would preside over their guests.

As soon as they were seated, all the Shadow Princes arose, saying with a single, strong voice, "Welcome home, Lara! May you dwell among us forever!"

Lara stood as they returned to their seats. "I thank you, my lords," she replied. And then with a wave of her hand caused a shower of fragrant rose petals and small pearls to fall upon the banqueting chamber. The female companions of the princes squealed with excitement, reaching for the jewels, and not a one touched the floor. Lara sat down and picked up her goblet, sipping delicately from it.

"That was nicely done," Kaliq said, dropping a kiss on her shoulder.

She turned and kissed his mouth, a sweet, slow kiss. "I am happier tonight than I have been in years, my lord. I did not realize how miserable I had been until I woke up a little while ago, and realized I was here, not in the castle of the Dominus. That this was my home. At this moment I never want to see Hetar or Terah again, but I know that is unrealistic, Kaliq. Still, for now I am content to remain here in Shunnar undisturbed."

The Shadow Prince caressed her face tenderly. "Aye, this is your home, my love, but we both know that your destiny is not to remain forever. Understand this, however, that I will be with you now wherever you go, Lara, my beautiful life mate. We will not be separated again."

She caught the hand touching her face, and kissed it. "Would you prefer I withheld myself tonight, my lord?" Lara asked him, her faerie green eyes searching his handsome face for the truth. She loved him, and would do what pleased him this one time. She smiled a soft smile at him.

"Aye, I would prefer it, but you cannot. You need the magic my brothers can give you through their passion. But most important you must not sublimate your faerie nature, especially now for soon you will need it," Kaliq said.

She wondered what he meant, but before she might question him the servants appeared bearing cold raw oysters, which both the men and the women consumed in great quantity. They were followed by poached fish, and shellfish brought each day from the seaside of the Coastal Kings via magical transport. Next, platters of roasted meats and poultry were brought along with large round plates containing heaps of slender green stalks of asparagus, bowls of red, green and purple lettuces, fresh bread and several different cheeses.

Everyone ate with excellent appetites. There was much laughter and witty conversation. When the main meal had been cleared away, the servants brought baskets containing green and purple grapes, slices of sweet gold, green and orange melons, plump apricots, dishes of red and black berries along with platters of honey cakes. The cups were now filled with a dark, sweet, potent wine.

As the couples fed each other the delectable sweets, lithe dancing girls in diaphanous silks ran into the banquet hall. The musicians seated in a corner of the hall began to play upon their drums, pipes, reeds and cymbals. There was an open space before the dais where Kaliq and Lara sat. It was surrounded by the other dining couches and small low tables. The dancers performed before them in that space for all to see. When they were gone the passion would begin. Looking about her, Lara could see that most of the guests were now naked or in a state of near undress

Cadi reclined upon a couch in the arms of a Shadow Prince who was now caressing her large breasts. Other Shadow Princes sat on the floor about the couch. One was already stroking Cadi's slender leg, his fingers inching closer and closer to her plump mons. Another was sucking upon her fingers, and the faerie's eyes were closed as she began to allow herself to experience pleasures with her lovers.

Lara smiled up at Kaliq. "I think Cadi will please those who seek to please her," she said. Then she gave a small shrug, and her garment disappeared. Reaching out, she touched his chest with a single finger, and the Shadow Prince's clothing was gone. "You first, and you last," she told him softly as Prince Lothair joined them, leaning forward to kiss her lips.

"You are the most beautiful faerie woman I have ever known," he said to her. "I envy my brother Kaliq, but then he loves you. I merely lust after you each time I see you." He smiled a most engaging smile at her.

Lara laughed. "As candid as ever, Lothair," she replied. "Be patient, and we shall take pleasures together, but I am in no great hurry, my lord. The evening is just beginning. We have much time ahead of us, do we not?" She smiled back at him.

"Ahh, cruel faerie, you are of a mind to tease me then," he said.

"Is not pleasure denied all the more sweeter for the wait?" Lara asked.

Lothair laughed. "You have learned well," he said. "Very well, then I shall go and taste a bit of that lovely morsel you brought for us this evening." He arose and joined those Shadow Princes surrounding Cadi.

Lara and Kaliq watched, amused, as the younger princes gave way to the sword master. He slid himself in next to Cadi upon the couch, gathered her into his embrace and kissed her a long, deep kiss. Cadi's arms came up to slip around Lothair's neck. She instinctively recognized a great lover, and had secretly had her eye upon him ever since they had entered the banquet hall.

"Why the little faerie vixen," Kaliq chuckled, picking up on Cadi's thoughts.

"Do not!" Lara scolded him. "Let them enjoy each other, and allow Lothair to think it is he who conquers her."

He ran a finger down her slender arm. "Do I conquer you, my love?" he asked.

"From the first moment you kissed me, Kaliq," Lara answered him honestly. "Mayhap even before. How I hated it when you sent me from Shunnar. But in hindsight I understand. There is so much more than just you and me."

"Aye, there is, but now is not the time to discuss it," Kaliq told her.

"When?" she queried him.

"In the days to come when you are rested, and your strength has returned," he promised her. "Now, however, I want to kiss you." And his dark head dipped to find her eager mouth. The touch of her petal-soft lips on his caused his head to spin with delight. They had been lovers on and off for well over a century, and yet he had never grown bored with his faerie woman. Each time was like the first time he had kissed her as they stood in the wide marble corridor of his palace, and she had told him of herself, and of Og, the giant who accompanied her. He had fallen in love with her at that moment. And he had never stopped loving her. Now he must divert his jealousy in order that she receive the diverse passions she needed from his brothers. His kiss deepened.

She felt him blocking his thoughts from her. At any other time it would have disturbed Lara, but she suspected she knew why he did it. He was one of the most powerful beings in the Cosmos, and yet he was capable of feeling invidiousness. Unlike mortals, however, the great Shadow Prince could put such emotions aside, and not act on his feelings. *Make love to me, Kaliq,* she said in the silent language.

Did you not tell Lothair that passion denied was sweeter? he teased her.

For Lothair perhaps, my love, but not for you and me, Lara replied. *Is it possible for either of us ever to get enough of the other?*

"No," he murmured in her ear, and licked it. Then he forged a trail of kisses down her jaw, her neck and across her shoulder.

Lara drew his head to her breasts.

He groaned as he buried his face between the round twin

orbs. He licked at her nipples one by one. Then Kaliq suckled upon them while a single finger ran up and down her slit until she was squirming. The touch of her hand communicated her needs to him.

Tell me your desires, my beautiful faerie lover, Kaliq said to her.

I need your tongue to love me, Lara told him.

The warm fleshy organ began to lick her belly with long, slow strokes. She sighed. He moved lower and lower until his tongue replaced the finger that had been teasing at her slit. He moved himself between her open legs, and opened her to his view. The dainty nub of flesh called her jewel was simply perfect. He was almost mesmerized as he stared at it so neatly placed between the deep pink walls of flesh now becoming wet and shiny with her need.

And then Lara felt another Shadow Prince straddling the couch behind her, and reaching around to cup her breasts in his hands. Leaning her head back, she saw Prince Nasim's smiling face, and she smiled back. His hands skillfully played with her nipples sending shivers of pure lust through her. Kaliq's mouth was on her jewel, licking gently at first, then sucking and sucking on her until between the two men her desire was beginning to blaze high.

Kaliq pulled himself up, his lover's rod visible to her half-closed eyes. He was hard, and the lust on his face was potent. Two other princes were suddenly there, each taking one of her legs to draw them back over her shoulders so Kaliq might delve deeply. Memories of the first time they had shared pleasures at a banquet assailed her as he drove himself deep into her sheath.

"Oh yes!" Lara breathed aloud. *"Yes!"* she encouraged him.

He rode her long, and hard, and when he had filled her with his juices, Kaliq withdrew, seating himself on the carpet next to the head of the couch. Lothair quickly took his place, filling Lara full of himself, groaning as the muscles within her sheath tightened about him, drawing his juices from him as they both screamed with their satisfaction at the encounter.

I want more! Lara said as, kissing her, he reluctantly arose.

Lothair laughed. *And we shall give you all you desire this night, Lara. Let me but rest and I will return to give you more of myself.*

She was awash in the most exquisite sensations. There was not a part of her that was not indulged by the passions of the Shadow Princes. They sucked on her fingers, her toes, her nipples and her throbbing jewel. They tenderly filled every open orifice on her body taking her singly, two at a time, and at one point she accepted three manhoods at once. And all three of the Princes released their juices in a single moment, causing Lara to swoon.

The rest of the evening was as these evenings always were, a dream of intense pleasures and sweet tenderness that left Lara gasping with her delight. The Shadow Princes generously gave her their passions, and those passions renewed her spirit, making her stronger than she had been in decades. Finally Kaliq was in her arms again, and it was just the two of them upon the wide dining couch. She caressed his face and kissed him gently. *I love you,* she told him simply as he entered her body joining them once again. *Only you, my lord Kaliq. Only you!* She saw the tears he quickly forced back just briefly fill his bright blue eyes. *Only you,* she repeated, and then let him sweep her away.

When the sun rose in the morning, the naked couples awoke slowly, pair by pair, and then arose to go off to their own private places. Lara and Kaliq sought the baths, and then he joined her in her bed to sleep. There was no sign of Cadi until they awoke in the early afternoon, and she came to say a meal was set up in the gardens for them.

"Did you enjoy the banquet?" Kaliq asked the faerie as he stepped naked from the bed. He donned the white cotton caftan with the deep blue embroidery that she handed him. "We do not have such affairs often, but your mistress needed to regain certain powers that only my brothers and I can give her."

"It was wonderful, my lord! I thank you for allowing me to come. Queen Ilona has spoken many times of your banquets. I never thought to experience one," Cadi said.

"I think you have intrigued my brother Lothair," Kaliq said mischievously.

"The sword master? I cannot deny he wields his personal weapon well," Cadi replied pithily. "I hope we will meet again."

Kaliq laughed. "I suspect your wish will be granted, Cadi," he told her. Then, turning back to the bed, he caught Lara's shoulder shaking her gently. "Wake up, sleepyhead. It's time to eat. Even a faerie woman needs more than one strength."

Lara rolled over looking up at him. "Feed me then," she responded.

"If I do you will never get up, and we need to talk, Lara, my love," he told her.

The green eyes grew wary. *"Today?"* she said.

He nodded.

"Do I not get a few days of respite, my lord?" Lara demanded to know.

"After we talk," he promised.

With a sigh Lara arose, taking the white cotton caftan with the blue embroidery from Cadi, donning it and then sitting down upon a small bench so Cadi could brush out her long tangled hair. When Cadi had braided the golden hair into a single plait, Lara joined her prince in the garden where a meal of roasted capon, saffron rice, mixed lettuces, yogurt, fruit, bread and cheese was awaiting them. Cadi filled their carved silver cups with sweet apricot-flavored frine and then disappeared from their sight.

"Eat first," Kaliq said to Lara. He took up the capon and tore it in half, taking one of the two large pieces for himself and slicing from the other what he knew Lara enjoyed. Lara filled their plates with the rest of the foods, and they ate quietly at first. Finally she could not wait any longer to learn what he had to say to her. Sensing it, he said, "Your son and his evil have begun to stir once again, my love."

Lara sighed. "Has Kolgrim rebuilt his armies then? Is he planning to reach for Hetar and Terah once again?"

"Rebuilding an army proved an impossible task," Kaliq said.

"Why? Certainly there are enough dark creatures in our world eager enough to profit from Kolgrim's greed for power and lands that they would pledge themselves to him," Lara replied. "Of course there is always the possibility of being killed in one of those little ventures the Twilight Lords so enjoy."

"The Dark Lands cannot provide Kolgrim with the armies he needs to overcome Hetar and Terah. They do not have enough women to breed soldiers upon. But when those two lands he covets combine their forces with the magic world, he has no chance at all of succeeding. Still there have been whispers of a more disturbing nature that indicate Kolgrim is planning something nefarious, Lara."

"Can he not raise up warriors full grown to battle us?" she wanted to know.

"He has tried over the last century to do just that. But he has failed, and now he considers something different. But what we do not know. That is why it was so important for you to leave Terah and return to Shunnar. Whatever it is Kolgrim seeks to do will be dangerous, for although Alfrigg has kept him in check until now, the old dwarf is probably nearing his end.

Without him Kolgrim's reckless nature will erupt, I fear," Kaliq told Lara.

"Has Alfrigg not trained a replacement for himself? He very much wanted to escape the burdens he carried for Kol these last few centuries. I pushed back the years from his aged body so he might guide Kolgrim long enough to find a successor and teach him what he needed to know. It was my reward to him for his aid," Lara said, concerned.

"Kolgrim will not let him go, nor will he even hear of someone taking Alfrigg's place as his chancellor," Kaliq replied. "Prince Coilen has been visiting the Dark Lands, watching and listening. If Alfrigg dies we will have serious difficulties with Kolgrim."

"Perhaps if I pay this dark son of mine a visit I can learn what he is thinking," Lara said slowly. "He is untrustworthy, of course, but he has always liked me."

Kaliq chuckled. "I know," he said. "He is quite fascinated by you, which fascinates me. Until a century ago he did not even know who you were, but from the first moment he laid eyes upon you he felt a bond with you."

Lara sniffed derisively. "He seeks to beat me at the game we of the magic world seem to play with each other and the mortals. If he ever had a triumph over me, he would no longer be interested in me, Kaliq. He is amusing, and clever, but his heart, if indeed he has a heart, is icy cold. He is like his father. He is filled with greed for everything, and with lust for everything. But if you sense that he is about to reach out again, we must learn to what purpose," Lara remarked. "I must go into the darkness to learn what I can."

Kaliq knew better than to forbid her, so he said, "If you go then I go with you."

"Are you that fearful for my safety, my lord?" He surprised her.

"If Kolgrim is attempting some mischief, my love, then

having you in his power would give him an advantage and but speed his wickedness," Kaliq said. "And he is capable of holding you captive, Lara. He will never harm you for you gave him life, and he holds fast to the family law of the Twilight Lords, which forbids the shedding of familial blood. But keeping a golden bird in a golden cage does it no harm. Remember how he tricked his twin brother, Kolbein, imprisoning him with Kol."

"I can't forget it," Lara admitted. "I am ashamed to admit that I thought it extremely clever of him."

Kaliq laughed. "It was," he said. "But it is evidence of how dangerous Kolgrim really is. If we cannot stop him, he will envelop the world of Hetar in a deep and terrible darkness from which they may never escape."

"Then we have to stop him, Kaliq," Lara said. "However we must first learn what wickedness he plans before we may take measures to prevent it."

"Let us first see what Coilen can learn," Kaliq suggested.

"Very well," Lara agreed. "But if he can learn no more than he already has, I must go into the Dark Lands myself to see what I can see."

They decided they would give the Shadow Prince known as Coilen a moonspan in which to ferret out any information that he could. But when the month had passed Coilen came to tell Kaliq and Lara that he could learn nothing. Whatever Kolgrim was planning he kept it to himself. Possibly the old chancellor, Alfrigg, knew, but he was not a man to gossip.

"There is nothing of any interest to report," Coilen said, "unless you are interested in hearing that it is said Kolgrim may take a mate. But that rumor comes up now and again. It means naught."

A chill ran down Lara's spine. "No!" she said sharply. "How long has it been since that rumor was last heard and bandied about?"

Prince Coilen thought for several long moments. "I don't think I have heard it," he said slowly, "in decades. It was spoken in the mating season after he disposed of Ciarda, and possibly a season or two afterward. But nay! I have not heard it in decades, Lara. Can it mean something?"

"Possibly," Lara answered him. "Has anyone new, anyone dark, been brought to the Twilight Lord's House of Women lately?"

Coilen shook his head. "Actually he has but few women. Many Darklanders hid their daughters after what happened in the wake of Ciarda's death."

"What exactly did happen?" Lara wanted to know.

"Kolgrim had his daughters, their mothers and any of his many women who might be with child, or were known to be with child, murdered. Then he put a spell on the remaining women closing their wombs to his seed and keeping them young. He slakes his lust with those few, but there have been no more children. It is reported he said he wanted no siblings challenging his son's right to inheritance one day."

Lara smiled grimly. "Ciarda's legacy," she said. "Had his half sister not attempted to usurp her brothers' place this would not have happened at all. Kolgrim is truly Kol's rightful heir that he could have been so heartless as to slaughter all those innocents to protect a son not even conceived by a bride not even known."

"That is the past," Kaliq said. "We must consider the present and the future."

"We will need to know if Kolgrim is truly planning a marriage for himself. Has the Book of Rule directed him to find a bride? Or has it told him the bride to seek? These are the questions we must answer before we can proceed, or even decide how to proceed," Lara told him. She felt stronger today. Stronger than she had felt in years. The Shadow Princes, in generously sharing their passions, had passed on to her a measure of their power. They did not, Lara knew, do this lightly. "I thought once," she said to Kaliq, "that my destiny was to unite Hetar's civilizations. Now I know it is to save them. But am I strong enough?"

"Only time will tell us that, my love," the Shadow Prince answered her.

"I AM BORED," MARZINA, THE YOUNGEST DAUGHTER of Lara, announced with a sigh. She was a very beautiful young faerie woman with long straight black hair and violet eyes. Seated by a small pool she combed her silky tresses with a mother-of-pearl comb.

"How can you be bored?" Ilona, Queen of the Forest Faeries, her grandmother, wanted to know. "There is so much to do in the forest. What happened to your lover?" Ilona was seated upon a delicately woven rug that had been laid upon the forest floor. "He was rather nicely made for a mortal. You have such a good eye, child."

"I sent him away," Marzina answered. "He was becoming as boring as my life now is, Grandmother. Perhaps I shall go home to Terah and visit my mother. I do enjoy seeing how it upsets the Dominus to have both of us in the midst of his court. I know his thoughts. He refuses to accept magic, and thinks we should both be long dead. It makes it very difficult to deny the existence of something when it is standing there in front of you." And she laughed mischievously.

Ilona laughed, too, but then she said, "Your mother has finally left Terah, and no sooner had she departed than the Dominus, her great-grandson Cadarn, began dismantling the southwest tower of the castle where she lived. I suppose he thinks if he destroys her home she cannot come back. But he will never get that tower down for each night after his workmen have left it I use my magic to rebuild the tower." Ilona chuckled. "The Terahns are beginning to be frightened, and Cadarn is quite frustrated. He even attempted to blow up the tower. Eventually he will simply give up. He may put Lara from his thoughts, but he will not destroy the evidence of her existence in Terah."

"I suppose Mother has gone to Shunnar," Marzina said casually. "She always runs to Kaliq when she weakens."

"Your mother has done great things for Hetar and Terah," Ilona said quietly. "Do not be angry at Lara because Kaliq loves her. He did from the moment he first laid eyes on her, Marzina. Your mother and Kaliq are life mates. They always were, but your mother had a path to follow, and she did."

"Mother has never been kind to me since Kaliq tried to seduce me. She blamed me, Grandmother," the young faerie said. Though she had lived over a hundred years, she looked no older than a girl of sixteen.

"Marzina, Marzina," Ilona chided her. "Kaliq did not try to seduce you. You made a very blatant attempt to seduce him. An attempt to which he did not succumb, I might add. And when your mother learned of it she was rightly and justly angry. It was a very naughty thing to do." But Ilona could not hide her smile. Still it disturbed her that Marzina could twist the truth to suit herself.

"You and Kaliq were lovers once," Marzina said.

"Whoever told you such a thing?" Ilona demanded.

"No one told me, Grandmother. But I know it to be true. Kaliq has lived for centuries, and so have you. And you and mother look alike. He could not have you for you were born to succeed Queen Maeve. So he had mother instead," Marzina said.

"My dear child," Ilona said, "I do not know how you wove such a tale, but unweave it, for it is not so. Kaliq and I have always been friends, but never have we been lovers. Oh, I will not deny I have always thought him an attractive creature. But as you have so rightly pointed out, Marzina, I was born to take my mother's throne. Kaliq was born to be Lara's life mate. Her destiny is entwined with his, and it was always meant to be. Your mother loves Kaliq as she has never loved another."

"Even my father?" Marzina demanded.

"She loved Magnus Hauk for the mortal he was even as she loved Vartan, lord of the Fiacre, in the same way. But Kaliq is magic as your mother is magic. Their passion is magic, and far different from any passion magic could feel for a mortal."

"I have never been in love," Marzina said.

"I know," her grandmother replied.

"But why?" Marzina wanted to know.

Ilona laughed softly. "You have not yet met the right one for you," she responded. "Oh, you have enjoyed pleasures with both mortal and faerie, but none was *the one*. When he comes into your life, Marzina, you will know it, I promise."

"Was your husband, Thanos, *the one?*" Marzina inquired boldly.

"Thanos? Gracious no, child. Thanos was the mate I needed to sire my heir. We have little else in common although I will admit he is a fine gentleman faerie, and he gives me no difficulty, nor does he cause scandal."

"Who was *the one* for you, Grandmother?" Marzina persisted.

"I am not certain there was ever a special one for me, child," Ilona said slowly, "but if I had to choose it would be John Swiftsword, who sired your mother on me. He was such a beautiful and exciting boy. And he loved me unconditionally, but his fate lay in Hetar, and mine lay in the Forest Kingdom."

"What if I never find *the one* for me, Grandmother?" Marzina asked her.

Ilona shrugged. "It does not matter if you do or not, child. A companion to take pleasures with is very nice. Love, however, complicates things, Marzina. Each of you must be totally unselfish, must be willing to sacrifice yourself for the other. I don't think I could have ever done it. I am selfish, and make no apologies for it. And I need no male of any species to succeed in life. No female should. Your mother and Kaliq are unique creatures. The love they share will do great things, Marzina. Do not be jealous of it. And better to be happily free than to be unhappily bound in a relationship you don't want or need, my child. You must continue to be an independent creature. Males are for pleasures, or if you want a child. There is no other need for them."

"I don't think I want children," Marzina said. "You have to invest too much of yourself in your offspring. Like you, Grandmother, I am selfish."

Ilona reached out and stroked her granddaughter's silken head. "You are faerie, my darling child. Pure faerie."

Aye, she was pure faerie, but she shouldn't be, Marzina thought. Not with a mortal for a father. But perhaps, as neither her twin brother, Taj, nor her sisters Anoush and Zagiri had magic, it was Marzina alone who had inherited their faerie mother's magic. They were long gone, of course. Sometimes it was as if they had never existed at all, Marzina considered, feeling a prick of sadness. Of course her big brother, Dillon, the king of Belmair, was all magic having had Kaliq for a father. And he lived.

Kaliq. How she had lusted after him, and if the truth be known, she still did. In her vivid imagination none of her lovers, mortal or faerie, could equal Kaliq. But he had made it very clear he wanted nothing from her, not even a single evening of pleasures. How it had wounded her pride to have him refuse her. He had done it gently at her first approach, but she had persisted, Marzina recalled, flushing angrily at the painful memory, until finally taking her by the hand he had brought her to a group of his brothers, saying, "This bitch is in heat. Cool her unseemly ardor."

What had followed had been a night such as Marzina had never known before or since. The Shadow Princes came by their reputation as magnificent lovers honestly. She experienced pleasures heretofore unknown to her, and her lust had been eased. But having tasted such passions Marzina had never stopped wondering about what pleasures with Kaliq would have been like. She never knew who told her mother of her attempted seduction of Prince Kaliq, but Lara had sought her daughter in the forests of Hetar and excoriated her cruelly for her behavior.

"It is bad enough you would betray me, my daughter, but to embarrass Kaliq, who had been so good to you is unforgivable!"

"'Twas he who approached me," Marzina lied. She was frightened by the way her mother was looking at her.

Liar! Do you think I do not know Kaliq, Marzina, that I would believe that ridiculous falsehood? Did you learn nothing from me? From your father? Magnus Hauk was the most honorable of mortals. When did I ever behave so disgracefully? You ought be ashamed of yourself, my daughter. Lara's words spoken in the silent language of magic were far more stinging than if she had voiced them aloud.

But something in Marzina would not let her apologize to her mother. Instead she glared haughtily at Lara and said, "You may think what you will, Mother. I know the truth of what happened." Why could she not admit her fault and ask her mother's forgiveness, Marzina wondered to herself. But she could not.

She could still see the look of anger and disdain in Kaliq's bright blue eyes when he turned her over to those half-dozen Shadow Princes. Not that she hadn't enjoyed herself with them, but it would have been better if he had beaten her and banned her from Shunnar. As it was, she hadn't been back since. And she envied Lara Kaliq's love and devotion. What they had together went beyond mere magic.

"How long has it been since you have seen your mother?" Ilona said, breaking into the girl's thoughts.

Marzina shrugged. "A few years, Grandmother. Taj's Farewell Ceremony. I could hardly believe that old man on the bier was my twin brother. Still he remained a handsome man like our father."

"Go and see your mother, child," Ilona told her granddaughter. "That pride of yours will be your downfall. Tell her you are sorry. Lara's heart is generous, and she will forgive you, Marzina. She loves you."

"Kaliq will never trust me again, I fear," Marzina said. "And I must admit to you, Grandmother, that I still find him attractive, and intriguing."

"Have you accepted the fact that he will never be yours, child?" Ilona asked.

Marzina nodded, and there was no guile in her now. "I know he is Mother's," she admitted with a dramatic sigh of regret.

Ilona laughed. "It is always difficult losing your heart to someone who loves another. But you are young, and you will survive. Now go and see Lara."

"I will think about it," Marzina said. Then she disappeared before her grandmother's faerie green eyes leaving her mother-of-pearl comb behind upon the velvety deep green moss.

Ilona shook her silvery-gold hair impatiently. The breach had to be healed between her daughter and her granddaughter. Something was about to happen, to change. She sensed it. Her faerie subjects felt it. The forest felt it. She had met recently with her counterparts in the faerie world. King Annan of the Water Faeries; King Laszlo of the Mountain Faeries; and Gwener, Empress of the Meadow Faeries. They, too, anticipated something momentous coming. But no one could imagine what it was. "Humph!" Ilona said aloud and, snapping her fingers, appeared before her daughter and Kaliq, who were sitting in Shunnar's main garden in the twilight.

Seeing the purple smoke that always presaged her mother's arrival, Lara quickly arose. "Mother! How nice to see you," she greeted her parent.

"You have to make peace with Marzina," Ilona said bluntly.

"Good evening, Ilona. Please sit and join us," Kaliq said, assisting the faerie queen to a comfortable chair. Taking a cup of berry frine from the air, he handed it to her.

"Kaliq," she purred at him. "You are always so welcoming. Now tell Lara she must heal this breach with Marzina." She sipped from her silver cup.

"Lara makes her own decisions, Ilona, and you well know it. What has Marzina done now that you are insisting she and her mother be reunited," Kaliq asked candidly.

"Marzina has done nothing for once," Ilona said. "It is just that I feel something is about to happen. Something of import. Something that will require us all to be united. Given Marzina's paternity I want her to remain on the side of the light," Ilona told them.

"So you sense it, too," Kaliq said quietly.

"We all sense it, in the meadow, in the mountains, in the water," Ilona told him. "The feeling is palpable, though we know not what it is."

"It is Kolgrim," Lara replied. "He intends to take a bride and sire an heir."

"What!" Ilona was surprised. "I thought he was to do that on the Darkling, his half sister, Ciarda."

"He tried for three mating cycles, but she failed him. He killed her, Mother," Lara said. Then she explained the murders Kolgrim had committed afterward.

Ilona was horrified. "He surpasses his father in evil," she remarked. "But who is this bride he means to take? And when?"

"We know nothing now, Mother. We are seeking to learn what we can. One of the Shadow Princes listened for several months but could learn nothing other than what we already knew," Lara told her parent. "Kaliq and I must go to the Dark Lands ourselves if we are to find out who the unfortunate girl is. We will attempt to prevent the marriage, of course. The longer we can keep Kolgrim from marrying the better."

Ilona nodded. "Of course," she said. "You must prevent your dark son from taking a wife and siring an heir. But first you must take Marzina back into your heart, Lara. She needs you."

"Then let her come and apologize to me for lying. I will let the rest pass for she has always been impulsive in her nature, but I cannot forgive the lie she spoke unless she asks, Mother. You know that you would not forgive it. What if Marzina had attempted to seduce Thanos, and then told you it was the other way around."

"Seduce Thanos?" Ilona's tinkling laugher bubbled up. "I would never believe such a thing, Lara."

"Nor did I believe that Kaliq had attempted to seduce

Marzina," Lara countered. "Would not the lie have angered you, Mother?"

Ilona's laughter died away, and she said, "Aye, it would. To disparage Thanos, who has been so good to Marzina, would be quite dreadful, Lara, even as her charge against Kaliq was quite wrong. I understand your anger, but you must forgive your daughter. If the darkness is once again on the move, Lara, then we do not want Marzina tempted into it. And given who her real father was, it could happen. We have done our best to make Marzina strong and good, but she still has a broad streak of recklessness that she needs to learn how to control."

Suddenly Kaliq reached out his arm seemingly into the air. The fingers of his hand closed partly, and with a sharp pull he brought Marzina into their midst. "We have an eavesdropper, it would seem," he said. His look was one of deep concern. "How long have you been listening, Marzina?"

Marzina's pale face was drained of its little color. She looked to her grandmother. "What did you mean *given who her real father is,* Grandmother?" Her young voice was shaking, and her violet eyes were wide with her fear.

Lara reached out to grasp Kaliq's arm. Her fingers dug hard into the muscle. Ilona made a small sound, not quite a whimper, not quite a moan. Her eyes desperately sought Lara's.

"Magnus Hauk was my father, wasn't he?" Marzina's young voice was pained.

Lara drew a very deep breath then let it out with a sigh. Letting go of Kaliq's arm, she reached for her youngest daughter, drawing Marzina into a gentle embrace. "Do you know how much I love you, impossible child?" she said, and she stroked the dark head. "Even when you do foolish things, and lie boldly to me, I still love you."

Marzina looked up at her mother. The warm arms about her

were comforting, and she felt safer than she had in decades. "Oh, Mama, I am sorry," she said. "Kaliq did not approach me. I approached him, and when he rebuffed me I was angry. I did not mean to lie, but I have admired him my whole life."

"I know," Lara said softly. "You are forgiven your lapse, my darling." She kissed the top of Marzina's head.

"But what did grandmother mean, Mama? Magnus Hauk was my father, wasn't he?" Marzina's eyes questioned Lara anxiously.

There was no way she could escape telling Marzina the secret she had kept for so many years. "You and Taj were born from my womb on the same day," Lara began. "You were believed to be fraternal twins. And Magnus Hauk believed that you were his child as was your brother. But you were not his child, Marzina. Newly pregnant with Taj, I was violated upon the Dream Plain by Kol, the Twilight Lord. You are his daughter," Lara told her youngest child.

"No!" Marzina cried out, and she looked to both Ilona and Kaliq to tell her it was not so, but they did not speak.

"There is more," Lara said, "and you must know it. Long ago as I summered in the New Outlands with the clan families, Kol, the Twilight Lord, kidnapped me and robbed me of my memories. He believed I was his chosen mate, and I believed I was his wife. He impregnated me with his son. Twilight Lords can only sire a single male heir although they can have many daughters. Kaliq helped restore my memories and told me that it was planned that I bear a son for Kol who would cause chaos within the Dark Lands. By means of my magic, now restored to me, I divided the child into two children. And indeed the birth of Kolgrim and Kolbein did cause eventual anarchy in the Dark Lands. I returned to my own life. The memories of the months in which I was gone were removed from us all to protect us. But Kol began invading my dreams, seeking to bring me back. Kaliq finally had to tell me what happened and restore the memories of my time in the Dark Lands so I might protect myself, because Kol was threatening to tell Magnus what had happened. I, however, told him first."

"What did my fath—what did the Dominus say when you told him?" Marzina asked her mother. She looked so vulnerable, so broken at that moment.

"He was furious. His pride was crushed. He railed at me, at Kaliq. At one point your grandmother threatened to turn him to stone he angered her so greatly," Lara said. "But then his anger and hurt cooled, for your father loved me."

"Do not call him my father!" Marzina cried. "He was not my father! My father was some monster who forced his seed upon you!" And she began to weep bitterly.

Lara wrapped her arms about her youngest child and, holding her tightly, rocked her back and forth. "Magnus Hauk never knew the truth of your conception, my darling. He believed himself your father, and he was your father. The only father you ever had."

"I am the Twilight Lord's sister then," Marzina said slowly, and suddenly she remembered a time long ago when she had first gone to live in the forest with her royal grandmother. She had learned how to transport herself by magic, and in her excitement had appeared in Lara's privy chamber, surprising her. Marzina had found her mother in conversation with two young men, but Lara had quickly magicked them away with little explanation. "That first time I learned how to transport myself…" she began.

"Aye—" Lara nodded "—I remember."

"I gained barely a glimpse of the two men with you. Their faces were identical, but one was dark, the other light." Marzina cudgeled her memory. "Which one of them became the Twilight Lord, Mother?"

"Kolgrim, the one with the golden hair," Lara replied.

"What happened to the other, the dark one?" Marzina persisted.

"Kolgrim imprisoned him with their father in a cell fashioned by the Shadow Princes," Lara explained. "Neither of them will ever be free."

Marzina felt cold. Tears still ran down her face, staining it, but she paid little heed to her tears. In these past few minutes her entire world had been turned upside down. "Then that is why I am all magic when neither Anoush, Zagiri or Taj had any magic at all about them," Marzina said thoughtfully.

"That is why," Lara told her, stroking the long black hair.

"Both light and dark inhabit my soul," Marzina remarked. "And the balance must be kept. Is that not so, Mother?" She looked into Lara's face.

"It is to be hoped, Marzina, that the light will overwhelm any dark within you, for in the battle to come we will need your help, too," Lara said.

Marzina was silent, and then she finally spoke. "Now I understand why I do the reckless things I sometimes do."

"No one is perfect," Lara answered her. "Even in the magic world. There is always a balance."

"How can you love me?" Marzina asked brokenly. "*He* forced himself upon you."

"It is true that you were not conceived from love," Lara told her youngest daughter candidly, "but from the moment I laid eyes upon you I loved you, Marzina. And Magnus loved you. Your whole life you have been surrounded by love, and it is love that makes you strong, and will keep you strong."

"But if fath—if the Dominus had known the truth, Mother,

would he have loved me? If he knew my sire was evil personified, could he have loved me?"

"Yes!" Lara spoke without hesitation. "He would have loved
you no matter. That I know for certain. Your father's heart was
a large one for a mortal, Marzina."

Suddenly the Queen of the Forest Faeries spoke. "Well,
Marzina, now you know the consequences of eavesdropping. I
hope you have learned your lesson. When I think how we have
all struggled to protect you over the years, and are you any better
for the knowledge you have gained this day?"

"I am sadder, Grandmother, but I am wiser," Marzina
answered. "Now I will work harder to overcome my sire's
heritage."

Lara hugged the young faerie woman. "There is far more of
the light in you than there is dark," she said. "But one thing,
Marzina. Kolgrim does not know the truth of your heritage. If
he learns it, he will attempt to turn you to him. He is very
charming and very persuasive. But he is far more wicked than
his father ever was. Be warned."

"I hope she will listen to you now as she never listened to
me," Ilona said irritably.

Lara shot her mother a fierce look, and seeing it, the Queen
of the Forest Faeries laughed aloud. "It is not funny, Mother,"
Lara said.

"Oh, but it is, my darling," Ilona said. "You have at long last
perfected my look of disapproval and righteous indignation. You
did it quite well, Lara."

Now Marzina giggled and Kaliq began to chuckle. Even Lara
smiled as she saw the humor in her mother's words. The worst was
over for now. Marzina knew the terrible truth of her birth, but
with constant reassurance and love she would recover and be all
the stronger, Lara was certain. Kaliq's voice broke into her thoughts.

"Marzina, your mother and I would like you to make your home with us," he said.

"But I am a Forest Faerie," Marzina began, then she stopped. "I don't think I know where I belong now," she admitted.

"You belong with your mother for now," Kaliq told her. "You belong in the light and sun of our desert."

"I need to be alone with this," Marzina said frankly.

Ilona looked worried at her granddaughter's words. This had to have been a terrible shock for Marzina, but it was true that she needed time to come to terms with it.

"I have the perfect place," Lara said with a smile.

"She should come back to the forest with me," Ilona insisted.

"Nay," Lara said. "She should be allowed the privilege of my own special place." Lara looked to Kaliq, who smiled and nodded.

"Aye, 'tis perfect, my love," he agreed.

"Where is that, Mother?" Marzina wanted to know.

"Zeroun," Lara told her.

"That isolated oasis?" Ilona said. "It's hot and sandy. Nay, Marzina needs the cool green forests to restore her spirit!"

"I think it is Marzina who must decide," Kaliq said. His eyes met Lara's and she nodded imperceptibly. Kaliq then caught Marzina's hand, and they disappeared.

Ilona stamped her foot irritably. "How like Kaliq to do something like that! Are you certain you can trust Marzina alone with him?" she said wickedly. "I am going home since my presence obviously isn't required here." And the Queen of the Forest Faeries was gone in a puff of royal-purple mist.

Lara laughed ruefully. How like her mother to say something hurtful when she couldn't get her own way. Unlike her grandmother, Marzina rarely made the same mistake twice. Lara reclined upon a couch and watched the rising moons of Hetar as about her the night birds sang softly, and the night blooms perfumed the warm air. She sensed Kaliq's return before he actually appeared by her side, joining her on the couch.

"She loves it and will remain for a few days," he said, dropping a kiss upon Lara's bare shoulder. "I've put a spell on the oasis so no one will find it while she is there."

Lara began to cry softly. "I didn't want her ever to know, Kaliq. I didn't want her to learn about Kol, or her brothers. And now I am afraid if she learns the truth, Kolgrim may very well learn it, too."

"Kolgrim will be too busy taking a bride and impregnating her with his son," Kaliq said.

"We know nothing until we have gone to the Dark Lands ourselves," Lara replied. "What we think we know is but whispers upon the wind. Tomorrow. We must go tomorrow, Kaliq. And there is only one way we will learn what we need to know. I will have to ask my son myself."

"He could lie to you," Kaliq reminded her.

"Aye, he could," Lara agreed, "but he has his father's ego and pride. He cannot resist sharing his cleverness with me. If I ask him, he will tell me some of the truth. The rest we will have to learn for ourselves. I know you would come with me, Kaliq, but if you do you must remain cloaked. He will not speak before you as freely as he will to me alone. And you know the Twilight Lords are incapable of detecting Shadow Princes, so he will not know you are there."

"Very well, my love," Kaliq said. "We won't learn everything, but what little we do learn will enable us to ferret out the rest."

They fell asleep together upon the reclining couch in the gardens, and when they awoke Lara sought out a balcony in Kaliq's palace that faced the rising sun. Pulling her loose gown from her, she stood, arms outstretched by her sides, her palms up, and allowed the great golden orb to bathe her. Its rays shot forth to fill her with strength, and she radiated light. It seeped into her flesh, and could be called upon later to protect her. When the sun had finally risen above the horizon, Lara left the balcony and went to bathe. Then Cadi dressed her in a beautiful white gown with long full sleeves and a rounded neckline. The serving woman fastened a gold rope belt about Lara's waist and slipped gold sandals upon her dainty feet. Brushing her mistress's long gilt-colored hair, she plaited it neatly, weaving delicate ropes of gold amid it so that the hair glittered even more than it naturally did.

When she was ready, she joined Kaliq. Together they broke their fast. He had bathed and was dressed all in white, too. His bright blue eyes sparkled in his tanned face as he fed Lara bits of melon, and she laughed at him, licking his fingers teasingly. He stopped, shaking his head at her in mock disapproval. "We have business to attend to first, my love," he said. "Do not distract me."

"Then do not treat me as if I were your special pet," Lara shot back as she buttered a piece of fresh warm bread and began to eat it.

"Your point is taken, faerie woman," he responded. "But I cannot resist you."

"I know," Lara answered him, grinning mischievously.

"Remind me to take a lover one day soon," he said wickedly.

"If you insist," she chortled. "Would you like me to choose her for you?"

Kaliq burst out laughing. "I do not know how your mortal husbands survived that sharp tongue of yours, my love."

"I thought you liked my tongue," Lara teased back.

"Stop! Stop!" he pleaded, laughing harder, and she laughed with him.

The meal finally concluded, they went to Kaliq's library, where he took a black onyx bowl from a cabinet and, taking up an earthenware pitcher, poured water from it into the bowl. The water lay crystal clear and still within the wide almost flat dish.

Lara waved her left hand above the water, saying as she did, "Show me Kolgrim."

The water darkened, and then clarified to reveal the Twilight Lord in his Throne Room consulting the Book of Rule while old Alfrigg stood by his side. The chancellor looked tired, Lara thought.

"Remember, my lord, you are to remain unseen," Lara said to Kaliq.

He nodded and then, wrapping his cloak about them, transported them to the Throne Room of the young Twilight Lord. Lifting the edge of the cape to allow Lara to be seen, it appeared as if she had simply stepped from the air itself.

"Kolgrim," she said by way of greeting.

The Twilight Lord looked up, surprised by the sound of her voice. Then he smiled broadly. "*Mother dear!* How nice of you to visit. How long has it been? A century?" Reaching out to catch her hand, he kissed it.

Lara felt an icy chill race down her spine, but she showed no distaste. "You have left your hair golden," she said. "I would have thought it better if you darkened it."

"My golden locks remind everyone who my mother is," he said with a smile. "I believe that to be a good thing, coupled with my father's features. Why have you come?"

Lara turned her eyes on the very elderly chancellor. "Greetings, Alfrigg. I would have thought you retired by now."

The old dwarf bowed low. "Greetings, Domina. Regretfully I can find no one who suits my lord, though, by Krell, I have tried hard."

Lara looked at Kolgrim. "If he dies, what will you do?" she asked.

"He will not die," Kolgrim replied. "I have put a spell upon him. I need him."

"You are truly a monster like your father," Lara said, feeling sorry for Alfrigg.

"Why have you come to visit me?" he repeated. "I doubt not there is a purpose in your sudden appearance." He smiled at her, and briefly Lara was reminded of his father, who now lay imprisoned beneath his own castle. Kolgrim was a handsome man. Tall with lightly tanned skin, his cheekbones were high, his nose long and straight and his mouth wide and sensuous. His had thick bushy black eyebrows above his dark gray eyes, which had long dark eyelashes tipped in gold. Like his predecessor, his eyes turned black with his deep thoughts. While his father's handsome face was more beautiful and his twin, Kolbein, looked just like Kol, Kolgrim's visage was stronger, more masculine. He favored the dark robes his father had once worn.

"I am told," Lara said, "that you seek to take a bride and sire your heir. I thought that Ciarda, your half sister, had been given that privilege."

The Twilight Lord's eyes grew black with his displeasure. "The bitch failed me. She was filled with a sense of her own importance but her womb was barren. And she never stopped nagging me. Her bones lie bleached and white below the ravine bridge. I can point them out to you if you wish to see them."

"It was too soon for you to sire an heir," Lara told him, controlling her urge to shudder at his dispassionate explanation.

"You are right, Mother! If only you had said so to me then," Kolgrim exclaimed.

"You would not have listened," Lara told him. "Children seldom listen when they set their minds to something."

Alfrigg smiled a small grim smile. Kolgrim was a great Twilight Lord, but had his mother taken any interest in him at all he would have been a greater one.

"Are you planning to marry?" Lara said again.

Kolgrim smiled slyly at her. "Perhaps," he said.

"What does the Book of Rule say?" she asked bluntly.

The Twilight Lord shrugged. "I would show you, but you couldn't read the words for they are in our ancient language," he told her.

"I do not need your book. All I require from you is an answer. Do you plan to wed, Kolgrim?" Lara demanded for a third time.

"I have already answered you, Mother. *Perhaps,*" Kolgrim said.

"*Perhaps* is not an answer. Eventually you must wed in order to sire an heir. The rumor currently making its way about our worlds is that you intend to take a bride soon. Where will this unfortunate bride come from, Kolgrim?" Lara's gaze met his and did not waver. She was stronger than he was, and she wanted to remind him of this salient point.

Kolgrim finally looked away from his mother, irritated. The faerie-woman mother was more powerful than ever, he thought. If he could but have that power! "The Book of Rule has not revealed the chosen maiden to me yet," he answered her honestly. Then his eyes danced devilishly. "Will you come to the wedding, Mother, and give us your faerie blessing? I promise you the grandchild I sire on this unknown will honor you as your Terahn and Hetarian grandchildren and great-grandchildren have not."

The barb stung but Lara struck back. "'Tis true they do not honor me, but my Belmairian descendants do. *My son's* wife has borne him beautiful children."

"I am your son, too!" Kolgrim cried out.

"You are your father's son," Lara said cruelly. "Farewell, my lord!"

She quickly stepped back, feeling Kaliq next to her. He knew what she wanted, and his cloak immediately made her invisible. She did not speak in even their silent language for if she had, Kolgrim would have known that someone else was there, as he was capable of hearing and speaking that tongue himself. The Shadow Prince simply transported them back home to Shunnar.

"He is every bit as devious as his damnable father," Lara said angrily.

"But he speaks the truth," Kaliq said. "If the book had already instructed him to the unfortunate who is to be chosen, he would have told you. He wants you to know that he is capable of being every bit the Twilight Lord his father was."

"He never really knew Kol, and he did not know me until he was grown, but other than his golden hair, he is all Kol. His instincts for evil are all there, Kaliq. But we must learn who the bride is before he has a chance to wed her."

"Until the Book of Rule reveals her to Kolgrim, we have no chance of knowing," the Shadow Prince replied. "This is a game of patience we have begun to play."

"We have to know when he knows," Lara said.

"I wish we could. There is something protecting the book," Kaliq told her. "I attempted to put a small spell upon it that would alert us each time the book was opened, but my charm was repulsed."

"It is powerful magic that would repel a Shadow Prince," Lara said slowly.

Kaliq shook his head. "It was a simple spell. I dared not create a stronger one lest Kolgrim be warned. Marzina at the age of six could have repelled my spell. The Book of Rule, however, is a living thing. If it felt it could not defend itself, it would cry out to its master for help. Coilen will remain in the Dark Lands within the castle. He will know when Kolgrim discovers who his bride is to be, and then we will know."

"We will have to be satisfied with that," Lara replied.

MARZINA RETURNED several days later. Her naturally pale skin was bronzed, and her violet eyes sparkled in her face. "Oh, I love the sun!" she told her mother. "Thank you so much for sharing Zeroun with me. I feel much better."

"And you will remain with Kaliq and me?" Lara asked.

"I will consider that I have a home here in Shunnar, aye," Marzina said, "but the mountains of Hetar above the northern end of the forests are where I have made a home for myself, and raised up a small castle. It sits high on the heights, and the view of our world is wonderful, Mother. You have never seen Fairevue, and I should like you and Kaliq to visit me one day when you can."

"You are safe there?"

"I have lived there for the last fifty years, Mother," Marzina said with a little smile.

"Alone?" Lara asked.

"Sometimes, and sometimes not. But I have servants, and a bevy of forest creatures who serve as my guardians," Marzina explained.

"Let me learn what I must about this prospective bride for Kolgrim," Lara said. "And then I will come and visit you," she promised.

"I am forgiven then," Marzina said pointedly.

"Aye, you are forgiven," her mother responded.

The beautiful young faerie kissed her mother's cheek. "Then I am gone," she said, and as she stepped away from Lara pale lavender mist enveloped the girl. When it cleared she was no longer there.

"I am glad you two are reunited with one another," Kaliq said, stepping from the shadows of Lara's day room. "Especially given the knowledge she now possesses."

Lara shook her head. "I fear her curiosity is going to get the better of her, my lord. She is going to want to slip into the Dark Lands and see her brother for herself. I can reason with Marzina to a certain point, but I live in terror of Kolgrim learning of her existence. He will use her to his own advantage if he discovers who she is."

"If we take her with us once, we will be able to control that situation," Kaliq replied.

Lara nodded. "You are right," she agreed.

"She will manage her own behavior for a time, my love," Kaliq said in sure tones. "It gives us time to learn what we must. Once we do, we will offer to show her Kolgrim."

"If I know my daughter, she will conjure him up in her reflecting bowl first," Lara told him. "But she will control her curiosity for a brief time." She leaned against him. "It will be soon, Kaliq. I can feel the change in the very air. It builds as if to a crescendo. From where will this bride come?"

"Be patient," Kaliq advised Lara. "Coilen will inform us when the Book of Rule speaks, and then we can act. But not before."

IN THE DARK LANDS the Shadow Prince known as Coilen stood invisible and silent in the Throne Room of the Twilight Lord, watching. Each morning Kolgrim came and opened the book. But nothing was written upon the fresh clean vellum page. Several weeks passed, and Kolgrim grew more and more impatient. Then one day when fierce storms battered the Dark Lands with great booms of thunder, and jagged sheets of lightning tore through the purplish skies outside the Throne Room's balustrade, Kolgrim came and opened the book.

Coilen could see from his vantage point directly behind the young Twilight Lord the words written upon the smooth paper. The Shadow Prince knew and read the mysterious ancient language of the Twilight Lords. Few could. Now his eyes scanned the page anxiously, surprised by what he translated. He put it into his memory so he might repeat it as it was written to Kaliq and Lara. Then he waited for Kolgrim's reaction to the Book of Rule's directive.

"Guard!" Kolgrim shouted, and a man-at-arms immediately stepped into the chamber. "Go and fetch the chancellor immediately," the Twilight Lord said.

"Yes, my lord," the man said, and he ran off.

Kolgrim was smiling and chuckling to himself. He could hardly wait to let Alfrigg see what wisdom the book had imparted to him. He waited impatiently, but knowing his master, the dwarf came swiftly.

"My lord, you sent for me?"

"The Book of Rule has a message for me this day," Kolgrim said. "Read it!"

Alfrigg stepped up onto the small step by the trifooted book holder. His rheumy old eyes scanned the lines written. Then he looked up, smiling at his master. "It is genius, all praise to Krell, Lord of Darkness, who guides us so wisely," Alfrigg said, smiling at his master. "We have never done something like this, but with the charm you have inherited from both your mother and your father you will accomplish your goal easily, my lord. *And,*" he added, "with no loss of life or resources to us." He shook his head wonderingly. "It is too perfect, is it not?" His smile grew broader.

"Aye, perfect, Alfrigg. But will Hetar cooperate with us, do you think?"

"I believe that they will, my lord. Hetar has fallen back into its old decadence, with one exception. They learned from that fraud the Hierarch a hundred years ago not to permit their underclass to suffer want and privation. They have kept them fed, housed and entertained ever since. It has cost them little enough to do it. And it permitted them to slide back into debauchery and greed. They want no wars with anyone. And if you can take Hetar without destroying its people and resources, so much the better."

KOLGRIM WALKED OUT ONTO THE COVERED
balustrade to view the storm as Alfrigg hurried off to attend to
business. Prince Coilen of the Shadows brought himself back to
Shunnar with a whispered command. Several weeks had passed
since he had last checked in with no news. Now he sent out a
silent signal to all of his brothers, materializing in Kaliq's banqueting hall as the others came. Kaliq and Lara were already there.

"We must wait for everyone," Coilen said.

Finally the Shadow Princes were all in the hall. Even the
oldest of them, Cronan, who had come from Belmair, hobbling
through a Golden tunnel for the distance was so great, and he
was frailer than ever. Several of his brothers helped him to a
straight-backed chair with sturdy carved arms and a cushioned
seat. Then as if a silent signal had been given, they all looked
to Kaliq, Lara and Coilen.

"Our brother has brought us disturbing news," Kaliq began.
He turned to Coilen. "Tell them what you have seen and heard."

"For weeks I have stood in the Throne Room of the Twilight

Lord, waiting for the Book of Rule to inform Kolgrim, the son of Kol, of his next move," Coilen began.

Lara was grateful he did not identify Kolgrim as the son of Kol and Lara although all the Shadow Princes knew she had borne him.

"Today the book finally revealed its plans, my brothers, Lara. It said, and I quote it exactly,

The Twilight Lord, Kolgrim, will seek his bride in the Hetarian House of Ahasferus. She who is to be your mate is the great-granddaughter of Cuthbert Ahasferus. She is one of three cousins, all aged sixteen, all beautiful, all descended from Ulla. But only one of these maidens has the power of Ulla. She does not know this power exists, or that it is hers. If you choose wisely, her power will become yours, Kolgrim. Tell Clan Ahasferus that you seek a virgin. Only the right girl still retains her virginity. It is lodged tightly within her silken sheath. You will need both her innocence and her hidden power to produce your successor. Find her and she will belong to you, and you alone for eternity. The son you father on her will be worthy of you, and your father before you.

"That is exactly what was written," Coilen said.

For a brief moment there was silence in the hall, and then old Cronan said, "It is time for the Shadow Princes to leave Hetar, my brothers. You must seek a new home. King Dillon will welcome you to Belmair until you have time to find this new home. Your valley will slowly disappear, and your palaces crumble."

Lara was shocked. "Why must this be, my lord?" she asked Cronan.

He turned his gaze to her and smiled. "There was always a chance that the darkness would finally come and swallow Hetar. This happens now and again when the light simply cannot prevail, though it tries its hardest to do so, my daughter."

"We have beaten back the darkness before," Lara responded.

He nodded. "Aye, you have."

"We can do it again!" she insisted.

"Not this time, Lara," Cronan said. "If Kolgrim weds this maiden, the child they spawn will be all-powerful. Even Kolgrim will not be able to withstand him."

"Then we must find the girl first, and prevent her marriage to Kolgrim," Lara said.

"We must try," Kaliq agreed.

Cronan smiled a sad smile at them. Then he sighed. "Sometimes," he said, "even goodness and light such as yours cannot overcome evil, my brother. You know this to be truth, but it does not mean we will ever stop trying." He turned back to Lara. "My daughter, we planned your existence carefully centuries ago. Your pedigree had to be exact with faerie blood outweighing mortal. You had to be so pure of heart that your faerie magic would be stronger than any before you. You were created for a dual purpose. To cause chaos in the Dark Lands by bearing Kol twin sons, and to create a new world that might be safe from the darkness for mortals. You have performed your task so far quite magnificently, but we creatures called Shadow Princes knew long ago that Hetar would eventually be overcome by the darkness. Your magic gave them the last opportunity they had to save themselves. They have not taken it."

"If you knew I would not succeed," Lara cried, "then what has been the point of all of this?" She could not quite believe what he had just said. There were many good people yet in the world of Hetar, in Terah, in the New Outlands. Still… She sighed a deep reluctant sigh. Cronan was extraordinarily wise, and not given to braggadocio.

"Do not despair, Lara, my daughter. You yet have a destiny to fulfill," Cronan responded in kindly tones. "Be patient. All will be revealed in its time." The old Shadow Prince looked to Kaliq. "You know what must be done, my brother. It is time. Within the next year the magic that is light must be gone from Hetar lest it be caught in the conflagration to come." He looked out over the Shadow Princes assembled. "Are we in agreement, my brothers?"

"We are!" they responded with a single voice.

"Kaliq, I would speak with you privily," Cronan said.

Lothair came up to where they stood. "Come, Lara," he said quietly. "Andraste is ready for you to try once again." He led her off before she might protest.

"She will attempt to prevent what is written," Cronan said quietly. "Let her. She will fail, but she must try if she is to finally accept that Hetar has written its own fate."

"This has all been quite a shock to her," Kaliq said.

"Of course it is," the elderly Shadow Prince said. "She has come to believe over the years that her destiny was to unite all of this world beneath one banner and live in peace." He snorted with derision then continued, "You will need every ounce of patience you possess and more to contend with her disappointment, my brother. But Lara must fulfill her appointed destiny before you may have your eternity together."

Kaliq laughed softly. "Aye, she will not give up her dream easily, but while stubborn her intellect is sharp. Once she is convinced herself that your words, though disturbing, are truth, she will do what she has been fated to do."

"And you will be with her," Cronan nodded. "Her destiny is your destiny, too, Kaliq, but then you always suspected it, didn't you." He smiled at his companion.

Kaliq smiled back. "I fell in love with her at first sight," he admitted, "and then I knew. She is making her home here in Shunnar now."

"She should," Cronan said. "What is to come is too strong and will harm her powers if she remains in the mortal world. You must tell her that, Kaliq."

"I will," Kaliq promised.

"Then I must return to my tower on Belmair. Your brothers will rest there before seeking out their new home," Cronan said.

"Where is that place?" Kaliq asked the ancient Shadow Prince.

Cronan shook his head. "Even I do not know that, my brother, but I do know I will never see it. I was the third of us to come from the ether, and it will soon be time for me to move on into that other world to be reborn once again. I will not return as a creature of the Shadows. Your son, Dillon, is the last of us. His son has magic, but not *our* magic. Our kind is fated to disappear. But you and your brothers have centuries ahead of you before that happens. And you will spend those centuries with Lara. *That* I do know, Kaliq." He arose slowly from his chair, and with a wave of his gnarled hand he opened a Golden tunnel. "We may meet again before the end of Hetar's time, my brother," he said. Then leaning on his staff he hobbled into the bright shimmering opening and down the tunnel until he was out of sight.

When the glimmering vortex finally closed, Kaliq knew that Cronan had reached his destination. He sighed. Lara still had her destiny ahead of her, but bringing her to that destiny was going to prove difficult. She loved this world, and she had done so much good for it. Yet despite her bravery and sacrifices Hetar had relegated her to legend. They had not learned their lessons, and had now infected Terah and the New Outlands.

Aye, there were good people among them, but even good people made bad choices. Kaliq sighed again, and then went to seek out Lara.

She was not with Lothair now. She had left Andraste, her singing sword with him and gone down into the valley of the horses, where their herds grazed. Looking down from the balustrade of his palace's main corridor, he saw her walking toward her old friend and companion, Og, the giant, who cared for the horses of the Shadow Princes. He might have listened to their conversation from where he stood so high above them. But Kaliq did not. Much of what was to come Lara would have to work out in her own mind, and in her own time. But he knew how very disturbed she was by Cronan's bleak pronouncements of what was to come.

Lara felt him watching her. Turning, she gazed up, but he was gone. She looked to the giant, calling his name. "Og!"

Og turned with a smile. Though small for a Forest Giant, due to an unfortunate childhood of near starvation, he was still a giant. His bright red hair was fading now, but his blue eyes were as sharp as ever. "Lara!" he greeted her with a smile, and then leaning down, he offered her his hand. Lara stepped into it, and Og raised it to his shoulder, setting her down gently where she might sit comfortably and speak with him. "I hear you have finally come to live with us here in Shunnar," Og said, sounding very pleased.

"It was time," Lara admitted, "and do not say past time, as so many have."

Og chuckled, for that was exactly what he had been about to say. "I would never even think such a thing," he prevaricated mischievously.

"I have come to bring you the news we have just received," Lara said, and then she went on to explain about Kolgrim, and what Cronan had said. "Of course he is the oldest, and the wisest of the princes," Lara admitted, "but I know we can overcome the darkness once again. And perhaps this time we must drive it from Hetar forever, even as Usi the Sorcerer was driven from Terah."

"I don't know, Lara," Og said thoughtfully. "If Cronan says Hetar is lost, then it is surely lost. The old fellow isn't one to make mistakes."

"The history of Hetar is not completely written, Og," Lara insisted. "With Kaliq's aid I can prevent the darkness from overcoming Hetar. Have we not done it before?"

"I wonder if the horses are to go," Og considered. "Would they take me with them? I shouldn't like to leave my horses, and what of my new helper, Lara?"

Lara shook her head. Og was a simple man with simple needs. "If they go, you will go with them, and Leof, too. What of your family?" she asked him.

"My wife and children are long dead, Lara. The few descendants remaining to me prefer living among my wife's desert folk. I do not know them anymore. The princes and my horses, they are my family," Og said. "And now I have the lad, too." He smiled.

"The princes would never leave their horses behind, and so it would seem they will not leave you behind, Og," Lara told him. "But I still believe such thoughts are premature, dear friend. We will save Hetar once again, and this time forever. The darkness may come, but the light will not be driven away. Remember there must always be a balance, Og. Balance is the key. We will leave the darkness a tiny corner."

"Perhaps you are right," he replied, encouraged by her assurance. "Now come and walk with me. Dasras has been awaiting your arrival. He is going to sire several more foals, Lara.

He has taken at least five mares into his keeping. The other two stallions in the herd are not happy, but as he sired them they cannot complain." Og chuckled. He walked slowly although his strides were long, and they had covered half of the valley before he finished his thoughts. "Ah, there he is."

"Dasras!" Lara called, having seen her horse even before Og spoke.

The great white stallion with the creamy mane and tail raised his head, and seeing Lara perched upon Og's shoulder, trotted over to her. "Mistress! You have come at last." His dark eyes looked up at her. They were filled with love.

"You do not seem to have suffered much in my absence," Lara teased her horse.

"As usual you have chosen a harem of beautiful mares for yourself, you old rascal."

Dasras whinnied and tossed his head. "If I must return to the valley of my youth, and be put out to pasture, my lady Lara, I should be comfortable, and have congenial companions," he said.

"Just because we have returned to Shunnar," Lara responded, "does not mean we have retired from the world, Dasras. The darkness is on the move again, and my son, Kolgrim, threatens the peace. We will have much to do, I promise you."

"I am glad to hear it," Dasras replied. "When do we leave?"

"Not quite yet, old friend," Lara said. "You have time in which to enjoy your new wives. Where is Sakira?"

Sakira was Dasras's favorite mare and had borne several of his foals.

"There, among the new ones," Dasras said. "I have not been to the valley in so long, and she knows all the mares. She helped me choose the new ones."

"She loves you greatly, Dasras, that she would do so," Lara told him. "Where is Feroz?"

"My son is one of the two stallions remaining here in the valley," Dasras replied with a chuckle. "He is not pleased to see me for his appetite for mares is every bit as large as mine. The other stallion I sired, Tekli, is an amiable, lazy fellow who should have really been gelded, but he is so beautiful and perfect in form that the princes kept him as he was created. His dam was a magnificent creature, and his foals are truly fine."

"I am pleased to see you so well acclimated again to the valley. I will leave you now. Remember that I will need you. Og will tell you when."

"Let me take you for a ride, mistress," the stallion suggested.

Lara laughed. "Very well," she replied, leaping from Og's sturdy shoulder onto Dasras's broad back. As her knees clamped his sides and her hand wrapped itself about a hank of his mane, the stallion whinnied and then began to trot away from the giant.

The trot gave way to a slow, easy canter, which then moved into a gallop. The stallion raced down the long broad valley, his hooves barely disturbing the grass beneath them. He did not unfold his wings to fly. He wanted to gallop, and he knew the woman upon his back did, too. He had heard the tension in her voice, and seen the concern upon her beautiful face when she had spoken to him. She had not told him everything, but she would eventually. For now it was just the two of them, as it had once been, galloping across a swath of green for the pure joy of it. He had heard her laugh happily as he had increased his speed from the canter to the gallop.

KALIQ WATCHED THEM from the covered balustrade of the palace. He knew the stallion's thoughts, and smiled. Dasras knew his mistress well and served her with skillful devotion. They were well suited, even as he and Lara were well suited.

A year. Cronan had said. Within a year the good magic must

be gone from Hetar or it would be overtaken by the darkness. Faerie posts would have to be sent out to every corner of their world warning of the chaos to come. There would be meetings to be called, decisions to be made regarding destinations. Faeries, giants, elves, gnomes and Shadow Princes all would need a new home. The magic population of this world hadn't been disturbed in centuries. And it would be difficult, Kaliq knew, for them all to leave.

It would be a great undertaking, and they had just enough time in which to complete it. But there could be some who sided with his beloved, and would waste time trying to save that which could not be saved. Kaliq sighed. He had hoped for a little time in which he and Lara might enjoy a peaceful existence together. Coilen would not be returning to the Dark Lands. It was too dangerous now, for Kolgrim would allow nothing to deter him from his purpose, which was to take a bride from the House of Ahasferus. A virgin with Ulla's magic at her command. But the poor girl would have no knowledge of her power, and Kolgrim would take it from her unknowing. The girl's single purpose, poor creature, was to give Kolgrim his only son and his heir.

Lara was suddenly by his side again. She stood on her tiptoes and kissed his cheek. She smelled of sunshine, fresh air and horse.

Kaliq wrapped his arm about her. "I watched you ride. You were happy again."

"Aye, 'twas like old times before this all began," Lara replied. "It was nice to go back, my lord, if only briefly. Now we have work to do."

"We will not send Coilen back for it is too dangerous," Kaliq told her. "We will simply have to wait for Kolgrim to make his first move. He must have the girl to wife, but how he obtains her is another matter."

"Do you think he will go to war?" Lara wondered. "He might simply kidnap her."

"Nay, I doubt he will go to war. It is a waste of his resources," Kaliq replied.

"We must know who this girl is. There are three of them, almost exactly alike. The one who is the chosen still retains her virginity. What if we tempted her with an irresistible lover, Kaliq. Most Hetarian girls take lovers once they have passed their fourteenth year. Why, I wonder, has this girl waited?"

"It doesn't matter why she waited," Kaliq said, "but she has."

"One of mother's faerie men could tempt her perhaps," Lara said slowly.

"But first we must learn which of these three girls it is," Kaliq reminded her.

"That is simple enough. Mother can choose three young faerie men to seduce the trio of cousins. The two who either have lovers or can be easily seduced will prove themselves not the girl in question. Once we know which of them it is, we can act," Lara told him. "But we must move quickly, for my son will not dally now that he knows what he must do in order to assure the darkness comes."

BUT KOLGRIM HAD already decided how he would gain his fated bride. His army was small, for the benefit of soldiering for the Twilight Lord was more often death than anything else. He had a small standing force just large enough to prevent anyone attempting to invade his lands. He would not go to The City, an army at his back. He might steal the girl, but he did not know who she was. He needed time to ascertain that. Nay. There was another, a more skillful way, and he would employ it.

He chuckled as he considered it. His imprisoned father would appreciate what Kolgrim was about to do, but Kol's companion, who was the young Twilight Lord's twin brother, would not. Now and again Kolgrim would take his reflecting bowl to observe his sire and his sibling. Kol was a sad figure, weakened by the loss of his magic, and the decades he had spent in the windowless dank stone cell. Kolbein, however, alternated between stamping about his prison swearing as he sought a means of escape, and sitting in a corner whimpering with his frustration. Kolgrim always enjoyed seeing him thus. But when the Twilight Lord finally triumphed and brought the darkness to the world of Hetar, he would transmit that knowledge to his father via his thoughts. Kol had never done him any harm, and indeed had favored him over his twin. He deserved that small bit of happiness in his declining years.

IN THE CITY THE LORD HIGH RULER PALBEN II was enjoying the Springtime. The Icy Season had concluded, and the early flowers, all shades of yellow from the palest to the deepest, were at their most vibrant. The flowering trees in the Golden District and the Garden District were in full and glorious bloom, their shades of pink, peach and white perfuming the air. The skies were a clear bright blue each day, and the sun warm upon his back. The breeze from the south was soothing.

Lord High Ruler Palben was a tall, slender man in his middle fifties with dark eyes and hair. He knew from the portrait that hung in the royal palace that he very much resembled his grandfather, Jonah, who had been Lord High Ruler some eighty years ago.

By rights Palben should not have been Hetar's Lord High Ruler. His grandfather, Jonah, had a son, Egon, from a first marriage. Egon, it had been predicted, would be a great soldier, but in the last war he had been too young to either fight or lead. And there had been no more wars. Egon turned to the pursuit of knowledge. It consumed him to the point of neglecting everything else. While he was a frequent visitor to the Pleasure Houses, he did not marry, nor did he produce any progeny. Hence, it was Egon's half brother, Palben I, who had inherited the throne of the Lord High Ruler when Jonah died.

Palben I had been the son of Jonah's second marriage to the Terahn princess, Zagiri. Zagiri was the daughter of the Dominus of Terah Magnus Hauk, and his wife. His great-grandmother was reputed to be a powerful faerie, but Lord High Ruler Palben didn't believe that for an instant. In fact, he did not believe in magic at all. He had never met his great-grandmother for after his grandmother Zagiri died she never came to Hetar again. It was rumored that she had been born in Hetar. He didn't really know, and she would be long dead by now, but his great-grandmother had been responsible for opening up the previously insulated Terah to Hetar.

The Lord High Ruler Palben's mood was a particularly good one this morning. He had, to his amazement, received a missive from the Twilight Lord of the Dark Lands. It had been delivered to his secretary, who had brought it to his master immediately. The Twilight Lord asked his permission to visit Hetar for talks he assured Palben would be mutually beneficial to both their lands.

Palben did not believe there had been any contact with the Dark Lands in more than a century. If the vague history he had been taught was to be believed, the Twilight Lords in the past had launched an unprovoked attack upon Hetar and Terah. They were, of course, a savage uncultivated group of ignorant barbarians. Still, the message he had been sent was exquisitely worded and beyond polite. Palben was curious.

He dictated a reply to his secretary.

"We would welcome a visit from the Twilight Lord Kolgrim. We will prepare for your arrival, and will await your coming in the month of the Full Summer Moons. Palben II, Lord High Ruler of Hetar."

"How shall I have it delivered?" the Lord High Ruler's secretary asked his master.

Palben looked confused then he said, "How was it brought to us?"

"I don't know," the man replied. "I found the envelope with the message on my desk when I arrived this morning, my lord."

"Put it in the same place then tonight before you leave," Palben said. "Whoever brought it came carefully, not certain of their reception. He will most likely return for the reply, but come secretly again. If the letter is still here in the morning, we will seek another way of answering my fellow monarch." He laughed. "It is all quite mysterious."

The Lord High Ruler kept peeking into his secretary's chamber until he finally retired for the night. The letter remained propped up on the desk to his great chagrin, but when he hurried to see if it was still there in the morning he found it gone. Most curious, he thought. He knew there was a mail service called faerie post, but he never used it. It was a silly name, and there were no such things as faeries. At least he had never seen one.

KOLGRIM HAD NOT USED faerie post. He had simply sent his missive via magic. He opened the message from the Lord High Ruler Palben, read it and smiled with evil satisfaction. He would be interested in meeting this mortal. They were distantly related actually for his half sister Zagiri, was Palben's grandmother. He wondered what Palben would think of that fact. The month of the Full Summer Moons would be a perfect time for wooing and seducing a maiden.

As the time grew closer for Kolgrim to make his visit, he sent messages to the Lord High Ruler requesting a northern exposure for his guest apartments. He would expect his servants' quarters to be nearby. And there must be a kitchen quarter for he was frequently hungry late at night. He did not like flowers, and so there must be none near him or in the chambers that he would occupy. His favorite frine was distilled from blackberries, he informed his host. And he was so looking forward to their meeting.

THE LORD HIGH RULER PALBEN gave his majordomo orders based upon his guest's preferences. He wondered if the Twilight Lord would bring a concubine or a wife with him. He decided not, as no mention was made of it. But would he enjoy having a Pleasure Woman at his beck and call? That could be decided once he met the man.

As the month of the Full Summer Moons drew near Palben grew more curious.

"I am told he is a dark lord," the First Lady of Hetar, who was named Laureen, said. "Is it wise to entertain such a man?"

"He has done nothing to incur our wrath," Palben replied. "He has politely requested permission to visit us. I see no danger in that."

"But why does he seek to meet with Hetar?" Laureen queried her husband.

"You ask too many questions, wife," Palben said. "Whatever he seeks of us, it is not your affair. He is coming to see me, not a mere woman. Attend to your household, to our children and grandchildren. That is your province, not diplomacy."

"I but wondered," Laureen said meekly. But she was an intelligent woman, and this sudden desire by the Twilight Lord to visit Hetar disturbed her.

"The Dark Lands are an unknown," Palben continued almost to himself. "It is a place of mountains, wife. What riches those mountains could hold! And they could be Hetar's," he said excitedly. "A new source of wealth, and I would be the one responsible for obtaining it. How I wish my father were alive to see this."

"If this Twilight Lord seeks you out, he will want something from you," Laureen said quietly. "I but fear for your safety," she added, so he would not scold her again.

Palben smiled benignly at his wife. Reaching out, he took her hand in his. "Of course he will want something, and I will want something in return, my dearest. That is the way of the world, is it not?" He patted her pretty plump hand. "Mayhap the Twilight Lord's mountains hold transmutes. Then we shall not have to depend upon Terah for them. I do not like this new young ambassador the Dominus has sent us. He is too arrogant by far. But old Amren is still here. He is the most skillful player of Herder I have ever played against. Perhaps if we make a pact with this Twilight Lord, we may relegate Terah back to where it belongs."

"Their Dominus is your kinsman," Laureen said softly.

"So it is said, but I have no idea what the connection between us is, my dearest. They are really nothing like us, the Terahns. I am told they have raised up a marble town mimicking The City. But no one lives there." He laughed. "What a waste of good resources to build a city where no one lives. I have also been told towns, little better than slums have risen up where our ships now dock. They are attempting to be like us, but no place can compare to Hetar. And the poorest of our own Hetarians are certainly better than any Terahn," he sneered. "I see an opportunity in the visit of the Twilight Lord, wife. A great opportunity."

THE MONTH OF THE FULL Summer Moons arrived. It was this particular year when Hetar's four moons would be visible and fully waxed at the same time. Pale green, blue, butter-yellow and copper-red, they would shine together over the city when the Twilight Lord arrived for his visit. Usually the four moons shone each in a different phase, but not this year. It had been some forty-three years since this quartet had waxed simultaneously. Festivals were planned throughout Hetar.

Kolgrim had decided to enter The City as any noble visitor would. To appear with all his retinue in a puff of smoke could frighten the Hetarians. He had not been out of the Dark Lands since he became Twilight Lord. Consequently he cast a stunning spell over his lands so all life was frozen in place. It would remain that way in his absence, and he didn't have to worry about any rebellions as Alfrigg was to come with him. He then created a retinue of well-trained, virtually silent servants who would serve their needs.

He materialized his royal train in a deserted wood several miles from The City. A small troupe of men at arms dressed in his black-and-silver livery rode ahead of him on matching dappled gray horses with black manes and tails that had been decorated with delicate silver chains and dark crystals. The soldiers' saddles were black leather trimmed with silver. Their polished silver helmets caught the sunlight, gleaming. Next came the flag bearers, and following them Kolgrim—wearing black leather pants, boots and jacket over a purple silk shirt—rode alone. Behind him his old chancellor was borne along in an ebony-and-silver litter chair carried by four liveried slaves with silver neck collars.

Following Alfrigg was the household of the Twilight Lord. All the servants wore black, silver and purple. Two dozen of them marched behind the chancellor. Others drove the carts accompanying the Twilight Lord. The carts contained his household goods and the gifts he had for the Lord High Ruler. Looking at the assembled train, Kolgrim added a group of musicians and dancers behind the men-at-arms, dancing amid the flag bearers, and before him. The dancers were both male and female, and very beautiful. He would give them to Palben in a seemingly careless gesture of generosity. The Lord High Ruler would be impressed, Kolgrim decided.

The Twilight Lord's impressive train exited the desolate wood following the road that, like all of Hetar's roads, led into The City. Forewarned of his coming by the Lord High Ruler, the guardsmen on the wall, seeing the great train sent immediately to Palben. When Kolgrim reached the gates of The City, he was welcomed and ushered through. A guide upon a fine dark bay horse was provided to lead him to the Golden District.

Kolgrim was fascinated by The City. The streets while dirty were lively, filled with noise and smells both pleasant and unpleasant. The citizens of The City gaped at the spectacle passing by them, and the Twilight Lord felt a sense of deep satisfaction. First impressions were most important. Reaching the entrance to the Golden District, they were again welcomed and led to the palace where Palben awaited upon the steps of the building to welcome his honored visitor.

The Twilight Lord's gaze quickly swept over this great-grandson of his mother's. There was nothing of Lara visible in him, and Kolgrim was very pleased to note it. The man was pure mortal and would have all of a mortal's weaknesses. The victory over Hetar was already his, Kolgrim decided. But still he must not judge too quickly. Palben might prove cleverer than he looked. He should know in a few days if this was so.

Dismounting his coal-black stallion, the Twilight Lord stepped forward, both of his hands outstretched in greeting. He was smiling his most winning smile. "My lord Palben, I greet you in friendship."

Palben was pleased by the Twilight Lord's words. The fellow did not seem at all a barbarian. "My lord Kolgrim, I greet you in friendship. Welcome to Hetar and my house!" He took the hands held out to him, squeezing them before releasing them. "We have prepared everything as you requested, but you will tell me if it is not correct. Tonight there will be a small banquet with a few of our more important citizens."

"I shall look forward to it," Kolgrim said, continuing to smile.

Palben took his arm, leading him into the palace. It was not a particularly grand home, Kolgrim thought, but it was lavish in its decor. "My wife, like all women, is curious as to why you have come. Our two lands have lived estranged for many years." The Lord High Ruler brought Kolgrim to a garden and indicated he should sit.

Kolgrim sat, and patting the bench next to him, invited his host to sit, as well. Palben did, and at once servants brought heavily carved gold goblets decorated with rubies filled with blackberry frine. The two men accepted the vessels and silently toasted each other before drinking. "I have come with a specific purpose," he told the Lord High Ruler.

"And what purpose would that be?" Palben asked. So it was not just a social visit. What could the Twilight Lord possibly seek from Hetar?

"I have come to take a bride," Kolgrim said quietly, and then he waited.

"*A bride?*" Palben was surprised.

"Aye, a bride," Kolgrim replied, smiling again. "There are few females in The Dark Lands, and none of rank from whom I could choose a wife. You see, my lord Palben, Twilight Lords can sire as many daughters as we choose, but only one son. My mother was a lady of high rank. I wish a bride of high rank." Kolgrim drank the frine in his goblet, and set it aside.

Palben nodded slowly. "Of course," he said. "I understand completely. And I am honored that you would come to me to help you find the proper lady."

"The Twilight Lords live by a specific code that is laid out in our Book of Rule," Kolgrim explained. "The book has directed me to choose my bride from the House of Ahasferus, my lord Palben. I am sure this family is of high rank, and known to you."

"My youngest daughter is eighteen," Palben began, considering that to have his family allied with this ruler would be an excellent thing.

Kolgrim held up his hand to stop the Lord High Ruler. "I mean no disrespect to you, my lord, and none to your daughter, who I am certain would make a good wife, but the Book of Rule has directed me to the House of Ahasferus. You will understand that I cannot go against the Book of Rule. It is our holy book."

Palben nodded sympathetically, but the truth was, he did not understand. He wondered what kind of a god the Twilight Lord worshipped. It certainly wouldn't be the Celestial Actuary. And in Hetar there was no holy book of which he knew. "Of course, if your holy book directs you to the House of Ahasferus, then it is there you must go," he said to Kolgrim. "The current patriarch of that house, Grugyn Ahasferus, will be one of my guests tonight. He is a magnate, and his family can be traced to the earliest days of Hetar. Will you allow me to speak with him first, my lord Kolgrim? Then I will introduce you. He has several granddaughters who are of marriageable age. The women of that family are noted for their beauty, too. While it is said all cats look alike in the dark, a man lives more in the light with his wife." Palben chuckled, giving Kolgrim a friendly poke.

Kolgrim joined his host laughing and gave him a friendly wink.

"You will want to see your quarters now," the Lord High Ruler said. He clapped his hands, and his majordomo appeared immediately. "Take Lord Kolgrim to his quarters. His servants are already settled, I hope."

"Indeed, my lord, aye," the majordomo said.

"A servant will come to fetch you and bring you to the banquet," Palben said.

Kolgrim bowed with an elegant flourish, and then without another word went off with the majordomo.

Palben rubbed his hands together, delighted. He could hardly wait to tell his wife of the reason for the Twilight Lord's visit. But Laureen said, "Thank the Celestial Actuary that he did not want our youngest child, my lord! I could not bear it if she were so far away." In actuality she was relieved, for she had watched the Twilight Lord's arrival from a window that fronted on the palace entry. He was the most handsome man she had ever seen, but he had made her shiver. She remembered that when she was small and misbehaved, her grandmother would say, *"If you do not behave, Laureen, you will be sent to the Twilight Lord, and live in his Dark Lands forever."* It was a common threat made to children of her generation.

"Well," Palben continued, unaware of his wife's genuine relief, "Grugyn Ahasferus will certainly be in my debt now. A match between one of his granddaughters and the Twilight Lord will bring our Hetar and the Dark Lands closer. I cannot speak for the citizens of that far place, but this ruler is a man of excellent breeding and good taste. Did you see his train, Laureen?

The horses' manes were braided with silver! The musicians and dancers were garbed in the finest silks. There have been rumors of great wealth in the Dark Lands." Palben paused, thinking. "I wonder," he continued slowly, "how we can profit financially from this possible marriage?"

"I am certain you will find a way, my lord," his wife answered.

"Aye, I will," he agreed, nodding. "Wear something beautiful tonight, my dear. I would have you shine before our guest."

He would sell me to this dark lord if he thought he might profit by it, Laureen thought to herself. "Of course," she answered her husband. "I have just the gown, my lord." Then she curtsied to him and hurried off.

The Lord High Ruler sat alone, and considered to himself what possible riches the Dark Lands held. He rubbed his hands together again gleefully. Tonight would be just the beginning of his personal triumph. Palben II would be remembered as Hetar's greatest ruler for bringing the Dark Lands into Hetar's circle of power. He could hardly wait for his guests to arrive. It was a small party, but the guest list was made up of the most influential men in Hetar. They would be fascinated by the handsome and urbane Twilight Lord. They would be astounded to learn what had brought him to Hetar.

And they would be fiercely jealous of Grugyn Ahasferus's good fortune. He would have to keep a tight line on his old friend Grugyn. There would be no marriage celebrated without the permission of the Lord High Ruler Palben. And it was going to cost the House of Ahasferus a goodly sum to gain their lord's formal consent. Palben chuckled to himself. He had been considering taking a second wife for some time. Perhaps he would wed another of Grugyn's granddaughters. Then he would have a blood tie with the Twilight Lord.

"My lord."

He looked up to see his body servant. "What?" he demanded, irritated at having been interrupted in the midst of his musings.

"You must come now, my lord, if you are to be ready on time to receive your guests," the man said, bowing low for he saw the annoyance in his master's eyes.

Palben arose. "Thank you," he said to the servant. "Is that new gold-and-silver robe ready for me to wear this evening?"

The servant nodded in the affirmative as he led his master away.

AT THE APPOINTED HOUR the Lord High Ruler of Hetar stood on the wide steps of his palace with Kolgrim the Twilight Lord greeting his guests. He was dressed in a light gray velvet robe with stripes of cloth-of-gold and cloth of silver. It glittered with his every movement. The robe had long wide sleeves with cuffs of gold. It was not a flattering design for it made him look leaner and more angular. But the robe was saved by a wide collar fashioned from gold and studded with rubies that sat upon his shoulders and his chest. Each of his long thin fingers was decorated with a bejeweled band, the ring of his office on the middle finger of his right hand. About his forehead was a gold band with a center ruby. His dark hair was close-cropped.

His guest of honor wore a robe of black-and-silver silk. It was simple in design, but elegant. About his neck was a heavy chain of gold and silver from which hung a round silver locket studded with sapphires. A band of silver with a center sapphire was set about his golden head. Kolgrim had about him an air of command that needed no luxurious ornament. The Hetarian magnates recognized it as they entered the palace with their women and were introduced.

Palben looked about his banquet chamber and felt well pleased. None of his guests was as well dressed as he was. Most had brought younger second wives, which but pointed out to him that without a beautiful young bride by his side he was losing prestige. Aye, he would have to take another wife. Laureen, while a pretty woman, was simply past her prime. And she had never been a great beauty. But her pedigree was without par, and her wealth was most satisfactory. She had been obedient and dutiful, giving him two sons and four daughters. However it was time her face was retired into the background where it belonged so he might enjoy a nubile, beautiful, young wife. She would probably be relieved for he knew she didn't enjoy these state dinners.

He had placed the Twilight Lord at his right hand at the table. Laureen sat on the other side of their guest of honor. Grugyn Ahasferus was seated at the left hand of the Lord High Ruler. As the meal progressed Palben leaned toward his friend and said, "You should know that Lord Kolgrim has come to Hetar to seek a bride."

Grugyn Ahasferus grunted an acknowledgment as he chewed on a piece of capon. "What has it to do with me?" he asked low, knowing Palben would not speak to him of this without a reason.

"He wants one of your granddaughters, Grugyn. Do you know what a coup, an honor, this is for your house?"

"Why one of my granddaughters?" The magnate's voice sounded disinterested.

"He will tell you himself. I have arranged for you to meet privily with him while my other guests are being entertained after the sweet is served. When I tell you, you will go to my own privy chamber. You know how to reach it, Grugyn, for you have often shared conversation and frine with me there."

"He's handsome. The girls would like that. Is he rich?"

"His train was magnificent when he entered The City," Palben responded.

"I heard. Men-at-arms in livery, banners, musicians and dancers. A goodly show to be sure, but such can all be hired," Grugyn said. "I need to know if he has the kind of wealth needed to ally himself to our house."

"An alliance between your granddaughter and the Twilight Lord would mean an alliance between Hetar and the Dark Lands. I am sure Lord Kolgrim is worthy, and such a marriage could mean great new wealth for us," Palben said meaningfully.

Grugyn's eyes narrowed briefly in thought. "Such an alliance would add to both your prestige and mine," he replied. "I would become richer than any in Hetar."

"And my position upon the throne could never be challenged," Palben murmured to his friend.

"I will listen to him with care and seek to gain the best advantage, but, between us, he can have one of the girls. A union between my granddaughter and the Twilight Lord will mean greater matches for her cousins." He smiled. "We are in agreement, my lord."

AS THE SWEET was served, and the guests distracted by an entertainer with a troupe of small dogs, Grugyn Ahasferus discreetly left the banqueting table. The Twilight Lord still sat murmuring in conversation with Palben. But when the magnate reached the Lord High Ruler's privy chamber he found Kolgrim awaiting him. "How...?" he began.

"Magic," Kolgrim said to him with a charming smile. "Sit down, my lord. My cousin, Palben, has told you why I have come to Hetar, has he not?"

"*Your cousin?* I was not aware that Lord Palben was your kin," Grugyn said.

"He does not know it," Kolgrim said with a chuckle. "It would be difficult for him to reconcile that his grandmother, Zagiri of Terah, was my half sister, that we shared the same mother, the faerie woman, Lara. After all, he rejects magic, doesn't he?" Kolgrim laughed aloud. Then he said, "But you know magic exists, Grugyn Ahasferus, for you are a descendant of Ulla."

"Magic is one of those subjects most Hetarians avoid these days, my lord Kolgrim. The Lord High Ruler does not believe, and therefore it is not fashionable to believe in it. But aye, I believe in magic and accept its existence in our lives." He motioned Kolgrim to a comfortable chair, seating himself opposite the Twilight Lord. Then, leaning forward, asked, "Why one of my granddaughters? If you wanted a Hetarian wife, there are any number of suitable young women available. Why one of mine?"

Kolgrim observed Grugyn Ahasferus carefully. Then he said with a candor that surprised even himself, "Because I have been directed to choose from among your family, my lord. The Twilight Lords live by the Book of Rule. And the book has instructed me to take a wife from among your three granddaughters. I don't know why, but I must follow what is written. These maidens are all sixteen. A good age for marriage. I do not know which I will choose, but it must be one of the three. And the decision must be mine. It cannot be made for me." Kolgrim glanced at his companion to see if he would accept his explanation. Oddly he had told the truth. He had just not told all of it. He hoped what he had said was enough to satisfy the Hetarian's curiosity.

"I understand," Grugyn Ahasferus said, and he did. When magic directed you, you followed whether you understood it or not. "Will your wife hold a place of honor in your kingdom, my lord Kolgrim? Will she be free to visit her family now and again?"

"First she must produce my son and heir," Kolgrim said. "Then she is free to do as she pleases, my lord. Her duty is to birth this child. It is a great honor, you know, for Twilight Lords have only one son. My wife will be showered with riches, and live like the queen she will be. I will never mistreat her," Kolgrim said.

"Perhaps I can help you to choose," Lord Grugyn said. "What sort of woman pleases you best?" Of his three granddaughters, two of the trio pleased him greatly. They were high-spirited maidens with a passion for pleasures that would certainly please any husband. The third girl, however, worried him. She was the most beautiful, it was true, but she was quiet and shy. She had, if his son was to be believed, never had a lover. She was definitely not the kind of girl a powerful ruler like the Twilight Lord would choose for a wife. Still, he would have to present her to this princeling, for Kolgrim knew there were three. But he would wait until the other two had had their chance to dazzle Kolgrim.

"I have no preconceived notions with regard to my wife," Kolgrim lied smoothly.

"Excellent, excellent!" Grugyn said, smiling. "Come to my home tomorrow afternoon, two hours after sun's peak. I will introduce you to my granddaughters, and you may take your time knowing each of them." He leaned forward and offered Kolgrim his hand in friendship. Then he added, "Of course your bride will be costly, my lord."

"I would expect it no other way," Kolgrim replied, smiling. "A perfect jewel is always well worth its price, my lord." Greedy, fatuous fool, he thought to himself.

The two men returned to the banqueting chamber. Grugyn

as he had come. And Kolgrim using his magic. The Twilight Lord had left a replica of himself seated within his chair, drinking, smiling, speaking. No one was aware that he had ever left the table. He nodded imperceptibly to Lord Grugyn as the other man reseated himself.

Grugyn Ahasferus smiled just ever so slightly in acknowledgment. He was not as stupid as Kolgrim thought he was. The magnate did indeed, as he had admitted to the Twilight Lord, believe in magic. And he knew the history of his family very well. The powers his ancestress Ulla had possessed passed into a single female in each generation of his family. Obviously one of his three granddaughters was the current host of this power, and Kolgrim wanted that power. Well, Grugyn Ahasferus thought to himself, he will pay dearly for it. I will want a monopoly on all the mineral rights in the Dark Lands, he thought to himself. There was surely gold and silver in those mountains as well as valuable gemstones to be had. And they would all be his. He would become the richest man in Hetar.

Of course there was Palben to consider. He would expect a substantial portion of Grugyn's spoils in exchange for his permission to allow a marriage to take place. Grugyn would not defy his old friend. Palben's power base was too strong. One enormous bribe, and Palben's cooperation would be far easier to obtain than with several large bribes, and an eventual betrayal. No. The Lord High Ruler and the magnate were old friends. They understood one another.

The question remained which one of his three granddaughters Kolgrim would choose. Each was sixteen. Each beautiful in face and form. But the girls all had very different personalities. Divsha was a blue-eyed blonde with large perfect breasts, who was sweet and gentle. She was a perfect Hetarian female, and there had already been a number of offers for her hand in marriage that the family was considering. Yamka was petite with dark auburn hair and amber-gold eyes. She was a lively girl, perhaps a bit too daring and reckless, but then her mother had been so at that age, too, yet once married became obedient and amiable. Grugyn expected Yamka would, too, and they already had, as with Divsha, several offers of marriage to consider for her.

To marry into the House of Ahasferus was an incredible honor. The descendants of Ulla were considered to have the finest pedigree in all of Hetar. Any magnate seeking one of Grugyn Ahasferus's granddaughters for himself or his son had best have an impeccable Hetarian lineage, and an obscene amount of wealth. The daughters of the House of Ahasferus were used to the best of everything, and nothing any of them had ever sought had ever been denied them.

Grugyn now considered his third granddaughter, Nyura, a tall willowy girl with long golden-red hair, and gray-green eyes. The only daughter of his younger son, she had always been a puzzle to him, and to their family. She was certainly obedient, but she was also quiet and introspective. She spoke little, but when she did it was obvious that she was very intelligent which, of course, was not a good thing in a Hetarian female. No man wanted to be outshone by a woman. There had been no offers for Nyura's hand in marriage so far. She would end up being some elderly magnate's second or third wife. A pretty trophy to display at public events and dinner parties. But they would obtain an equally good bride price for Nyura as they would for her cousins, Divsha and Yamka.

As they were transported home in their lavish gold litter with its royal-blue velvet curtains, Grugyn Ahasferus told his wife, Camilla, of his conversations this evening with the Lord High Ruler and with the Twilight Lord. A plump woman with a still-pretty face, Camilla listened, the fat beringed fingers of one hand tapping gently on a pillow as he spoke, her light blue eyes thoughtful.

"He is not Hetarian," she finally said. "And what do we really know about the Dark Lands? They have been an inhospitable, mysterious part of our world for centuries. Now suddenly this man claiming to be its ruler comes to The City and says he wants one of our granddaughters to be his wife. I would know more before I entrust a member of our family to a virtual stranger."

"I believe he is who he says he is," Grugyn replied. "He has magic."

Camilla Ahasferus's face grew wary. "My lord," she began in a warning tone.

"He has magic," her husband repeated meaningly.

"That does not make him who he says he is," Camilla said.

"What possible proof could you require that would satisfy you, wife?" Grugyn Ahasferus looked irritated. "One of our granddaughters is going to be elevated to the rank of a queen. I am well pleased."

"Then I am well pleased, too, my lord," Camilla Ahasferus said softly, smiling as she saw the building anger drain from her husband's face. Of course she was not. And she would seek to learn what she needed to learn before she would allow one of her granddaughters to be given in marriage to a stranger.

"I have invited the Twilight Lord on the morrow to come meet the girls," Grugyn Ahasferus told his wife.

"Only present Divsha and Yamka," Camilla suggested. "Nyura is too somber, especially when the three are together."

"He knows there are three," Grugyn Ahasferus responded. "I will display all of them. Remember that the choice is his to make, not ours."

She shrugged. "You are right, my lord," she agreed. "How did he know of our granddaughters?" she asked her husband. He told her, and Camilla listened carefully. If this fellow was who he said he was, and if he proved worthy, she considered, then perhaps a marriage alliance with him could turn out to be a very good thing. Yet how was she to learn what she needed to know? That would prove the difficult part.

BUT THE NEXT MORNING GRUGYN Ahasferus sent a message to Kolgrim asking him to visit on the following day. Then he sent for his two sons and his daughter, who was Yamka's mother. When they came later that day, he told them of the Twilight Lord's request. His daughter immediately began to cry. Grugyn ignored her.

"Mother is concerned he may not be who he says he is," his older son said.

"I believe he is," Grugyn Ahasferus replied. "Palben is far to canny a man to be taken by a fraud. But more importantly, I have seen the man's magic."

"We would be fortunate if he chose Nyura," his younger son said. "I don't know who we will get to marry such a serious girl."

"I don't want to lose my Yamka!" Grugyn Ahasferus's daughter wailed.

"Yamka and Divsha are my choices," Grugyn Ahasferus said. "He won't be able to resist either of them and will have a difficult time choosing. Nyura is lovely, I will grant you, but she is, as you have pointed out, my son, too serious. Now send my granddaughters to me by nightfall. I want them ready to greet our honored guest when he arrives tomorrow morning." And Grugyn Ahasferus dismissed his progeny.

His three granddaughters arrived at exactly sunset. Each

came with her serving woman and a trunk. Divsha and Yamka giggled together while Nyura smiled at the pair indulgently. She was not at all like them, and she knew it. She did not want to be like them, for together they had fewer brains than a cobblestone in the street. But she was fond of them, as they were of her. They understood each other, having grown up together.

Their grandmother saw they were given a sleeping draught almost immediately. She did not want them up laughing and talking all night. They must be well rested, and their beauty at its peak come morning.

The Lady Camilla instructing them, the serving women woke their charges just before dawn. The girls were bathed, their hair washed and subtly perfumed. Divsha's scent was rose. Yamka favored honeysuckle. Nyura preferred the more sophisticated fragrance of the night-blooming lily. The girls were then garbed in identical simple sleeveless white silk robes with plain round necklines. Divsha's gown was belted with gold. Yamka's with copper. Nyura's with silver. Their hair was dressed in the same way, long and unfettered, so their beauty would be equally displayed to the Twilight Lord.

He arrived at the appointed hour garbed in a black-and-silver robe. His eyes lit with pleasure at the sight of the three maidens who stood with their grandfather waiting to greet him. "My lord Grugyn," he said, bowing politely.

"My lord Kolgrim, welcome to my home. And here are the three precious flowers of my house to greet you. This is Divsha. She is the oldest born in the first month of the Icy Season." He drew the blonde girl forward, pleased to see she kept her eyes lowered as she should. "And this is Yamka, born in the last month of the Icy Season." Yamka bounced forward, her eyes sparkling with excitement, but she quickly lowered them, seeing her grandfather's slight frown of disapproval. "And here is

Nyura, who has only just turned sixteen this month." Nyura silently came forward and made her curtsy.

"Exquisite," Kolgrim said, smiling at Grugyn Ahasferus as they moved into the house. "I will interview each separately, of course, my lord. Have you a chamber in which I may do this?"

"Will you make your decision so quickly then?" Grugyn Ahasferus asked, surprised. "I thought a few days would be necessary."

"I can learn what I need to know today, and then the marriage date must be set. In a few months the mating season frenzy will be upon me. It is then I must impregnate my wife if I am to have a son within the year."

"Of course, of course," his companion replied. "Would you prefer an inner chamber, or one opening into the gardens?" he inquired politely.

"An inner chamber," Kolgrim replied. "And I shall speak with your granddaughters in order of their age."

Divsha smiled smugly at her two cousins. She had no doubt she would be chosen to be the Twilight Lord's wife and queen.

"Go to your grandmother, Yamka, Nyura," Grugyn Ahasferus said. Then he led his eldest granddaughter and Kolgrim to a small interior guest chamber, ushering them inside. There was a roll-armed upholstered couch in the room, and a table with a decanter and four goblets. "The frine is blackberry," he told Kolgrim, who nodded his thanks. "When shall I send the other girls to you, my lord?" he asked.

"When I have learned from Divsha what I need to learn, she will come to fetch Yamka next, and Yamka will fetch Nyura," the Twilight Lord said quietly.

Grugyn Ahasferus bowed politely. "It shall be as you require, my lord," he said, and then he backed from the chamber, hurrying off to join his wife.

When he had departed, Kolgrim walked to the door and turned the key in its lock. Then he turned back to Divsha, who smiled at him coyly.

"Would you like to see my breasts?" she asked him sweetly.

"Aye, I would," Kolgrim said, and pointing a finger at her, removed her gown.

Divsha squealed with surprise.

"I want to see all of you," he told her, seating himself on the couch. "Come here now, and sit upon my lap so I may inspect you more closely."

Obedient, she complied immediately. "You are a wicked man," she said to him.

"I am indeed," he agreed, a big hand slipping beneath her to feel up her bottom.

Divsha squealed again. "Ohhh!" she exclaimed.

His other hand began exploring her large round breasts. The skin was both soft and firm to his touch. He squeezed a breast, and her fair skin immediately bore the mark of his fingers. She was finely made. Bending, he kissed her nipple, licking it, then taking it into his mouth to first suck upon it, then to bite down on the tender flesh.

"Ohh, that hurt!" Divsha complained.

Raising her head, he kissed her, and her tongue immediately snaked its way into his mouth. She fell back into the curve of his arm, and almost at once he began to explore her nether regions. She was already wet with her lust, and so he pushed two fingers into her, moving them swiftly back and forth until she released her juices to him. She was not a virgin, but Kolgrim wasn't disappointed. He meant to have pleasures of the girl before he sent her back to her grandmother. Divsha's eyes were closed.

Kolgrim smiled. "Seat yourself upon me now, Divsha," he said. He had magicked his own robe away, and his manhood was already standing tall. He lifted the girl and sheathed himself within her.

Divsha's eyes opened and widened with his entry. "You are too big," she whimpered.

"Ride me!" he commanded her sharply. "You certainly have been taught how to please your lover, wench. Do so now!"

Divsha obeyed him, clamping him between her thighs as her body rose and fell with the rhythm of their shared lust. He grasped her big round breasts, squeezing them until she was gasping for mercy. He gave her none, only easing his hold on her as his juices filled her, and Divsha fell forward, clinging to him "Ohh, my lord," she murmured as she licked his ear. "You are so masterful. Never have I known such."

Kolgrim lifted her off him, restoring their garments with a snap of his fingers.

It had been a pleasant interlude, and she was a beautiful girl. But she had certainly not been a virgin, and the Book of Rule had said his bride would be a virgin. His fingers might have been mistaken, but his manhood had probed her deeply. Her maidenhood was long gone from her. "I have enjoyed your company, my lady Divsha," he told her, kissing her hand as he led her to the door, unlocked it and gently sent her on her way. "Go to your grandmother now. Have Yamka sent to me so I may conduct my interview with her next. I am sure we will meet again before I depart Hetar."

"Have I pleased you," she simpered coyly, certain she had.

"You have," he agreed, and closed the door on her.

When Divsha reached her grandmother's day room Yamka departed immediately. The blonde girl was disappointed she had no time to share her experience with her cousins, and gloat over how she had pleased him. Yamka almost ran from the chamber in her eagerness, Divsha noted.

"Enter!" Kolgrim called at the slight knock upon the door. Yamka stepped into the room, and Kolgrim again locked the door.

Yamka smiled slyly at him. "Did you fuck Divsha?" she asked, amused. "I am told she is rather dull when taking pleasures. We have shared several lovers."

"What a bad girl you are, Yamka, to speak so disparagingly of your cousin," the Twilight Lord chided her.

"Ohh, I am very bad, my lord," Yamka agreed. "Do you mean to spank me for it?" Her amber eyes glittered gold and danced with anticipation.

He snapped a finger at her and her gown dissolved away.

"Ohhh!" Yamka exclaimed, surprised, and in a half crouch tried to shield her breasts and mons from him with her hands.

"Aye, I can see you are a bad girl to deny me the sight of your luscious body," Kolgrim said. And Yamka was indeed luscious. Like Divsha her breasts were round, though not as large. Her hips were rounded as well, and he suspected her bottom would be plump and round, too. "Come here!" he commanded her in a hard tone, and when she quickly obeyed him he said, "Over my lap, wench. If you accept your punishment with good grace then I shall have a fine reward for you." His big hand descended upon her fat buttocks with a satisfying smack.

"Ohhh!" Yamka cried out. "Oh! Oh! Oh!" and she wiggled atop his knees.

Kolgrim continued spanking her bottom until it had turned a beautiful and burnished red sheen. Then standing, he yanked her to the rolled arm of the couch, put her over it and, grasping her hips in a firm grip, thrust his lustful rod as deep as he might go. She was not a virgin. But he was not disappointed. She was a most glorious fuck, and released her juices twice for him. Drawing his cock from her female sheath, he found her rear passage, and began to push himself in there.

"Ohhhh!" Yamka groaned. "I have only had one man there!"

"You have one now," Kolgrim said pushing himself as far as he could as his sac slapped against her bottom. But he knew she lied, for her rear passage had been easily penetrated. He moved within her once or twice, and released himself.

Several minutes later he restored her garment, and sent her back to her grandparents. He had not even kissed her lips. Now he waited for the third girl. What was her name? Nyura, yes, Nyura. He knew Hetarian girls were permitted to start taking lovers at the age of fourteen. Both Divsha and Yamka had obviously not wasted any time in availing themselves of this privilege. How could this third girl still be a virgin? Yet he had never heard of the Book of Rule being wrong. His lust had been well fed with the first two of Grugyn Ahasferus's granddaughters. He must treat the third as if she were an untried virgin until she proved that she was not. "Enter!" he said at the knock upon the door.

Nyura stepped into the chamber. She did not appear particularly nervous even when he locked the door. Nor did she cry out when he magicked her robe away. Instead she stood quietly so he might view her charms, turning slowly for him. Kolgrim felt the lust he had thought satisfied suddenly beginning to burgeon once again. "Do I please you, my lord," Nyura asked him softly. "My breasts are not as large as Divsha, nor my bottom as plump as Yamka's, I fear."

Slender and shapely, she had the most perfectly proportioned body he had ever seen in all of his life. His eyes devoured her. Her breasts would just fill his palm.

He suspected his two hands would span her narrow waist. The twin halves of her bottom were like ripe firm peaches. Her limbs were slim and shapely.

"Come and sit by my side," he invited her, and Nyura came

without hesitation, turning her face to him, smiling. He took the heart-shaped face between his two palms and kissed her mouth. Her lips were like rose petals, soft and delicate. Her breath was sweet, and he realized with shock that no man's lips had ever touched hers before his. His kiss deepened. He could not help himself, but Nyura slipped her arms about him without hesitation. He ran his tongue along her sensual full lips, and they parted for him. Kolgrim's heart was beating wildly. No female had ever given him this kind of a reaction.

Enboldened he pushed his tongue into her mouth. Shyly Nyura touched his tongue with hers then sighed. Kolgrim began to stroke the beautiful body in his embrace. She did not flinch as his hand caressed her breasts, fondling them gently, tweaking the perky little nipples that froze beneath his fingers. He moved swiftly, eagerly down her torso, her belly, arriving at her smooth mons. A single finger slid easily along the shadowed slit, and she trembled. He heard himself reassure her, kissing her mouth again. The finger insinuated itself though the fleshy folds, and Nyura stiffened.

"My lord?" she murmured nervously.

"I will not hurt you, Nyura," he promised her, even as he found her tiny jewel. "No, my pet, I will instead give you a taste of pleasures." The tip of his finger flicked back and forth, back and forth over the little nub.

Nyura moaned softly as her flesh began to tingle, the sensation building until she thought she could bear no more and whimpered for his mercy. She knew what he was doing, for while she had withheld herself from men she was a Hetarian girl. None of the women in her family withheld information of this nature, and both Divsha and Yamka were always comparing the attributes of their lovers.

Then Nyura gasped at the tingling burst, and she was weak with a pleasure she had never before experienced. His finger

moved down slightly to insert itself into her sheath. She stiffened again with her anticipation.

"I must ascertain something, my pet," he whispered to her
as she lay in his lap, her eyes closed tightly. The finger moved
deeper, and suddenly Nyura winced. He immediately stopped.
"You are a virgin," he said.

Nyura's eyes flew open. "Of course I am. You are meant to
take a virgin for a wife, my lord. Why do you think I never took
a lover? I but waited for your coming."

"What!" He was astounded. What did she know?

"I knew I was meant to be your bride," Nyura said. "You need
the power of Ulla that I possess to add to your own powers. My
ancestress came to me when I was a child to tell me this. We will
wed, and I will give you Ulla's powers for your own, my lord."

Kolgrim laughed aloud. "Why did you not tell me this
sooner, Nyura?" he asked.

"What? And spoil my cousins' dreams immediately? Nay, my
lord. I have waited my whole life to see the look on their faces
when they must face the fact that I have gained the prize, and
not them. Did you enjoy taking pleasures with them?"

"I found them quite ordinary," he told her, for he knew it
would please her. This exquisite quiet girl had a delicious dark
streak running through her. "Yamka swore when I had her ass
that she had only entertained one man before me there, but I
knew she lied."

"Indeed she did," Nyura said. "Being ass-fucked is quite her
favorite perversion, my lord. I shall be fascinated to see what it
is all about."

Her words drove him into a wild excitement. "I must have
you, Nyura!" he cried.

"Nay, my lord, you cannot. You must wait until our wedding
night, for a pure virgin is very much prized here in Hetar and

incredibly rare. The taking of my virtue will bring great and special prestige to my family. It will be publicly announced that I am a virgin. You must take my maidenhead before witnesses so all know it is no lie. You will not mind that, will you?" she teased him wickedly.

Kolgrim's cock was so hard he thought it would break off. To fuck her first and do so before an audience, would be a magnificent start to their marriage. But he would not remain in Hetar once they were wed. The mating frenzy that would come upon him shortly must be carried out in his own land. He wouldn't take her ass until then, for he wanted his lesser rod to be the first penetration of it. He closed his eyes in an attempt to cool his lust. "The wedding must be soon, Nyura," he told her. "I want your family to have all the prestige due them, but I want you in my bed sooner rather than later."

"You will tell my grandfather then that I am your chosen one, my lord, and that the wedding is to be set seven days from this day," Nyura told him.

"The Dark Lands are very different from Hetar," he said, not knowing why he bothered to say it. She was his. It was foretold.

"I know," she said. "You have lots of wonderful storms. I will be happy there with you, my lord."

"Let us join your grandparents now, and I will tell your grandfather of my decision," Kolgrim said. He restored her robe, unlocked the door to the chamber and hand in hand they went to find Grugyn Ahasferus.

Nyura led the Twilight Lord to her grandfather's sitting room, where he waited with his wife, Lady Camilla, Divsha and Yamka. The young woman entered, bowing first to her grandfather and then curtsying to her grandmother, who held out her hand to the girl. But Nyura did not take it.

"I have made my decision as to which of your granddaughters I shall take as my bride and my queen," Kolgrim said to Grugyn Ahasferus.

"So quickly?" the magnate replied.

"Your granddaughter Nyura meets my criteria and that of the Book of Rule," Kolgrim said. "She is a virgin, and she descends from Ulla."

"You mean she has Ulla's gifts," Grugyn Ahasferus remarked astutely. "Both those virtues will cost you dearly, my lord Kolgrim."

"Name your terms, but the marriage must be celebrated in seven days' time," Kolgrim responded.

"I thought you liked *me* best," Divsha said, tears springing to her eyes.

"You are a most charming companion, my lady Divsha," Kolgrim said.

"Did I not please you well?" Yamka demanded to know.

"You pleased me very well even if you lied to me." Kolgrim chuckled. "Your ass was far too easy to breach, my pretty."

Yamka flushed and stamped her foot angrily, but said nothing more.

"Did I not tell you to use the tightening lotion?" her grand-mother hissed at her.

"I will want the mineral rights to your mountains," Grugyn said.

"Forty percent of the ore you mine will come to me," the Twilight Lord said. "And I will take all of the jewels you find while seeking the metals."

"I want the transmutes," Grugyn answered him.

"We will split them fifty-fifty," was the quick reply. "But the rest of the jewels are mine."

"My granddaughter is a prize worth having, my Lord Kolgrim, is she not?"

Grugyn said slyly.

"That you give me a pure virgin will shower honor and

prestige upon your house," Kolgrim replied, also slyly. "When I have her maidenhead her screams will echo throughout your hall so your guests may know the truth. You will choose the witnesses to her defloration yourself, my lord. And have a bloody sheet to fly from your housetop shortly thereafter. I am taking your granddaughter and making her a queen. Do you think any of her gifts are greater than mine? I am Kolgrim, sired by Kol on Lara, a faerie woman. My powers are enormous and they are strong. If I wanted, I could take the girl and give you nothing. But I am of a generous nature, and so I have come as any suitor would to sue for the hand of Nyura."

Sixty percent of the mineral ore, half of any transmutes he found. He would shortly be the richest man in Hetar, Grugyn Ahasferus thought excitedly. Taking Kolgrim by the arm he said in a low voice, "Palben will expect a share of what I have. Let me tell him of our agreement, my lord."

"So you may lie to him and keep a greater share for yourself, of course." Kolgrim chuckled. "Why not? Nyura is worth it. Reverse the percentages for him, and tell him you are getting forty percent, then give him twenty. What you do about the transmutes is your business." He chortled again. If Grugyn Ahasferus was an example of Hetar's ethic, this world would fall into his hands like a ripe peach when he was ready. But not until after Nyura had birthed his son. He clapped Grugyn upon his back. "We are agreed then?"

"We are agreed," came his reply.

"I believe this calls for a toast," Lady Camilla said. She looked to Divsha and Yamka. "You may go home," she said, dismissing them. Then she put an arm about Nyura's shoulders. "Come, child, let us celebrate this magnificent betrothal you have made. We are very proud of you. Our quiet little granddaughter catching the heart of a powerful man," she gushed.

"The Twilight Lord has no heart, Grandmother," Nyura said bluntly.

"Nyura!" Lady Camilla reproved the girl. "Apologize to Lord Kolgrim."

But Kolgrim laughed, and catching up Nyura's hand kissed both the back of it and the palm, then the soft inside of her wrist. "She already knows me well, my beautiful bride-to-be," he said. "There will be no illusions between us."

Lady Camilla shrugged. "You are both too clever," she noted.

"Nothing is settled until the Lord High Ruler approves this match," Grugyn Ahasferus reminded them. "Tomorrow Lord Kolgrim and I will deal with Palben. Then we may prepare for the wedding feast."

"The bribe must be large," Lady Camilla said, "and Palben should not know that Nyura is the inheritor of Ulla's powers. Any thought that there might be another more powerful than he will cause him to block this alliance."

"If he knows of Ulla's powers he will not believe in them. Palben does not believe in magic," Grugyn reminded his spouse.

"Then he is a fool," Lady Camilla responded tartly.

Kolgrim chuckled to himself. He actually liked these mortals who would be his relatives. They were greedy and thought only of themselves.

THE LORD HIGH RULER was pleased to receive the Twilight Lord and Grugyn Ahasferus in his privy chamber the next afternoon. He smiled toothily at them. "I take it you bring me happy news, Grugyn, my old friend," he said.

"I have come to seek your permission for my granddaughter Nyura, only daughter of my younger son, Zenas, and his wife, Sabine, to wed with Lord Kolgrim," Grugyn said.

"And what will be paid you for the girl?" Palben asked.

"I may mine minerals and ore in the mountains of the Twilight. Sixty percent of what I mine will go to Lord Kolgrim. The remaining forty will be mine. I will give you fifteen percent of the profits from the minerals and ores. I may also keep all the transmutes I find. I will give you thirty percent of those, my lord." Grugyn looked expectantly to the ruler.

Palben was silent for what seemed a long time, and then he said, "I will accept your offer on one condition, my old friend. I want your granddaughter, Divsha, as my second wife. I have consulted on this matter with the First Lady Laureen, and she is agreeable. I will expect Divsha to give me children so that our offspring, and those of my lord Kolgrim will be blood kin through their mothers." He smiled broadly again. "Is that not an excellent idea, my old friend?"

Grugyn Ahasferus was briefly rendered speechless. Then he managed to say, "This is a great honor you do my family, my lord Palben."

Kolgrim was surprised. He had underestimated Palben. The man was clever. With the proper amount of fear instilled in him and training in how to serve, he would prove an excellent minion, the Twilight Lord decided to himself. "The nuptials could be celebrated together," he suggested. "I am certain such loving cousins would want to be at the weddings. Once I return with my bride to the Dark Lands she must concentrate her entire being on giving me my heir. We will not come to Hetar for some time. If you would not mind sharing the day, my lord Palben," Kolgrim said, "we might take our brides in seven days." Seeing Palben hesitate, the Twilight Lord continued, "I can but imagine the joy you will have with a beautiful young bride to share pleasures with, my lord. I know I can hardly contain my anticipation."

Lust sprang into Palben's eyes. "Aye, aye," he replied enthusiastically, "I agree! The marriages will be celebrated together."

"Nyura is a proven virgin," Grugyn said. "You know the fuss surrounding such a thing in the case of a bride, my lord. It will bring great notoriety to the House of Ahasferus. I would not want to overshadow your own nuptials. Perhaps you could wed the day before, and then my Lord Kolgrim the day after."

Palben considered his friend's words. "Aye," he finally said. "You are right. Nothing should overshadow the wedding of the Lord High Ruler. It is settled then! I will wed the day before him."

Grugyn bowed low. "I will inform my family of this double good fortune," he said. He then turned to Kolgrim. "You will not see your bride until your wedding day, my lord. It is custom here in Hetar. I hope you will understand."

"Of course," Kolgrim replied. "I have some other business to conduct before the marriage. I will take this time to do it."

Grugyn Ahasferus hurried home to tell his wife this latest news.

CAMILLA THREW UP HER HANDS in frustration. "Two weddings in a week? It will require a miracle. Have you sent to our eldest son to tell him this good news? Divsha, the Lord High Ruler's wife!"

"Second wife," Grugyn said. "She will have no title but *Lady*. She won't like that, I fear. Nor will she be pleased to learn she is to become the Lord High Ruler's property. Still in all she is a clever wench. She will find a way to make a success of this."

"It will cost us dearly to pacify her," Camilla noted sourly. "It would have been better if we had just matched her with the son of another wealthy magnate."

"Divsha is a good Hetarian woman. She has been brought up properly and will do what she is told for the good of her family," Grugyn replied.

"She wanted the Twilight Lord, and will demand much of the

family to go to the Lord High Ruler's bed smiling," Camilla insisted.

"We will give her everything she wants then," Grugyn said. "Do you know what these marriages mean, wife? We are not only about to become the richest family in Hetar, but our power base will be greater than I had ever imagined. I will no longer be just Palben's friend. We will become blood kin by this marriage, and blood kin to the Twilight Lord, as well. The House of Ahasferus will be the most influential in our world. Could you have ever imagined such a thing, Camilla?"

As the realization of his words hit her, she staggered with shock. "Grugyn! What have we done?" she half whispered. "You are the cleverest man in Hetar, my lord, to have engineered such a coup."

He accepted her praise, but the truth was, he had done nothing. The Twilight Lord had come to him. The Lord High Ruler had come to him. His only contribution was in having three beautiful sixteen-year-old granddaughters.

"We must do something for Yamka," Camilla said. "She will be devastated by her cousins' good fortunes. Of course we can't duplicate such magnificent matches for her, but we must find someone worthy."

"Go and speak with her then, and reassure her," Grugyn Ahasferus said to his wife. "We cannot have our daughter's child unhappy, and she certainly will be at this turn of events. But she must not remain unhappy long. I won't have her sulking about on the wedding days, taking the attention from the bride."

"I will go and find her immediately," Camilla said, and she hurried off.

WORD SPREAD QUICKLY throughout The City of the two great marriages about to take place. In the residence that housed the members of the High Council, the Shadow Prince Nasim heard first. Going to his private apartments, he expeditiously transported himself to Shunnar and found Kaliq. "News, my brother! Bad news!" he greeted him.

"What news?" Kaliq asked. "Lara, come quickly!"

"What is it?" She was at once by his side.

"Nasim brings news from The City," Kaliq told her.

"What has happened?" Lara asked Nasim.

"Kolgrim came to The City. He had sent to Palben to request he be allowed to visit," Nasim began. "It is the purpose of his visit that is most interesting."

"He came for his bride," Lara said. "And he has found her, hasn't he?"

Nasim nodded. "Nyura, granddaughter of Grugyn Ahasferus, daughter of his younger son, Zenas, and his wife, Sabine. He had his choice of three of Ahasferus's granddaughters, but he chose this one."

"She has Ulla's power then. The question remains, does she know how to use those powers? Few of Ulla's descendants ever did. Villia tried, but all she accomplished was attracting the Darkling Ciarda. What is known of this girl?"

"Little," Nasim said, "other than she is a virgin. She is fair to look upon, Lara, but her two cousins are actually more spectacular, and they have been enjoying lovers since they reached fourteen. But not this girl, which is why little is known of her."

"Something more must be known of her," Lara said.

"Of Divsha and Yamka I can tell you much," Nasim said. "But this girl has kept to herself. I, myself, only saw her recently because of the fuss that was made when the three girls were brought to their grandparents' house to be inspected by Kolgrim. They came through the streets of the Golden District in separate litters proceeded by musicians and dancers. I was there visiting a friend, and we watched the procession. She found the whole thing most amusing, given the reputation for enjoying pleasures that two of the maidens have. The third girl, however, she knew nothing about. I caught a good glimpse of her as her litter went by. Slender, fair, red-gold hair, a serene beautiful face. My friend named each of them as their conveyances passed us by. This is all I can tell you."

"So he has found the girl," Lara said thoughtfully. "The marriage must be stopped. I wonder if this girl realizes she has powers. She might not want to share them with a husband, and especially not a powerful husband. If she is a true Hetarian, she would want to keep those powers for herself even if she didn't know how to use them."

"She is a Hetarian girl, Lara. She has been taught total obedience to the men in her life," Kaliq reminded her quietly.

"You can argue this until the end of time," Prince Nasim said. "You have no other choice than to go to Hetar and deal with the girl directly."

"Nay," Lara told him. "I do not want to go to Hetar, for Kolgrim is there now. He always senses when I am near him. He would seek me out and make it appear as if I were involved in this marriage of his and approved it. Nay! We will bring the girl to us on the Dream Plain tonight and learn what she knows of her gift. Then we will deal with it."

NYURA! NYURA! COME TO ME, CHILD, LARA CALLED.
She stood among the swirling mists of the Dream Plain. The
girl should be asleep in her own bed now, and she would be
alone. Lara hoped Kolgrim had not set some spell about her to
keep her safe from other magic. Certainly they had not aroused
his suspicions yet. *Nyura! Lara* called again. *Nyura, come to me.*
Then to her relief she heard the girl's voice.

Who calls me? a young voice asked. *Where are you?*

Come forward, Nyura, Lara said. *Let us speak face-to-face.*

The mists grew thinner as Nyura walked barefoot in her
simple white night garment, and then she saw the woman before
her. She was a beautiful, slender creature with golden hair, pale
green eyes and a sweet smile. *Who are you?* Nyura asked.

I am called Lara. I am Faerie, and I wish to speak with you.

You are my lord Kolgrim's mother! Nyura said excitedly.

I am, though I am not proud of it, Lara responded. *I am told you
are to be his bride, Nyura. Why do you wish to ally yourself with the
darkness, child?*

It is my fate, Nyura said quietly. *When I was very young the shade of my ancestress Ulla came to me. She told me I possessed certain powers that had once been hers. She told me I must not take lovers when I turned fourteen for I was meant to be a virgin bride for my husband one day. She said he would be the Twilight Lord. She said my purity and my powers would help him to conquer our worlds. She said that I would stand by his side and rule with him. She said I would give him a son who would be all-powerful. Should I have eschewed such a fate, my lady?*

The Twilight Lord seeks to bring the darkness to our worlds, Lara said.

Nyura shrugged. *It matters not to me, lady. I shall rule by my husband's side.*

Nay, you will not, Lara told her. *The Twilight Lords do not share their thrones with anyone, let alone a female. Kolgrim imprisoned his twin brother rather than share. In the Dark Lands females are considered lowly creatures. Their only uses are pleasures and childbearing. And there are few females, for Nature has consigned more male offspring to the ordinary among them. The Twilight Lords, however, can only sire a single son, though I gave Kol two in order to create chaos and hold the darkness at bay.*

A single son is all that is needed, the girl replied simply. *Does my betrothed have many daughters by his Pleasure Women?*

He had many daughters, but he murdered them, and their mothers decades ago. He wanted no daughter of his to spring up and challenge her brother for the throne the way his half sister did to him, Lara told the girl. *How can you pledge yourself to a creature who would slay his own blood? The law of the Twilight Lords forbids spilling the blood of kin, and yet Kolgrim did so.*

With good reason, my lady, Nyura replied. *You have told me the tale yourself of how his sister tried to usurp his rights. I am glad he did it, for now I shall not have to worry about such a thing happening to my son. Besides, those women were not his blood kin, and their offspring were just females,* Nyura said.

Lara was horrified. This girl had no heart. She was beautiful but cruel beyond imagining. This was going to require stronger measures than they had thought.

I would go now, Nyura said. *I am tired.*

Will you tell Kolgrim we have spoken? Lara said.

Nyura smiled. *Nay, lady, for then he would prevent us from speaking again, and I think we may want to speak again. Farewell for now!* The mists quickly surrounded her, and she was gone from Lara's sight.

Lara forced herself awake, sitting up with a gasp. "The girl is evil personified," she said to the Shadow Princes who surrounded her bed, awaiting her awakening. "She has the face of an innocent, but her heart is dark." Then she went on to explain her conversation with Nyura, concluding, "We must kidnap this girl, and put her where Kolgrim cannot find her. If the Book of Rule says she is the chosen mate, then he cannot sire a son on another. It must be done now. We cannot trust her not to tell him, though she has said she would not. I could see she was already in love with him."

"Taking her will cause difficulties in Hetar," Kaliq said.

"Hetar sought to make an alliance with Kolgrim by giving him a daughter of a premier house of the land in marriage. Let them see the consequences of their actions in doing so," Lara told her companions.

"But where can we hide the girl that Kolgrim will not find her?" Lothair asked.

"We must not bring this darkness into Shunnar," Kaliq said quietly.

"We will hide her right under their noses," Lara replied. "Be assured they will not find this hiding place, and if they get close we can easily move her to another location."

"Where?" Prince Nasim asked.

"Only Kaliq and I will know that," Lara told him. "You must

return to Hetar as you are a member of the High Council. Rest assured that when it is discovered the girl is gone you will be questioned, my lord. You will be able to say truthfully that you do not know where she has been taken. Return now to the Council Quarter." And before Prince Nasim could speak Lara sent him back herself. This was not a time for debate, and Nasim did love an argument.

The other Shadow Princes chuckled softly at her actions. Wrapping their cloaks about themselves they vanished, leaving Lara and Kaliq to speak alone.

"Where?" he asked her, reaching out to take her hand and kiss it.

"In the Outlands there is a place known as the Crystalline Falls. If the Hetarians have left the falls as they once were then we can hide her in the tiny cave behind the waters," Lara told him. "Let us go and see."

He wrapped his white cloak about her, and they were transported to their destination. Lara was relieved to see that the great waterfall still flowed, and was as pristine and beautiful as ever. The great soaring trees of the ancient forest around the falls had once been cut down in Hetar's greed for wood, but the Forest Faeries led by the queen's husband, Thanos, had replanted the trees. Then Thanos had put a spell upon them, which made it impossible for the hand of any mortal to fell a tree within those woods. The forest had regrown, and remained untouched for the last eighty years.

The pool below the falls was as clear and beautiful as ever, surrounded by its moss-covered rocks. Lara led Kaliq down a narrow path invisible to mortal eyes and stopped the flow of the water briefly to allow them to slip through a small opening and walk along a narrow ledge that led them to a cave. The waters flowed again as they stepped inside. Dark and cool, the cave was little. Its roof was no more than eight feet in height. It was nine feet in depth and ten feet in width. The chamber was a perfect rectangle with a stone shelf that ran across its rear wall.

"We will enclose her in a glass box," Lara said.

"In a dreamless sleep," Kaliq added, nodding.

"It is close to dawn in The City," Lara pointed out. "Let us do this thing now before she awakens. Kolgrim cannot see her again."

"Weave your spell, Faerie Woman," the Shadow Prince told her.

> Bring the Dark Lord's bride to me,
> Nyura will my captive be.
> A dreamless sleep is now your fate,
> You will not be Kolgrim's mate.
> Sleep surrounded by the light,
> Hetar be safe from Kolgrim's might.
> This spell cannot, will not be broken.
> Faerie Lara has now spoken!

As her words echoed about the cave and then died away, a beautifully carved glass container decorated with gold, a dark green velvet mattress within, appeared upon the stone ledge. The box pulsed gently with light. Within it Nyura in her simple white robe lay sleeping.

"The light will not extend beyond the box and cannot be seen from the outside even at night," Lara explained to Kaliq. "To be safe I will ask you to set a spell that will close the opening to the cave so it cannot be found accidentally, my lord."

Kaliq walked across the floor to peer into the glass box. "She is lovely," he noted.

"How tragic that she was born to advance the cause of evil."

"But we have stopped the evil once again," Lara said triumphantly.

"Nay, my love," Kaliq said quietly. "Kolgrim will not let this pass. If the Book of Rule says this girl is his mate, and will produce his son, he will move the heavens above to find her. We have but slowed his progress."

"Why do you insist on believing Cronan's prediction," Lara demanded angrily.

"It is not Cronan's alone. It was written in the stars aeons ago, Lara, my love," Kaliq said, and wrapping them in his cloak, he returned them to Shunnar. "Remember the tale that Master Bashkar told you when you studied with him. He told you how Hetar began as a world of fog and clouds. How we Shadow Princes came from those mists, how the Forest Lords descended from the tree spirits, the Midland folk from the earth spirits as did the Outland Clan families, and the Coastal Kings from the sea. The Terahns descend from a combination of earth and hill spirits. And when the mists cleared the world was revealed to be beautiful beyond any other. But its beauty eventually attracted evil spirits. They came to claim the part of Hetar that is now called the Dark Lands, but they have always wanted it all.

"It was then that the battle between light and dark began. The light has always had the advantage for it had most of this world before the evil discovered it. But as the mortals grew more intelligent, less simple and pure of heart, evil began to exert its influence. Wealth is not a bad thing if it is shared with the less fortunate. Greed, however, is evil in its purest form. Some mortals are more fortunate than others. But those who are, cannot count themselves any better than their less fortunate brothers and sisters. Are all Hetarians equal? Only in the eyes of the Celestial Actuary is that so. Those who work harder and succeed are entitled to greater stature, provided they do not abuse those who are not as lucky," Kaliq said. Then he continued.

"In the beginning Hetar's neat division of its citizens was good. The people were never hindered from advancement based on the caste into which they were born. But then Hetar became fixed in its own system, using wealth for power, holding back men who might advance its world. Evil grew stronger. We Shadow Princes, and the Faerie Races sought to give Hetar a final chance. You were born to save them, but when it became evident you could not, then your destiny was turned to another direction. Cronan has not condemned Hetar. They have done it themselves."

"What will happen to Hetar then?" Lara asked.

"Before a year has passed the Magic Races who have protected this world will be gone from it," Kaliq said.

"But I have stopped Kolgrim," Lara protested once again.

"You have delayed him," Kaliq repeated. "That is all, my love."

"I cannot believe there is no hope for Hetar," Lara said. "I will remain until I know it for certain."

"And I will be by your side," he promised her. "Our fates have now been joined."

"If we cannot remain in Hetar where will we go, Kaliq?" she asked him.

He shrugged. "I do not yet know," he told her.

"If you do not know, then perhaps it is not meant we leave," Lara said hopefully. Her faerie green eyes were filled with unshed tears. "I am so ashamed to have failed Hetar." The tears overflowed and slid down her cheeks.

"You have not failed, my love," Kaliq said, taking her into

his arms to comfort her. "It is Hetar, and its people, who have created their own fate by following a well-traveled path that they have traveled before. For twenty-five years after the Hierarch came and went, Hetar improved itself. But as their world grew prosperous once again, they began to fall back into their old ways. Hetar has been come bloated with greed, and ripe with its own debauchery. They have put magic from their lives in an effort to make themselves all-powerful. They have forgotten and ignored their own history. The magic surrounds them, and yet they deny its existence. They give the Celestial Actuary lip service, but nothing more. They have become a people without belief, for if they believed in anything at all they would be afraid. Very afraid."

"There is still hope, Kaliq," Lara persisted. "Tell me there is hope."

"I still believe in miracles, my love," he told her. But he hid his thoughts from her, for he knew for certain what she could not yet come to accept. Hetar was doomed. Then changing the subject he said, "You should speak with Dillon, for Belmair will need to host Hetar's magic. You have done all you can do here for now, Lara. I think a visit to a world that still believes will renew your spirits."

"Tomorrow," Lara said. "I will go tomorrow, my lord. Tonight I would spend with you alone." Reaching up, she touched his handsome face, smiling when he caught her hand to kiss the palm.

"Let us go to Zeroun," he suggested, "and watch the moons rise. They will all be visible tonight before they return to their usual cycle. We will eat, play in the water and make love the night long, my darling."

"Yes!" Lara agreed, and before she could say another word he transported them beneath the awning before the silk tent at the oasis.

Laughing, Lara dissolved her garments, ran across the soft golden sand and flung herself into the water. Kaliq quickly joined her, and they played together, splashing each other like children. She dove beneath the waterfall, and he followed, catching her in his arms, their bodies melting into one another, their lips meeting as they kissed and kissed. Beneath the falling water the pool grew shallow until they could stand on the sandy bottom once again.

Sliding his hands beneath her buttocks, Kaliq lifted Lara up as she put her arms about his neck. His kisses touched her lips, her cheeks, her eyelids as his manhood slipped slowly, slowly into her sheath. His control was amazing. Inch by gradual inch he deliberately pressed himself forward. When he could go no farther he stopped, standing so still he might have been a stone statue.

Lara could hardly breathe as she waited. His superior length and thickness pulsed within her. She squeezed him with the muscles of her sheath. His manhood throbbed with a fiercer beat. Lara clasped him more tightly, and a small groan escaped him. "Ahh," she responded, well pleased with herself.

Faerie witch! he scolded her softly. Walking from beneath the little waterfall, he put them onto the sand of the pool's edge laying her upon her back as he crouched between her open thighs. He unclasped her hands from about his neck, pressing her arms back over her head and beginning to piston her with slow deep strokes of his manhood.

Lara sighed, wrapping her legs about his torso, her ankles locking themselves. Her eyes were closed, and she let herself experience the delicious nuances of each thrust as he delved deeper into her sweetness. *I adore you, my lord,* she whispered to him. *Ahh, yes! That is perfect! Do not cease, I beg you, my darling Kaliq!*

He brought her to perfection once, and then withdrawing from her gathered her into his arms so he might stroke and kiss her. He loved her round breasts, and could have suckled forever upon them. The contours of her body were familiar, and yet he never grew tired of caressing her. Her skin was so soft, and never failed to arouse him.

Lara returned his ardor, her own hands unable to remain still. She clutched at his strong shoulders. Her nails skimmed down his long back. She smoothed her hand over his tight hard buttocks, then reached beneath him to fondle his sac, her palm rippling beneath the soft and tender flesh as she moved the tiny jewels within about.

Do you mean to slay me, faerie witch? Ahh, how I love you!

Their lips met again, the kiss deepening until she was almost faint with the simple pleasure his hands and mouth were giving her. And then he was inside of her again, and Lara cried out with delight as they climbed passion's peak together, and their lust exploded in a wild burst of satisfaction that left them both weak and sated for the moment within each other's bodies. They lay together upon the warm sand, dozed for a short time and then awakened hungry for the evening meal. Entering their pavilion, they found themselves garbed once again in soft silk and wool robes, for the desert nights were cool. Awaiting them was a meal of roast lamb, minted rice, warm bread, butter and fresh fruit upon the low table. Lying among the pillows, Kaliq and Lara fed each other, talking softly to each other as they ate and drank the sweet apricot frine.

Why could it not be like this always, Lara wondered? Why had she not come back to Shunnar sooner when these days might have seemed as if they would go on forever? Now they were once again engaged in a battle with evil. And it was to be a far more subtle conflict this time. Lara knew exactly what her dark son was doing. He meant to conquer Hetar by insinuating himself into their society. Unlike mortals he had the time that they did not. She found she had a grudging admiration for Kolgrim in this. But what would happen to Terah?

"What are you thinking?" Kaliq asked her.

"If you are right we but delay Kolgrim," Lara began. "But when this marriage is finally accomplished, what of Terah and its people? What of the Clan families in the New Outlands, my lord? What will happen to them?"

"Kolgrim has not the military might for war, and neither has Hetar any longer. What remains of the Mercenary Guild is used to guard the caravans of the Taubyl Traders, or litters of the rich these days. Their ranks are decimated now for there are better ways of earning one's bread. A mercenary's life has never been an easy one. As for the Crusader Knights, they have grown old, and there hasn't been a tournament in decades to recruit new potential leaders. What was once a well-trained military force is now a remnant of elderly men practicing upon a parade field once a week. They collect their pensions from the government, and are content. If Hetar learned one thing in the time of the Hierarch, it was to keep their population fed, housed, warm and entertained. If the people have no complaints, then they have no will to rebel against authority," Kaliq said wisely. "And in the end it is less expensive for those in power. They may continue to make their profits with no one to gainsay them.

"Now they have begun to infect both Terah and the New Outlands with their greed. Once the Taubyl Traders discovered the Obscura, and sailed across it to explore what might be there, the New Outlands were doomed. The Ore and the Jewel gnomes bring their goods directly to the docks that the Felan have built on the sea for transport to Hetar. They now compete with the Terahn artisans for Hetar's business. The gnomes can sell their goods cheaper because they not only mine them, they create the jewelry and other goods. And the gemstones and ores they sell to Terah now cost more because the gnomes keep the lion's share for themselves," Kaliq told her.

"I did not know this," Lara said. "I kept to myself because my family had become so wary and uncomfortable of me. I stayed mostly within my own chambers and gardens, but for rides with Dasras. If the Dominus had but come to me, I could have suggested ways to mitigate the damage to Terah." She sighed. "Oh, Kaliq, how I have failed them!" Tears sprang into her eyes.

"Nay," he said, brushing the droplets from her cheeks. "They drove you away, and even had you known, it is unlikely they would have listened to anything you said. Remember the Terahns' stubborn insistence that women are not wise enough to advise. And as their population has never been a large one, without strong leadership they, too, were doomed."

"How could it have come to this?" Lara wondered aloud once more.

"You are dealing with mortals, my love," he reminded her.

"There is mortal blood in me," Lara said.

"Not enough," Kaliq told her. "But even if you were pure mortal I should love you," he said gallantly.

She gave him a quick kiss and a smile, but then grew serious. "What will Kolgrim do when he discovers Nyura missing?"

"I suspect his first emotion will be anger. Then he will realize that we know his plans," Kaliq said, "and it will become interesting. Cronan said we have a year, but no more. We may not even have that. But we need time to evacuate the magic to Belmair. Will you speak with King Dillon?"

Lara nodded. "I have borne four sons," she said. "One was

ordinary, but dear to my heart. One is good. Two are evil. And I have Marzina to consider, as well. If she cannot contain her curiosity about Kolgrim, I fear greatly for her fate."

"Marzina has her own destiny to follow," Kaliq said. "And while she will be curious about Kolgrim she will be careful, too, for she knows he is dangerous."

MARZINA WAS CURIOUS ABOUT this brother she had suddenly learned she had. She sat in the little hall of her home and stared into her green malachite reflecting bowl. *Show me Kolgrim,* she ordered. The water grew cloudy and dark, then cleared, and she saw him. She thought him extraordinarily handsome, but she could also feel the danger that emanated from him. His powers were strong, and growing stronger. *Let me hear what he would say, but keep me safe from him this day,* Marzina softly murmured the spell.

"She knows!" Kolgrim shouted. "Only my dear faerie-woman mother could have done this, would have dared to do it, Alfrigg! How in the name of all the demons living and dead did she find out?"

"You are certainly correct, my lord," Alfrigg said calmly, ever the voice of reason, "but how she learned of your plans is not important. What is important is that we find the Lady Nyura before the season of the mating frenzy comes upon you."

"She is certainly at Shunnar," Kolgrim said slowly. "And it is one place into which I cannot gain entry. So I must bring my dear mother to me. But how?"

"That is simple, my lord. You must gain her attention by taking something that she holds dear," the elderly chancellor said.

Kolgrim snorted. "What?" he said. "The Terahns no longer know or respect her, and it is the same everywhere. She frightens them all, and so they pretend she doesn't exist. Her children are all dead but for the King of Belmair. Since he is half-Shadow I cannot touch him without bringing down the wrath of the princes on myself. Even Nyura is not worth that, Alfrigg. We will simply have to find her."

"The faerie woman, Lara, has another living child," Alfrigg said softly.

"Indeed," Kolgrim said. Then he thought. "Surely you don't mean Magnus Hauk's youngest daughter?" he said. "The little half-faerie girl I once saw? She must surely be dead by now, Alfrigg, or a doddering elder at best."

"Magnus Hauk was not her father," Alfrigg said quietly. "Kol was."

Marzina swallowed hard. Her identity revealed, she could be in danger, but fascinated, she continued to watch and listen to the conversation between Kolgrim and the old dwarf, who was now smiling at his master for having revealed to him something previously unknown but of great value.

Kolgrim's mouth fell open with genuine surprise. "How?" he asked.

"Your faerie mother was newly pregnant with Magnus Hauk's son when Kol caught her on the Dream Plain and ravaged her. He loved her, and was angry she preferred her mortal mate to him. Princess Marzina was conceived then. That is why your father was imprisoned, my lord. He broke the law of the Dream Plain. When your sister was born her maternal grandmother, Queen Ilona, declared she strongly resembled a Nix ancestor with her dark hair and pale skin. No one considered arguing the point. It was believed that the two children born from the faerie woman's womb at the same time were fraternal twins. How could it be otherwise?"

"Another sister," Kolgrim said slowly, and his gray eyes darkened.

"Not a half sister as the Darkling Ciarda was, my lord. You share both parents with Marzina of Terah," Alfrigg pointed out. "She is true blood, not half blood."

"What of her powers? Could our mother use her against me, Alfrigg?" the young Twilight Lord asked his chancellor. "Is she beautiful?"

"I have not seen her since she was a child," Alfrigg said, "but her untrained powers were then great. Now I would imagine she is a power to be reckoned with, but your faerie mother will not use her against you. Remember, she is the light, and she loves this daughter well. But if your sister were in your power, my lord, I imagine that your faerie mother would reveal to you the location where she has hidden your betrothed."

Marzina stood. Picking up the reflecting bowl she emptied it with shaking hands into a planter. She needed to reach her mother, and quickly. But suddenly in a clap of thunder and flash of lightning Kolgrim stood before her, smiling. Marzina shrank from the hand he held out to her. "I will not go with you," she said.

"Ah, you were listening to us, were you?" he replied. "In mortal society they consider it rude to eavesdrop, but we don't consider it that at all, do we, my pretty one? How on earth would we learn what we need to know if we didn't listen at doors?" He laughed at the guilty flush suffusing her face.

Mother! Mother! Hear my plea! Cease all else and come to me! Marzina said.

"She can't hear you, Marzina. I put a spell about your house as I came. I certainly don't want our mother interrupting us. You know, of course, who I am."

"You are Kolgrim, the Twilight Lord," Marzina said.

"And your brother," he added with a charming smile.

"I did not know that until recently," Marzina replied.

"How did you learn it? I would have thought our mother would not want to share that information with you," Kolgrim remarked. "Unless, of course, she means to use you against me, little sister. Does she?"

"I overheard her speaking with Grandmother," Marzina said low.

Kolgrim burst out laughing. "You were eavesdropping!" he chortled. "It must have been quite a shock to learn that the revered Magnus Hauk was not your sire."

"He was my father!" Marzina cried angrily. "Do not ever say he wasn't!"

"I will agree that he believed you his own child, and raised you thusly," Kolgrim said. "But it was my father's seed that gave you life. We are blood kin, little sister, and as such I can never, by our own laws, harm you."

"Yet you murdered your own concubines and their children without a moment's hesitation or remorse," Marzina surprised him by saying. "You violated your own laws, my lord. There is no way in which you can justify such bestiality."

"I wanted my son to have no sisters threatening his rights as the Darkling Ciarda threatened mine and my brother's," Kolgrim responded. "Other than Ciarda the women were no kin of mine."

"And the children?" Marzina pressed him. "They were your blood."

"Females, and barely formed most of them," he said casually. "They had some of my blood in them, but *you,* Marzina! I look at you and can see that the light does not claim you entirely. Stand with me little sister, for I mean to conquer this world of Hetar." His gray eyes blazed with excitement. Reaching out, he caught her hand in his, and before she might protest there was a flash, and Marzina found herself standing in the middle of a strange room.

She gasped, surprised, whirling about. She could see beyond an open balustrade the jagged purple snowcapped peaks of a range of mountains that seemed to go on forever. The skies were a reddish-dun color filled with lightning. Marzina did not need to ask where she was. The Twilight Lord had brought her into the Dark Lands. It was terrifying and beautiful all at once. She was fascinated in spite of herself.

"Now, little sister, you are going to be my guest until my marriage is celebrated and consummated," Kolgrim said in perfectly pleasant tones.

"Take me back immediately!" Marzina snapped at him, knowing even as she spoke that he would not obey her. But she had to try.

"Now, sweeting, you know I cannot do that," Kolgrim said. "Mother has hidden my chosen bride away. I might find her for myself, but I do not choose to waste the time when it's easier to simply take something that our mother values instead. *You!*" he chortled. "Unless, of course, you know where Nyura is. Do you, sweeting?"

"No! I didn't even know you had chosen a bride. Why doesn't Mother want you to have her?" Marzina asked him candidly.

"She is a descendant of Ulla, and carries her powers," he answered. It was not necessary to say more, for being of the magic world Marzina would understand the rest.

"It has taken aeons to get to this point," Marzina said thoughtfully. "The mating of a descendant of Ulla's with a descendant of Jorunn's."

His eyes lit up with pleasure at her intelligence. "You understand the ramifications," he said, smiling at her. While he believed that ordinary women were beneath the male of the species, Kolgrim knew that some women could be their equal, or close to it. His mother was one of these women. This little

sister he had so newly discovered was obviously proving to be
another. He could actually talk with her, and he had to admit
to himself that he had been lonely for another with whom he
might speak on equal footing. "Then you also comprehend why
I must regain custody of Nyura. Soon the season of the mating
frenzy will come upon me, and she is the chosen one even as
our mother was once our father's chosen one."

"If you can only sire one son, and it must be on the chosen
one, then why can't you just wait until you find the girl?"
Marzina asked. "And who chooses your bride for you?"

"The strongest son is sired during the season of the mating
frenzy," Kolgrim explained to her. Then he said, "Come, and
I will show you the Book of Rule. It directs me in all my important actions," he said as he beckoned her across the chamber
where the book sat upon its stand. Opening it, he saw new
words upon the page.

The Faerie Maiden who is your kin can aid you in all you
do. Or destroy you. She cannot be harmed no matter her
direction. Win her over, and the victory is yours.

"I realize that you cannot read the words, for only certain of
us can comprehend this ancient language of the Twilight,"
Kolgrim said.

"What does it say?" Marzina asked him innocently, but to
her surprise the words upon the parchment page were quite un-
derstandable. Still she knew it was wiser to keep this knowledge to herself.

"It directs me to treat you well as my guest while you are here,
little sister," he told her, lying with such charm that had she not
known better she would have easily believed him. He smiled
warmly at her.

"Oh. I expected it would be something with far more portent," Marzina replied, sounding quite disappointed.

He laughed. "The Book of Rule is not always portentous," he said. "Just sometimes." Then changing the subject, he asked, "Do you like my Throne Room?"

"It is beautiful," she responded. "I like the black, the gray and the silver."

"You see," he said. "You will not be unhappy here, little sister."

"You cannot keep me here, my lord," Marzina said.

"Ah, but I can," Kolgrim told her. "I have put a lock upon your magic. You cannot leave until I let you leave."

Return me now from whence I came. I do not choose to come again, Marzina said. But nothing happened. She remained where she was. The girl grew very pale. Until now very few had been able to thwart her magic. Her grandmother. Her mother. Prince Kaliq. And they had not interfered with her in years. "*My mother* will punish you for this," Marzina said, in what she hoped passed for a hard and strong voice. "You have overstepped your bounds, my lord."

"You are brave," he told her admiringly. "I only intend keeping you until *our mother* releases the lady Nyura, my bride, to me. She will resist for a brief time, of course. But that will allow us to become better acquainted, little sister."

"I have no desire to know you better, my lord," Marzina said.

Kolgrim laughed. "You are a poor liar," he responded. "You wanted to know all about me, which is why you watched me in your reflecting bowl. I could sense your eyes on me, which is why I was able to catch you so quickly, little sister."

"You did not even know about me until the dwarf told you," Marzina replied. "Who is he? He is very old."

"Aye, he is. He has served several Twilight Lords before me

as chancellor. His name is Alfrigg. He would spend his declining years tending his mushroom and nightshade gardens if he could, but I have found no one to replace him," Kolgrim told her. "I have never known him to keep a secret from me before, but I forgive him for he saved this secret for the time I would need it the most."

"Return me to my hall," Marzina said. "By taking me you have set yourself up against a host of those who would gladly destroy you."

"No," Kolgrim said. "I want my bride returned to me first."

Marzina sighed. "I shall be here a long time then," she told him. "Where am I to sleep? You took me just before the dinner hour. I am starving. Do you mean to starve me then?"

"Will our mother sacrifice you needlessly, little sister?" he asked her. "I mean to have Nyura to wed and bed. Her path was chosen centuries ago."

"You mean to bring the darkness to the world of Hetar, *brother*. You intend to bring it forever, but the good in our world will not allow you to do so," Marzina said.

"Nay, little one. I will only lead Hetar into the darkness. It is the son Nyura bears me who will keep it there," Kolgrim told her. "That is why our mother is so desperate to stop me. But she will not this time. She lingered too long among the mortals. And worse, she behaved like them except in the privacy of her own chambers. They no longer believe in her, or in the magic world. They do not even believe in their own mortality. Status, power, wealth and lust have become their deities. They will follow any creature who promises them more of it, and I will. I do not have to bring the darkness to Hetar. They will bring it upon themselves."

"Yes, yes, but where am I to sleep?" Marzina demanded of him.

Kolgrim laughed aloud again and held out his hand to her. "Come, and we will eat. Then you will be shown to the quarters that will always be yours when you come to visit me, little one." He smiled warmly at her as he led her from his Throne Room down a beautiful dark marble corridor to a small, intimate dining room.

Marzina could not help herself. She took his hand, and he gave it a little squeeze. She had to admit that he was, as she had been warned, a very charming man. She knew she was going to like him in spite of herself. His manners were impeccable as he seated her. Who had taught him, she wondered. "When are you going to send for Mother?" she asked him as a silent servant ladled soup into a bowl before her. She took a spoonful, and it tasted of the earth and the forest. It was delicious.

"I'm not," Kolgrim said. "She and Ilona keep a close eye on you, although you have not been aware of it. They will both know soon enough that you are missing. It will not take Mother long to know with whom you are currently residing."

"And then she will come and get me," Marzina said as she tore a piece off a warm loaf of bread, dipping it into her soup before popping it into her mouth.

"She will come, little sister, but she will not take you from me," he told her.

"Why not?" Marzina asked him.

"Because you will be where she cannot retrieve you," Kolgrim told her. "She must first return Nyura to me so our marriage may be celebrated. Then I will release you."

He smiled at her. "Don't worry. I promised our mother long ago never to harm any of my blood, and I have not. Now eat your supper, little sister."

The soup was followed by a platter of some kind of fish, lying upon a bed of dark green leaves and thin slices of lemon; a capon roasted to a golden-brown, and stuffed with sweet and tart fruits; a stew of venison in a rich wine gravy that was filled with leeks, mushrooms and slivers of carrot; more fresh warm bread, butter and two cheeses. When it had all been cleared away a sponge cake soaked in sweet wine and covered with rich thick cream was served.

"My aunt is fond of cake like this," Marzina remarked as she enjoyed the sweet.

"Ah yes, the beautiful dragon Nidhug," Kolgrim replied.

"You've seen her?" Marzina was surprised.

"When Ilona finally invited Nidhug to her domain because the egg in the dragon's nursery hatched a faerie child, and not an infant dragon," Kolgrim said, "I came to see for myself. Of course no one knew I was there." He smiled. "Have they produced any other children, Prince Cirillo and Nidhug?" he asked her.

"There is another egg in the nursery nest, but it is believed that one is Nidhug's successor, and will not hatch until a thousand years before her time as guardian of Belmair is to come to an end," Marzina told him. "It will take the Great Dragon of Belmair that length of time to teach her heir all he will need to know."

"Fascinating," Kolgrim said, shaking his head. Then, seeing she had finished, he asked her, "Are you ready to see your chamber, little one?"

"I am tired," Marzina admitted.

"Come along then," Kolgrim said, standing up. He led her from the dining room down another wide marble corridor. At its end was a single door. Opening it, he ushered Marzina into the chamber. "It is simple, but I thought you would prefer it. Your own home is without ostentation. You may come and go within my palace whenever you choose. However, be advised that if you are not in this place when our mother arrives to discuss matters with me, you will be magicked back here immediately, and the chamber door will be locked. Do you understand, Marzina?"

"Of course," she answered him. "But if you think you can keep Mother from retrieving me, you are mistaken. Her magic is far stronger than yours, my lord."

"We shall see, little sister," he told her. Then, bending, he kissed her cheek and was gone, closing the door behind him.

Marzina looked about her. The chamber was windowless. The floors were smooth stone as were the walls. It was more a dungeon cell but for the comfortable furnishings. There was a curtained bed draped in lavender velvet and covered in soft furs. Beneath it she noted a delicately painted chamber pot. At the foot of the bed was an iron-bound trunk. Lifting its rounded lid, Marzina was surprised to find it filled with beautiful robes made from a mixture of silk and fine soft wool. The colors, however, were mostly dark. Forest-green, deep blue, black, lavender and a rich purple. She let the lid fall shut and, going to the door, turned the handle. It opened, as Kolgrim had said it would. Marzina was surprised but pleased he had not lied to her.

Shutting the door, she continued her inspection of the chamber. It had a large fireplace that burned scented wood that perfumed and warmed the room. In the coals of the hearth was a dark bronze basin and pitcher of water for her bathing. There was a small round candle stand by the bed with a thick taper in a carved silver taperstick with its own snuffer attached by a delicate chain. A dark wood sideboard stood against one wall. Upon it was a silver tray with two decanters and a single silver cup. There was also a bowl of fresh fruit, and a little plate of honey cakes. Nothing was lacking within the room that a guest would need, Marzina thought.

Lying across the foot of the bed, a soft night garment of white cotton was ready for her. She wondered if she was being watched but then decided it didn't matter. Before Marzina prepared herself for bed, however, she tried her spell once again. *Return me now from whence I came. I do not choose to come again.* But nothing happened. That was twice now she had caught Kolgrim in a truth. She would not have thought such a thing possible of a Twilight Lord.

With a sigh of resignation she took the basin and pitcher from the hearth, set them on the sideboard, poured the warm water into the vessel and bathed. When she was finished she was surprised to see the water drain away from the basin. With a little laugh she put them back, noting as she did that the pitcher was full again. Then Marzina took off her gown, donned the night garment that had been laid out for her and climbed into the bed. It was as comfortable as it looked, and deciding there was nothing else she could do, Marzina fell asleep. It had been a very long day.

Watching her in his reflecting bowl, Kolgrim smiled to himself. While love was not an emotion he usually experienced, he had come in the few short hours he had known her to adore this younger sister of his. When their mother released Nyura, he would keep his word and release Marzina to her. But he meant to win Marzina to the dark side. What an asset she would be to him. And it would certainly break their mother's faerie heart. He smiled again.

8

"SHE IS GONE!" ILONA, QUEEN OF THE FOREST Faeries said to her daughter as she materialized in burst of purple mist.

Lara looked up. "Good morning, Mother," she said. "Who is gone?"

"Marzina! Marzina is gone! I went to Fairevue to discuss some matters of great import with her, and she was gone, Lara. She was there two days ago her old body servant says, but then the next morning she was gone."

"Kolgrim!" Lara said immediately. "Kolgrim has her. He knows how much I love her. He has taken her in exchange for Nyura."

"To wed?" Ilona sounded scandalized.

"Nay, nay. The Book of Rule has chosen Nyura as his mate," Lara said.

"Will he harm Marzina?" Ilona asked her daughter. "He does not know she is his sister, after all."

"Alfrigg knew and has undoubtedly told the Twilight Lord the truth by now, which is why Kolgrim acted so swiftly to steal

Marzina. Nay, he will not harm her," Lara said. "But I can guarantee you, Mother, that he has some wicked plan in mind. He needs Nyura back quickly for the season of the mating frenzy is almost upon him. The fiercer the frenzy, the stronger the child he will spawn on Nyura. He cannot wait."

"You must go to him at once!" Ilona said.

Lara could not help but laugh. "Did you believe I would wait. Aye, I will pay Kolgrim a visit to learn his terms and decide how we may delay him," she said. "Tell Kaliq where I have gone. I will not linger long in the Dark Lands." Then in a puff of lavender mist she was gone.

"Mother!" Kolgrim smiled toothily at her as she appeared in his hall. "How lovely of you to pay me a visit." Stepping forward, he took up her hand and kissed it.

Lara glared at him. "Where is Marzina?" she demanded without any preamble.

"My little sister?" he said, smiling again at her.

Lara was silent a moment. There it was. Out in the open at last after all these years. "Aye, where is your sister?" she said wearily. "I know you have not harmed her, Kolgrim, but I also know that you have her."

"She is a charming girl," he said. "I mean to win her to the darkness. Her blood is equally divided, Mother. The decision is hers to make. She will be mine eventually."

"Never!" Lara replied. "You will not blacken and steal her soul from her, Kolgrim. My daughter is filled with the light. She will always be."

"My blood began as hers did, Mother. Equal parts light and dark, yet the dark triumphed in me. I am my father's son. I might have been my mother's son, but that you deserted me and destroyed my father in the process," he accused her. "The Book of Rule had declared you his true mate, and he loved you."

"Oh, Kolgrim, do you not yet understand that the Book of Rule was manipulated by the magic world, even as I was, in order that your father mate with me and give me his son. He stole my memories from me to accomplish this, and when the Shadow Princes saw my memories restored I did what I knew had to be done. I divided the child in my womb into two in order to cause chaos in the Dark Lands. And after I birthed those twins I fled back to my own world where the memories of that time here were hidden from me so I should not go mad. I was another man's wife. I had other children who needed me."

"I needed you!" he told her, anguished. It was the first honest emotion she had ever seen him exhibit and Lara was surprised.

"Your father wanted only one thing from me. An heir. I gave him two. But he could not leave me alone. He tugged at those hidden memories, until finally the Munin had to restore them all. Then I carried the burden of them, of those months with your father here in the Dark Lands, and it was painful beyond all else, Kolgrim," Lara said.

"You put us from your thoughts," Kolgrim accused.

"I did," Lara said bluntly, "because had I not, I should have gone mad. I despised your father and what he did to me here, and afterward on the Dream Plain, but it did not negate the fact that I had borne two little boys, and then left them to a terrible fate. But your father would have never let either you or Kolbein go, and I could not remain."

"Did you ever love us?" he asked pointedly.

"I could not allow myself to love you," she answered him candidly.

He nodded. Then he said, "Return Nyura to me, and I will return Marzina to you. I will not promise you, however, not to take her from you."

"You will try, but you will not succeed," Lara told him. "Marzina is my child, and she is of the light, Kolgrim. As to Nyura, since I know you will not harm your sister I shall wait a while before returning your bride to you."

His handsome face darkened. "You know I must mate her soon," he said meaningfully. "The marriage must be celebrated soon. You know the reasons."

"Aye, I do," Lara told him with a small smile. "But a son is a son, Kolgrim. Don't you think that is so?"

The young Twilight Lord shook his head ruefully. "Mother, dearest mother," he began. "How little you must think of me. My powers lack a certain strength outside of the Dark Lands, it is true, though they are increasing each day. But here in my own castle my powers are strongest. Did you think it would be as simple as I have Marzina, you have Nyura and we will make a civilized exchange? Nay, it will not. If I return my sister to you before the wedding, you will find a way to conceal her while snatching Nyura from me once again. That will not happen. I will return Marzina to you after the wedding has been celebrated in Hetar. And the wedding will be celebrated in a few days' time. Come," he beckoned her. "Let me show you what will happen if you do not return Nyura to me in a timely manner. Marzina is sleeping now, and so she will not be frightened."

Kolgrim led Lara from his hall, and after several turns they entered a long corridor lit by torches that were set in iron holders bolted to the stone wall. At the end of the corridor he stopped before a single small wood door. With a wave of his hand the wall before them became transparent so the chamber beyond was visible to their eyes. Looking into it, Lara thought it was very comfortably furnished, and she saw her daughter sleeping soundly in a fine high bed. Kolgrim pointed a single finger at the chamber, and suddenly all its walls and even its floor and ceiling were translucent.

"It is a glass cube," he said, "attached firmly to my castle. It hangs over the endless canyon that separates this structure from my House of Women. If the magic holding this chamber is released then it will fall into the canyon."

"You cannot harm her!" Lara cried softly. "She is your blood, not just by me, but by her sire as well, Kolgrim!"

He smiled sweetly at her. "She would not be harmed, but she would face eternity within a glass cube, falling deeper and deeper into a bottomless pit, mother dearest. I seriously doubt any magic—yours, mine, the Shadow Princes—could save her from her fate once the chamber began its descent. But of course you are welcome to attempt a rescue. Or you can return Nyura to me immediately. I am not an unreasonable man so I will give you a day in which to make your decision," he said.

"You are a monster!" Lara cried, looking into his handsome face. Then she turned to look back at Marzina, but the wall had become stone once again.

Mother, return from whence you came. I'll call when you must come again. Kolgrim spoke the spell silently.

"MY LOVE!" KALIQ CAUGHT HER as she literally fell into his arms, sobbing. "What has happened? What is the matter? Speak to me, Lara!"

"Lara, why do you weep so bitterly," Ilona demanded.

"He is Kol's son," Lara sobbed, "and his father would be proud of him."

"Does he have Marzina?" Kaliq asked. "But of course he does, and he wants Nyura in exchange. We can delay him, my love. He won't hurt Marzina. You know it."

Lara swallowed back her tears. She pushed back the fear he

had engendered in her heart and soul. Then she told her mother and her life mate of her visit to Kolgrim. "He is ruthless. He will not hesitate to send my daughter into an agony of an eternity."

"But can we trust him to return her once he has his way," Ilona wondered aloud.

"What choice do we have?" Lara said. "But I do believe if he gets his way he will release Marzina to us. He wants the triumph of luring her to the dark side, of hurting me. He wants to win this new war he makes for Hetar. I must attempt to warn Palben. I must get him to listen to me."

"He will not," Kaliq said quietly. "Palben will take a second wife tomorrow. She is another of Grugyn Ahasferus's grand-daughters. Her name is Divsha. Your great-grandson is a clever man, my love. He will now be able to publicly claim a blood tie with the Twilight Lord for he does not know he already has one."

"If Hetar and the Dark Lands are united by marriage, what will become of Terah?" Lara fretted. "Did not Grugyn Ahasferus have three granddaughters? What of the third girl? If she is not wed, then I can make a match with Terah. Cadarn's oldest son is not wed. Did not Anoush predict that one day I would unite the worlds? And if the three are united and bound by familial ties then perhaps we can prevent Kolgrim from overwhelming all in his damnable darkness," Lara said excitedly. "All three of them will be busy attempting to overcome the other two, and rule alone."

"It is possible," Ilona said slowly but her voice held little conviction.

Lara would not be content until she had accomplished it, Kaliq knew. But she would not change the fate assigned this world. Yet until Lara could be convinced that all was lost, she would not move forward and could not meet her destiny.

"You will have to move swiftly. Cadarn will not be easy to sway, and you may not convince him. You know he will not acknowledge our world of magic," the prince reminded her.

"Then you must come with me and convince him that it does exist," Lara said.

He nodded in agreement.

"I will come, too," Ilona said. "We must dazzle this foolish mortal publicly so he is unable to deny the evidence of his own eyes."

Lara laughed. "Whenever I made magic," she said, "that is just what he did. He would declare the air poisoned, or the cheese bad."

"Not this time," Kaliq said. Lara was wrong, but he would aid her to the best of his ability until she could admit it. "You must look the part," he told her. *Make this faerie woman fair so no one can deny her there.*

And Lara found herself clothed in a beautiful bejeweled robe of cloth-of-gold. Her long gilt hair was braided with thin plaits intertwined with delicate gold and silver chains filled with tiny sparkling gemstones and pearls. About her forehead was a narrow gold band, an oval emerald in its center. Ilona waved a languid hand, and a pair of iridescent wings sprouted from Lara's shoulder blades.

Lara chuckled. "Why, Mother, you never gave me wings before," she said.

"Mortals have certain ideas," Ilona told her drily. "Today we will cater to them."

And a pair of pearlescent wings popped from her back. She was garbed in a royal-purple and cloth-of-gold silk gown, her gold crown of office upon her golden head.

Kaliq had transformed himself into his all-white trousers and bejeweled white tunic. Upon his dark head he wore a small turban, a bloodred ruby and three plumes at its center. A small gold dagger, its hilt decorated with diamonds was stuck into his wide sash. A white satin cloak lined in cloth-of-gold floated out of the air, fastening itself onto broad shoulders. His dark leather boots rose to his knees. "I think we are all ready now," he said. He nodded to an attending servant, who brought a reflecting bowl to his master. Kaliq gazed into it and then said, "They are in the Great Hall of the Dominus's castle, celebrating Cadarn's birthday. Ilona, will you go first?"

"Of course, my lord," the Queen of the Forest Faeries said with an arch smile.

THE RAFTERS OF DOMINUS Cadarn's Great Hall shook with the clap of thunder as Ilona appeared in their midst. "Greetings, kinsman," Ilona said.

A second clap followed the first, and Lara appeared. "Cadarn," she said.

And finally Kaliq stepped from what appeared to be thin air. "My lord." He bowed, flourishing his cape as he did so.

The silence was palpable. Those in attendance to celebrate the Dominus Cadarn's birthday stood with open mouths. What they were seeing could not possibly be. Surely this was some entertainment. But there were a few in the hall who still believed in magic, and for them what was happening was marvelous. They recognized the magical trio, and were excited to learn why they were here and what was to come.

"How do you explain us away, my lord Dominus?" Kaliq asked Cadarn. "Is the air poisoned? Then open the windows and doors here, but we will still remain. Perhaps it is something you all ate this evening? Even if you purge yourselves we will remain before you. Deny the evidence of your own eyes, Cadarn, son of Amhar, grandson of Taj, great-grandson of

Magnus Hauk. Look at us, and say we do not exist," Kaliq said in a deep and commanding voice that boomed about the silent chamber.

"Who are you?" the Dominus asked, his voice shaking slightly.

"I am Prince Kaliq of the Shadows," came the answer. He drew Ilona forward. "And this is your great-great-grandmother, Ilona, Queen of the Forest Faeries. You know your great-grandmother, Domina Lara, widow of Magnus Hauk."

"It is not possible," Cadarn said low. He had been relieved when Lara departed Terah. He could now relegate her to history and legend. But here she stood before him with her two companions, and he was finding it difficult to say they did not exist.

"Reach your hand out, mortal, and touch us," Kaliq said. "We are real. It is time you admitted to it. We come to help you, for the darkness is threatening once again."

Cadarn kept his hand by his side. "We need no help," he said icily.

"That I should ever live to see a Dominus of Terah not just stubborn, but stupid, as well," Lara said to him. "Magic exists, you lumpish fool! And while you look the other way, Hetar and the Dark Lands are making an alliance against you. The Twilight Lord will wed a Hetarian noblewoman. The Lord High Ruler makes that girl's cousin his second wife. If you are to survive this disastrous union, your son, Vaclar, must wed Yamka, granddaughter of the great Hetarian magnate, Grugyn Ahasferus."

"Vaclar will marry a proper Terahn wife," Cadarn said.

"Do you not understand, Cadarn," Lara said to him. "Hetar and the Dark Lands will take Terah into their keeping. You, and all of your people will be enslaved. The darkness threatens Terah!"

Prince Vaclar stepped forward. He bowed to the uninvited

guests. "There is yet no betrothal made on my behalf," he said to his father. "If what the Domina Lara says is true then it would behoove us to take her advice, my lord father."

"These creatures before us do not, cannot exist, Vaclar. Your imagination has been triggered by something in the air."

Lara's hand flashed out, and she slapped the Dominus Cadarn's face. The sound of the blow echoed throughout the hall.

His hand flew to his cheek, and then Cadarn shouted, "Arrest this woman! She has struck the Dominus a blow."

"If I do not exist, Cadarn, then I cannot have struck you," Lara said quietly. "Nor should you have felt the blow, nor should the imprint of my fingers be upon your face, but it seems to be." A small looking glass appeared in her hand. "See?" she said.

He peered into the mirror. Her mark was clear upon his cheek.

Prince Vaclar snickered just slightly.

The Dominus Cadarn sent him a dark look. "I am willing to acknowledge that you exist," he said to the trio before him. "But you are certainly an anomaly from a time past that now haunts this hall."

Prince Kaliq laughed aloud. "We have indeed visited this hall in times past, my lord Dominus, but we are no ghosts." He held out his hand. "Take it, and see that I am flesh and bone, even as you are. The Domina Lara seeks to help you, Cadarn of Terah. She has always acted in Terah's best interests. She returns now to do so."

"Is she pretty?" the Terahn prince asked. "This Hetarian maiden."

"I have not seen her," Lara answered truthfully.

"Who is she then that you would have me wed her?"

"Her grandfather is the most wealthy and influential man in

Hetar," Lara explained. "Grugyn Ahasferus has three grand-daughters. One will wed the Twilight Lord. Another will become the second wife of Hetar's Lord High Ruler. If Terah is not to be left out, you must wed the third. Hetar, Terah and the Dark Lands will then all be linked by a blood tie. It is vital to Terah's survival that this link be forged."

"I will do it then," Prince Vaclar said.

"You do not have my permission to make a marriage," the Dominus Cadarn said.

"And when you wed it will be to a good Terahn maiden."

"Were you not listening, my lord father? Would you permit Hetar to gain this advantage over us? When two are linked, the third is likely to be the object of their scorn," Prince Vaclar told his father. He turned to Lara. "The girl has a rich dower?"

Lara smiled. "She certainly will, but you will have to convince her grandfather that you are the man for her. Your great-uncle Amren will know more than I do."

"I can't have my heir living in Hetar," the Dominus Cadarn spoke up.

"He will return home from Hetar with his bride," Lara said.

"She must become Terahn in her ways," the Dominus continued.

"She will. Hetarian wives are most obedient, my lord," Lara murmured.

"How will you accomplish this marriage?" Cadarn asked.

"Your son will come with us," Ilona spoke up. "Your brother and your uncle will certainly have invitations to the Lord High Ruler's wedding. They will bring Terah's heir with them as his father's personal representative. Palben will be quite pleased by this. You are kin, after all, even if you have forgotten it."

"We are kin to Palben? How?" the Dominus inquired.

"His grandmother, Princess Zagiri of Terah, and your grandfather, the Dominus Taj, were brother and sister," Ilona explained. "How can you be so ignorant of your own history, Cadarn of Terah?" She sniffed dismissively.

About them the Terahn court watched and listened, fascinated. With their Dominus and his heir in conversation with these unusual beings, Cadarn would have a difficult time denying the existence of magic in the future. But those who knew him best understood that he probably would. Cadarn did not like being proven wrong.

"His garments are all wrong," Ilona said, staring at Vaclar. "He is not royal enough." She waved her hand over the Terahn prince, and he was suddenly garbed in dark blue velvet embroidered with gold. "What do you think?" she asked Kaliq and Lara.

There was an audible gasp from the Terahns.

"Too severe," Lara said, looking to Kaliq. "Don't you think so, my love? He is young, and passably fair. He must appear distinguished and wealthy without any sign of ostentation. What do you think of this?" She waved her hand at Vaclar, and the dark blue became a lightly bejeweled sky-blue velvet tunic that reach below his knees. The sleeves and hem of the garment were trimmed in pale fur. Beneath it he wore cream-colored stockings embroidered in gold. "He has Magnus's coloring, and I think these colors suit him better. The girl will fall in love with him on sight," Lara said with a smile.

"And her grandfather will immediately appreciate the quality of his garments, which indicate a man of taste and wealth," Kaliq noted.

"His hair needs a little bit of a wave to it," Ilona said. She ran her hand over Vaclar's dark gold head, and it grew wavy, one small curl escaping to fall over his forehead. It was very flattering. The Queen of the Forest Faeries looked the young man over from head to toe. "He needs silver buckles on his shoes," she said, and put them there. "And a short velvet cape." It appeared on his shoulders. "There! He is ready."

"Ready? Ready for what?" Cadarn asked nervously.

"The sun is rising over The City now," Lara said to him. "We are taking Vaclar to the wedding of his kinsman, the Lord High Ruler Palben II, my lord."

"Are you mad?" Cadarn now shouted. "Look outside the windows of this hall. It is night, not daybreak."

Ilona shook her head wearily. "How can he be so ignorant?" she asked her companions. "Magnus wasn't ignorant at all."

"Terah has fallen back into its old ways," Lara replied. "Do you think Vaclar needs a chain and pendant, Mother?"

Ilona looked at the Terahn prince with a critical eye. "Aye, I think you are right, darling." *Chain appear upon his chest so this prince will look his best.*

"Oh, that's much better," Lara said as the heavy gold chain with its jeweled pendant appeared about the prince's neck, falling upon his doublet.

The Dominus was staring, bug-eyed.

Kaliq stepped next to him. "Hetar and Terah occupy the same world, my lord, but each is on a different side of that world. Consequently when it is day in Hetar it is night here in Terah. Our sun can but light one half of our world at a time."

Cadarn nodded slowly as he struggled to digest the Shadow Prince's words. "Then how will you reach The City in time for the festivities?" he ventured softly to Kaliq.

"We will use our magic," the Shadow Prince said quietly. "Do not fear, my lord. We will return your son to you safely in several days' time." Then, flourishing his cape to enclose Lara, Ilona and the young Terahn prince, he took them to the beautiful mansion in the Golden District of The City where Prince Amren had lived with his Hetarian wife for many years.

AMREN'S WIFE, CLARINDA, shrieked with surprise as the quartet appeared in the hall as they were seated breaking their fast.

Terah's former ambassador arose from his High Board and hurried to greet the unexpected guests. "Grandmother, welcome to my home," he said, taking her hands in his and kissing them.

"He has manners," Ilona said, looking Amren up and down. In his youth he would have been a handsome young man, she thought. Now she found him distinguished.

"This is your great-grandmother, Queen Ilona." Lara introduced her mother. "This is Taj's younger son, Mother."

Amren took up Ilona's hands to kiss. "I thought she was your sister, Grandmother," he said, giving Ilona a winning smile.

"And he has charm," Ilona cooed.

"This is Prince Kaliq of the Shadows," Lara continued, "and I'm sure you recognize your nephew, Vaclar."

"Indeed I do, and I see you have personally attended to his wardrobe," Amren said approvingly. He turned to his wife. "Finish your meal, my dear. My guests and I must speak privily. Come with me," he said to the others, leading them quickly to a book-lined chamber that overlooked a green and spacious garden. "Sit, sit," he invited them, "and tell me why you are here."

"Palben marries a granddaughter of Grugyn Ahasferus today. Tomorrow the Twilight Lord weds another of that family's maidens. One remains. You must help me to arrange a marriage between that last of Grugyn's granddaughters and the Dominus's son and heir. That way Hetar, Terah and the Dark Lands will be bound by a blood tie. No one will have an advantage over the other."

"I know that we are already related to Palben," Amren said slowly.

"But Palben does not know it, nor would he acknowledge it. His knowledge of his family ties is as scant as Cadarn's," Lara said. "We need to forge a new tie. The remaining of Grugyn's granddaughters must be furious at being overlooked. She is certainly complaining to her family. Offering the magnate the crown prince of Terah for this remaining granddaughter will appeal to him. It will also bring honor to his house. I am sure that Lord Kolgrim paid a high price for Nyura, and Palben was clever enough to ask for another of these girls for a second wife, binding him by blood with Lord Kolgrim. If Terah is left out in the cold, what is to prevent Hetar and its new ally from invading our lands and enslaving our people?"

"Indeed," Amren Hauk said thoughtfully.

"Do it quietly, Amren. Get Palben's permission to pursue a match today while he is in a good mood with this new marriage alliance. Tomorrow the Twilight Lord will marry Nyura and take her back to his castle immediately after the wedding feast. He will remain there until he is certain she is with child. And while he is distracted, Vaclar will marry his bride. Kolgrim means to bring the darkness to our world, Amren. But his own laws forbid his harming kin. Perhaps we can stop him by making this triple alliance."

"And if we cannot?" Amren asked quietly. "Unlike my late brother and my nephew, I know the history of our worlds, Grandmother. I know the battles you have fought, and won. But I sense something is different this time. What is it?" His turquoise-blue eyes had not faded, though he was over seventy now. They reminded her of Magnus's eyes, Lara thought.

Tell him, Kaliq murmured in her ear. *Tell him everything.*

He can't be entirely trusted, Lara replied. *He will do what is best for his own interests, Kaliq.*

Cronan says Hetar is doomed, Kaliq reminded her. *But perhaps there is a small chance we may save it once again although to what purpose I do not know.*

"There is much you do not know, Amren, and most of it I don't think you would believe," Lara said, smiling. "The sorcerer Usi had two concubines, Jorunn and Ulla. Both were with child when he sent them away, not so much to protect them, but to protect the offspring he had sired on them. Jorunn came to the Dark Lands, and from her loins came Usi's son, who has fathered this line of Twilight Lords. Ulla went to Hetar, where she bore a daughter who married into the House of Ahasferus. Since that time one female in each generation has possessed the magical powers that Usi bestowed on Ulla. In the current generation it is Nyura who holds those powers. Kolgrim wants her powers."

"And when he gains them," Amren said slowly, "he will become all-powerful. Aye, I see, Grandmother. But in the past the Twilight Lords' powers were good, but never great. His father, Kol, must have wed with magic to produce such a strong son. Do you know who Lord Kolgrim's mother is, Grandmother?"

"I am Kolgrim's mother," Lara told him.

"You!" Amren's handsome face was shocked. "How…"

"I was kidnapped, and my memories stolen. I was told I was Kol's wife. The magic world had planned it carefully because I was meant to cause chaos in the Dark Lands. When my memory was restored I found myself with child, and my purpose in the greater scheme of things was explained. I used my own magic to split the child in two, so that I bore twin sons to Kol. Such a thing had never happened. I came back to my own world. Kol disappeared and has not been seen since. His chancellor hid the twins so no one would harm them. They grew up not knowing who they really were. Then one of Kol's daughters learned the secret, found them, told them who they were and set them against one another. She planned to rule the Dark Lands herself, but in the end Kolgrim overcame her and his brother, Kolbein. That was over a hundred years ago, Amren. Magnus Hauk had only just died, and your father, Taj, become Dominus of Terah."

"Did Magnus Hauk know what happened?" Amren asked her.

Lara nodded. "I could not keep secrets from him," she said. "But as for the rest of our worlds, their collective memory of what had happened was erased. We wanted peace, and Kolgrim was too new to his position to cause difficulty."

"But now he is not," Amren said. "Why not simply stop the wedding?"

"Palben would not agree," Lara told him.

Amren thought a moment and then said, "Nay, he would not. The advantages to Hetar, to himself, are too great in his eyes." He looked at her with admiring eyes. "I will keep your secrets, Grandmother. I am honored that you shared them with me."

Lara nodded her thanks then said, "You have served Terah with honor, Amren. I am proud of you, and know that Magnus Hauk would be proud, as would your father, my son, Taj. Do not forget your heritage, whatever happens. Terah has always walked in the light. May it continue to do so."

"And Hetar, too," he replied. "They are not bad people, Grandmother. Just heedless lovers of everything that they can wrap their hands about."

She nodded at him. "Age has helped you become a good man," Lara said.

"Or perhaps it is the faerie blood in my veins," he replied with an amused smile.

Lara laughed. "Perhaps," she agreed.

"If you two are through chattering," Ilona said impatiently, "there is much to be done this day."

"I will take Vaclar with me to the wedding," Amren said, "and see he is introduced about to all the people he should know. His uncle Cadoc must be advised of the heir's arrival. I will send a faerie post immediately." He turned to his wife, who had just appeared at the door of the chamber. "Clarinda, my dear, see that Prince Vaclar is fed before we must leave for the festivities."

"What of these people?" the lady said, looking nervously at Lara, Kaliq and Ilona.

The Queen of the Forest Faeries glared at the poor woman. "I am not *people*," she said irritably. "I am a queen, you foolish mortal female." Then with a clap of thunder and a puff of purple smoke, Ilona was gone.

Amren's wife staggered and held on to the doorjamb to keep from falling. "Oh my!" she said in a weak voice, her eyes locked upon Kaliq and Lara.

The Shadow Prince stepped forward and gallantly put a hand beneath the lady Clarinda's elbow. "Please do not let us distress you, my lady. We have but come to help." He led her to where Prince Vaclar stood. "May I introduce you to your husband's great-nephew, heir apparent to the throne of Terah, Prince Vaclar. Your Highness, this lady is your great-aunt Clarinda. She will see to your comfort before you must leave for the Lord High Ruler's wedding."

Vaclar bowed with an elegant flourish and, taking the lady's hand, kissed it. "I am delighted to make your acquaintance, my lady great-aunt," he said.

Soothed by the Shadow Prince's gentle voice and normal

behavior, the lady Clarinda was eased in her mind. "Your Highness," she said curtsying to Vaclar.

"Dear great-aunt Clarinda," Vaclar said, smiling at her, "we are family. You need not curtsy to me."

"Oh nay, dear boy," the good woman answered him. "It must never be said that a Hetarian lady of rank such as myself forgot her manners in the presence of royalty." Then she brought him up to the High Board and called to her servants to feed him immediately.

"We will leave you to do what you must," Lara said to Amren.

"If I need you," he answered her, "how can I find you?"

"You have but to say these words. *Grandmother Lara, hear my plea. Cease all else and come to me.* If you call me, Amren, I will come." Then she put a hand on his arm. "Thank you," she said to him. Then Lara disappeared in a puff of lavender mist.

Amren blinked. Her mode of transport always surprised him. He looked about for Prince Kaliq, but the Shadow Lord had also departed. Amren Hauk chuckled softly to himself. How foolish he had been. How foolish his whole nation was that they had put magic from them. Magic existed. And it was fascinating.

RETURNING TO SHUNNAR, LARA immediately turned to Kaliq, who was by her side. "I believe we have begun this campaign well, my lord. We shall again defeat the Twilight Lord, and all his ilk. I will not let the darkness come! *I won't!*"

The Shadow Prince took her into his arms. "You are a brave faerie woman, my love," he told her. She was brave, he thought. But her efforts this time were for naught. Still Lara was not a woman who would blindly accept a fate she could not live with for she was an optimistic creature of light and of hope.

He stroked the soft gilt-colored hair beneath his big hand.

Soon the exodus would start, and the magic would slowly slip away from Hetar, leaving it vulnerable to the darkness. Kaliq wished it were otherwise, but Hetar now must accept the fate it had carved out for itself. Lara would resist until the bitter end, he suspected. But then they would depart into the Cosmos. His beautiful faerie woman would help to create a new world. She would shed tears for Hetar, but she would also be happy again because they would be together.

Lara looked up into his handsome face. "You are thinking," she said with a small smile. "I can almost hear the cogs and wheels within your head."

"You have devised a clever plot, my love," he told her. "If we can get Vaclar wed to the last of Grugyn Ahasferus's granddaughters, the bond between Hetar, Terah and the Dark Lands will be unbreakable at least for the generation to come. Kolgrim will not be pleased. I'm certain he meant to pit Hetar and Terah against one another to their detriment. But now, my love, you must return his bride, Nyura, to him. Our time is short, and he will take his revenge upon Marzina if you do not."

"I know," Lara replied. "I will go now. Do not come. He will not harm me."

And suddenly she was gone from his arms.

"MOTHER!" KOLGRIM LOOKED UP from his throne where he had been seated. "Will you tell me now where I may find Nyura so we may be wed tomorrow?"

"Release Marzina to me, and I will," Lara said. "You know my word is good, Kolgrim. You cannot harm your sister by your own law."

"Allowing the chamber in which she is housed to drop into the endless abyss would only make it impossible for you ever to see her again. Nor could she escape for I have put a spell upon the chamber. Her magic does not work there. Now where is Nyura?"

"Well hidden in a place you cannot find, Kolgrim. Now release Marzina, and Nyura will be safe in her own bed again. They will be coming soon to awaken her for her cousin's wedding to the Lord High Ruler," Lara said in a calm voice, but her heart was pounding violently. This was a battle of wills between them, and she knew her son did not like to lose such battles. Especially to a woman. She smiled encouragingly at him.

Kolgrim laughed. "Very well," he said. "Soon enough your influence over this world will weaken and then fade altogether. The power will be mine, Mother dear. I can afford to be generous to you this time."

Outside Kolgrim's Throne Room the skies darkened from pale gray to dark gray. The clouds thickened as the winds rose. Thunder rumbled in the distance, and jagged lightning flashed. *Marzina, to me!*

And there was her daughter standing between them.

"Are you all right?" Lara asked the young faerie woman, putting her arms about her youngest child.

Marzina looked dazed. "What happened?" she asked.

Lara took her daughter's face between her two hands. "Look at me, Marzina. Focus your eyes on my face. You're still half-asleep." She looked to Kolgrim. "A bit heavy-handed with the sleep spell, weren't you, Kolgrim?"

Marzina's violet eyes began to clear. "Oh!" she said. "Yes! I came to see my brother, the dark one. Are you angry with me, Mother?"

Lara sighed. "Of all my children you are the most impetuous," she said. "Aye, I'm angry, but I'm also relieved."

"Kolgrim wouldn't harm me," Marzina said. "We're blood kin."

"He thought nothing of violating the law to kill his half sister, Ciarda," Lara reminded her daughter.

"Ciarda was foolish, Mother. I am not," Marzina replied boldly.

"I have upheld my end of our bargain, mother dear," Kolgrim purred. "What about your end?"

"Look in your reflecting bowl, my lord," Lara instructed him.

Kolgrim walked over to the black onyx vessel, waved his hand over it and saw Nyura as she wakened in her bed. She wore but a thin night garment, and her breasts were quite visible to his eye. His cock hardened beneath his robes. Soon those breasts would belong to him, for his pleasure. He watched as two servant women hurried into Nyura's bedchamber followed by her mother.

Looking at his own mother, he said, "How can I be certain what I see is real?"

"You will just have to trust me, Kolgrim," Lara told him. "Come, Marzina."

"I can take her back at anytime," Kolgrim said.

"Of course you can," Lara replied. "But so can I." Then she and Marzina were gone from his sight.

Kolgrim laughed softly. His mother was a magnificent opponent. He was almost sorry that this time he would win in the battle between the light and the dark. And when he did, he would take her powers for himself. She owed him a debt for having deserted him and his brother in their infancy. For leaving them to be raised by traitorous giants, and vicious Wolfyn. Aye! Her magic would be his. And when it was, he would make his mother love him as she had loved the children she had born to Kaliq, to Vartan and to Magnus Hauk.

He knew the magic inhabiting Hetar even now plotted their departure. They understood that this world would now belong to him. But his mother would not leave Hetar. Lara loved this world, and she would be convinced that she could save it as she had saved it from his father. She would remain. He was convinced of it. Aye, Lara would remain. And if she did then Marzina, his little sister, would remain, too.

"My lord."

Kolgrim looked down to see his chancellor. "What?" he demanded irritably. He disliked having his thoughts interrupted.

"My lord, you must prepare to return to The City for the wedding of your kinsman, the Lord High Ruler, and the Lady Divsha. Palben has scheduled your marriage to the Lady Nyura for two days from now, not tomorrow. Will you remain in The City?"

"I shall remain there," Kolgrim said. "I wish to see the pleasures Hetar has to offer me, Alfrigg, for soon I will be a married man."

"Marriage should not deter you from your pleasures, my lord." Alfrigg chuckled.

Kolgrim laughed darkly. "It will not," he agreed. He grew thoughtful for a few moments before posing a query to his chancellor. "Shall I impregnate Nyura immediately, or give her time to grow used to my attentions. She is a virgin, after all."

"But she is also a Hetarian," Alfrigg said. "Once she has been introduced to the joy of pleasures she will become greedy for them. Time, however, is of the essence in this matter. The season of the mating frenzy is a short one. A few days, but no more, can pass before you must seed her with your heir."

Kolgrim nodded. "I agree. I shall grow quickly bored with her anyway. But once she has proved fecund, then I may depart her bed. Nothing can prevent her from bringing this child to term." His dark gray eyes turned to look directly at his companion. "Do you take pleasures, Alfrigg?" he asked the old dwarf. "You have a wife?"

"My wife is dead these many years, my lord, but I have three nubile concubines who serve their purpose well, and please me," the chancellor answered. He was a little disturbed to have his privacy invaded by his master. But then Kolgrim was different from other Twilight Lords. "My lord," he reminded his master, "the time grows short. Shall I instruct Drug to pack your trunk?"

"Aye, and remind him my wedding garments must be carefully stored," the young Twilight Lord said. He turned back to the onyx reflecting bowl, where Nyura was now being prepared to attend her cousin's wedding. She sat before her dressing table admiring herself as a serving woman brushed her long reddish-blond hair. He observed her vanity, and smiled. She had the face of someone pure, but Kolgrim saw the wonderful darkness in her, and was excited by it. Sexually he was a creature who needed more than one woman to attend to his lust. Nyura would come to bore him, he knew. But intellectually she would be a delightful companion he decided.

NYURA SMILED AT HERSELF in the looking glass. She sensed eyes other than those in the chamber upon her. It would be Kolgrim, of course. In just two days' time she would be his bride, and she could hardly wait. Oh, let her cousin Divsha preen and brag about being the second wife to the Lord High Ruler. Divsha thought her position would be greater than Kolgrim's wife. But then Divsha thought that only Hetar existence meant anything. Divsha, of course, was wrong. But she would learn that soon enough.

"Enough!" she said to the serving woman plying the brush. "It is almost time for me to go and attend my dear cousin, the bride. Do you think she will like my gown?"

"She will be most jealous," the serving woman said, "for all eyes will be upon you today, my lady mistress."

Nyura laughed. "And that is as it should be," she said, well pleased. *For soon I shall be mistress of all the worlds, and Divsha will bow to me.*

WHEN THE THE LADY LAUREEN, THE FIRST LADY
of Hetar, stepped from her apartments, she found herself face-
to-face with the Twilight Lord. "My lord!" she said, surprised.
Her hazel eyes swept over him admiringly. He was certainly an
extraordinarily handsome young man. He stood several inches
over six feet, and his dark gray eyes were a most startling contrast
to his golden hair. He was wearing a long silk gown of rich lavender embroidered heavily with gold threads and studded with
small amethysts and diamonds of the finest quality. Lady Laureen
was an expert on gemstones and recognized the excellence of
the tiny jewels. How the creator of the garment had found so
many perfect stones amazed her, and she was frankly envious.

"I thought, perhaps, you might allow me the great honor of
escorting you to the wedding, my lady," Kolgrim said, smiling.

Behind her Lady Laureen heard her ladies twittering with excitement. She smiled back at the Twilight Lord. "How very kind
of you, my lord. Aye, you may escort me." She took the silken-
clad arm he offered. Her husband was taking a young woman

for a second wife. How fitting that this handsome, powerful young man be her escort. "But perhaps you should be escorting little Nyura," she simpered at Kolgrim.

"The choice between a rosebud and an exquisite bloom is a difficult one, I will admit," Kolgrim said gallantly, "but soon the bud will be mine to keep. For today I prefer the more mature rose. Besides you and I shall be the envy of all the guests, which is certain to irritate the bride."

"Ohh, my lord," Lady Laureen giggled, "you are quite naughty."

"If you take pleasures with me later, my beauty, you shall see for yourself just how naughty I can be. *And,* how naughty I can make you be." His gray eyes darkened, and fastened onto her hazel eyes.

Though Lady Laureen blushed, she never lost the rhythm of their steps as they walked through the palace toward the great hall. But she did not answer him, for she had no idea what she could possibly say to such a bold invitation.

Kolgrim hid his amusement. Aye, the fair Lady Laureen could be tempted, and she could be seduced. He would take advantage of her weaknesses tonight while her husband played with his new toy. Divsha would keep her new lord and master quite busy, for she was a greedy and ambitious girl. And when the morning came, all would awake satisfied. He chuckled softly, and the woman on his arm flushed a deeper hue as if she had heard his thoughts.

THE GREAT HALL OF THE Lord High Ruler was built of snow-white marble. The round marble pillars holding up its domed roof were streaked with gold. The floor was made from squares of striated green marble ranging from a medium to a dark hue. Tall arched windows going from just a foot above the floors almost to the ceiling could be seen beyond the pillars. They offered views of the greenery, trees and lake within the Golden District. Gilded twisted poles were fastened to the tops of every other pillar, and from them hung silk tapestries depicting scenes from Hetar's history both real and fictional. The entryway was hung with portraits of Hetar's past rulers. Its only emperor, Gaius Prospero, and his beloved third wife, Shifra, who had mysteriously disappeared. The first Lord High Ruler, Jonah, and his first wife, Villia and his second wife, Zagiri, Princess of Terah. The second Lord High Ruler, Palben I and his wife, Coralyn. The bridegroom was already planning to have his portrait painted soon with both of his wives.

The large chamber, which was used only for high state occasions, was crowded with Hetar's wealthy and important citizens eagerly awaiting the bride. At one end of the hall was a raised dais of purple-and-gold marble. Upon it stood the chair of office of the Lord High Ruler. The wooden chair was square with a low open back, and narrow twisted arms that turned under at their ends. Its legs matched the arms, and there was a purple velvet cushion with gold tassels at each of its four corners upon the caned seat. To the right of the chair was a low tufted rose velvet stool for Hetar's First Lady.

A murmur arose from the guests as Lady Laureen now entered the hall. She was garbed in a beautiful gown of pale yellow with a low square neckline and wide flowing sleeves. The neckline was edged in a band of gold decorated with pearls and orange transmutes as were the wide cuffs of the sleeves. Her rich brown hair with its auburn highlights was braided, and the braids twisted into an intricate design upon her head. About her forehead was a band of gold centered with a large orange transmute. She glided through the chamber on the arm of the handsome Twilight Lord, who led her to the dais where Palben stood. The Lord High Ruler smiled a welcome to his first wife.

Lady Laureen curtsied low, her skirts billowing out like the petals of a flower. "My lord husband," she said to him, "I greet you upon this happy day."

Palben took the hand that Kolgrim now handed him and kissed it as his wife stepped up on the dais, and settled herself upon her stool. His wedding garments were fashioned of cream-colored silk, a simple round-necked robe with straight sleeves, decorated with golden threads and sewn all over with diamonds. Upon his dark head was a circle of gold studded with multicolored gemstones.

Kolgrim bowed. "My lord," he said politely and then stepped to one side of the dais as a flourish of trumpets sounded, announcing the arrival of the bride.

The guests turned eagerly as Divsha, escorted by her father, Balint, and her grandfather, Grugyn Ahasferus, entered the hall. The bride was garbed as the groom was in a gown of cream-colored silk with a round neck and straight sleeves decorated in gold and jewels. Her golden hair was braided in half a dozen narrow braids, and upon her head was a wreath of sweet-smelling flowers. Her beautiful hands rested delicately upon the arms of her male relations as she seemed to float toward the dais, eyes lowered.

Kolgrim glanced at Palben and saw the lust in his dark eyes. He looked to the Lady Laureen, reading her angry thoughts, although her pretty smooth face showed no emotion. The lady, Kolgrim knew, was not pleased that her husband was taking a second wife, but Laureen had acquiesced because she loved Palben. Later, after the bride and bridegroom were put to bed, Kolgrim would help the First Lady of Hetar to ease her fury and jealously.

The bride had reached the foot of the dais. Hetar no longer had any religious authority, so the marriage would be formally celebrated between the consenting parties and their families. Head lowered in a gesture of perfect submission, Divsha knelt before the Lord High Ruler as Grugyn Ahasferus put the girl's hand into his.

"We give you this maiden to be your wife," the patriarch of the family Ahasferus said in a loud voice that carried throughout the hall. "Will you accept her?"

"I accept Divsha of the family Ahasferus as my second wife with all the privileges and rights that it entails," Palben said.

Divsha's father, Balint, turned to face the guests. "You have heard," he said.

"We have heard!" the guests responded.

"Then it is done," Balint said.

Palben raised up the kneeling girl and kissed her hard on her lush mouth. Divsha felt his hard cock against her leg and smiled up at him, her eyes meeting his for the first time. Without a word to her Palben passed the bride to the First Lady of Hetar.

"You are welcome into the house of Jonah," Lady Laureen said, kissing Divsha upon both of her rosy cheeks. "Our fates are now intertwined, Divsha."

"Thank you, my lady," Divsha said prettily. She knew her place for now.

A servant brought an even-lower tufted velvet stool than the one that Lady Laureen sat upon. He set it down to the right of Hetar's First Lady, who signaled the girl to seat herself. Then the guests began to come forward to pay their respects to the trio sitting upon the dais. Divsha was angry that her place was so publicly lower than the first wife's. But her beautiful face showed only happiness. Palben and Lady Laureen's children came to welcome her. Two of their sons were grown.

The third was half-grown, as were his two sisters. They were closer to her in age than her bridegroom. Divsha smiled brightly at them all, considering her stepsons might prove entertaining eventually.

When all the wedding guests had greeted Palben and his two wives, the Lord High Ruler stood, and standing before Divsha, raised her up to lead her into the large dining chamber where a feast had been prepared for all. Kolgrim was quickly at Lady Laureen's side, smiling boldly into her eyes as he escorted her to her seat at the High Board, and took the chair next to hers. Startled by his quick actions, Lady Laureen decided his attentions to her were pleasant, considering that her husband was practically drooling over his new bride.

The dining chamber was filled with laughter and the smells of roasting meats, game and poultry. Servants dashed to and fro with platters and bowls containing salads, vegetables and at least three different rices. One was yellow. Another white with bits of green seaweed to accompany the large plates of broiled fish, and prawns. The third, reserved for the High Board, was purple with thin pieces of gold leaf tossed in it. Rich wines from the vineyards of the Outlands were served, and the goblets and cups were never empty. Some of the ladies preferred strawberry frine. The cups of the bride and groom were well laced with aphrodisiacs so their night would be a memorable one.

At one point in the meal Kolgrim surreptitiously flipped the hidden latch on his ring of office, emptying into Lady Laureen's cup a small substance that would relieve her of any inhibitions to his attentions. Then he let his hand slip into her lap. Slowly, slowly, he drew her skirts up until he was able to slide his hand beneath and fondle her plump mons. The lady had obviously played such a game before, for she gave no indication at all to what he was doing. Indeed she carried on a lively conversation with him as a single finger pushed through her moist nether lips to find the jewel of her sex and begin to worry it.

"That was nice," she said, smiling at him as her juices flowed, wetting his hand.

"'Tis' but a taste of what is to come, my lady," he told her, putting the finger he had been using in his mouth and sucking it free of her juices. "Umm. Delicious," he said.

"Should you not be spending at least some time this evening with your lovely betrothed?" Lady Laureen asked him. "She is not looking particularly happy right now seated alone with her family. I think I might excuse you for a short time, my lord. You know your way to my apartments," the First Lady of Hetar purred with a small smile.

Again Kolgrim read her thoughts. She was hot to take pleasures with him, and he was more than ready to oblige her. "I hesitate to leave you alone," he said, nodding in the direction of Palben, who was now feeding his bride some bit from his fingers, and laughing with delight at something Divsha had said.

Lady Laureen made a small moue with her mouth. "I am not used to sharing him publicly," she admitted. "And it is all your fault, my lord. He would be bound to you by blood, and so he has wed Nyura's cousin."

"We are already related by blood," Kolgrim said, knowing his words would sting her deeply. "His grandmother, Zagiri of Terah, was my half sister. The faerie woman Lara is our mother. Did you not know that?"

Lady Laureen paled. "Nay, I did not. I wonder if Palben did?"

"How could he not know of our connection?" Kolgrim replied. "You Hetarians are very invested in your families and family connections."

"Come to me later," she said to him. "I must know more."

"As must I," he said, smiling as his eyes dipped to view her breasts swelling over her neckline. He put the thought into her head of his tongue licking between the valley separating those two luscious rounds, and she flushed, sighing, causing him to chuckle. Then he arose, and catching her hand up, kissed it. "Until later, my beauty," he told her.

NYURA SAW THE TWILIGHT Lord leaving the High Board, and her heart raced with excitement. Then her pretty lips set themselves in a line of disapproval. He had left her alone with her family, embarrassing her before all the Hetarian court while he fawned over Lady Laureen. And now he dared to come toward her, smiling warmly? She knew that women in the Dark Lands had fewer rights than those in Hetar, but she would be its queen. Certainly she would not be treated as an ordinary woman. She had Ulla's powers, and Kolgrim needed those powers. He expected her to give them to him, but she would not. If he pleased her, treated her well, she would allow him the use of her powers. Nyura had realized that to relinquish her gift would be to render herself powerless. She would be more than a womb. As Kolgrim drew near, she hid her thoughts from him.

The Twilight Lord suddenly felt a wall spring up between them. How adorable she was, he considered as he took both her hands in his and kissed them. She was jealous, of course, and sought to hide the childish emotion from him. "My love," he said by way of greeting her. "Forgive me for neglecting you this day, but the poor First Lady has been feeling forgotten amidst all this celebration."

"It is not her day," Nyura said coldly. "It is my cousin Divsha's wedding day. Lady Laureen cannot always be the center of attention. She must share her husband and the limelight now, my lord."

"What if you had to share me?" he asked her.

"Will you take a second wife?" Nyura asked him nervously.

"I will have only one wife," he answered, pleased to see her discomfort. "But I keep concubines in my House of Women."

"Concubines do not count," Nyura said, feeling relieved.

He laughed. "I am glad you think so," he told her. "Now, will you forgive my disregard of your most beautiful self, my love?" He tipped her face up to his, smiling.

"Oh, very well," Nyura said, feeling the heat of his gaze warming her. "You are far too charming for your own good, my lord. And I am too quick to forgive you, I fear."

"May it always be so, Nyura," he said in reply. Then he leaned forward and brushed her lips with his. "I wish this were our wedding day, our wedding night," he said meaningfully. "I long to instruct you in the ways of pleasure."

"And I long to be your pupil, my lord," Nyura said. "After our wedding night may we return home to the Dark Lands. Our son will be strongest if he is conceived in his own castle in the land he is meant to rule."

He sat down next to her on the trestle bench, sliding an arm about her slender waist so he might draw her closer to him. His hand slipped into the neckline of her gown to cup a nicely plump breast. His tongue licked her ear and blew softly into it. Then he pinched the nipple of the breast he was fondling, delighting in her sharp intake of breath. "Now, Nyura," he murmured low to her as he withdrew his hand from the opening of her gown, "I am going to put my hand beneath your skirts."

"*Here?* With all watching?" Nyura didn't know whether to be shocked or thrilled by his outrageous daring.

"No one will notice unless you draw their attention to what we are doing," he said. "They are far too involved with each other and the feasting. This is your first lesson in the complete and perfect discipline you must give me." Beneath the trestle his hand began to draw her skirts up until he was able to slide his hand between her thighs. Her legs parted slightly for him. Finding her nether lips, his fingers began to play with her.

Nyura could not believe how exquisite the torture she was undergoing was. She held herself still while carrying on a conversation with her cousin Yamka. Yamka had been sulking the entire day. Now Nyura whispered to Yamka exactly what Kolgrim was doing. "His fingers are very skillful," she said softly.

"Is he frigging you yet?" Yamka asked in equally low tones. Suddenly her amber eyes were alight with excitement.

"Nay, he is playing with my jewel. Oh, Yamka! I want to scream, it is so delicious, but I must show him that I can be obedient."

"Raise your ass slowly and lean forward just slightly," Kolgrim whispered.

Nyura repeated this command to her cousin as she complied.

"What is he doing? What is he doing?" Yamka demanded to know.

"*Oh!*" Nyura's gray-green eyes grew round with surprise. "*Ohhh!*"

"Tell me, tell me!" Yamka begged.

"He has put a finger in my sheath, and one in my rosehole," Nyura confided low.

"Together! He is moving them back and forth, back and forth. Oh, Yamka, I do not think I can bear it! It is so wicked! So good!"

"You must bear it! It is your duty, cousin!" Yamka hissed back. "Oh, I am so envious of you, Nyura! Here Divsha has just been wed to Palben, and you will marry in two days to the Twilight Lord. Will I ever be wed? If I am, I will not have the prestige that you and Divsha have. They will match me with some magnate's second or third son, who only wants me for my dower portion."

Nyura's head was spinning with the pleasure Kolgrim's wicked fingers were giving her as she sat stoically at the trestle table filled with her relatives all of whom, except Yamka, were unaware of the sweet torture she was undergoing. "Palben has only married Divsha because he wanted to be related to Kolgrim. Oh, he'll enjoy pleasures with her, but he loves Lady Laureen. He will pay little attention to Divsha except when his cock needs a good workout," Nyura said candidly. "And the Twilight Lord marries me to make an alliance with Hetar and to get a son. Do not envy either of us, cousin. Oh! Oh! Ohhh!" she gasped softly.

"Did he give you pleasures?" Yamka asked avidly, licking her lips with her excitement. "You are so fortunate, Nyura."

"Aye, he has given me pleasures," her companion replied low, and then she turned to Kolgrim. "Was my behavior as you expected, my lord?" she asked him.

"Aye, you behaved quite well, my love," he told her. "I am pleased to see how disciplined you are, Nyura. I commend your obedience to my will." He arose from the bench. "Come," he said, holding out his hand to raise her up. "There are several rooms of entertainment to be seen. It will be several hours before the Lord High Ruler and his new bride depart these festivities. Let us go and see what has been presented for our delight."

She walked with him. In one room they found dancers entertaining the guests who stood about watching. In another there were two animal acts in two circus rings. One man worked with several brown-and-white patchwork bears, who tumbled and played with round balls. The second ring contained a tiny woman in tight red pants and a matching coat, managing a troupe of equally tiny horses. They came to a third room, where several beautiful Pleasure Women were publicly diverting male guests with their skills. The room was crowded and hot.

"Have you ever viewed this manner of entertainment?" Kolgrim asked Nyura.

"Nay," she replied. Her eyes did not know where to look next, for she was frankly fascinated by what she was observing. "I have seen these things only in books since I chose to retain my virtue while waiting for you, my lord."

"I mean to have you keep your virginity until our wedding night, but you should learn what will be expected of you, my love." Looking about, he saw a lovely Pleasure Woman who had just entered the chamber. Kolgrim signaled to her to come over.

Recognizing him, she glided across the floor and bowed. "I am Mava, my lord Kolgrim. How may I serve you?" The Pleasure Woman had light golden-brown hair, soft gray eyes and a beautiful ripe body. She smiled at them in a pleasant manner.

"My bride is a virgin," Kolgrim began.

"Indeed, my lord, how fortunate for you," Mava replied.

"I wish her to see what awaits her," Kolgrim said.

"Of course, my lord," Mava answered him, and she immediately fell to her knees before him, opening his deep lavender robe, reaching for his cock.

"Teach her what to do, Mava," Kolgrim told the Pleasure Woman. "And when I have been properly prepared, you and I will take pleasures together so the Lady Nyura may see what she must do in two nights time. Kneel down next to Mava, my love," Kolgrim said to Nyura, "and follow her instructions."

Fascinated to learn what was to come, Nyura obeyed and

fell to her knees before the Twilight Lord. She looked curiously to Mava.

The Pleasure Woman smiled. Then she said, "Sometimes a man needs a bit of encouragement, although I suspect your betrothed does not. Still, it cannot hurt to learn all you can about passion." She drew Kolgrim's cock from his robe, admiring its length, for she had seen many cocks in her day and thought his a particularly fine one. "He is flaccid, and of no use to either himself or me in this state."

"What can you do?" Nyura asked.

"Take his cock into your mouth, my lady. Be careful not to bite or score him with your teeth right now," Mava said. "That's it. Take him all in, and now begin to suck him. Find a good strong rhythm, and suck him hard." She watched as Nyura followed her careful instructions. After a few moments she said, "Cease now, but hold his cock with your thumb and your finger. Either your pointer or your forefinger will do. Lick gently around the tip, my lady. Slide your tongue beneath the ridge of the head. Lick his length up and down several times."

"He's getting quite big," Nyura noted. "I like the taste of you, my lord."

Mava chuckled. The girl was nicely lustful. "Take him back into your mouth, my lady, and began your sucking rhythm once again." When Nyura began to gag on Kolgrim's thickness and expanded length, Mava advised, "Relax your throat, my lady. He is large, but you can take him all in easily with practice." She looked up at the Twilight Lord. "Put your hand on her head, my lord, and instruct her as to your desires. Be aware of his hand, my lady. Do not lose yourself in the sweetness. Do you wish her to drink your juices, my lord?" Mava asked Kolgrim.

"Nay," he said.

"On one occasion he might request that of you, my lady. You should be aware of it. Tonight he wishes to couple, and I will take your place. Your lord will tell you when you must release his cock, and you must obey immediately so as not to spoil his pleasure or yours in the future."

Nyura listened carefully, all the while sucking hard on Kolgrim's thick and lengthy cock. She had taken Mava's advice and made a strong effort to relax her throat. When she did, she was able to take him all in. From his heavy breath and soft groans she knew he was enjoying her first efforts.

"Cease, Nyura!" His voice was rough and hard.

She immediately released her hold on him, and as she did she realized that Mava had taken a position upon a low double couch. Nyura sat back on her heels to watch.

"Well done, my lady," the Pleasure Woman complimented her. "Now watch as my lord Kolgrim fills my sheath with his cock, and we take pleasures together. This is what you will be expected to do in two nights," Mava told her as Kolgrim now covered her ripe body, sinking his cock deep into her, causing her to sigh with delight.

Fascinated, Nyura watched as the two bodies moved together in a wild rhythm. Kolgrim's cock flashed back and forth, and as it did Nyura felt a tug in her own nether regions. The woman beneath her betrothed began to moan as her crisis overtook her. Her legs wrapped themselves around the Twilight Lord's torso. After a few moments her body shuddered and convulsed. Kolgrim withdrew from her. His cock was still hard.

Nyura stared, fascinated. "She did not pleasure you, my lord?"

"Aye, she did, but I need more," he told the girl. "On your knees, Mava," he told the Pleasure Woman, who immediately complied, and reentering her sheath, his hands gripping her plump hips, Kolgrim pumped and pumped the woman to a shrieking crisis. Still his mighty cock stood hard and straight.

"If she cannot pleasure you, my lord," Nyura said nervously, "how can I?"

Kolgrim chortled. "You and I will enjoy pleasures together, my love. I am particularly lustful today. On your back, Mava, with your legs over the edge of the couch, my girl," he instructed the Pleasure Woman. Then standing, a single hand upon his partner he thrust into her, moving back and forth, back and forth until with a deep groan he released his juices even as Mava cried out her third round of pleasures.

Mava's eyes opened, and she sighed gustily. "Thank you, my lord. I admit to you that I have never enjoyed fucking as much as I have just enjoyed it."

He smiled at her, raising her into a seated position now. "You are an excellent instructress, Mava." Then he turned to Nyura. "Did you enjoy your lessons, my love?"

"I did, my lord, very much," she told him.

"Excellent then, let us move on. There is a punishment room, I believe," Kolgrim said. "Sometimes when passion grows old, gentle pain can be introduced to revive it. Is that not so, Mava?"

"Indeed, my lord, it is. Perhaps your lady could benefit from a small lesson," Mava said. "I suspect our interlude has aroused her, but she forces it away. She should not deny herself or you, should she, my lord?"

"She should not," Kolgrim agreed. He took Nyura's hand. "Come, my love." Following him into another room, Nyura saw several of the guests partaking in rather bizarre activities. One man's bare bottom was being flogged by a woman holding a tied bunch of birch twigs. His buttocks were scarlet yet he cried to her, "More! More!" A beautiful woman was having saw-toothed clips attached to her nipples as she was suspended from manacles that hung from the ceiling. There were two women shackled and bent over padded bars while two gentlemen plied thick leather straps to their posteriors. The women cried out as they were whipped, but neither sounded as if she were in pain. Then one of the men threw his strap aside and, lifting his robe to display a rigid cock, began to fuck the woman he had so recently punished.

"Fascinating," Nyura remarked. "What have these people done to merit punishment from their partners."

"Little, if nothing," Kolgrim told her. "The pain they inflict or have inflicted upon themselves restores their lusts. And some of them grow to enjoy it. Come," he said, seating himself. "I will give you a tiny taste. Put yourself over my knee."

"I do not think so, my lord," Nyura said. "Such activities do not appeal to me."

"Nyura," Kolgrim said in a low even voice, "you cannot disobey me, my love. Now put yourself over my knee, for you are to be spanked for this disobedience."

"Oh, do not make me," she pleaded mischievously, for she sensed he would enjoy forcing her to his will.

"Wench, you but compound your misbehavior," he told her, reaching out and yanking her over his knee.

"Oh! Oh!" Nyura cried softly. Then she gasped as he pulled her gown up, and she felt the air upon her backside. Then his hand descended, delivering a stinging blow, and she squealed, wiggling wildly.

He placed one hand in the small of her back and continued spanking her until her bottom was a fine glowing pink. Turning her over onto her back, he pushed two fingers into her sheath, which was already dripping with her juices. He thrust the two digits back and forth until she moaned her surrender to him.

Then sitting her up, he kissed her a long, slow passionate kiss, his tongue insinuating itself into her mouth to stroke hers. She moaned again against his lips as he withdrew the two fingers. "Was that exciting?" he murmured in her ear as he drew her gown down.

Nyura opened her eyes. "Aye," she said.

"When we are wed I will strap you now and again," he promised her. Kolgrim was pleased. Nyura was proving herself to be worthy to be his wife. Her lusts were great. Untutored, she was an eager learner, and he would enjoy her briefly before impregnating her. He wondered what she would say when she discovered his two cocks. Would that make her fearful? But no, he decided. She would relish them, and give him everything he desired. This girl, he decided, would never bore him. "We had best return to the dining chamber, my love," he said to her.

"I am eager for our wedding now more than ever," Nyura told him.

THE DAY WORE ON, AND THEN as night fell it came time for the bride and groom to be put to bed. Much merriment ensued as Palben and Divsha were escorted to their bedchamber. Once there, the gentlemen divested the Lord High Ruler of all of his garments, leaving him naked, while the ladies did the same to Divsha. There was a great deal of good-natured bantering back and forth by the guests.

Then came Lady Laureen bearing in her hand a large-footed gold cup, its base studded with rubies. Standing by the bed, she offered it first to Palben, and when he had drunk his fill Lady Laureen presented the goblet to Divsha, who also drank deeply. "May your union be fruitful," the First Lady of Hetar said in a neutral voice. Then turning, she left the bridal chamber, followed by the rest of the guests. Her mouth tightened as the door closed and Divsha's voice was heard saying, "Oh, my lord, you are so virile!"

Kolgrim watched, amused, as he accompanied Nyura. His eyes met those of Lady Laureen, and he nodded almost imperceptibly. Finding Grugyn Ahasferus in the crowd of courtiers, he brought Nyura to him. "I am returning your granddaughter to you, my lord, lest I be tempted before our wedding night," he told the magnate. Then he kissed Nyura's lips gently. "I shall not see you until our wedding ceremony, my love," he said. "Dream of me until that day." Then he left her.

"You are an extremely fortunate girl," her grandfather told her. "And your good fortune has already enriched this house more than I could have ever imagined. Divsha, Palben's bride. You to wed the Twilight Lord. And now I have received an offer for Yamka from the Dominus of Terah's son. All three kingdoms related by blood ties through the children you will bear your husbands. I could have never envisioned such a thing, Nyura. The house of Ahasferus will not only be the richest house in Hetar, but our power will be increased threefold."

"Yamka is to be married? She said naught to me today. Indeed she did nothing but complain," Nyura remarked.

"She does not know yet, and you must say nothing." Grugyn Ahasferus chuckled, well pleased. "I must speak with her parents for she will have to live in Terah. But one day she will be Terah's Domina. They will have to pay a premium for her, of course. She is a most valuable commodity. Still, he is a most handsome young man, Prince Vaclar. Yamka will not be displeased.

"Lord Amren brought him to the wedding today, introducing him to your grandmother and me. Then Ambassador Cadoc made the suggestion that a marriage between our family and his would be a profitable venture for us all. I would not have thought Lord Cadoc that astute for I find him narrow-minded.

I suspect the whole thing is my friend Amren's idea, but it is an excellent one, don't you think?" He actually didn't care what she thought, but Nyura was his favorite granddaughter, and she was surprisingly intelligent for a female.

"My opinion does not matter, Grandfather," Nyura said, confirming his faith in her, "but I think you are a brilliant man to arrange such stellar matches for us. The House of Ahasferus will be well served by our unions. I know Divsha and Yamka will do their best, as will I, to continue to serve the house of our birth."

Grugyn Ahasferus patted Nyura's delicate little hand and nodded. "You are a good girl," he told her. "And cleverer than the other two. Lord Kolgrim is powerful, Nyura, and he means to be even more powerful once he has Ulla's powers. Tread carefully, girl, and obey him without question except when it interferes with us."

She smiled at him. "Of course, Grandfather." She did not tell him of her decision to withhold Ulla's powers from Kolgrim. Nyura sensed retaining Ulla's powers would guarantee her a greater measure of safety than giving them up. Suddenly she was alert, and a tingle raced down her spine. She thought they were being watched, but glancing about, she could see no one.

"I will take you home myself," Grugyn said to the girl, and called for his litter.

Lara and Kaliq listened to Grugyn Ahasferus and his granddaughter from the shadows, invisible to the two Hetarians. Satisfied that all was going as it should, Kaliq whisked them back to Shunnar, where the sun was just rising across the desert sands. The air was clear and cool, and in the skies above a hawk soared screeching loudly as he flew. Seeing it, Lara was reminded of Vartan of the Fiacre, her first husband, a mortal who could shape-shift taking the form of a hawk when he did.

"Anoush's prediction will come to pass," Kaliq said. "You have united the worlds, Lara, my love."

She was silent for a moment. "Aye," she replied. "But this world is small, Kaliq, and eventually it would have all come together. It is true I have touched each part of it. Hetar. Terah. The Dark Lands. But my influence has faded away now. Why? The magic world tried to teach these mortals who inhabit these lands that war was not a solution. That there was enough for all." She laughed bitterly. "At least that lesson took, after the era of the Hierarch. Hetar sees that all its people are fed, clothed and housed. But none of them has any purpose. The magnates and the merchants continue on as they always have. The Crusader Knights are few now for there are no challenges left to conquer. I had hoped Hetar would change and grow. It has not."

"I know," he replied. "Change is difficult, Lara. It takes courage for a leader to stand up and effect it. Such men and women are not being born into Hetar or Terah."

"I cannot just give up, Kaliq," Lara told him. "But for the first time in my existence I do not know what to do. If I curse Nyura's womb, or put a spell upon her so that she does not produce Kolgrim's son, he will know the blame lies with me. He will harm Marzina. Oh, he will not spill her blood, but dropping her into the bottomless ravine would be worse than death for Marzina, and for me. And I will not give Kolgrim that pleasure, for to see me in pain would pleasure him."

"He wants you to love him," Kaliq said. "That is natural for he is your child."

"How can I love him?" she asked despairingly. "I hated his father. His birth, and that of his twin, was an aberration."

"The birth of your sons has helped to keep the darkness at bay for over a century," Kaliq reminded her.

"To what purpose, my lord? Cronan says that Hetar is doomed. That within the next few months the darkness will claim it, and the light will go out of this world," Lara said. "So why did the magic world use me to birth Kolgrim and Kolbein? One has lived to rule. The other lives imprisoned. What has it all been for, Kaliq?" She gazed up at him, her beautiful faerie green eyes wet with her tears.

"You gave the world of Hetar the opportunity to turn back from the brink of its own destruction. You showed them the way when you defeated Kol, the previous Twilight Lord, in the battle for The City. For a few years, I believed that they could make this world the place it should be. A place of peace and plenty. A place where all races, mortal and magic, could live together, respecting each other and our different customs. A place where we would all have a purpose and that purpose would be to the good. But it did not happen, despite all we did to make it so."

"So now we will desert Hetar because it hasn't lived up to our expectations?" Lara asked him. "How does that make us any better than the mortals we have tried to protect, my dear lord?"

"Perhaps that has been our mistake," Kaliq told her. "Mayhap we should not have interfered in their growth. But we did. We tried to help, and it only made it worse, for mortals, it seems, are their own worst enemy. We did not create them so we cannot accept all of the blame for their behavior."

"If we leave them, what will happen to them?" Lara wondered.

"The darkness will overtake the world of Hetar. But even in the darkness, my love, there is always a pinpoint of light. And if that tiny light is strong and someone nurtures it, it will grow, and perhaps one day it will overcome the darkness that will take this world shortly," Kaliq said.

Lara put her arms about his neck, and laying her head against him, she wept softly. Finally when she had eased her grief she asked him, "Where will we go, Kaliq?"

"First to Belmair, for the darkness will not touch that world for many centuries to come. The magic that lives on this world will evacuate Hetar and regroup there to consider where we will make our new home. The Cosmos is vast, Lara, and there are many worlds. I think, however, we will find one that is not inhabited, or perhaps make one for ourselves. We will cloak it from mortal eyes so we may live in peace without fear of the darkness," Kaliq told her.

"I will not leave until I must," Lara said. "Perhaps I may foil Kolgrim, if not entirely, a little bit." She nestled against him, breathing the familiar fragrance of him. It soothed her, and she was overcome by calm. Lara still could not quite believe with all of her heart that the world of Hetar was doomed. Perhaps there was something she might do to buy her world more time.

"You are plotting," Kaliq said. His voice held a hint of amusement.

"It isn't polite to intrude on another's private thoughts," Lara scolded him, but she was smiling. Then she said to him, "We are going to Kolgrim's wedding, Kaliq. It will please him, and perhaps I can in that way delay the inevitable."

Kaliq shook his dark head. "You are not a faerie woman to give up easily or without a fight, are you, my love? Very well, we will go to Kolgrim's wedding."

"Is Lothair still serving on the High Council?" Lara asked.

"He is for the interim, but when our brothers depart for Belmair, he will withdraw, too," Kaliq said.

"Have him inform Grugyn Ahasferus that the Twilight Lord's mother and her life mate will attend the wedding. Then he is to tell Palben that we will expect accommodation for several nights at the palace. We will arrive tomorrow," Lara said.

Kaliq laughed heartily. "We will create quite a stir amid a kingdom that espouses an official policy that magic does not exist. Shall we make an entrance like we did last time, my love? Or shall we be polite, and just pretend we are normal guests."

"That will depend upon our reception," Lara said. "I think Dominus Cadarn and his wife, the Domina Paulina, should also attend Kolgrim's wedding. Have Lothair tell the Lord High Ruler that they will also need accommodation. It is time my descendants met face-to-face. Perhaps if they know one another their blood tie will help them in the darkness that Kolgrim means to bring. Oh, I wish I could prevent his wedding, Kaliq. Is there no way? No way at all?" she asked. Then her eyes narrowed.

"I gave him life, Kaliq. Could I not take that life away?"

"At the cost of your own soul, my love? And it would change nothing, for with Kolgrim's death both Kol and Kolbein would be freed. Their joint reign would be a far more violent and cruel one than Kolgrim's will be," Kaliq told her. "Despite his strength of will, Kolgrim has inherited some of your good, Lara. He shuns it, to be sure, but it still exists deep within him. It is why he showed you Marzina's fragile prison, and gave you the opportunity to be reasonable with him rather than just simply releasing his sister into the bottomless ravine, and then demanding Nyura's return. Kolgrim is the child you created from the one Kol gave you. Kolbein is his father's son. He inherited nothing of you, Lara. He is pure evil. Far worse than any Twilight Lord ever created, even Kol," Kaliq explained. "When you split the unborn child within you, most of the evil remained with the first infant, Kolbein. Only some of it burgeoned with the second baby who was Kolgrim. That is why he has always felt an affinity for you where his twin did not. And that is also why you have felt an affection for him that you could not, would not admit even to yourself, Lara."

"He is Kol's son, Kaliq," she quickly replied.

"He is your son, also, my love. For all his wickedness, Kolgrim is your child, too," Kaliq told her. "I think you clever to attend his wedding and give him what he wants. Your love and your respect."

Her eyes filled with tears again. "I have tried so hard not to care for him," she admitted to Kaliq. "He should not have my love! He should not!"

"But he does, Lara," Kaliq replied. "And you are, as always, an amazing faerie woman that you can admit to it honestly."

"Do not dare to tell Ilona!" Lara said. "She would destroy me where I stood if she knew I harbored any affection for Kolgrim. And I do not understand why I do, Kaliq."

"It is that tiny bit of mortal within you, my love," he answered her. "Mortals may be foolish, but they are good creatures at heart." He kissed the top of her golden head. "Now, if we are going to that wedding and we must stop in Terah to convince the annoying Cadarn that he must go, too, then we had best hurry. But first we must eat. I am ravenous. And then we must rest. We may be magic, but we are not indestructible."

She stroked his handsome face. "Aye, food, rest, a few pleasures, a bath. And then I will be ready to face The City, and my descendants." She smiled seductively up at him. "But which shall we have first, my lord?"

IO

"IF YOU CANNOT MAKE UP YOUR MIND, MY LOVE, then perhaps I shall do it for us," Kaliq said teasingly. "Remember that I am ravenous?"

"But for food or pleasures?" she teased back, laughing softly.

"Ahh, faerie witch, I know what you would have me say, but I tell you, both!" Kaliq answered her with a chuckle. With a wave of his hand he transported them to her bedchamber and onto the bed, where a tray of tempting foods awaited. They were both now quite naked. "Pity the poor mortals who cannot indulge their twin appetites at the same time, Lara, my love." He caught up her hand, kissing it tenderly, then kissing the inside of her wrist, as well.

Lara caused a strawberry to appear in her upturned palm. He smiled at her as their eyes met, his white teeth carefully picking up the strawberry and eating it. When he had swallowed she pulled his head toward her, kissing him, her tongue finding his, murmuring with delight as she tasted the strawberry, breathing the fragrance of it into her own mouth. "Delicious!" she said softly, magicking the tray to the sideboard as she lay back, and three more berries appeared in the shallow chasm between her breasts.

His dark head bent, and one by one he plucked the straw-berries with his teeth, crushing them so that juice ran from between her breasts, down her belly and into the cleft between her nether lips. His tongue followed slowly, thoroughly, licking up the juice, pushing between those tempting folds of flesh to touch her hidden jewel. His fingers spread her open so he might have greater access to the prize, which he taunted and teased with delicate licks, then stronger strokes of his tongue until she was writhing and moaning softly with his attentions. When her juices began to come forth for him, Kaliq raised up his head, pushing two fingers slowly into her sheath, moving them rhythmically back and forth until Lara sighed with her small release. Leaning forward, he kissed her lips passionately.

Her arms wound about his neck as Lara drew him close. "You have but whetted my appetite, my lord," she said to him. "Now you must satisfy that appetite." Then she swiftly rolled him onto his back. *Bind my love so he must yield! And let him not raise his shield! But let him a strong weapon wield!* Lara silently invoked her spell before Kaliq might check her.

Surprised, he found himself spread upon her bed, arms and legs bound with silk. The Shadow Prince burst out laughing. "In all our years together, my love, you have never been so bold," he told her.

"You delight in teasing me, my lord, and so I thought perhaps you should be teased instead," Lara told him.

"I am faint from hunger for food," he said to her pleadingly.

She pinched his muscled arm. "You do not seem too slender to me," Lara said.

"I shall be unable to *wield a strong weapon*," he said, quoting a piece of her spell.

"I can make you strong, my lord," Lara told him as she slithered between his shapely legs. Reaching up she undid her long gilt-colored hair from its plait. Then, moving her head, she trailed her long, soft tresses across his torso several times, watching as his manhood, already interested in play, twitched. "Ohh," Lara purred, "I think your *weapon* considers battle, my lord."

"You will have to do more than just tickle me with your hair, faerie witch," he taunted her.

Lara complied, positioning herself so she might play with his cock. She caressed it. She held it between two fingers and slowly licked its length several times, making him groan for the heat from her tongue was delicious. Lara took him into her mouth and suckled upon him until he was so swollen she could no longer contain him between her lips. Releasing him, she burrowed beneath the standing pillar of hard flesh, finding his sac, again licking, finally taking it into her mouth, her tongue rolling the twin seedpods about their container of cool flesh. Then Lara sucked hard thrice, and Kaliq actually cried out, a sound of both pleasure and pain.

Releasing him, she pulled herself up and, positioning him between her thighs, lowered herself onto his cock until he was fully sheathed, and her buttocks rested upon his muscled thighs. Lara began to ride him slowly. "You will not release your lust, my lord, until I give you permission," she warned him.

"And if I do?" he demanded to know.

"Then I shall see you chained to my bedroom wall and forced to watch while I take my pleasures with Lothair," Lara said wickedly. "You know how he lusts after me."

"Faerie witch!" he growled at her. "Without my permission you are no longer free to indulge your passions with anyone but me!"

"Oh, beware, my lord! I am faerie, and you know our natures are hot," she replied mischievously. She began to ride him harder and harder.

Kaliq struggled to contain his lust for her. He was perfectly capable of releasing himself from her spell, but he could see the delight she was taking in having the upper hand in their passion. "I could go deeper," he said softly, "if our positions were reversed, my love. You have made your point. Do not deny us perfection."

Lara said nothing, but his bonds were released as suddenly as they had been set upon him. As he rolled her onto her back she raised her legs, putting them over his broad shoulders, and hooking her ankles behind his neck. Kaliq plunged deeper and deeper into her sweet softness with his hard cock. Bending his dark head, he captured a nipple and sucked upon it.

A fierce thrill raced through her entire body, and Lara screamed softly. Her head was spinning with the beginnings of pleasure. Her breath came in quick little bursts and she tingled all over as her whole being centered itself on the long thick peg of flesh plunging in and out, in and out in perfect rhythm. *Kaliq! Kaliq! Ohh, how I love you!* she told him in their silent language. *We will take pleasures together, my dear lord! Now! Oh, now, I beg you!* Her scream was one of pure delight as he roared with equal satisfaction, their love juices mingling within her body. And then Lara swooned, which she had not done in many a decade. What they had just shared had gone beyond perfection.

Kaliq could not believe the pleasure they had just attained together. He had known from the moment he met Lara that he would never tire of this female, but she constantly amazed him. He held her tightly in his arms, his lips softly kissing the top of her golden head. *I love you, but then you have known that for decades, my darling. Never were life mates more suited than you and I. Whatever happens, I know that we will never be parted, Lara, my love. We are one.* He stroked her hair as she nestled against him in a state of complete contentment.

Finally Lara sighed and said, "I am ravenous! Where is that tray?"

His chuckle was deep and rich. "Are we eating in bed?" he asked her.

"Remember we just have time for a bath, and either food or a nap before we must go and fetch the Dominus and his wife."

"I think food will serve me better. Cadarn can irritate me even well rested," Lara said. "I need the strength that taking pleasures with you, and a good meal can give me."

He magicked the tray back, and they ate. Then he left her to bathe, and Lara went to her own bath. Her women were waiting, and thoroughly pampered, she called to Cadi to bring her a gown. The faerie serving woman came smiling, holding out a beautiful gown made from a mixture of silk and fine cotton, bright green in color and embroidered with gold and silver threads.

"Your heritage is that of a Forest Faerie," Cadi said. "Tonight you will wear one of the forest's greens. It would please your mother, my lady."

Lara nodded her approval. The gown was styled in the fashion of the desert kingdom. Its neckline was round with a keyhole opening. Its sleeves were long and wide, the broad cuffs decorated with the gold and silver threads matching the narrow band of embroidery at the neck. It was not fitted, but rather hung gracefully from her shoulders, not quite touching the floor. She would have matching green silk slippers.

"Tonight," Cadi said, "I have a new hairstyle for you. It is more elegant, as this occasion demands, mistress." She brushed out Lara's long tresses then, pulling it back, coiled it tightly and fastened it with gold and silver hairpins. When she had finished she stood back, admiring her handiwork, saying, "Do you like it, my lady?"

"I do!" Lara replied. "I look quite sophisticated, which may make my great-grandsons feel more at ease with me." She turned her head this way and that, admiring herself in the mirror. "Where are those wonderful barbaric gold ear loops, Cadi? The ones with the tiny diamonds threaded on them."

Smiling, Cadi handed them to her mistress. Then she took each of Lara's hands in turn, and pushed several gold and silver bangles up her arm. "And you'll need rings, too," she said. "I thought the heart-shaped ruby with some simple bands on one hand, and the star-shaped sapphire Prince Kaliq gave you on your other hand."

"And Ethne about my neck on her gold chain," Lara said of her guardian spirit who lived in a crystal star that had always hung about Lara's neck. She preened before the mirror again. "I look as I should," she decided aloud.

Cadi chuckled. "You had best hurry," she said. "It is close to sunset in Terah, and you will want to catch the Dominus before he goes to bed."

"I hope his day has been an easy one, for I can guarantee that the Ahasferus family has arranged a spectacular wedding for Nyura and Kolgrim."

"You honor the Twilight Lord," Cadi said quietly.

"I do what I must to keep the darkness at bay a little longer," Lara replied.

"The Forest Faeries have begun to leave Hetar for Belmair," Cadi volunteered.

Lara sighed. "Is my mother still here?"

"Queen Ilona will not leave until she is assured that all of her people are safe. The faerie races of Hetar have carefully arranged their evacuation. Your mother has been in touch with King Annan, King Laszlo and Gwener, Empress of the Meadow Faeries. The Forest faeries are the last to depart Hetar."

"The others are already gone?" Lara was surprised. Could they not have waited to see if she might stop this new threat?

Cadi nodded. "Old Prince Cronan spoke with each of them, and they listened. I am sorry, mistress."

"Nay, the darkness is coming now, and I know it. But I had hoped...." Her voice trailed off.

"For aeons the light has brightened Hetar, and I am sure it will one day again, mistress," Cadi said. "But for now Hetar has sealed this world's doom. Eventually the good will lift its head and begin its rebirth here. But first the darkness will come. It has happened before this in other worlds, and it will happen again in worlds unknown to us. But the light cannot be stopped, my lady. It will return! It always has."

Lara took her serving woman's hands in hers and looked into Cadi's pretty face. "Thank you," she said softly.

"Lara!" Kaliq called from the garden where he now awaited her. He was garbed in his usual white, but today his tunic was decorated with silver thread and black pearls. On his feet he wore silver slippers rather than his leather boots.

"I'm coming," she said, hurrying from her chamber to meet him.

"Ah, my darling," he said, his eyes lighting at the sight of her in her green gown, "how beautiful you look. The color suits you well."

She stepped to his side. His arm went about her, and then Cadi watched as they disappeared before her eyes. They reappeared in the Great Hall of Terah's castle, much to the discomfort of Cadarn and his wife, Paulina, who were seated alone at their High Board.

"Greetings, Cadarn," Lara said. "We have come to fetch you to the wedding of the Twilight Lord and his bride in Hetar."

"We cannot reach Hetar in time for that wedding," Cadarn said irritably.

"Great-grandson, you continue to disbelieve the evidence of your own eyes. Do you think you are dreaming?" Lara asked. Stepping up to him, she pinched his arm.

Cadarn yelped, and yanked the arm away from her.

"You will need to look more like the Dominus of Terah than you do," Lara said.

"What do you think, Kaliq?"

"He has Magnus's eyes," Kaliq noted. "Turquoise-blue brocade with gold beading, I think." The Shadow Prince turned his eyes to Domina Paulina, a pretty woman with fair skin, dark brown hair, and gray-blue eyes. "Rose silk for the lady," he said, nodding to Lara.

Then together they clothed the Dominus and Domina of Terah in magnificent garments. On Cadarn's head an elegant gold crown studded with green transmutes appeared. Paulina's dark hair was magically dressed in a series of bejeweled plaits, and about her forehead a gold circlet with a large pink pearl in its center appeared.

The Terahn couple gasped in both surprise and shock.

"How…" Cadarn said.

"Oh really, great-grandson, please do not be so silly," Lara told him. "'Tis magic. Now listen to me, you irritating creature, so you do not appear any more ignorant than you already are. Your great-grandfather, Magnus Hauk, sired three children on me. You descend from our only son, Taj. The Lord High Ruler, Palben, descends from our eldest daughter, Princess Zagiri, who married the Lord High Ruler Jonah. Do you understand?"

"This is truth?" Cadarn asked.

"Why would I tell you if it weren't?" Lara demanded of him. "You are blood kin to Hetar's ruler, Cadarn."

"If we are kinsmen, then why must my son, Vaclar, marry a Hetarian girl?" Cadarn wanted to know. "You said it was to make us all kin."

It was easier to make it simple for him, Lara realized. "The patriarch of the greatest family in Hetar, the clan Ahasferus, has three granddaughters. All are sixteen. One marries the Twilight Lord today. Two days ago another became your cousin Palben's second wife. And shortly Vaclar will wed the third girl. You need to be kin to the Twilight Lord, for he is a powerful being who will shortly rule this entire world. If you are his kinsman, he is unlikely to harm you and your family."

"What do you mean the Twilight Lord will rule this entire world?" Cadarn demanded to know.

"The darkness is coming, and it will overtake Hetar and Terah," Lara said.

"Why can't you stop it?" Cadarn wanted to know. "You have stopped it before."

"Ahh," Lara replied softly, "so you admit to knowing and believing in my accomplishments, great-grandson. I thought magic did not exist."

He ignored her taunts. "I thought you were all-powerful, Great-grandmother," he said. "Have you lost your magic then?"

"My magic can only exist in the light, Cadarn. For almost a century and a half I have kept the darkness at bay. But everything has its season. Even the darkness. The Twilight Lord was born of two powerful magic beings. Kol, the last Twilight Lord, was his father. Mine was, most reluctantly, the womb from which he sprang. I was born for the express purpose of causing chaos in the Dark Lands, Cadarn. Twilight Lords can only produce a single son, though they are known to have many daughters. Once Kol had impregnated me I split the infant in my womb in two so that I birthed twins instead of a single son. Then I returned to my own life, leaving Kol with two sons and much difficulty." Lara thought it better not to go into explicit detail with Cadarn. "The Dark Lands spent many years in anarchy and lawlessness until the twins came to manhood, and Kolgrim triumphed over his brother, Kolbein."

"And this Twilight Lord is more powerful than you? Than the Shadow Princes?" Cadarn asked her.

"It is not that he is more powerful, Cadarn. He has yet to even realize his full powers, but he is strong. The dissolution in Hetar, and now Terah, has played into his hands. I cannot save a world that does not believe it needs to be saved. And so the darkness will overtake you. To help you before I leave Hetar, I have united these three branches of my family. It may protect you until the light can come again," Lara told him. "Now do you understand why Vaclar must wed Yamka Ahasferus?"

Cadarn nodded slowly. "Aye, I understand," he said, "although I am not certain I completely believe your tale."

"Whether you believe me or not isn't important, Cadarn, just as long as you unite your family with that of Kolgrim and his bride," Lara replied. "Your son's children will be blood kin to the children Kolgrim sires on Nyura. This will keep Terah safer than if you were not related. You may even keep your position as Dominus."

"What do you mean I may even keep my position?" he said nervously. "I was born to be the Dominus of Terah, as my father, grandfather and great-grandfather before me."

Lara sighed. The sound was part sadness, part exasperation. "The darkness has tried for centuries to conquer this world," she said. "Until now it was not possible. Do you remember the story of Usi the Sorcerer?"

Cadarn nodded slowly. "A child's tale," he scoffed.

"All tales have an element of truth in them. Some more than others," Lara told him. "Usi was real. Before the heroine Geltruda defeated him, Usi impregnated two of his concubines. One he sent to his brother in the Dark Lands. It is from the son of Usi born of Jorunn that Kolgrim descends. The maiden he marries this day descends from the female line of Usi, born to Ulla. She possesses certain powers that Kolgrim needs to complete his conquest of this world. Only by joining your blood with Kolgrim's blood can you save Terah, but you will answer to an evil master in return."

Cadarn Hauk was pale as the impact of her words bored into him. "And you say you will leave us at this terrible time, Great-grandmother," he said low. "Why now when we will need you so desperately? *Why now?*"

"I have no choice," Lara told him, realizing as she spoke that what she was saying was the absolute truth, and understanding for the very first time what Kaliq had been attempting to tell her all along. "The magic that has existed in this world is powerful, but our magic is pure and golden. We can fight the darkness just so far, but when it reaches a point where it can overwhelm us, we must retreat or die. And the death of good, or light, but strengthens the darkness and its evil. Your world invited the darkness into its midst. We tried to warn you, but you would not listen, even going so far as to deny our existence or that of our magic."

The Domina Paulina began to weep. Turning a tearstained face to Lara, she held out her hands. "Help us, faerie woman!" she pleaded.

Lara shook her head. "Uniting the three major rulers of this world by blood is the only help I can offer you now. You must help yourselves if you wish to destroy the darkness. Now we must go. The day will have begun in Hetar." She looked to Kaliq.

"Palben's palace, my lord?"

He nodded. "Clasp hands with us," Kaliq said to Cadarn and Paulina. "Do not be afraid. When the day is done we will return you safely home." The sure and commanding tone of his voice calmed the Dominus's fears. But it was Kaliq's warm smile at the Domina that eased hers. Certain they were all now linked together, Kaliq transported them to the Hetarian Palace of Palben in The City.

They reappeared in the Lord High Ruler's private dining salon, where he and his two wives, Laureen and Divsha, were now breaking their fast. Divsha shrieked as four magnificently garbed people appeared before the High Board. She reached out to cling to Palben, who shook her off irritably.

"Good morning, Great-grandmother, my lord Kaliq," the Lord High Ruler said. As annoying as these sudden appearances of theirs were becoming, he was getting used to them, he realized. They seemed almost natural.

"Good morning, my lord," Lara greeted him. "I have brought your cousin Cadarn Hauk, Dominus of Terah and his wife, the Lady Paulina, to meet you. They will attend the wedding today of my son and Nyura Ahasferus. And afterward they will conclude the negotiations for the marriage of their heir, Prince Vaclar to Yamka Ahasferus."

Palben's first wife, Lady Laureen, immediately arose, coming down form the High Board to greet their visitors. She curtsied to them all, and after briefly greeting Lara and Prince Kaliq said, "Welcome to Hetar, kinsfolk! We are most pleased to receive you. I even believe there is a small resemblance between Dominus Cadarn and my husband. Lady Paulina, what a beautiful gown. The color is both pleasing and flattering."

"Yamka is to marry a prince who will one day be Dominus?" Divsha said petulantly. "That isn't fair! Nyura weds a ruler. Yamka weds a ruler-in-waiting, and I am just a second wife?" She stamped her foot angrily. "But I am the most beautiful of us." Divsha burst into fulsome tears.

Palben's lips narrowed in irritation as his second wife had her small tantrum. He made no attempt to placate her. While he enjoyed their bed sport his only rationale in marrying her had been to unite himself with the Twilight Lord, for he had taken Lara's warning to heart. To his mind Divsha was nothing more than his personal Pleasure Woman, although he suspected she would cost him a great deal more.

Looking at him, Lara was reminded of her late son-in-law Jonah. His grandson not only resembled him, with his severe demeanor and cold eyes, he obviously had his icy nature, as well. Briefly she felt sorry for Divsha. Then she turned to Lady Laureen. "We shall need a comfortable chamber to refresh ourselves before the wedding," she said.

"Of course, Great-grandmother," Palben's first wife said. "I will take you myself, and be assured that we will provide you transport to Grugyn Ahasferus's home, though it be just across the park." She led them to a bright sunny chamber, and instructed two servants to see to their comfort. "I must go and change for the wedding. I shall also have to soothe and cajole Divsha, for she shall surely now refuse to come."

"Perhaps," Lara said, "it would be better if she didn't."

"Nay," Lady Laureen replied. "It would reflect badly upon my husband if his brand-new second wife was not at this important wedding. It is my duty to see that Divsha behaves herself. I saw how you looked at Palben, Great-grandmother. You know who he resembles, both in features and in spirit. He won't placate Divsha, but he will expect her obedience for that is a wife's duty. And if she does not give it, he will beat her. It would not do to have her make an appearance with that fair skin of hers marked and bruised."

Lara nodded. "What a pity Hetar's women lost the rights that they once found," she said. "You would have been a leader if that movement still existed."

"Did you ever know a Pleasure Woman named Gillian, Great-grandmother?" Lady Laureen asked Lara.

"I did," Lara responded. "She was a great lady, head of the Guild of Pleasure Women for many years. Why do you ask?"

"I am her descendant," Lady Laureen said. "I never knew her, of course, but she was always spoken of with great respect among the women of my family."

"Faerie blessings on you then, descendant of Lady Gillian," Lara said. "I counted that lady my friend."

Lady Laureen colored prettily. "Thank you, Great-grandmother," she said, and then she hurried off.

Kaliq sighed. "I am sorry that those whose hearts and souls are good will be caught in what is to come," he said.

"I know the others must go," Lara murmured low, "but why can we not stay, my lord? If we all leave, where is the light to come from?"

He shook his head. "We have another destiny, Lara, my love. We have done all we can do here. You know it even if your heart cannot admit it."

She nodded sadly, but tears filled her faerie green eyes, glistening as they caught in her dark lashes like tiny crystals.

He put a comforting arm about her, and she rested her head against his shoulder.

Cadarn Hauk watched, intrigued by the scene being played out before his eyes. But then he looked about him, seeing the richness of Palben's palace, and enviously began to consider how he might obtain such luxuries for his own castle. Next to him his wife admired the gown that had been magically produced for her, and wondered if she would be allowed to keep it. She had never seen such wonderful silk, and how did they get such a perfect color? The jewels sewn about the neckline and on the cuffs of the gown had to be worth a small fortune.

"If Vaclar is to marry this Hetarian girl, we are going to have to redo the entire castle, my lord," Lady Paulina whispered to her husband. "The few things we have imported from Hetar are nothing compared to this palace. And today we will see how another of these Hetarians lives. If it is as magnificent as this palace, then we will be put to shame bringing this young noblewoman into our midst unless we can at least equal their splendor. We must convince her family to let her bring whatever she desires with her when she weds Vaclar."

"And the marriage must be celebrated in Terah, as he is my heir," Cadarn said, "so we will have to do what needs to be done, and quickly."

Lara heard their words, and was astounded. Their world would soon be taken by the darkness. Evil would abound. And Cadarn and his wife conversed as if everything was going to remain the same. Had they not understood what she had told them? Or mayhap they did not believe what she told them.

It is too much for their mortal minds to fully comprehend, Kaliq said in the silent magical language. *It is not that they don't believe you. They simply refuse to understand. They can only survive by going on with their lives as they always have. Change is the most difficult circumstance for mortals to effect.*

It is breaking my heart, I fear, Lara replied.

He held her tightly. *Again that tiny bit of mortal blood rouses itself in you. But that is why you have become a powerful faerie entity, my love. You sympathize with them even if you don't fully under-stand them.*

She relaxed against him, and he felt the tension that had been building up in her ever since they reached Terah, and then Hetar, draining away. *I need faerie bread.*

Alas, I have none with me so you will have to satisfy yourself with Hetarian fare.

Lara laughed, causing Cadarn and his wife to cease their chatter. Looking about the chamber, she called to a servant. "I need food and drink," she told the woman.

"At once, my lady!" the woman said, hurrying off.

"Is there time?" Cadarn asked. "Is not this wedding soon?"

"Palben and his wives were not garbed for the occasion," Lara told them. "It will be several hours before we go. They will bathe and dress. And of course the second wife will have to be placated in some fashion for having realized her cousins are making better matches than she believes she has."

"She seemed quite outspoken and spoiled," Lady Paulina noted. "Quite unlike the Lady Laureen, whose manners and un-derstanding of her place I quite admired."

"Divsha Ahasferus is undoubtedly very spoiled, for she is a child of the wealthiest house in Hetar. Palben married her for the same reasons your son, Vaclar, will marry Yamka Ahasferus. To bind himself by blood to the Twilight Lord. He will have to get a child on her of course to do that, but he will. I see in him much of his grandfather Jonah, and Jonah was a man who always did what must or needed to be done," Lara said drily. "After the infant is born Palben will give her a home of her own here within the Golden District, and a potent sex slave to amuse her while she raises their child. She will receive all the respect due a second wife who is Ahasferus born, and Palben will not have to be annoyed by her. Divsha will survive quite well."

"Oh! Our poor son to have to marry into such a family," Lady Pauline said, distraught. "And she will despise Terah certainly, and hate our castle, which is very old-fashioned when compared with this beautiful palace!"

"The girls are not sisters, but cousins. They have been raised by different parents. I am sure you will find Yamka Ahasferus a nice girl," Lara tried to assure Lady Paulina.

"What choice have we?" Lady Paulina cried.

"You don't!" Lara said sharply. "Unless, of course, you wish to have your husband's kingdom completely taken over immediately by the Twilight Lord. Do you not comprehend that as long as you are kin to him he will give you a modicum of respect. Without that kinship Terah will cease to exist! This marriage Vaclar makes will save Terah. Yamka will have to make do like any other bride coming into her husband's home."

"Lara." Kaliq spoke gently to her. *Be calm. The woman cannot help but be what she is. A vain and foolish mortal. Be patient with her.*

I am hungry, and not of a mind to be patient with this Terahn woman who cannot see her world collapsing around her, yet frets that her furnishings aren't fashionable enough. Ohh, I am weary of these folk, Kaliq!

I know, he said. "Ahh, here are the refreshments for us." He turned, smiling at Cadarn and his wife. "You must be hungry and thirsty, too, as we took you from your evening meal."

"Oh, how beautiful the dishes are!" Lady Paulina trilled. She picked up a plate decorated with a floral design. "Look, Caddie, you can see through the china. We must have plates like this for the castle." She turned to Prince Kaliq. "Do you think we might remain a few days here in The City, my lord? I must visit the shops."

"I am certain that when the Ahasferus family learn you are here to personally take part in the negotiations for your son's marriage, they will want you to stay with them," Kaliq said. He was at his most charming. "If you remain, I shall see you have a trunk of the proper garments for your stay. And I shall return you to Terah when you wish to go."

"Paulina, I cannot leave Terah without my governance," Dominus Cadarn said.

"Ohh, Caddie, just two days? Terah will not fall apart in two days," Lady Paulina pleaded prettily. "And if this young noble-woman is to be our new daughter, we really should get to know her family."

"Two days, but no more, and only so I may oversee Cadoc and my uncle's negotiations for this marriage," Cadarn responded sourly.

As husband and wife spoke back and forth Lara suddenly realized that her passion for this world, her desire to save it, was not as strong as it had previously been. Was Kaliq right? Of course he was right. She could not recall the last time, if ever, when he had been wrong.

The door to the guest chamber opened suddenly. *"Mother! I was told that you had come, but I would not believe it until I saw you with my own eyes."* Kolgrim, the Twilight Lord, stepped into the room and, coming over to her, kissed her on both cheeks.

"I was unable to resist wishing you my felicitations," Lara said drily.

Kolgrim laughed aloud.

"This is your son?" Lady Paulina twittered.

Kolgrim's changeable gray eyes looked directly at Lara, waiting for her answer.

"Aye, this is my son," Lara finally said.

"He is very handsome," Lady Paulina replied. "How fortu-nate his bride."

Bertrice Small

"And extremely wicked, are you not, Kolgrim?" Lara taunted him.

The gray eyes darkened slightly. "No one knows my character better than my dearest mother," he agreed. "Is that not so, Mother? She felt so sorry for my betrothed, she stole her away and hid her from me. Only when I threatened to destroy my sister did she relent and return Nyura to me."

Lady Paulina tittered nervously not knowing whether to believe him or not. "Oh, my lord," she finally said. "You surely jest."

"Not at all, Lady Paulina," Kolgrim said, smiling at the woman.

Lady Paulina shuddered delicately, suddenly realizing this beautiful young man was a dangerous man. She reached out for her husband's hand.

But the Twilight Lord had already turned away from her. She was pretty, but too old for his taste although he just might take pleasures with her when he brought Terah under his control. He could see that Cadarn would need to fully comprehend who the master was. He would take the woman before her husband, making him watch as he forced her to cry out with delight. Nothing broke a man more than seeing the woman he loved violated by another man…and enjoying it.

What evil are you contemplating? Lara silently asked.

He told her and watched as distaste flooded her beautiful face. Then he said, *I am glad that you came, Mother. I could but wish my father were here to see my triumph.*

There is no triumph yet, Kolgrim. You but wed Ulla's descendant.

The child she bears me will be the greatest Twilight Lord ever born, Mother. The darkness will hold the world of Hetar in its grasp beyond time as even we of the magic kingdoms know it. And you cannot stop it this time. You will be forced to accept my rule as will everyone else, Kolgrim said.

We shall see, my son. *We shall see,* Lara responded coolly.

You must stand by my side when I wed today. It is Hetarian custom that the parents of the bride and groom be by their side to give them to each other.

He grinned mischievously at her, and Lara suddenly saw the boy he once was. The boy she had never known, or wanted to know. There was a poignancy in that knowledge, and then she felt Kaliq reach out to take her hand in his. He had understood, of course. *You cannot give away what you never had,* she told the young man before her. *But I have come today, and so I will do you honor, Kolgrim, son of Kol. You will not be shamed before these people or before those who are your blood kin even without these marriages.* For a brief moment she thought she saw a glimmer of tears in his eyes, but then the illusion was gone.

"I am pleased to see you all," Kolgrim said jovially. "Now I must go and prepare for my wedding. But before I go I would tell you that I may have four witnesses of my own choosing at the defloration ceremony. I invite you, my lord Dominus and Domina, and you, Prince Kaliq and my dear mother, to be my witnesses. Will you accept?"

"Of course we will accept, my lord," Prince Kaliq said, speaking for them all. "We are honored to have been asked." He bowed toward Kolgrim.

Kolgrim flashed them a bright smile, and then was gone from the chamber.

"What in the name of the Great Creator is a defloration ceremony?" Cadarn wanted to know.

"Tell them," Lara said, swallowing her laughter, for she knew when her great-grandson and his wife learned they would be horrified.

"The bride is a virgin, which as you know is quite rare in both Hetar and Terah. When a girl who has known no man before is wed here in Hetar, her virginity is taken before a group of chosen witnesses because it is thought to bring honor to her family. The bride's family chooses four witnesses, and the groom chooses four," Kaliq explained.

"That is barbaric!" Lady Paulina declared. She turned to her husband. "Caddie, we cannot do this! We cannot!"

"Of course we can," Dominus Cadarn replied calmly. "The Twilight Lord has honored us, wife. If it is to be as my great-grandmother says, and I have no cause to disbelieve her now. We must keep on the good side of our kinsman Kolgrim."

"I will *not* be party to such a thing," Lady Paulina cried.

"You will do as you are told," Cadarn said in a cold hard voice. "If you do not, if you embarrass me, embarrass Terah, we will return home immediately. And when we get there I will see you are beaten for your insolence. You will be imprisoned till you die in Great-grandmother's old tower, which refuses to be destroyed. Then I will divorce you and take a younger, more obedient wife. You will never see your children, or your grand-children again. Do you understand me, Paulina?"

Cowed, she bowed her head. "Yes, my lord," she said meekly.

"Do not feel sorry for the bride, Lady Nyura," Lara said to her great-grandson's wife. "She is aware of this custom. She chose to keep her innocence until she wed. I do not believe she knows it, but it has something to do with the powers she possesses. They would have been weakened by her sexual activity if she had indulged herself prior to marriage. Whether she sensed it, or the shade of her ancestress led her, we will never know. And she is pleased to bring honor to her family by her sacrifice."

"Every virgin screams the first time," Cadarn said in matter-of-fact tones.

"But to be taken before witnesses," Lady Paulina said weakly.

"There will be no intimacy between them prior to the defloration," Lara explained. "Their passion is not for our eyes. We are there to attest to the honesty and the value of the bride who saved her virginity for her bridegroom. Kolgrim's cock will be stimulated by several skilled Pleasure Women while at the same time Nyura is brought to a state of readiness by several equally skilled sex slaves purchased for just this occasion. When bride and groom have been properly prepared, they are brought together and complete the defloration with the aid of the Pleasure Women and the male sex slaves. It's actually a very civilized ceremony. If everyone involved does their job properly it will be over quickly. Then Kolgrim and his bride will disappear behind closed doors. The sheet upon which the deed was done is then brought back to the hall to be displayed to all the wedding guests. Then our part in the ceremony is over."

"Did you really steal his bride away and hide her?" Cadarn asked Lara.

"I did," Lara admitted. "I would have been very happy to keep Kolgrim from this marriage to Nyura Ahasferus, but it was not to be."

"What did you hope to accomplish by such an act?" Cadarn asked.

"This girl he is to wed was not chosen casually," Lara said. Then she explained to them about the Book of Rule, and how its pages wrote themselves, directing each Twilight Lord in his behavior. "I hoped to stop this marriage in order to save Hetar, but Kolgrim charmed my youngest daughter, Marzina, and menaced her."

"I thought he did not kill blood kin," Cadarn said.

"He did not intend killing her. What he planned was far worse. She was in a room of glass that Kolgrim threatened to release into a bottomless cavern outside of his castle. Marzina would have been trapped, unable to escape, and condemned for eternity. As I have a particular fondness for this daughter," Lara told Cadarn, "I gave him back his betrothed wife, and he gave me back my child."

"How cruel!" Lady Paulina said softly. "I could see the evil in his eyes. The poor maiden who is to be his wife."

"Oh, she is quite delighted with her fate," Lara said. "Do not grieve for Nyura."

"Let us make ourselves comfortable until we are called to the wedding," Prince Kaliq said, seating himself upon a velvet couch, drawing Lara down beside him.

"Indeed," Cadarn agreed. "If this wedding is like all weddings, it will be a busy day." He sat himself upon another velvet couch, patting the cushion by his side.

Lady Paulina accepted his invitation.

Let silence reign among us all and quiet be until the call, Prince Kaliq silently murmured the small enchantment. At once Cadarn and his wife fell asleep where they sat. "There has been enough talk," he said by way of explanation to Lara.

"Agreed," she replied. "They won't listen anyway. They do try, but they are so quickly led astray. They are beginning to sound more like Hetarians than Terahns. I can only imagine what Magnus would say."

"I think he would be very surprised to see what is happening in Terah. His son should have never allowed the Hetarian trading vessels to come to Terah. The kingdom was safer when the Terahn ships met the Hetarian ones at sea and transferred the cargo," Kaliq noted. "I will never understand why Taj did not listen to you in the matter."

"He was seventeen," Lara remembered, "and determined to escape the influence of his mother, the Shadow Queen. His grandmother, Lady Persis, persisted in irritating him about my position. She simply could not stomach a woman in a locus of power. And so to prove to her that he was Dominus and my authority was nonexistent, he allowed the Hetarian trading vessels to dock in Terah. Then he cajoled his uncles into declaring him old enough to rule alone, and that was the end of it. He had no respect for my advice after that, although he loved me. And then Persis died, and begged him on her deathbed to choose a traditional Terahn wife. His swore it, and his aunts acted swiftly." Lara laughed ruefully. "After that my power among the Terahns began to wane. There was nothing I could do."

Kaliq shook his head. "These mortal folk are determined to go their own way, and now here in the world of Hetar we must let them do just that. I am only sorry for the hurt they did you, Lara, my love. And now today we must watch as this marriage brings them closer to the edge of destruction. They will eat and dance and celebrate, not knowing until it is too late just what they have done."

THE DOOR TO THE CHAMBER OPENED AGAIN, AND a servant in splendid red-and-gold livery standing in the portal announced, "My lords and my ladies. The litters to take you to the wedding await you. If you will follow me, please." And he bowed to them.

Awaken refreshed! Kaliq released the Terahn ruler and his wife from the spell he had set upon them earlier.

"Must have dozed off," Cadarn said. "Nothing like a little nap to refresh one."

His wife nodded in agreement as she stood brushing nonexistent wrinkles from her beautiful gown. Then she took her husband's arm and they followed the servant.

Lara and Kaliq came behind them, smiling at each other with amusement.

As they came out into the great entry foyer Lara remembered the first time she had been in this place. Strangely it did not seem so very impressive now as it had then. As they exited the palace into the late-morning light they found two magnificent litters awaiting them. Large enough to comfortably carry two adults, they were of carved ebony decorated with pure gold designs, upholstered with soft golden leather and hung with gold-colored and spangled silk gauze draperies.

"Look at the tassels on the pillows," they heard Lady Paulina exclaim to the Dominus as she climbed into the transport. "Do you think the jewels are real? Caddie, we must have a litter like this made for ourselves when we get home. Our litters are too plain by far. What will Vaclar's bride think of us with such ordinary litters?"

They did not hear Cadarn's reply, and Lara was more interested in the four young men who bore each litter. They were identical in face and form. "Are you brothers?" she inquired of them.

The men nodded in reply. Then they all opened their mouths to reveal they had no tongues and could not speak.

Lara saw their plight then asked, "Magic effected this perfection you all bear. Did it also take your tongues and with it your power of speech?"

Again the bearers nodded in unison.

"Are you well treated otherwise?" Lara wanted to know.

They nodded.

"Then I shall restore your ability to communicate without anyone realizing that you can," she said. *Hear my voice this very day. Hear what all your brothers say. Speak to them within your head. This is magic you need not dread.*

A look of wonder suddenly lit the eight bearers faces, and Lara smiled.

"Take us to the wedding now. You will be able to speak with each other in this manner from this moment on. Those who rendered you voiceless will never know you have the power to communicate again," she told them. Then Lara climbed into the litter.

Thank you, faerie woman! Thank you! one of the bearers said. *You are welcome, my friends,* Lara said. She moved slightly to accommodate Kaliq, who had climbed in beside her. "How barbaric to take their tongues from them so they could not tell of the magic that made them identical. Some bad faerie did this. I hope it was not one of our forest folk. I will have Mother investigate."

"And how Hetarian of the Lord High Ruler to have handsome identical bearers for his litters. I wonder how many more of them there are," Kaliq wondered. "No matter. I have enabled any unknown to us to have the gift of mind speak. I will tell these bearers, and they can bring the news to the others."

They felt their litter lifted up, and the bearers set off at a swift trot across the green park that was the Golden District. Looking at Lara in her green gown, Kaliq felt a surge of desire and was startled to find her gaze on him. Closing his bright blue eyes, he began to imagine them making love within the litter. Catching his thoughts, Lara joined hers to his. They were naked, lying stretched out against the soft golden leather of the interior of the litter. He sat propped up by the many pillows, his great cock filling her as she sat facing him, her arms entwined about his neck, her breasts pushing against his chest. They moved together in perfect rhythm as the litter jogged along. And then their passions peaked simultaneously. They sighed, and opened their eyes, smiling at each other.

"That was delicious," Lara murmured to him, laying her head upon his shoulder.

"An appetizer for later when we have returned to Shunnar, and I may spend hours enjoying your beautiful body, your sweet lips, Lara, my love," Kaliq told her.

"If mortals knew all the things we could do they would be

so envious," Lara chuckled mischievously. "Their perceptions of magic are far too simple."

They felt the tempo of the bearers slowing down and, looking through the sheer draperies, saw they were coming up a curved driveway. On either side of the path great tall bushes filled with round, deep pink flowers lined the way. Then suddenly a view of Grugyn Ahasferus's home was revealed to them. A low two stories, constructed of cream-colored marble, and generously colonnaded, it had two wings separated by a third single-storied section. Its exterior was almost as magnificent as the palace, but Lara wagered with herself the interior would be far more glorious. As long as the Ahasferus family was wise enough not to display their great wealth too publicly they were safe from Palben's wrath. No one but those few invited into both homes would ever be able to compare the two. And they would not dare to do so if they valued their lives.

The litter came to a stop and was set down gently. Kaliq emerged, holding his hand out to Lara, who then stepped forth. *Tell any others who have been afflicted as you have in the service of your masters that they can now use the mindspeak of the magic world, my friend,* Kaliq told one of the bearers.

There is no way in which we can thank you for this gift, my lord, the bearer said with tears in his eyes.

Fight the darkness that will soon come with good, Kaliq replied and then he turned to escort Lara into the great mansion of Grugyn Ahasferus.

The master of the house and his wife, Lady Camilla, having been advised of these most important guests, were awaiting them in the entry rotunda of the house. Cadarn had wisely waited for Lara and Kaliq despite his wife's insistence they go ahead. Lara nodded her approval to her great-grandson as they passed him by to meet Grugyn Ahasferus and his lady.

"We are honored by your presence, Prince Kaliq of the Shadows," the patriarch of the family said, bowing. "And by yours, as well, my lady Lara. I remember my grandfather, Cuthbert, speaking of you when I was a child. May I present my wife, Camilla, whose line of descent is through the eldest daughter of Sir Rupert Bloodaxe, who fathered your late son-in-law, Jonah," Grugyn Ahasferus explained.

Lara bowed slightly in recognition of his greeting. "Faerie blessings on your house this day, Grugyn Ahasferus," she said to him.

"We much admire your son, lady," he responded.

Lara smiled slightly. "Kolgrim is an interesting young man, well not really so young for he passed the century mark several years ago."

Lady Camilla paled. "He is old? But he looks no more than a man of thirty."

"His vanity would revel in your words, lady," Lara told her. "Twilight Lords age far more slowly than do mortals. But my son will keep your granddaughter young as long as she amuses him." Her words were cruel, and Lara knew it.

It would not, however, faze Lady Camilla. Tomorrow mattered little to Hetarians. Today and prestige was most important to them; and today Lady Camilla's granddaughter would wed a powerful magical being who ruled over his own land. No one else in Hetar could say that. She smiled coyly at Prince Kaliq, who kissed her hand. Lady Camilla had heard that Shadow Princes were great lovers. Of course that was legend. Shadow Princes didn't exist. Magic didn't exist. At least according to the powers that be. And yet here was a Shadow Lord kissing her hand, and she had just spoken with a faerie woman who was said to exist only in legend, and yet she was real. It promised to be a very wonderful and very exciting day. Lady

Camilla focused on greeting the Domina of Terah, who was wearing one of the most beautiful gowns she had ever seen.

The thoughts in her head, so filled with self-importance and misinformation, boggle my mind, Kaliq.

You are harsh in your judgments, my love, he replied. *But that is because you are angry with what is happening. Do not be, Lara. We have done our best for Hetar. We can do no more, and so we will move on to new pastures and new adventures.*

Then let us go now, Kaliq! I cannot watch this travesty.

Nay, we must yet remain, he told her. *Our task here is not quite finished. Today you will give Kolgrim what he has always wanted of you. Your love and your approval. In doing so you weaken him, although he will not realize it. It means that one day the light can return to this world. And when it does it will hopefully be a better place.*

So in the end I do defeat the darkness, Lara said softly.

Nay, 'twill not be you who defeats it here, Lara, but by giving your love and favor to Kolgrim this day you will set in motion what is to be.

And then what? Lara asked.

And then, my darling, we will ride Dasras together into the Cosmos. There is more, of course, but better you live it than I tell you of what is to come, he said with a smile, his blue eyes twinkling at her for he knew what she would say next.

You know I hate mysteries, Kaliq! Lara said, and Kaliq laughed aloud.

"Mother!"

"Marzina! What are you doing here?" Lara wanted to know.

"Kolgrim wanted me to come, and frankly I couldn't resist. The forest is almost emptied out of all of our race. Grandmother and Thanos will be the last to go, for they are so responsible. And I think Grandmother is sorrowing a little over Hetar. Dillon has offered them a permanent refuge on Beltran if they want it. I must admit the forests there are magnificent, but Grandmother is not ready to settle herself just yet," Marzina said. "I love your gown, Mother! The green is wonderful and exactly like the White Oak leaves of spring in the forest. Hello, Kaliq."

"Marzina," he said, amused by her chatter.

"I do not know if I want you to become so friendly with Kolgrim," Lara said to her youngest daughter.

"Why not? He is my brother after all. Not half brother, but *my brother,*" Marzina said meaningfully.

Lara sighed. "If I could have prevented it, you would have never known that, my daughter. And Kolgrim is evil as he was meant to be. When your grandparents leave the forest I want you to go with them, Marzina."

"You cannot plan my fate, Mother, as you could not plan that of your other offspring. Dillon went to Belmair. Anoush returned to the Fiacre clan family where she felt happier. Zagiri defied you, ran away and married the man she loved. Taj listened more to others than to you. He committed the worst sin of all by marginalizing you, Mother. I have my own destiny to follow, and I will."

"And just what is your destiny?" Lara wanted to know.

"I have absolutely no idea. I simply listen to the voice within, who guides me even as Ethne sometimes guides you," Marzina said airily. "Whatever my destiny is I am not afraid of it. Unlike you, I like enigmas." And she laughed her tinkling laughter.

"This is your brother's wedding day," Lara said, "and so you and I shall not quarrel, Marzina. But you must leave Hetar with the others."

Marzina, her violet eyes dancing with merriment, kissed her mother's cheek. "Have you seen all the handsome young men here today? I am in the mood to take pleasures with several of them."

Kaliq chuckled. "You are a naughty faerie maid," he teased her. "Try not to break too many hearts today, Marzina."

"Mother!" Kolgrim strode forward. Garbed in black silk decorated with silver, he was very handsome. He kissed her on both cheeks. "Thank you for coming."

"I always attend my sons' weddings," Lara said. "My daughters either run away, or stay unmarried."

"Marzina is too beautiful to marry," Kolgrim said. "I shall build her a House of Men in the Dark Lands next to my House of Women. She may keep her male concubines there for pleasures."

"What a grand idea!" Marzina said, clapping her hands. "You are the best brother any girl could have!" She threw her arms about him so she might hug and kiss him.

Lara felt an icy ripple race down her spine. Marzina was the most reckless of all her children. That, she supposed, was Kol's doing. But her daughter must not ally herself with Kolgrim. He was a fascinating man to be sure, but he must not take Marzina with him into the darkness. *He mustn't!*

"I have a favor to ask of you, Mother," Kolgrim said.

"What is it?" Lara inquired of him. He wanted a favor from her? Curious.

"Marzina has already agreed to stand with me, but I would have you, too."

Lara's first instinct was to say no. But then she heard Ethne, her guardian spirit, speaking to her. Only Lara could hear her when she spoke.

Say yes, my child! Ethne's voice was most plain.

Why? Lara asked surprised.

Because it is important to him, and it is important for you to do so, Ethne said. *Trust me, my child, as you always have.* The crystal star on the end of the chain about her neck glowed with its golden light.

Has Kolgrim bewitched you, Ethne?

Nay, my child, he has not the power for that. Now tell him aye.

"I will stand by your side, Kolgrim," Lara told the Twilight Lord.

His handsome face mirrored his delight at her words. "Then you do love me!" he said excitedly! "Sometimes I speak with Kolbein in his imprisonment. He says you will never love me, but you do. *You do!*"

"Do not press your good fortune, Kolgrim," Lara said tartly. "I will stand by your side, and gladly give you to Nyura, but I have said naught of love."

"You would not have come today, nor would you stand by my side if you did not love me," the Twilight Lord insisted.

Lara said nothing more. She did not wish to quarrel with him, and she wondered to herself if she did indeed have some tender maternal emotion where Kolgrim was concerned. He was after all flesh of her flesh. She was surprised that he cared if she loved him or not. And then she considered that, like her, he had a tiny drop of mortal blood within him. Perhaps that was why it meant so much to him that she love him.

"You look beautiful today, Mother. Every inch the forest faerie," he complimented her.

"Thank you," Lara replied. How odd this all was. It was almost as if it were a normal day and a normal wedding of a normal couple. She would have never considered that one day she would stand publicly by Kolgrim's side, admitting to any who asked or saw them that he was her son. But then, it didn't matter any longer. Those from whom she had hidden this truth were long dead, and Hetar was doomed. After today it was unlikely she would see Kolgrim again. "Does your father still live?" she asked him.

"Do you care?" he countered.

"Nay," she admitted candidly. "'Twas just curiosity."

"He yet lives," Kolgrim told her. "Shall I tell him you asked?"

Lara laughed wryly. "It pleases you to taunt him, doesn't it?" she said.

"He abandoned us even as you did," Kolgrim said.

"He didn't abandon you. He was imprisoned for violating the laws of the Dream Plain," Lara said. "You know that, Kolgrim. Alfrigg saved you and your twin by placing you with Dark Land families who knew nothing of your birthright so they could not use you. Nor could anyone else. This is ancient history. You are the Twilight Lord."

"And now I am about to conquer the world of Hetar," Kolgrim said. "Look about you, Mother, at these mortals who drink and jest and believe everything is as it has always been, who think it will always be this way, that nothing will change. Neither Palben nor Cadarn would listen to you when you warned them, would they?" He laughed darkly.

"They deserve well what I will bring them. Even now in the Purple Mountains, a volcano, so long dormant that no one remembers it once existed, bubbles, preparing to erupt. And it will tonight at the very moment I gain first pleasures from my bride. It will do quite a bit of damage, wiping out towns that once belonged to the Piaras and Tormod Clan families along with several large vineyards planted on the mountainsides. It will set the forests there afire, and many lives will be lost."

"You can stop it," Lara said to him.

"Actually I cannot," he said. "I haven't quite gotten complete control of the natural forces belonging to this world. I will eventually gain a mastery of it all."

"He did not set this into motion himself, Lara," Kaliq said, "even if he will enjoy it and use it to his own advantage," the Shadow Prince told her.

At that moment a servant came to tell them that Kolgrim was needed with his family to stand upon the dais that had been set up in the center of the rotunda. Nyura was about to make her entrance with her family. The many guests were seating themselves on either side of the aisles that had been formed with curved removable benches. Kaliq found a place on an edge near the front as Lara and Marzina followed Kolgrim and the servant to their designated place. The hall grew silent. Lara thought how beautiful it all was as she stood upon the dais, looking out over the hall and all the guests. Sunlight poured in through the open dome of the rotunda turning the space into a golden chamber. All around the circular space footed urns rose up, each holding large white wicker baskets of colorful blooms. Beyond the rotunda was a great dining hall where they would all adjourn after the ceremony. Two liveried serving men already stood before it, awaiting a signal to open the twin bronze doors. Marzina reached out to take her hand, and Lara squeezed the hand in hers.

A flourish of trumpets announced the arrival of the bride and her family. They advanced down the long aisle centered on the dais. The bride was extremely beautiful. She was clothed in a long, fitted cream silk gown, the skirt of which ended in a long train edged in gold lace. The neckline of the gown was round, its bodice sewn with tiny clear crystal beads and pearls. The long fitted sleeves came to a point at the end of her delicate wrists where they met her slender hands. Her pale red-gold hair flowed loose, and her head was topped with a delicate low white-gold tiara set with diamonds.

The bridal party was preceded by a troupe of musicians playing upon reed instruments, small drums and bells. These were followed by a group of slender young dancers—both male and female—in little silk gauze garments that left nothing to the imagination, who pranced and gamboled before Nyura and her family, flinging rose petals and fragrant violets as they came. The bride carried a basket of woven gold containing samples of all the wealth she would bring to her husband. It was filled with gold and silver coins, pearls, gemstones, pieces of different fabric and a parchment scroll listing all the land, livestock and slaves belonging to the bride. She carried it proudly, and Lara saw she noted quite clearly the envy of certain of her guests as she passed by them.

Beauty, and the untried powers Kolgrim needed. And Lara suspected the girl was intelligent. She would have to be to have listened to the shade of Ulla and kept herself pure for her husband. A virginal bride in Hetar was unique for the need for pleasures was ingrained in them. At the age of fourteen many Hetarian girls felt desire rising in them, and became sexually active. Others began earlier, but by sixteen when they were ready for marriage Hetarian girls were thoroughly experienced in passion. Oddly, young Hetarian men did not become active until they were sixteen or seventeen.

Pleasure Houses peopled by male slaves and catering to young women had become quite popular in The City. Parties were held in these houses by many parents for their daughters. At any time there was certain to be one or two male sex slaves who became particularly popular. Being deflowered by one of these slave men brought a girl great prestige. Consequently their services were considerably more costly than the other male sex slaves. Nyura, however, had proved the exception.

The bride had now reached the dais with her parents and grandparents. As marriage in Hetar was a business transaction, the ceremony would be presided over by Grugyn Ahasferus himself. Dressed in burgundy silk trimmed with black ebony beads and gold embroidery, he stepped up onto the dais, turned and looked about.

"We have come today to unite my granddaughter Nyura, daughter of my son Zenas, to Kolgrim the Twilight Lord, son of Kol," he said in solemn tones. "Is there anyone present who would object to this union? Speak now or accept what is to be." Grugyn Ahasferus's gaze swept the hall, although he did not expect any objection to this union. Satisfied that all would proceed as planned, he now said, "I speak for the family Ahasferus. We give this maiden in marriage to Kolgrim." He drew the bride onto the dais and took her hand to hold out.

Lara and Marzina spoke in unison. "We speak for the family of Kol. We give this man in marriage to the maiden Nyura." Lara drew Kolgrim up onto the dais and, taking his hand in hers, put it into Nyura's hand.

Grugyn Ahasferus nodded, pleased. He put his two hands over the clasped hands of the bride and the groom. "Then it is done. Kolgrim and Nyura are united in marriage."

A mighty cheer arose from the guests in the rotunda. The banquet and day-long entertainments would follow until night fell, and the defloration ceremony was performed. Only then would the day be over. The avenue outside of the Golden District had been closed off to all but foot traffic this day. The family Ahasferus had provided a generous feast of meat, bread, frine, sweet cakes and even Razi, a narcotic drink that was so popular in Hetar. All the citizens of The City were invited to partake, and they came.

The main wedding banquet would not be served until late afternoon. Until then wine and light refreshments were brought forth for the guests to enjoy. In several chambers off the rotunda entertainments were set up. There were musicians and dancers, and in part of the garden a small circus performed. One chamber was devoted to any gentleman who wished to avail himself of a Pleasure Woman. In another chamber there were male sex slaves for the ladies. There was little privacy in these rooms, but the guests did not care. They were filled with wine, and they could enjoy pleasures for free with some of the most skilled Pleasure Women and male sex slaves in The City. A scream of agony brought the guests hurrying to an open chamber where unfortunate slaves had been chosen to be beaten until they died.

Kolgrim and his lovely bride delivered the first cruel blows. They taunted one another as to who could deliver the most brutal smacks. On the edge of the crowd Lara overheard two women gossiping.

"I've heard that the servants in her father's house are quite terrified of her," one matron said low to another. "She is said to quite enjoy whipping any who offend her, and has become expert at it."

The other matron nodded. "Grugyn quite indulges her for she is his favorite, I'm told, and asked for this entertainment in particular. Have you placed your wager on which one will die first yet?"

"Oh I have. I think the man with the bald head will last longer than the other fellow."

Lara was horrified by what was now considered entertainment in Hetar, but more so by the fact Nyura apparently had a vicious streak. Aye, she was the perfect bride for Kolgrim, and she regretted more than ever being cajoled into taking part in this travesty.

I want to leave now, she said to Kaliq, who was suddenly by her side.

You cannot, he told her. *It would reflect badly upon you to do so.*

Did you see what they are doing? They are beating two poor slaves to death, and they consider it entertainment, Kaliq! I cannot believe they have come to this!

I have taken care of it, my love, he told her. *I have transported the spirits of both slaves to a safe place until it is time for them to perish. The bodies hanging between the whipping posts will bleed and struggle. They will scream, and the wedding guests will be content that they are suffering enough, but the two slaves now feel nothing more. Come away now, and do not distress yourself. The gardens here are beautiful, and quite empty right now. Let us go outside, and away from the crowd.*

Aye, the scent of blood in my nostrils is making me quite ill, Lara told him, clinging to his arm. They exited the rotunda, walking down a hallway and out into the lush gardens of Grugyn Ahasferus. *There is too much wickedness here, Kaliq. I swear that it is weakening me.*

It is not just this house, but all of Hetar now, my love, Kaliq told her.

They found a marble bench in a part of the garden distant from the house. There were several tall trees and rosebushes about them. They sat quietly in the sweet air as birds sang around them, and colorful butterflies flittered back and forth. Lara sighed and rested her head on Kaliq's strong shoulder. They remained that way for some time in the fragrant quiet, the sounds of revelry from the house quite distant.

But then a servant hurried toward them. He bowed. "My master asks that you join the bridal party at the High Board, my lord, my lady."

"We will come at once," Kaliq said, smiling at the servant. He stood up, drawing Lara with him. "Come, my darling. This day will be over soon, and we may return home to Shunnar." Then he led her through the gardens back to the great mansion as the servant hurried ahead of them.

The rotunda was empty as they walked through it, following the liveried man into a Great Hall and to the High Board at the far end of the room. The hall, like the house, was marble.

The painted ceiling was held up by a colonnade of slender pillars that encircled the entire hall. Beyond the hall were floor-to-ceiling windows that looked out upon the parkland of the Golden District. The High Board was set with a large white linen cloth and several gold candelabra. The table settings were all gold. The goblets crystal, rimmed in gold.

"Ahh, my dear lady Lara, my lord Kaliq," their host greeted them. "Please sit yourselves next to the bridal couple," he invited them, smiling broadly. "What a happy day for us all, is it not?" But he didn't wait for Lara to answer him, turning instead to the Dominus Cadarn, who sat on the other side of Lady Camilla.

"Mother, you look lovely today, if I have not already said it," Kolgrim murmured. "Where did you get to? We missed you. Marzina became quite troubled when she could not find you. She was much admired for the way she plied the whip on our entertainment slaves. Several gentlemen were quite entranced by her skill." He chuckled.

"You are vile!" Lara hissed at him. "How did you manage to get your sister to partake in that disgusting display. I would not have thought it of her."

"Oh, she was hesitant at first, but she has come to love me well and wanted to please me on this special day," he said. "I understand her, Mother, and quite delight in bringing the wickedness out in her. It has always been there, but then you knew that, which is why you have tried so hard to influence her, to keep her true heritage from her."

"She is leaving Hetar, Kolgrim. As soon as her grandparents are ready to depart, she will go with them," Lara said.

He laughed softly. "Nay, she will not leave Hetar, Mother. She wants to stay with me and be part of the new world that I will create. She is almost mine now," Kolgrim taunted Lara.

"Nor will you depart Hetar, for you will not leave Marzina. You love her."

Lara closed her eyes for a brief moment. When she opened them again he was surprised to see the steely resolve in them. "Marzina will leave Hetar, Kolgrim. And so will I. Do not attempt to thwart me in this for I will win the battle for my daughter's soul. You do not want to go to war against me, *my son*. You will regret it if you do."

"You cannot destroy me, Mother," he said.

"You are right, Kolgrim, I cannot. But I can cause you more difficulties than you can ever imagine. Remember it is Shadow Prince magic that contains your father and your twin brother, Kolbein, within their prison cell. I am forced to face the fact that Hetar is doomed to the darkness. But I don't have to make it easy for you, do I? Leave Marzina alone. I shall not warn you again, my lord." She smiled sweetly into his surprised face then, reaching for her goblet, drained it down.

Kolgrim smiled back at her. A tight smile. "Keep my sister then if you can," he said. "I have more important matters to attend to than that hoyden. I have a son to create. Do you remember when father mated with you? Did you scream with the pain?"

"What a nasty boy you are," Lara taunted him back. "At least I wasn't a virgin like the delicate Nyura. Will you mate her tonight? If you do, you cannot touch her again until the Completion Ceremony. I assume you will want to enjoy her for a while, but then your time is short, isn't it, Kolgrim."

He laughed now. "You are right, of course. But my House of Women is newly stocked and will keep me amused until Nyura is free from her duty to me."

"How fortunate for you, dear. I hope Nyura isn't the jealous type. If she is, your life will not be pleasant. You must treat her with especial care once she carries your only son," Lara purred at him. "I will say this about your father. He was always most courteous to me. But then I did not try his patience."

Kolgrim laughed. "He was too lenient with you, Mother. And then you broke his heart. I shall not be quite so forbearing."

Now it was Lara who laughed. "Kolgrim, you have much to learn of women."

"My lord—" Nyura put a proprietary hand on her bridegroom's arm "—you are ignoring me, and for your mother. What will people think?"

Lara chuckled low and turned to speak with Kaliq, who had been listening to her discourse with Kolgrim. "I believe I am temporarily better, my lord," she said.

"He is far more dangerous than you realize," Kaliq said softly.

"I know it," Lara said, "but as long as he does not know I know, our battles are less apt to be violent. He will finish this charade to suit Hetar. But come the morrow, Grugyn Ahasferus will find his granddaughter and her new husband gone. He only has a few more weeks in which to impregnate her. After that he will be forced to wait until the next mating season. And anything could happen in that time. The Book of Rule can be fickle. If Nyura does not conceive quickly, her usefulness to Kolgrim could be over. Remember, he had no compunction about killing Ciarda."

"I am relieved you are not plotting to prevent Nyura's conception," Kaliq said.

Lara shook her head. "My faerie heart has hardened. I no longer care what happens to this world of Hetar, especially given what I saw today. That depravity and cruelty should play a part in the joy of a marriage celebration is more than I can bear. How can I give my magic to mortals like that, Kaliq? My only care now is for us, for Marzina, for our family. We must quickly remove Marzina from Hetar. Kolgrim says he will leave her to me, but I can see into his black heart. He means to have his sister. He believes if he keeps her I will not leave her. And, though he says it not, I believe he intends to take my magic from me if he can."

"Aye, he would," Kaliq said slowly. "Nothing will ever be enough for Kolgrim, I fear. The tiny bit of mortal within him weakens him though he knows it not, my love."

"A toast! A toast to the bride and bridegroom!" Grugyn Ahasferus stood up, goblet in hand.

The guests all arose and drank to Kolgrim and Nyura a dozen times over as the lavish meal progressed. There were prawns broiled in butter and wine. Platters of fish from the Sagitta, caught only that morning and delivered by faerie post to the kitchens of Grugyn Ahasferus, were served on beds of watercress with carved lemons surrounding them. There was venison, wild boar, game birds of all kinds, ducks, geese, pheasant, quail and tiny ortolans among them. Green salads, fresh breads in all shapes and sizes, butter and cheese were in abundance. Then a great cake soaked in wine, covered with thick whipped cream and filled with berries was served to each guest. The goblets were never allowed to be empty; soft music from a musicians' gallery never ceased playing, but finally the meal began to come to an end.

Dancers began to weave their way among the trestle tables where the guests were seated, finishing before the High Board, where they entertained all. A choir of castrated men and boys sang for the wedding party. And beyond the colonnade the sun set, and night came. It would soon be time for the defloration ceremony. Nyura's mother and Lady Camilla arose, discreetly nodding to the bride. Without a word she got up and followed them from the hall.

Kolgrim leaned over. "Do not forget that you three are my witnesses," he said to Lara, Kaliq and Marzina.

"Who are the others?" Prince Kaliq asked, curious.

"The Lord High Ruler, Dominus Cadarn and Prince Vaclar," Kolgrim answered them. "The Domina begged to be excused and her husband has relented. Of course her parents and grandparents would be there if tradition permitted, but they must be in the hall with the rest of the guests. The witnesses must be unbiased and six is enough."

"I think it's barbaric," Marzina remarked. "The poor girl must be terrified. Losing one's virginity should not be a traumatic experience."

"You speak from experience, I assume," Kolgrim teased her.

Marzina laughed. "My first lover was a friend of my uncle Cirillo. He was most charming and gentle. I thoroughly enjoyed his company for some months, but then I grew curious and tried my first mortal."

"What a naughty girl you are, Marzina," Kolgrim said, looking directly at Lara.

"I'm a faerie, Kolgrim. And faeries are naughty," Marzina replied pertly.

"You are only half-faerie, sister. The other half of you is Darklander, and Darklanders are naughty, too," Kolgrim told her.

A small shadow passed over Marzina's pretty face. "I had not considered that bit of my heritage," she said.

"Perhaps you should," he murmured low.

"Perhaps you should cease tormenting your sister," Lara said in an even voice, and put an arm about Marzina. "Your promise I see is worthless, Kolgrim."

He laughed mockingly at her. "I did not have your good example growing up, mother dear," he taunted her. "Perhaps if I had I would be a different man."

Now it was Lara who laughed. "Nay, you would be as you are, Kolgrim. Your father's son. But Marzina is my daughter first." Her arm tightened about the girl.

"What are you two quarreling about?" Marzina wanted to know. "Oh, you smile and you laugh, but I know you are squabbling."

"Our mother wishes to control your fate," Kolgrim quickly said, knowing that Lara was overprotective of her daughter, and that Marzina sometimes resented it.

"Nay," Lara responded before Marzina might speak. "I want *you* to control your fate, but your *brother* seems to believe he can speak for you, and I object to that. You are perfectly capable of managing your own life, Marzina, although I will admit to being surprised by it," Lara concluded, almost laughing aloud at the surprised look on Kolgrim's face that she had so neatly and swiftly turned the tables on him.

The outrage Marzina had been prepared to aim at her mother she now directed toward Kolgrim. "How dare you presume to speak for me?" she demanded of him.

"I only thought…" Kolgrim began.

"Do not think for me, either," Marzina said icily. "Really! What is it with the male of any species that they believe themselves superior to the female? I should leave you right now, but that I am a woman of my word, and have promised to be a witness for you, Kolgrim. I will not embarrass you before these mortals, though you deserve it."

"If you are wise, you will say nothing further," Prince Kaliq murmured so that only Kolgrim could hear him.

Kolgrim fell silent. About them the wedding guests continued drinking and watching the entertainment. When the defloration ceremony was completed they would simply leave Grugyn Ahasferus's house, the wedding day and its celebration officially over. But until then, they waited, drinking, watching, talking. Lady Camilla and her daughter-in-law returned to the hall, going directly to Kolgrim.

"Your virgin bride awaits you, my lord," Lady Camilla said. Then, "The witnesses will follow me to the observation chamber." She turned and they arose and Lady Camilla led them to the far end of one of the house's wings, ushering them into a small chamber. Two tiers of seats faced a curtained wall. Lady Camilla drew the curtain back to reveal a transparent glass that gave a full view of the room on the other side. "You will hear what happens as well as see," she told them, "although they can neither hear nor see you. As you know, virgin brides are a rarity in Hetar, but we are not uncivilized. The couple will have the illusion of privacy. After the bride is deflowered a servant will collect the proof of her perfection and bring it to you." She looked directly at the witnesses. "My lady Lara, may I ask you to bring the evidence back to the dining hall yourself. Your history with Hetar makes you, and I mean no offense to others here, the most trustworthy of the witnesses."

"I am honored," Lara replied, nodding respectfully to Lady Camilla. She had no quarrel with Hetar any longer, and there was no harm in being civil.

"Thank you," Lady Camilla said. "Now I must bring the bridegroom into the Nuptial chamber." She hurried from the little room. The witnesses seated themselves.

"Given this display," Dominus Cadarn said, "the Ahasferus family cannot object to our traditional Terahn wedding ceremony."

"What's so different about it?" Palben asked, curious.

"The betrothed couple are married before their guests at dawn as the sun rises, *naked,*" Cadarn answered his cousin. "Once they are pledged they are clothed in wedding garments, but naked shows they are free of all impediment. It's a very ancient tradition, and Vaclar's wedding will be presided over by the High Priest from the Temple of the Great Creator. But Yamka will at least have privacy on her wedding night."

"Most brides do, except those who so childishly clutch their virginities to themselves," Palben answered. "But if they insist they are pure they must prove it before witnesses. It brings honor to their family that they have made such a sacrifice as denying themselves pleasures while other girls their age enjoyed themselves." Then he leaned forward in his seat. "Oh, look! The facilitators have entered the Nuptial chamber."

"Facilitators?" Prince Vaclar said.

"The defloration is done as quickly as possible," Palben said. "The couple does not wish any passion they might share to be viewed. The object is to remove Nyura's virginity so the bridal couple may enjoy pleasures together. But Kolgrim can hardly fling himself upon his bride and violate her rudely. There are three facilitators at such a ceremony. Two are male sex slaves. It is their task to prepare the bride, to see that her juices flow so that her bridegroom may have an easier passage. The third facilitator is a Pleasure Woman. It is her chore to make certain that Kolgrim's cock is firm and upstanding so he may perform his duty swiftly and with dispatch. Once that is done the couple is escorted to a private chamber for the night," Palben explained.

Marzina shuddered delicately. "I don't care what you say," she remarked. "The whole thing is simply barbaric."

"I am inclined to agree," Prince Vaclar said, and Dominus Cadarn nodded.

"Nonetheless, it is our custom in Hetar, even as naked bridal couples are yours in Terah," Palben responded tartly. How dare these two foreigners criticize Hetar? Hetar was the more civilized world, and always had been. What was Terah but fjords and farmlands. A place of simple artisans and craftsmen. They had nothing that Hetar had. They might not be savages, but they were certainly not urbane.

"My goodness, those two sex slaves are well hung," Marzina noted. "Perhaps I shall take advantage of their services afterward. Who owns them, I wonder?"

"They come from the Pleasure Mistress Helena's house," Palben told her. "They are quite well-known for their expertise. When we are finished here I will arrange it for you, my lady Marzina."

"Actually I am your great-aunt," she told him mischievously knowing how the presence of magic upset him. "I thank you for your aid. It shall make this day a perfect one, nephew."

Palben flushed at the word *nephew*. She was young and beautiful. Hardly a creature one would think of as a great-aunt. He had actually been considering the possibility of seducing her. But she was not a child, after all. She had been his grandmother's sister. It was just too disturbing to even consider.

"IT'S BEGINNING," PRINCE KALIQ SAID, BREAKING into the Lord High Ruler's thoughts, and freeing him from his distress.

The witnesses turned toward the viewing window. The bride, naked now, was laid upon the large bed that was covered with white silk and scattered with several plump pillows. Her slender, delicate arms were spread and bound with blue silk cords to the narrow bedposts above her head.

"Why has the girl been bound?" Lara inquired. "What is to come is no surprise to her. Why is it necessary to restrain her."

"The defloration needs to be done in relatively short order," Palben replied. "By restraining her, she is prevented from acting on any last-moment panic on her part."

Lara shook her head disparagingly. Nyura didn't look in the least panicked.

The two male sex slaves now joined her upon the bed. They kissed her lips in turn. Then each moved to play with one of her breasts. They kissed and suckled, kissed and nibbled upon her nipples. Their hands stroked her voluptuous young body. Now one of the pair moved to kiss Nyura's mouth once again. His kisses were slow and deep. It was obviously he was quite good at what he was doing, for the girl's body began to move slightly as his kisses grew more heated, evidenced by his burgeoning cock against the bride's shapely leg.

The second male sex slave began to lick and kiss the girl's torso, moving slowly down until he reached her plump rosy mons. His hand reached out to squeeze it several times, and the witnesses heard Nyura make a small sound of surprise. Then the sex slave pulled the girl's nether lips apart, licking the insides of them, seeking out that tiny nub of flesh that, properly cajoled, could offer small pleasures. Nyura began to make little whimpering sounds.

Lara's eyes moved to where Kolgrim stood naked. In his arms was one of the most beautiful Pleasure Women she had ever seen. The body Kolgrim caressed was flawless and perfectly proportioned, with two lovely round breasts, a narrow waist from which flared two rounded hips and smooth, plump buttocks. He kissed the woman passionately as her hands caressed him seductively, touching him in places that brought a virile man to full lust.

The Pleasure Woman finally eased from the Twilight Lord's embrace and slipped to her knees before Kolgrim, taking his manhood into her mouth. They watched as her cheeks moved slowly, rhythmically, in and out. It was obvious she was taking her time with him in order to bring him to a perfect pitch. Kolgrim's eyes closed with the ecstasy she was giving him. His large hand with its long elegant fingers dug into the tangle of her thick dark hair, kneading her head.

On the bed Nyura's little cries were becoming urgent as the sex slave between her legs worried her little jewel with a skilled tongue.

The Pleasure Woman held up her hand and, releasing the enormous cock she had been sucking, said, "Is the bride prepared and ready for her bridegroom? I cannot hold him back any longer."

"She is ready," the sex slave licking at Nyura said, backing away from the girl. Both he and his companion arose from the bed, each taking one of the girl's legs and pulling it up and back so her sex was fully accessible to her bridegroom. The two slave men had done their work well. Nyura was wet, her juices copious and visible to the witnesses in the other chamber.

The Pleasure Woman took the Twilight Lord's great hard manhood in her hand and led him to the bed. Kneeling next to the bride, she guided Kolgrim's cock to the opening of Nyura's sheath. "The prize awaits you, my lord," she said, sliding off the bed.

Kolgrim looked into Nyura's face. He saw in her face that her lust matched his. It would have pleased him to tease her for a bit, and while he could not see the witnesses, he knew they were watching; he could feel their eyes upon him, their antic-ipation. He wondered if his mother was remembering his father at this moment. Did she recall her mating when she conceived him? Or was it that time upon the Dream Plain when his father had ravaged her, impregnating her with his sister?

His thoughts excited him even more. His cock ached. He pressed it a little way into her sheath. She squealed, and he saw a sudden fear in her eyes. He pushed a bit farther, and met the resistance of her maidenhead. The knowledge that his would be the only cock to ever know her almost caused him to lose control of himself.

"It hurts," she whimpered at him.

"Does it?" He smiled into her face, drew his throbbing cock back and thrust forward hard. He felt her maidenhead give way as he ripped it asunder. Her scream was so loud that it was heard in the banqueting hall, and Nyura did not cease screaming for several long moments as her bridegroom thrust over and over and over again into her. But then her cries died away, and instead they heard her moaning as Kolgrim brought her the pleasures she had listened to other woman gush about since she was twelve, and old enough to understand, at least partly, what they were discussing.

He pumped her for several more deep strokes, and then his body stiffened momentarily as, groaning, he released his juices into her. Reaching up, he undid the bonds holding her, nodding to the two sex slaves to release her legs. Then, standing up, he smiled down upon her. "You did well, Nyura."

Dazed she looked up at him. "Did I please you?" she asked softly.

"You have much to learn, but I will teach you," he said. "Get up now, Nyura. The evidence of your honesty must be presented to our guests so they may go home. Then so will we, my pet."

Nyura managed to gather herself together. She climbed from the bed. Looking down at the large stain of blood upon the white coverlet, she appeared startled. There was blood upon her thighs, too. Ripping the silk from the bed, she handed it to the Pleasure Woman, who bowed politely. Then with the two male sex slaves the three facilitators left the chamber.

"Our part in this is over," Palben said. "Will you all agree that the bride's claim to virginity was a legitimate one? And that the bridegroom was not cheated?"

His companions nodded.

"Then we will return to the banqueting chamber with the proof," the Lord High Ruler said.

Stepping into the corridor from the viewing room, they

found the three facilitators waiting for them. The Pleasure Woman bowed to Lara, handing her the bloodied coverlet.

"Thank you," Lara said, nodding to her.

The Lord High Ruler snapped his fingers at the two male sex slaves. "You belong to the Pleasure Mistress Lady Helena?"

"We do, my lord," one replied.

"Tell your mistress that this noble young lady would avail herself of your services this evening. You are to both come to the palace."

"Yes, my lord," was the reply.

"Why thank you, nephew," Marzina said, smiling sweetly at him.

Behave yourself! Lara scolded her daughter, but her mouth was smiling.

He lusts after me because he sees me as young and fair, Marzina said. *And it truly troubles him, Mother, because I am his great-aunt.* She swallowed back a giggle.

They reached the banqueting hall. Lara entered and walked directly to the High Board, followed by the other witnesses. Moving to the table's center, she was lifted atop it by the four male witnesses. Once there Lara unfurled the white silk coverlet, its crimson bloodstains now beginning to turn brown. "The bride was true!" she cried.

The banqueting hall erupted in cheers, and as she was helped down from the High Board she saw Grugyn Ahasferus being congratulated. Lara shook her head in wonder. Hetarians encouraged their daughters to take pleasures early so they might be contented wives; they loved their Pleasure Houses; yet one maid who retained her virginity was celebrated for it on her wedding day though she had been scorned for it in the years prior.

"Are you coming back to the palace with me?" Marzina asked her mother.

"Nay. I think Kaliq and I will go home to Shunnar. Will you come and see us soon, my darling? I need to speak with you."

"Is it about Kolgrim?" Marzina asked cleverly.

"Aye, it is," Lara responded candidly. She would not lie to her child now. Not when what she must say was so important. She wanted Marzina's cooperation.

"I will come," Marzina replied, "but, Mother, you must not worry about me. I know what Kolgrim is. *Really is.* I know as much as he desires a family, a little sister, he would kill me if it suited his purposes. I am aware of it."

Lara nodded. "I trust your judgment," she said.

"Now let me go. Those two delicious sex slaves are awaiting me, and I am eager to take pleasures with them," the young faerie woman said with a twinkle in her violet eyes. "Do you think they are as sturdy as they look?"

"You will tell me when you come to Shunnar," Lara told her daughter.

Marzina laughed and, turning, hurried away.

"Great-grandmother!" Dominus Cadarn had come to her side. "We need your help in the matter of my son's betrothal."

"Your uncle is expert in all matters Hetarian," Lara said. "Can he not help you?"

"It is he who calls for you," Cadarn said.

"Very well, I shall come." She turned to Kaliq. "Will you wait or go home?"

"I will await you in Shunnar," he said, bending to kiss her mouth. Then, stepping away from her, he swirled his cloak about himself and disappeared.

Cadarn's mouth fell open. "What happened to him?" he asked.

"He returned home, which I should like to do, so take me to Lord Amren so we may conclude the matter of Vaclar's marriage. If I know your uncle, there is something he knows the Hetarians will consider unpleasant, and he wants me to press the point."

The wedding guests had all gone, and the house was virtually empty but for the family and their servants. Cadarn led Lara to a large library where Grugyn Ahasferus was now seated with her grandson, Prince Amren. She nodded to them both then said, "Well, what is it that I am needed for, my lords?"

"Will you not be seated, Domina," Grugyn Ahasferus invited Lara. "And I have not thanked you for being witness to my granddaughter's defloration ceremony."

Amren rolled his eyes at Grugyn's polite speech. The Hetarian magnate was just attempting to get on the good side of his faerie grandmother. "They want the wedding here in The City," Amren said, his tone annoyed. "But the wedding must be held in Terah, in the castle of the Dominus. Lady Yamka will one day be Terah's Domina. Her marriage must be celebrated where she will rule."

"Has neither of you heard of the word *compromise?*" Lara asked them tartly.

"She must be wed here among her family," Grugyn Ahasferus said.

"Nay, she must be wed in Terah," Prince Amren replied.

"She can be wed in both places," Lara told them. "Let the first marriage be performed here in this house in the hour before sunset. Then I will transport them by means of my magic to Terah in time for the sunrise ceremony that is our tradition."

"But what of the wedding feast?" Grugyn demanded. "Is my family to be made a laughingstock because we do not celebrate Yamka's marriage as we have celebrated the marriages of my other two granddaughters?"

It would be one of the last things she did for them all, Lara thought. "Both Terah and Hetar will have their feasts," she told them. "In Hetar you will celebrate within your banqueting hall for it will be night. But if you walk from your hall through a magic tunnel we will provide, you will find yourself in Terah celebrating in the gardens of the Dominus's castle in the morning light. Neither of you will be embarrassed before your families and friends. Indeed you will be envied in both lands that magic made such a thing possible even though you all claim that magic no longer exists," she mocked them.

Grugyn Ahasferus's brow furrowed as he considered her words. "Indeed," he finally said, "there has certainly never been a wedding such as this one will be. And none will be able to duplicate it. Aye! You have given us the perfect solution, Domina Lara."

He looked to Prince Amren. "My lord, are you in agreement?"

"I am!" came the reply.

"You must have Dominus Cadarn's permission for this," Lara said quietly, realizing that the two old men were leaving Terah's ruler out of the matter.

"Of course! Of course!" Prince Amren quickly agreed. "Nephew, will you give us your formal consent to celebrate the marriage of your son and heir, Vaclar, to Yamka Ahasferus, in both Hetar and Terah?" His tone was properly deferential.

The Dominus's ego now properly soothed, Cadarn looked at the two men, and said, "I will agree, my lords. You have come up with a clever solution."

"It is the Lady Lara who has found the solution," Grugyn Ahasferus said, "and I am grateful to her. This will be a good marriage, my lord Dominus. My granddaughter has been properly raised, and knows her place, as I have previously said."

"Aye, it is Grandmother's magic that will make this all possible, nephew," Prince Amren said quietly. Why was Cadarn so antagonistic toward Lara, he wondered.

"When would you celebrate this marriage?" Lara asked them. "Soon?" It has to be soon, she thought. Before Kolgrim moved to bring the darkness. Terah needed to be doubly related to the Twilight Lord by then.

"A month," Grugyn Ahasferus said. "The bride needs to gather together her dower portion. The house must be prepared, and another feast planned."

"Yamka must be isolated during that time," Lara said. "She has taken lovers in the past, but now is not the time for her to decide to have a final spree of lust before she marries. It is of vital importance that any child she bears carries both her blood and Vaclar's. I will keep her safe myself."

"Certainly, Domina Lara, we may be trusted to keep Yamka safe," Grugyn Ahasferus said pompously.

"I will not negotiate with you in this matter, my lord," Lara told the magnate. "And it is already done. I have transported the sleeping girl to a safe haven. When she awakens it will be her wedding day."

Prince Amren grinned, unable to help himself. Even Cadarn was forced to smile.

Suddenly a knocking sounded upon the library door, and it opened to reveal Lady Camilla. She was most distraught. "They are gone, Grugyn!" she cried.

"Who is gone?" the magnate demanded irritably. The faerie woman's high-handed tactic had irritated him, although he suspected she had done a wise thing.

"Nyura and Kolgrim! They are not in their bridal chamber," Lady Camilla said.

"He has taken her home to the Dark Lands," Lara said quietly.

"But the entire week is filled with parties for them," Lady Camilla protested.

"Kolgrim has done what he needed to do, and what was expected of him. He has married your granddaughter and completed the defloration ceremony," Lara said. "That done, he has taken his bride and returned to his castle in the Dark Lands."

"But he did not say his farewells," Lady Camilla said in a disappointed tone.

"I did not raise him, and so I cannot be responsible for his manners," Lara said. "However they are usually better than this. I suspect he was simply anxious to get Nyura to some place quiet and private where they might take pleasures together."

THAT WAS EXACTLY WHAT Kolgrim had done. The Hetarian ceremonies had both irritated and bored him. In a few days' time, ten at the most, he would have to seed Nyura with his son. Once that had happened she would be forbidden to him until the child was born, and they performed the Completion Ceremony. The few days they had together he wanted to spend taking pleasures with her, not attending parties in their honor. How wasteful of time these Hetarians were. And so when the witnesses had departed he had put his arm about his bride and magicked them into the bedchamber that would be hers in his castle in the Dark Lands.

Still dazed from her first adventures in pleasures, Nyura looked up at him, confused. "Where are we?" she asked.

"We are home in my castle," Kolgrim told her.

"But we cannot leave Hetar yet," Nyura protested. "There are events planned in our honor, my lord. It would be rude for us to just disappear."

"I did not ask for events in our honor, Nyura," Kolgrim said. "You know why this marriage has taken place. I told you that the Book of Rule chose you. Perhaps you do not fully comprehend your situation. It is the mating season for me. It is in this time, and this time only, that I can release the seed into your womb that will become my son. Twilight Lords only sire a single son in each generation. You are the one chosen for the honor of bearing that son. In a few days I shall seed you. And after that we will not come together as man and wife until after my son is born. Nothing can endanger you while you carry the child. This child will descend from Usi the Sorcerer on both sides of his lineage. He will be a special child, Nyura."

"Why must you seed me so quickly," Nyura pouted. "I have waited sixteen years to taste pleasures. I want more of them!"

"The time is circumscribed in the Book of Rule for your seeding," he replied.

"Couldn't we do it next month, or next year?" she pleaded.

"Nay, it must be within the next ten days, Nyura," Kolgrim told her. "And on the night I seed you, you will give me the gift of Ulla to add to my own powers."

"Nay," Nyura said. "There is no set time for me to pass my powers to you, my lord. I will give them to you when the child is born, but not before."

"You would defy me, Nyura?"

"Nay, my lord, never," she swore. "But the shade of Ulla visited me before our wedding and advised me to wait," Nyura lied smoothly to him. "As you must obey your Book of Rule, so must I obey the shade of Ulla. If I do not, my gift will be rendered worthless to you. Neither of us wants that, my lord, do we?"

Kolgrim laughed. "I think you lie to me," he said, "but you know I dare not take the chance that what you say is truth. You play a clever game, Nyura. Now tell me, do you like your chamber? It was once inhabited by my dear mother."

Nyura looked about. The chamber was spacious. There was a great hearth opposite the large bed that was covered in luxurious furs. On the far side of the room was an open colonnade, but as it was night she could make out nothing beyond it. The furnishings were few, and rough. The bed, a sideboard, a table, two chairs. "I am surprised that your mother could live in such a rough chamber," Nyura told him. "I cannot be comfortable here until I furnish this place to suit my needs, my lord."

"Which you are free to do," Kolgrim told her.

"I must have my furnishings from Hetar," Nyura insisted. "I will never be happy without my own things about me, my lord."

"In a day or two I will escort you myself to The City. You may choose whatever pleases you." He remembered she had said at their first meeting she could be happy in the Dark Lands. Kolgrim almost laughed with the memory.

"But it will take months for it to be brought here," Nyura said petulantly.

"Ah, I forgot that you were brought up to deny magic, my beauty. My magic will bring you whatever you desire in the same day, Nyura. Will you be happy then?"

"Oh yes!" She giggled. "Having a husband who is magic will be quite convenient. I shall be the envy of my cousins Divsha and Yamka." She snuggled against him. "You are so good to me, my lord. May we take pleasures again tonight?"

"We shall spend the next several days taking pleasures, Nyura. I want to make up to you the missed opportunities you suffered while you waited for me. And there is much you have to learn. Losing your virginity was pleasurable, but traumatic, too. Now I will show you all the delights you can enjoy with me. Your cousins have had other lovers. But I am the only lover you will ever have, Nyura. You understand that, don't you?" His hand wrapped itself tightly into her long golden-red hair, forcing her head back so he might look into her beautiful face.

"Why would I want another lover?" she asked him innocently.

"Each man is different in his ability to make love, my beauty. I, however, am an expert in the arts of passion. You will never be unhappy with me, so when your cousins visit you and brag on their lovers I do not want you to be jealous," Kolgrim said.

"Neither of them will take lovers again until they have given their husbands children," Nyura said. "As we are assets to our husbands, so are they assets to us."

"How practical," Kolgrim replied drily. Then he bent to kiss her ripe mouth, his other hand moving down her body so he might push two fingers into her sheath. She started, but the Twilight Lord held her tightly by her hair while his fingers mimicked what his cock would soon do. She released her juices to him quickly, and his kiss deepened with his approval. Like all Hetarian women she was a lustful creature, and he would mold her lust to suit his own. He broke off the kiss and pushed her to her knees. "Open your eyes, Nyura, and view my manhood. I have what no other male, even the great Shadow Prince Kaliq, has. Twilight Lords possess two rods. The dominant, which is now before your eyes, and the lesser, which is released upon my command."

Nyura stared at the long peg of flesh hanging before her. "It was bigger earlier," she noted to him. "Does it expand and contract?"

He chuckled. "It does indeed."

"What does the other rod look like, and why would you need two?" she asked.

"The other rod is so I may possess both of your lower entries at the same time," he told her. "As for what it looks like, you shall see for yourself very shortly. Now take the dominant rod into your mouth and suckle upon it," he commanded her.

Fascinated, Nyura obeyed, listening as he instructed her. Both her cousins had told her that men enjoyed being sucked upon.

"Be careful with those little teeth of yours, my beauty. Use your tongue. Run it about and beneath the head. Ahh, that's it." He was astounded by her natural skill. He knew she would have never involved herself in any, even the most innocent, sexual activity while keeping her virginity. Nyura was no fool, and knew the dangers of such play. He came close to groaning as she began to suck him deeper into her mouth and throat. She never hesitated, and Kolgrim closed his eyes, briefly allowing himself a moment of pure unadulterated enjoyment. But then as his dominant rod lengthened and grew hard, he felt the lesser of his rods stirring. "Cease, and sit back upon your haunches, my beautiful Nyura, and observe what happens."

She obeyed instantly. His dominant rod thrust straight out almost touching her face. It bobbed just slightly as from beneath it his lesser rod began to emerge. Much longer than the dominant, and slender, it was hard to the touch of her fingers, which could not refrain from touching it. Its tip was pointed and shaped like an arrowhead.

Nyura shivered looking at it. She could almost feel the lesser rod piercing her fundament. A small stream of her juices ran down her thighs. "I never imagined such a thing as two rods," she said slowly.

"I would have you taste it tonight," he said to her. "It should not return beneath the dominant unsatisfied, my beauty.

"How can we accomplish it?" Nyura asked, genuinely interested. The thought of having herself filled with two rods was beyond exciting.

"Come to the bed with me," he said, drawing her up from her knees. "It requires a special method to accomplish what you desire."

They climbed onto the bed of soft furs together. While she thought it a bit barbaric and savage, there was something about the touch of the furs on her naked body that Nyura decided was quite exciting. She lay stretched out upon her back waiting for him to begin. The lesser rod was now iridescent with a silvery sheen. Its arrowhead glowed brightly. It was the most living thing she had ever seen.

Kolgrim clapped his hands once. Two thin silver chains with manacles at their ends dropped down. The restraints were lined in silk and lamb's wool. "This will help you to attain the proper position," he explained as he fastened the manacles to her ankles.

"Oh my!" Nyura exclaimed when he had finished. Her legs were spread wide, drawn up and back almost over her shoulders so that both of her orifices were revealed.

He clapped his hands again, and a second set of silver chains and manacles dropped down. Kolgrim fastened them to her wrists. "Now," he said, "you are properly displayed, and ready for mounting, my beauty."

"My cousins have told me of something they call bondage," Nyura said. "Is this bondage, my lord?"

"A form of it," he said. "Now be silent. My rods have a need for you." He slid between her outspread and raised legs.

Nyura watched, fascinated, as the lesser rod, far longer than the dominant, found her rear orifice and pierced it. "Ohh!" she squealed as it pushed into her. Her gray-green eyes grew wide as she felt it filling up her rear channel. When it was fully sheathed she felt it throbbing within her. Nyura thought it exciting. Yamka and Divsha would be so jealous when she told them. "Ohhhh!" she gasped as his dominant rod thrust hard and deep into her female sheath. Her head began to spin as he pumped her savagely and her juices flowed furiously, bathing his steaming manhood as he used her. Nyura screamed with her pleasure. She struggled against the restraints about her wrists. She wanted to clutch at him, claw him. Raising her head, she sank her teeth into his shoulder, biting hard.

Kolgrim laughed aloud. His lesser rod, encased within her rear passage and throbbing, now began to match the rhythm of the dominant rod. They moved together within her twin sheaths. Nyura's mouth fell open as she gasped for air. And then both rods found the tiny spot within a woman's body known to give unrivaled ecstasy. They touched it from both sides at once. Nyura shrieked and shrieked with the pleasures pounding her body that would not stop.

The Twilight Lord laughed again and released his lust into her as she lost consciousness beneath him. Satisfied for the moment, he lay back as the Lustlings came forth to release Nyura from her bonds, and then bathe the sex of both Kolgrim and his bride. When they had departed Kolgrim raised himself up upon an elbow and looked at the girl by his side. He was pleased with her. She had not shown fear but for a moment when he had deflowered her. And now her second time she had accepted both of his rods without a whimper. Was it possible that his mate was his match in bed sport? How unfortunate he must seed her so quickly, but he had moved as quickly as he could.

The Book of Rule had taken its time in telling him who his bride was, and then it had only told him where to look. Well, once she had borne him his son he would see if she was worth keeping. If she was, he would give her the gift of never growing old. When their powers were matched he could do it. While she knew she had Ulla's powers, she didn't know what they were or how to use them. But he did. He was more amused than angry that she had said she would keep her powers until she birthed his son. He supposed she felt it gave her a small advantage over him. Foolish little mortal.

Finding himself actually tired, Kolgrim slept briefly. When he awoke, Nyura was still sleeping. Let her, he thought, rising from her bed. He had plans to make, not the least among them was winning his sister, Marzina, to his side. Power seemed to surge through him. No one could stop him from obtaining what he wanted. And he wanted Marzina. She was intelligent, even for a woman, with a delicious reckless streak that delighted him. The idea of her magic combined with his excited him.

She was his family. Not like their father dying painfully, helplessly and slowly in his captivity. Not like his twin brother, still looking about the small enclosure he shared with their sire for a way to escape so he might drink himself to death while taking pleasures and causing havoc within the Dark Lands and beyond. Not like his beautiful and powerful mother, who had never loved him. Nay, none of them were family. But Marzina was, and he wanted her. Nyura would enjoy her companionship for the serving women would not suffice. And Marzina would help him raise his heir. She would be charmingly and foolishly fond of the boy, as she should be. As he had never been doted upon.

And the promise he had casually made to his mother to leave Marzina to her? Kolgrim laughed aloud. His mother should certainly know from her own personal experience that Twilight Lords did as they pleased, not as others wanted. So he would not underestimate Lara. She would be on her guard against him. He smiled. But he would have Marzina, her powers, and in time his mother's powers. No one could defeat him. *Not now!* And he laughed aloud once more.

LARA SHIVERED. HER WHOLE body had suddenly gone cold, and she grew pale.

"What is it?" Kaliq, who lay next to her in their bed, asked, concerned.

"I don't know," Lara replied. "It was if something dark and icy washed over me. Kolgrim does not mean to keep his promise to me, Kaliq. About Marzina. I know he wants her to remain here with him as he brings the darkness into our world. And I don't know if I can stop him." She looked surprised by her own words. "Oh, Kaliq, I really don't know if I can keep Kolgrim from taking Marzina into his power!"

"It isn't up to you now, my love. Marzina for all her girlish appearance is a woman long grown. She lives in her own castle and conducts her life as she wishes," Kaliq said in soothing tones. "You have done your best by her. Your mother and I have done our best, too. She has her own fate, her own destiny. You cannot help or save her from whatever lies ahead. You have to concentrate on what you must do. There is naught left for the magic here in the world of Hetar."

"Anoush, Zagiri, Taj, my three mortal children are all long dead to me, Kaliq. All I have left is Marzina," Lara said. "Dillon rules Belmair with Cinnia. I have nothing to do with their lives. I just have Marzina."

"And Kolgrim," he reminded her.

"Kolgrim is his father's son," Lara replied bitterly, "and Kol would be proud of him, for he is evil like his father. Charming as Kol was, but even more evil."

"You cannot change him, or save him," Kaliq said patiently. "He is what he was meant to be, but he has a weakness."

"Kolgrim? Weak?" Lara looked dubious.

"He is half-faerie, my love, with just the tiniest touch of

mortal blood in his veins. And that is his weakness. He will bring the darkness to Hetar, but it is his son who will be far more dangerous, for in Kolgrim's son the blood of Usi runs twice as thick because of Nyura's ancestry," Kaliq explained.

"But if we could prevent Nyura from conceiving," Lara said hopefully, "then perhaps we could foil Kolgrim."

"The Book of Rule has ordained that she is his mate. Once it was believed it was Ciarda, but Ciarda failed because the magic of the Shadow Princes caused her to fail. We bought Hetar what time we could after the Hierarch departed so they might improve themselves, yet they did not progress, falling back instead into their old ways. If Hetar is to ever rise again it must fall into the darkness completely, and suffer the consequences of its failures," Kaliq explained to Lara. "Until mortals can learn from their errors they will always be doomed to end in the darkness. They are intelligent creatures, and yet their egos overcome them more times than not. Still, I have hope for them. This world is not the only world they inhabit. Their race is spread throughout the Cosmos, my love."

"Are they any better in those other worlds?" Lara asked him.

He nodded. "Aye, in some worlds they have progressed, but in others they have not. And there are a few I am told by others of my kind where they are even worse than Hetar," Kaliq said. "I do not want you to grieve for Hetar, Lara. Like you, it has its own destiny. For a time your destinies were joined. They are now severed, and you must move on with me."

"When?" she asked him.

"We have a little time left here," he replied. "It is up to the Shadow Princes to oversee the evacuation of the magic from Hetar. Kolgrim will not stop us for without other magic his becomes supreme."

"Marzina must leave Hetar, Kaliq. Please help me in this. I

do not want to control my daughter's life, but you know how rash and incautious she can be. And Kolgrim means to keep her here. He wants her magic for himself. I know it!" Lara looked distraught as she spoke.

"Let me speak with her, my love. You know that as much as she loves you, you chafe her," the Shadow Prince said gently.

Lara laughed. "You do not have to tell me what I already know, my lord."

Kaliq chuckled. "Go and visit your mother before the forest is emptied of faerie magic," he suggested to her. "It will probably be the last chance you get."

Lara nodded. "I will go today," she said.

He wrapped his arms about her, and they made tender love to one another. Their passion, while heated, was comforting and familiar. They stroked each other's bodies. They kissed long deep kisses until they were both dizzy. And when they finally came together the pleasures they took from each other were sublime. They lay together afterward in a sweet stupor, until finally Lara took the initiative and rose from the bed.

Kaliq lay watching her as she bathed herself in a basin. He loved her body, and always had. She was the most beautiful creature he had ever seen. She dressed herself in a simple loose gown of green, belting it with a twisted silver cord, plaiting her golden hair afterward into a single braid.

When she had finished she came to the bed, bent and kissed his sensuous mouth. "Are you awake now?" she asked him softly.

"How could I not be, having watched you bathe and dress. You gave me a lovely entertainment this morning, my love," Kaliq told her.

"I will return in a few days," Lara told him, "but if you need me, you know where I am, my lord." Then she kissed him again, and turning, she opened a Golden tunnel and hurried into it. The tunnel closed quickly behind her.

He would miss her, but her absence would give him an opportunity to speak with Marzina alone. He would visit her at her home in the forested mountains. Marzina was less apt to feel the pressure he meant to bring to bear upon her in her own personal environment. He could give Lara the closure she was going to need with Marzina without interfering with the beautiful faerie girl's own fate. Arising from the warm bed they had been sharing, the Shadow Prince walked from Lara's apartment across their shared garden to his own quarters, where his servants were waiting to help him bathe and dress for the day. There would be a breakfast set out beneath the portico in the garden when he was ready for it. He disliked eating alone these days for he had grown so used to having Lara with him. He wondered how her visit with Ilona would go.

LARA HAD EXITED THE GOLDEN tunnel into her mother's private day room. Ilona was seated in a cushioned window seat looking out into her forest. Lara walked over to her, kissed the faerie queen's rosy cheek and sat next to her in silence for the next few minutes. Finally the Queen of the Forest faeries spoke.

"Do you know how many centuries I have looked out these very windows into my forest? Four and a half," she continued, answering her own question. "It pains me that I must leave, but there is no choice. Our race cannot survive in the darkness. We need the light of the stars, the moon, the long days of sunlight."

"I'm sorry I have brought this upon you," Lara said.

"Nay, nay," Ilona quickly protested. "If Hetar had been able to change, no Twilight Lord could have brought this upon us. It is the fault of those damned mortals!"

Lara laughed softly. "Will you take Dillon's offer, and relocate to Belmair, Mother? Moving away from the familiar and comfortable is difficult, but Beltran is a beautiful province filled with forests. I believe you could be happy there."

"Aye, we will take Dillon's offer, but we shall also seek out another world eventually, where it will not be known that we reside. You know we Faerie folk like our privacy. We do not like mortals to be aware of us. Gwener has already located her people, the Meadow faeries, in Beldane. Annan has chosen Belbuoy, for it has several fine rivers and many streams for his Water Faeries. King Laszlo likes the mountains of Belia for his Mountain Faeries. It is all a great inconvenience, Lara, but it was bound to come sooner than later. Has the wedding been celebrated? What a word to describe the marriage of a Twilight Lord who will bring the darkness upon us." She laughed wryly.

"Kaliq said you are overseeing the evacuation of all the magic folk," Lara said.

"Aye, I am, and a difficult task it is, I want to tell you. Finding homes, if even temporary ones, for elves, gnomes, giants ad infinitum is not a simple task. The mountain gnomes in the Emerald Mountains have decided they will remain. Gulltop speaks for both the Ore and the Jewel gnomes now. He says they are few, and old. They are used to the darkness, but will disappear into the mountainsides until the light comes again. They will not labor for the Twilight Lord."

"The light will come again, Mother?"

"Oh, Lara, the light cannot be extinguished entirely. Even in the darkness there is always a small flicker of it somewhere. And eventually that flicker will grow and grow until the darkness is pushed back into the Dark Lands, and the light rules again," Ilona said to her daughter.

"Then why must we leave?" Lara wanted to know. "Could we not hide like the gnomes of the Emerald Mountains?"

"Oh, my darling," Ilona said. "It will be centuries before that happens. Once the darkness takes hold of a world it is difficult to overcome it. Gnomes, used to living in their tunnels, can survive that time. We of the other magic races cannot. We need the light if we are to thrive. All the good magic there is in Hetar must leave it."

"Kaliq said he knows my destiny, but he will not tell me," Lara said to her mother.

Ilona laughed. "He probably does," she said.

"He says we are to be together, for now our destinies are one," Lara continued.

"Does he?" Ilona wasn't surprised. Kaliq had always loved her daughter, and would of course share whatever destiny Lara had. "You are fortunate in your life mate, my daughter. He is the greatest of the Shadow Princes, next to old Cronan."

The door to the chamber opened, and a slender young girl entered. "Aunt Lara! How wonderful to see you again! Will you be coming with us to Belmair?"

"I imagine I will," Lara said. "I am certain your mother is glad you are returning home, Parvanah."

"I suppose so," Parvanah said, shrugging. Parvanah was the daughter of Lara's brother, Prince Cirillo and his wife, the Great Dragon of Belmair, Nidhug. And she was her grandmother's heiress after her father.

Cirillo and Nidhug had left an egg to hatch in the dragon's nursery cave in the mountainous province of Belia well over a century ago. The dragon that would hatch from it, a young male, would one day take his mother's place as Belmair's Great Dragon. The Queen of the Forest Faeries had finally and reluctantly accepted the fact that her only son and heir loved the female dragon. But she was distraught when he could not seem to settle upon a faerie maid to create an heir who would follow him as ruler of the Forest Faeries once his mother was gone. And then one day Nidhug had told her lover that she was about to lay another egg. They had both been surprised for the egg in the mountain nursery was destined to follow Nidhug. There should have been no others.

But the dragon could not restrain herself, and she laid this new egg upon their bed. It was pale pink imprinted with deeper pink roses. And it was smaller than her other egg. Both Nidhug and Cirillo watched in astonishment as the egg cracked itself open and within the shell lay a tiny female faerie infant waving its dainty fists and cooing. Ilona was called immediately. She examined the child carefully and pronounced, "She is pure faerie, although I don't know how this is possible. Look on her back. Do you see the wing buds?" And then Ilona named her granddaughter Parvanah, telling Cirillo, "She will follow you and one day be Queen of the Forest Faeries."

Now fourteen, Parvanah was a perfect Forest faerie in appearance but for her eyes, which were like her dragon mother's, dark with gold-and-silver swirls and thick purple eyelashes. She bowed to Ilona. "The evacuation of the Meadow, Water and Mountain Faeries is now complete, Grandmother. I have sent our soldiers into those areas to make certain that no one was left behind. The areas are clear now. The returning guards said you could feel the loneliness. Isn't it sad?"

"Aye," Ilona said quietly. "It is indeed sad. It would appear, my daughter, that you have come to the forest just in time. Tomorrow our own people will begin their departure. We are through with Hetar."

"I KNOW THIS IS HOW IT MUST BE," LARA SAID, "BUT I am still unhappy over it."

"We will revisit our history in the forest tomorrow," Ilona said. "It is important that we say our goodbyes. And you will see how low the Forest Lords have fallen."

"I don't know if I want to revisit that particular place or time," Lara said.

"Nay," her mother replied. "You must. Do not fear. They will not see us or even know we are there."

"Why don't you like the Forest Lords, Aunt Lara?" Parvanah asked.

"I will tell you one day in the hall of your kinsman, King Dillon," Lara promised the girl. "It is an unhappy tale."

"But you had a happy ending," Parvanah said. "Prince Kaliq," she sighed, "is a delicious man, aunt. To have such a life mate is surely wonderful!"

Lara thought a moment, and then she laughed. "Aye, it is wonderful to have such a life mate, my love. Thank you for re-minding me."

"Let us have our meal now, and rest," Ilona said. "Tomorrow will be a trying day for both of us, my daughter. Parvanah, you have done well. Tomorrow you will oversee the departure of our elves, brownies and the few gnomes who will go. Run along now, dear."

Parvanah curtsied prettily to her grandmother and her aunt as she left them.

"Will any of the gnomes leave?" Lara asked curious. "I thought they chose to remain, Mother. Gulltop speaks for them all now, and he isn't one to change his mind easily."

"Aye, the youngest among them, males and the few females young enough to still breed will leave Hetar. They are not a large race, and so I have suggested this in order that their kind not be lost. There are few gnomes on the other worlds, and their skill at finding ores and jewels is quite special. I have spoken myself with Gulltop on this matter. It was not an easy negotiation, mind you. He is almost ten centuries old, and not easily persuaded any longer, if he ever was. But I was finally able to convince him of the wisdom of sending some of his people with us by pointing out we could not know how long the darkness would last. If it held Hetar captive for too long his younger gnomes would be too old to breed, and their race would certainly die out. That he understood. And so those five centuries and younger will come with us."

"You look tired, Mother," Lara said.

"I am," Ilona admitted. "This has been a terrible undertaking for me, and for Thanos. Your stepfather has exhausted himself seeing that the rare species of flora and fauna native to Hetar are removed to Belmair that they may continue to propagate. Too much darkness will kill much of what exists upon this world, for an endless Icy Season will set in. But let us not speak anymore on so unpleasant a subject." Ilona waved her hands over the low table before them, producing two plates of faerie bread and cups of forest berry frine. She sighed, reaching for the faerie bread and tearing off a chunk. "I am ravenous of late with all this work. Umm! Roasted meat!"

"Mine is capon," Lara replied. "I do love faerie bread, Mother! I adore that it can be anything you want it to be."

When they had finished eating, they slept side by side on Ilona's great bed. Lara awakened once during the night to find the moonlight streaming into the chamber across the bed. She arose and went to look out into the forest, seeing a small herd of does led by a great antlered buck grazing in the clearing of grass outside. Sadness overwhelmed her. The last Autumn would come soon, and then the Icy Season would be upon Hetar. But no spring would follow it. Eventually, much of what had been Hetar, mortal beings, creatures, the land, would suffer and die, or be changed forever. What would Kolgrim do when he had nothing but a dead world to rule? Or would he find a way of keeping his subjects alive, and at his mercy? And would the light come to Hetar again one day as Kaliq and her mother insisted it must? The tears began to slip down her face as Lara returned to the bed, sleeping fitfully until the dawn broke.

Ilona was up first. She magicked a bowl of faerie bread for herself. This morning it tasted like roasted apples and porridge with a hint of sweet cinnamon. She saw the dried tears on the beautiful face so like her own. Lara had wept in the night, and briefly Ilona's cold faerie heart felt sympathy for her firstborn child. One of the reasons Lara had been born was to save Hetar. The fact that she had been unable to weighed heavily upon her, for she did not quite understand that the magic world had always considered her success unlikely. They had planned a far greater destiny for her, which she would soon learn. Finished eating, Ilona arose and shook Lara awake. "Magick yourself something to eat so we may be on our way. We have much history to visit today," the beautiful queen of the Forest Faeries told her now-half-awake daughter.

Like a child, Lara did as she was bid while Ilona sent for Parvanah, and gave her her instructions for the day.

When Parvanah had gone off, Lara asked her mother, "Why did you not ask Marzina to take on these tasks?"

"Parvanah will succeed me after her father," Ilona said. "Unless, of course, Cirillo steps aside from the succession, which he threatens to do every now and again. After all these years you would think the fires of his passion for Nidhug had banked. If anything it burns even brighter. My children, it seems, have a great capacity for love," Ilona noted a trifle drily. "Parvanah needs to know how to rule, and the great responsibility being a queen entails. Marzina has another path to follow entirely. I love both of my granddaughters equally, but Parvanah will be queen. She needs me more than Marzina. Your daughter has had the advantage of learning not just from me, but from you and Kaliq, as well. Parvanah has only me."

Lara swallowed down the final sip of apricot nectar. "I am ready, Mother," she said. Then she sighed. "It is a beautiful day in the forest. What shall we visit first?"

"We begin, as I told you last night, with the fall of the Forest Lords," Ilona replied. "Take my hand, Lara, and remember. No mortal eye can see us." Then, catching her daughter's hand in hers, Ilona uttered the silent spell.

Take us back in time to see,
This bit of faerie history.

Suddenly they were in a clearing deep within the forest. A beautiful pale colored roe deer with a jeweled collar about its neck dashed into the clearing, panting. Lara could hear the baying of the dogs close by, and the shouts of huntsmen upon their horses crashing through the woodland. The deer stood gasping for breath, for she had led the hunters a merry chase the whole day long. Both dogs and horsemen burst into the clearing simultaneously. The dogs surrounded the deer, snapping and barking, while the mounted men quickly drew their bows, notching them with arrows.

But the roe deer changed suddenly into a beautiful young faerie woman who laughed at the surprise upon the rough faces staring down at her. "How foolish you Forest Lords are," she mocked them. "Did it not occur to you that a roe deer with a jeweled collar about its neck was of the magic world? Do you usually waste a day chasing after such creatures?" And she laughed again at them.

Following their leader, a young man who was called Ubel, the men dismounted. The lust they had had for the hunt was dissolving into lust of another kind as they viewed the beautiful faerie woman, who was arrayed in sheer golden diaphanous garments, the jeweled collar twinkling about her slender white neck. They stared at her.

Lara and Ilona both could feel the fear suddenly rising in the faerie woman who was called Nixa. Her powers had been exhausted keeping herself in the form of a roe deer, and leading the chase the day long. It was then Lara realized that had the Forest Lords not been so full of themselves that day, the history of Hetar might have been different. But the hunters were angry at the faerie woman who had made fools of them. And they would be forced to return home empty-handed.

"You owe us a forfeit, faerie woman," Ubel snarled at her.

"I cannot change your stupidity into intelligence," Nixa told him foolishly.

The hunters surrounding her growled, fully understanding the insult directed at them. Instinctively they moved closer to her. Lara could smell the lust on them, and saw several cocks, Ubel's among them, pressing an outline against their trousers. Then without warning the young man's big hand shot out, catching at Nixa's long blond hair.

He flung her to the mossy earth. The faerie woman's head hit a small rock rendering her too dizzy to defend herself as, standing over her, Ubel loosened his garments and fell to the ground, his knees pinioning her tightly. He tore her sheer clothing from her so that she was completely naked. Then, taking his cock in his hand, he positioned himself as she began to regain full consciousness. As her startled eyes met his, Ubel thrust himself hard into the faerie woman's sheath, eliciting a single scream from her.

What a beast he is, Lara said. *Much like Durga who violated me.*

Each of these men violated Nixa not once but several times, Ilona replied. *We need not watch it all. It is disturbing and painful. Here is how it ended.*

Nixa lay bloodied and battered upon the mossy forest floor. Some of the hunters had not only ravaged her, they had beaten her, as well. Satisfying himself for the third time, Ubel ripped the jeweled collar from the faerie woman's neck. Then, taking his knife from its sheath, he slowly slit her throat, taking pleasure as the deep slash he inflicted filled up with bright blood. He noted it was tinged with streaks of green. Then, rising, he straightened his garments and signaled his men to mount their horses.

As the sound of the hooves disappeared, Ilona said in their silent language, *Now let us go to the hall of the Head Forester, Ruggero, and see how he dealt with the Queen of the Forest Faeries, my mother, your grandmother, Maeve.*

And with those words Lara found herself and her mother observers in a familiar chamber, the hall of the Head Forester.

She shivered, for though it had been decades since she had been in that hall as a captive, the memory was yet unpleasant. The Forest Lords sat eating and drinking. There was much laughter that night, and Lara saw that the Head Forester's wife now wore the bejeweled collar that had belonged to Nixa.

There was a thunderclap, a burst of violet smoke, and Lara saw her late grandmother, Maeve, Queen of the Forest Faeries appear before the High Board of the Head Forester. Lara had only known her maternal grandmother briefly in the time before she faded away, when she was so delicate and frail she could barely been seen clearly at times. This Maeve, however, was powerful and filled with life. She was tall with hair so gold it glittered and bright faerie green eyes. Dressed in the colors of the autumn forest, red and gold, she pointed an elegant finger at Ruggero.

"For centuries we have lived in peace together sharing the forest, my lord. Today, however, your men committed rapine and murder. For that you owe the Forest Faeries a forfeit, though whatever you may give us will not make up for the cruel death of the faerie woman Nixa," Maeve said. Her anger was palpable, but she restrained it for the alliance between her people and these mortals had been a long one.

"Come, Maeve, and be reasonable. If she had teased the hunting party but briefly and then disappeared, there would have been no ill feeling toward her. But she taunted my men the day long. We are deep into Autumn, and every day we lose is food lost for the Icy Season to come."

"Justice demands a life for a life," Maeve said in a cold hard voice. "I want five of the hunters who ravaged and killed poor Nixa in exchange for her life. Our value in the Cosmos is greater than yours, though you will not understand that. It is fair."

"She got what she deserved, and it should stand as a lesson

to your faerie folk to cease their teasing of our foresters. You call it playfulness, but it is not. Your young faeries torment us, and it must now cease."

Lara could see her grandmother was holding back her anger. "Return Nixa's jeweled collar to me then, Ruggero," she said.

The Head Forester's wife tugged his sleeve and Ruggero said, "Nay, Queen Maeve. It will serve as a forfeit for my hunters' wasted day."

"A final time I ask you for justice, Ruggero of the Forest Lords. If you will not give me five of your hunters then give me the leader of this pack of wild dogs you set upon one of my people. *And* I will have the collar returned," Maeve said. "I will give you a month's time to reconsider your decision."

"No amount of time will ever make me turn over any of my people to you, Queen Maeve! What is done is done, and you must abide by it."

As Lara watched she could see her grandmother's fury and outrage burst forth even as Og had said when he had first told her the story.

Maeve now raised her left hand. "I curse the Forest Lords, Ruggero. You who are so proud of your pure heritage, who call yourselves the oldest race in Hetar. From this day forward, the women of your kind will never bear children. Neither sons nor daughters. If you wish to propagate yourselves, you will have to mate with outsiders. Your bloodlines will be tainted, and in a few generations it will cease to dominate. All traces of what you were will disappear. The daughters you create with these outsiders will be infertile, or only capable of bearing daughters. Those of your women now carrying babies will miscarry, or the children will be born dead. Your name, Ruggero, will be cursed, for your unwillingness to render me justice has brought this upon you and your kind."

Then Maeve pointed a long finger at the wife of the Head Forester, and the jeweled collar about her neck tightened until the woman was strangled to death. There wasn't a sound in the hall for the Forest Lords and their women had been rendered silent with the terrible fear suddenly engulfing them. Maeve held out her hand, and the jeweled collar flew into it. "Farewell, Ruggero!" she said coldly and disappeared in another clap of thunder and violet smoke as a great wailing arose from those present.

It's even more dramatic than when Og first told me, Lara said to her mother. *Grandmother Maeve was most impressive and at the height of her powers.*

She was, Ilona agreed. *But of course when the Forest Lords realized the reality of her curse they sought the Forest Faeries out and burned our halls. We did not always live so deep in the woodlands. Afterward it was said we should have and not consorted at all with the mortal races. Let us look at more of our history.*

Suddenly the hall of the Head Forester was gone, and Lara found herself watching as her parents met. She recognized her father at once, even though she could not remember him being quite so young. His adoration of her mother, and Ilona's love for him touched Lara. Then the scene faded, and they were again in the palace of the faerie queen, but it was not Ilona's palace. It was Maeve's, and Lara's grandmother was speaking with Ilona, who was weeping.

"Cease this foolishness, Ilona," Maeve said. "You knew when you chose this mortal for a lover that his only use was his seed, and the need to create your daughter."

"But I love him, Mother!" Ilona cried out in a desperate voice.

"*Love?* Pah!" Maeve said scornfully. "Faeries do not love, and those who are foolish enough to do so suffer the consequences,

Ilona. You are my heir. And it is time you returned home to take up your duties and to learn from me what you will one day need to know when your time to rule comes."

"If I must give up John then at least let me bring Lara with me, Mother!" Ilona pleaded. "You know what will happen to her if she is left among the mortals. Hetarians disdain and look down upon children with faerie blood."

"Lara must grow up Hetarian," Maeve said in a stony voice. "How can she understand mortals if she does not. Nay, Lara will remain with her father. Bid your lover farewell, Ilona, if you must, but it is now time for you to begin your training."

The scene was gone, to be followed by a short one in which Lara saw her mother touching the gold chain with the crystal star containing her guardian spirit about the neck of an infant girl. Ilona was weeping softly. Then both she and the scene disappeared.

Oh, Mother, Lara said. *I never really understood how difficult that was for you.*

It was probably the hardest thing I've ever done, Ilona admitted. *Even leaving your father was not as bad. He never knew it, but I blessed him with the ability to wield a sword. And with the proper training it allowed him to become the greatest swordsman Hetar had ever known. There was none before him, nor after him. He was unique in Hetar's history, although his name has now been forgotten by those wretched mortals.*

Lara patted her mother's hand in an attempt to comfort her. *What shall we see next?* she asked her mother in an attempt to distract her from the sadness.

I will show you the Forest Lords as they are today, Ilona responded.

And they were suddenly in the forest again. Lara saw at once the ruins of the great homes that had been built high in the enormous trees of the woodland. The village beneath the trees with its wooden, thatched-roof cottages that blended into the greenery of the forest was half in ruins. Those cottages still standing were in ill repair. The only well-kept structure in this particular village was a tavern. There had been no tavern in Lara's time. Men lay drunk and in half stupors on the benches before the building.

Lara's eyes swept the square. The stone fountain was badly damaged, the once-clear water it offered was now cloudy and murky. Slovenly women were even now dipping their buckets into the water and filling them up for it was the main source of water for this village. The women, Lara noted, did not have the proud look of the Forest. Maeve's curse had obviously come full circle, she realized.

At the end of the village there had been a square stone building, which had been a bathhouse. It was now completely in ruins. The stone benches were gone, but the outline of the stone bathing pool was still visible, though it was filled with rubble and other garbage. Lara shook her head sadly. *They are no longer what they once were. I am shocked to see such deterioration. They appear to have forgotten their heritage and their customs, Mother. Let us move on. Certainly I was not happy here, but what it has all become is very tragic to behold.*

It is, but they brought it upon themselves, Ilona replied. Then she magicked them back to her own palace in the deep forest.

"You did not show me the Forest Giants' fate," Lara said when they were once again settled comfortably with cups of mint tea and a bowl of little sugar cones. She picked up a cone, dipped it into her cup and quickly ate it.

"The end history of Og's people was too tragic to behold," Ilona told her daughter. "You knew the brutality and cruelty of the Forest Lords for yourself. I did not need to show you more of it. But they have greatly contributed to the downfall of Hetar."

"The City seemed peaceful enough when we visited for Kolgrim's wedding," Lara noted. "But then the magnates learned one thing from the Hierarch. They learned to take care of the people. Everyone I am told is housed, fed and clothed. No one goes without."

"What the High Council of Hetar has done is both good and evil," Ilona told her daughter. "Aye, no citizen wants for anything, but they are virtually idle now. Each family is given an allotment of paper money each month. With this paper they buy whatever they need or want. The Council has made it the legal tender of the land. And the magnates continue to hoard their gold, their silver, their jewels. But few of the people still possess this coin. All the merchants and shopkeepers are required to accept this paper they call money. The Council did this because there was no work any longer for the majority of the population in The City. In the Midlands and Outlands the farms and vineyards are worked as always. But in The City there is no work. The paper is legal tender, and accepted even in the Coastal Kingdom. Even Terah accepts it. Did you not know that, my daughter?"

Lara shook her head. "As Magnus Hauk's widow there was nothing I did not have," she said. Then she sighed. "How out of touch I became, Mother."

"It was easier for you," Ilona told her daughter. "You should have left Terah years ago. The longer you remained, the more frightening you became to them. When your life span is so short, having one among you who does not age is probably hard to accept," Ilona considered. "But I have not told you the worst of Hetar. Do you remember the old Tournament field of the Crusader Knights?"

"Aye, I do," Lara replied. "I remember my father winning his victory on that field, and hence his place among the Crusader Knights."

"Well," Ilona said, "they have built a wall about it, and seats for spectators to come and watch. The Crusader Knights hold tournaments in which they battle against other knights, not of their order, to the death. And there are fights between men and women using whatever weapons they can, including their fists. These are also to the death. It is quite savage and disgusting," Ilona said.

"Why on earth would any man or woman involve themselves in such enterprise?" Lara asked, truly horrified.

"For silver, gold, copper and bronze coins," Ilona said. "There are a few licensed shops in The City that are permitted to take coin. The goods they carry are special and greatly coveted. But you can only enter those shops if you have the coin to pay. The magnates are still cleverly pitting the people against one another for their amusement, and the people love these spectacles. Razi kiosks surround the amphitheater. The customers drink deeply of the drugged frine, which is ridiculously inexpensive, and then go into the stadium to cheer their favorites on. Sometimes they are so drunk they leap down onto the playing field. If they do, they are considered fair game. They are caught and tortured before the spectators in a variety of unpleasant ways. Then the player who can make the victim shriek and scream the most is awarded a bag of coppers."

Lara shook her head. "This is worthy of Kolgrim," she said sadly. Then she dipped another sugar cone into her mint tea and consumed it before drinking down the liquid in her cup.

"Aye, he will encourage this evil to even greater heights," Ilona said. Then, changing the subject, she asked, "Has he mated his bride yet?"

"I don't believe so, but his mating cycle is coming to an end shortly. He must do so soon. I'm sure he will find me to tell me when it is done," Lara replied.

"You must leave Hetar with the rest of us, Lara," Ilona responded. "You know you cannot withstand the darkness alone, my daughter. If you remain, he will take your magic from you, and you cannot allow that to happen."

"I know," Lara told her mother. "But it is Marzina I fear for. Kolgrim has developed a strong attachment to her."

"He barely knows her," Ilona scoffed.

"That is true," Lara agreed, "but once he learned he shared not just a mother with her, but a father as well, he suddenly decided he must have *his family* about him. He addresses her as *sister*. I know Marzina is intelligent, and she does understand that her brother is an evil creature. But as he is fascinated with her, she is equally intrigued by him. You know how reckless she can be, Mother. And I will not leave Hetar until I know Marzina is safe on Belmair with you."

"Do not fear, Lara," the Queen of the Forest Faeries said. "I can reason with Marzina, and I promise you she will come with us. We will be gone within the month. The last Autumn has begun, and once it has ended, Kolgrim's power will be strong enough to begin to bring the darkness."

Lara set her cup down. Her eyes were filled with tears. But Ilona watched proudly as her daughter hardened her cold faerie heart. "There will be other springs on other worlds," she said. "Hetar will come to regret its own foolishness."

"Kolgrim's victory will in the end be a hollow one. The light cannot be extinguished forever," Ilona said quietly.

The door to the queen's privy chamber opened, and her consort, Lara's stepfather, Thanos, stepped into the room. He was pale and looked exhausted. "Is there more of that tea?" he asked the two women, and Ilona at once magicked him a steaming cup, which she handed to him. He sat down in a comfortable chair and sipped the minty brew.

"You look so tired, my lord," Lara said. "Mother has told me of your great efforts in removing the rare flora and fauna from Hetar to Belmair."

"It is just about done," Thanos replied. "It has been hard, but worth it. These plants and creatures will die out in the darkness to come. I could not bear seeing that happen. Nidhug has been most generous, offering her garden as a transplant nursery. I pray all of what we have taken will survive." He dipped a sugar cone in the hot tea and quickly ate it. "And the creatures we have removed are managing to overcome their confusion at being taken from the places of their ancestors. We have done our best to place them in similar environments. Many of the beasts on Belmair are related to those of Hetar." He yawned several times, his faerie green eyes began to close, his blond head drooped, and he fell asleep where he sat.

Ilona reached out and took the cup from his elegant hand before the remaining tea spilled. Then without another word she transported her consort to his bed. "He has a truly amazing touch with all he loves, and he does love the flora and the fauna," Ilona remarked with a fond smile. "He is really a perfect mate for me."

"You mean he allows you to do as you please," Lara said with a chuckle.

"Aye," Ilona agreed. "He has done his duty as my consort. He gave me a son, appears with me on formal occasions and leaves me to rule without interference. Thanos is really quite perfect for me, as Kaliq is for you."

"I do not rule anything," Lara said. "I am no queen."

"You have your own destiny, my daughter, and Kaliq is a part of it. Be glad for it, Lara. In the morning you will go home to him. I will not see you again until we have safely evacuated to Belmair. Make your farewells to the forest of your ancestors before you leave tomorrow."

"You will not forget about Marzina, will you, Mother? Kolgrim must not have her! I could not bear it if he did."

"I will keep my promise to you, Lara. Marzina will come to Belmair with me," Ilona, Queen of the Forest Faeries, promised her only daughter.

KOLGRIM, HOWEVER, HAD PUT aside his plans for his little sister, Marzina. The time had come for him to seed his new bride. Nyura was proving a delightful sexual partner.

So far he had not found her hesitant to perform any act. Even after having her virginity taken, Nyura retained a look of innocence. Kolgrim found it particularly exciting, and her interest in playing sex games with him was a delight. While she had retained her virtue she was Hetarian. She had been taught and trained in all manner of games to keep lovers amused and satisfied. His bride, Kolgrim quickly learned, was not only adept but enthusiastic regarding such activities.

She loved being the captive ravaged by the enemy general. She equally enjoyed being the cruel mistress of a sex slave. She would whip his bottom lightly in this particular scenario, but then the sex slave would turn on his mistress and violate her. And she enjoyed being spanked, playing the naughty girl, teasing him wickedly until he mounted her and rode her to exhaustion. Kolgrim could not believe his good fortune in the bride the Book of Rule had chosen for him.

But now the matter of creating his only son was at hand. And for that special night he decided he would begin the process by bringing two of his concubines from his House of Women.

"This will be a most extraordinary night for you, my darling," Kolgrim told Nyura. "Tonight I will seed you, and in several months' time our son will be born. But I must remind you from this night on I will not touch you. We will next come together at the Completion Ceremony when we join our bodies publicly before our people, Nyura. I want you to always remember this night, however."

"What shall we do to make this night memorable?" she asked him.

"You have never flinched from anything I asked of you," he began, "and so this night I will ask you to share the beginning of your passion with two of my concubines."

Nyura smiled slowly. "You wish to see me make love with other women, my lord? Is that what would please you?"

"Aye, 'twould please me greatly," he answered her.

"Rather than two of your concubines, why not invite my cousins Divsha and Yamka to join me," Nyura suggested wickedly. "I know you have fucked them, for each could barely wait to tell the tale after you chose me for your bride."

Kolgrim smiled a slow smile at her. "You have an unusual talent for exciting me, my pet," he told her. "I should very much like to see you with them."

"Then use your magic, my lord, to bring them to us," Nyura said sweetly.

And Kolgrim did. Both of Nyura's cousins were astounded to suddenly find themselves in the castle of the Twilight Lord. Divsha was particularly delighted for she had been in the midst of being lectured by the Lord High Ruler's master of protocol on how she should behave at Yamka's wedding. Yamka was equally pleased, for she had been put into an enchanted sleep in her parents' home from which Kolgrim now awakened her. She welcomed a final adventure before she must marry and become a staid Terahn matron.

When told what would be required of them, the two cousins chortled, quite pleased.

"Nyura watched us for months before she became bold enough to join in," Divsha said. She turned to Nyura. "Do you remember the first time we did it together."

"She released her juices so quickly," giggled Yamka. "I hope she has learned better with you, my lord."

"Show me what you did with her that first time," Kolgrim suggested to them.

The three cousins stripped off their robes, and taking hands to form a circle, raised their hands and came together for a kiss. Then Divsha took Nyura into her arms, her lips playing with the lips beneath hers while Yamka reached out to fondle Nyura's round breasts. Kolgrim stretched out upon the enormous bed and watched the trio through half-closed eyes. For a time they kissed and fondled each other's bodies. Then finally the three young women fell upon the bed near Kolgrim.

They took turns mounting each other, and playing at being the male. They kissed each other on both lips and body. They licked and sucked upon each other's lust orb. The three beautiful bodies intertwining with one another delighted him. Divsha with her big round breasts. Yamka's delightful plump bottom, and his exquisite mate, Nyura. Their long hair, red-gold, blond and dark auburn mingled as they pleasured each other. Kolgrim watched avidly, his arousal becoming more evident as each moment passed. Finally with a wave of his hand he froze Divsha and Yamka, removing them temporarily from the bed to sit on floor cushions. Their blue, green eyes were unseeing.

Stretched out upon the bed, Nyura smiled at her mate. "That was a delicious interlude, my lord." Her lips were swollen with her cousins' kisses, and her sex was slick and wet to his dark gray eyes. "I am ready to receive your seed, my lord. Come! For I need you inside of me," she whispered eagerly.

Kolgrim smiled down at her. "Do you love me, Nyura?" he asked her. A single finger of his hand stroked her slit lightly.

"Aye!" she answered him without any hesitation. "You are my world, my lord. I waited sixteen years for you. I am proud to be your chosen one."

The finger found her lust orb, still half-swollen from her recent love games. He began to play with her, rubbing it, pinching it, until Nyura was squirming beneath his hand. Then when she began to moan Kolgrim quickly thrust two fingers into her. Nyura arched her body, attempting to gain relief, but he would not give it to her. He watched her struggling on his hand to reach surcease, but his goal was to fire her lust into an almost-unquenchable blaze.

"Pleasure me!" she begged him.

"You have said you would bear my son, Nyura," he replied. "Do you understand that in creation there is pain, my pet?"

"I will do whatever you desire, my lord, if you will just give me pleasures," Nyura promised him. "*Please!* I am burning for you."

Kolgrim withdrew his fingers from her, and stroked her hair. "There, my pet, I will reward you shortly, but for now I want of you what your cousins had of you." He put his dark head between her legs, and with his forked tongue began licking her lust orb.

"Ohhh, my lord!" Nyura sobbed as her lust began to burn higher.

The tongue slid deep into her wet silken sheath, stroking its walls, readying her for his entry. Nyura had no idea of what awaited her. Despite his own burgeoning need he had to make certain her body was perfectly prepared to receive his seed. Her juices were already flowing, and she moaned with her need. He felt the tiny sharp nodules beginning to erupt all over his cock. This only happened when a son was to be created. "Tell me you love and desire me, Nyura. Tell me again that you would gladly conceive my son," he murmured hotly into her delicate little ear.

"Oh, my lord, how can you doubt that I love you? I do! I do! And I want you so desperately that I shall die if you do not soon fuck me! Seed me, I beg you! Seed me and give me your son, Kolgrim, my love! *Seed me now!*"

He did not hesitate, but drove himself hard into her. The sudden show of surprise within her gray-green eyes, her scream of pain, aroused him further. All the hidden nodules on his thrusting cock bloomed, their sharp points caressing her throbbing wet sheath cruelly. Nyura's nails dug deep into his shoulders and raked down his back, bloodying him. Kolgrim's mouth met hers in a searing kiss, his forked tongue wrapping itself about her tongue and squeezing it hard.

He ceased his movement briefly, and with a silent command the silver chains with their manacles dropped from the ceiling over the bed. Kolgrim quickly fastened the manacles about each of Nyura's ankles, careful not to dislodge himself from her. The chains drew themselves back up as soon as she was secured. "And now, my pet," he whispered to her, "we will begin again."

"You did not tell me there would be pain," Nyura sobbed.

"But I did, my pet. I warned you that in creation there is pain, and now there will be more pain than you can imagine. And you will scream for me, for only your cries of agony will force my seed forth from me to create my son."

"*Our son!*" Nyura said, and then her screams filled the chamber as he began to thrust deeper and harder into her. At first she thought she would die before he was finished, but then suddenly Nyura realized her own lust was building as a result of the pain. She gasped, and then she sank her teeth into his shoulder, biting down with all of her strength.

Kolgrim howled as a fresh wave of almost-unbearable lust rose up in him. He leaned back just briefly as she released his shoulder and slapped her hard several times. Nyura hissed ferociously at him, and laughing, he pistoned her all the harder, causing her to scream again, yet her cries now were more from her anger. But he needed her pain to succeed. Closing his eyes he felt himself growing in length and more nodules coming forth. Nyura's scream now echoed pain again.

Outside the bedchamber a storm arose suddenly. Lightning flashed, and the thunder crashed louder than he had ever heard it. He caught her hands and pushed her arms above her head, pinioning her. His eyes opened to stare down at her. Her eyes were closed as she struggled to let the pain of their creation wash over her. "Open your eyes and look at me, Nyura!" he growled at her.

"I cannot!" she sobbed. The pain was terrible.

"Open your eyes! If you fail me this night I will kill you, my pet! Now open your eyes and look into mine," he commanded. "If you are a good girl I will give you pleasures, Nyura. Now open your eyes!"

Her blue eyes looked up into his and she cried out with the pleasures that suddenly overwhelmed her. "I love you!" she cried out to him. "I love you!" And then Nyura realized that he no longer saw or heard her. He was concentrated on creating the child. The pain returned threefold, and she screamed. With each shriek he thrust into her harder and deeper, deeper and harder. Over and over and over again. Then suddenly his juices flooded her, hot and potent, its single seed bursting forth to bury itself in her womb, digging down, eliciting a single pained cry from her as it settled itself. The manacles unfastened from about her ankles, disappearing with their chains. Nyura's legs fell to the mattress. She was more exhausted than she had ever been in her life.

The Lustlings hurried to refresh their private parts.

Kolgrim arose from her bed when they had finished. "You have been properly seeded, my pet. We will not come together again until the Completion Ceremony."

"Will I not see you at all?" she asked in a quavering voice. "I love you."

"I know that, my pet," he said, his tone more kindly. "We will eat together, and we will talk together when I have time. But we will not take pleasures until after my son is safely delivered. Nothing must endanger the child."

"My cousins?" Nyura said, pointing to the frozen silent figures of Divsha and Yamka. "Will you return them home now?"

"Not quite yet," he said with a small smile. "The marriages contracted by you and your cousins bind us as family. I am even bound by blood to Cadarn and Palben. But before they are returned home I mean to seed both Yamka and Divsha with a daughter. The female seed will remain dormant within them until after they have each borne their husbands a son. After a year has passed my seed will bloom in each of their wombs. They will bear my daughters and one day those daughters will wed with their cousins. My daughters will become Domina of Terah and First Lady of Hetar." He chuckled, very well pleased with himself.

"But what of our son?" Nyura wanted to know. "Who will he wed?"

"Only the Book of Rule can tell him that when the time is right. It will be several centuries before our son becomes the sole ruler of the World of Hetar, my sweet Nyura."

And then it dawned on Nyura that she was nothing more than a mortal chosen to bear an immortal. She began to weep. Immediately Kolgrim was back at her side. "What is it?" he wanted to know. "Why do you weep? You must not be unhappy. It will harm the child."

"I am mortal. I will never live to see my son's success," Nyura sobbed.

"Is that all that troubles you?" Kolgrim laughed. "When you give me Ulla's powers, Nyura, I will be able to give you a lifetime that matches mine if that is what you wish, my pet," he promised her.

Nyura sniffed. "Really? And you would do that?"

"Of course I will, my sweet." He kissed her on her forehead. "We will be together always. Now I must go lest I break with tradition. Sleep well, and I shall see you on the morrow when we break our fast, Nyura." Rising, he walked over to where Divsha and Yamka sat unseeing and silent, and snapped his fingers. The two young women immediately arose and followed after him.

In the corridor outside of Nyura's bedchamber he found his chancellor waiting.

"It is done, Alfrigg," he told him.

"Excellent, my lord," Alfrigg replied. He looked curiously at the naked women.

Kolgrim chortled, and told him how he had brought his mate's two cousins to her bedchamber, and for what purpose. Then he explained what he would do with the two women now. "The mortals I allow to have some certain power in this world will be my own blood," Kolgrim said in a satisfied tone.

"Your plan is truly inspired, my lord. Your daughters will manipulate their husbands to your wishes, giving you and your son an easier world to manage," Alfrigg said. "My lord Kol would be so proud of you."

"I mean to send my father and brother a cask of wine to celebrate Nyura's seeding. After I finish with these two I shall do it. Have the cask brought to my library, and prepare a note of explanation that I will attach to it."

"At once, my lord. May you enjoy the rest of your time with your mate's toothsome cousins, if my lord will permit me to say so," Alfrigg said, smiling.

Kolgrim laughed. "You may say it, Alfrigg. You are ancient, but not without eyes." Then the Twilight Lord walked down the corridor followed by the naked Divsha and Yamka. Entering his private bedchamber, he snapped his fingers, and the two women were immediately aware again. He laughed at their surprise, and then told them that Nyura was now carrying his heir.

"Then why are we still here?" Divsha asked him.

Kolgrim explained his plan to her and to Yamka. They giggled conspiratorially when he finished and, taking his hands in theirs, led him to his bed. Soon the three bodies were entwined in sexual play, and when Kolgrim had finally satisfied his lust on them, and the Lustlings had bathed them, he sent them home.

But not before Yamka said, "How can you be certain I will give Vaclar a son first?" And Divsha nodded.

"I can be sure," Kolgrim said with a smile. "I will soon be the master of this world, and you can trust in what I say, my pretties."

14

LARA AWOKE WITH A START. SHE WAS HOME AGAIN in Shunnar, and Kaliq was by her side. She sat up gasping for breath. She had heard the screams, and knew immediately what the sounds portended.

"What is it?" Kaliq asked, immediately awakened when he sensed her distress.

"He has mated her," Lara said. "I heard her screams in my dream state. In just a few months she will give him his son."

"We will be long gone," Kaliq said quietly.

Lara found herself still torn with her need to save Hetar, and her awareness that she could not. It was painful for her, and once again she questioned her life span. What had she really accomplished? If the Twilight Lord was to have Hetar after all, what had it all been for? She understood from what she had been told that her birth, carefully planned by the magic powers of this world, had only been an opportunity to change Hetar's fate. The chances were that she would not succeed, for as strong as she was Lara knew she was a young power by the standards of the

Cosmos. But what had she done wrong that she had failed? She questioned herself over and over again yet could find no answer. Finally after several days she asked Kaliq.

"You did nothing wrong," he said to her. "Why do you believe you have?"

"Should I not have been able to hold the powers of darkness off longer?" Lara said. "Why did you all tell me I must wait for my destiny? If you had told me what was involved in the first place, perhaps I could have overcome the evil now encroaching upon Hetar and Terah. I am young, I know, but with each year I grow stronger. Why was my birth not planned sooner, Kaliq? If I had been born earlier then I should have had the time I needed."

"Our warrior had to be born of a specific bloodline, Lara. It was not by chance your faerie mother mated with John Swiftsword, a man thought to be mortal by his fellow Hetarians, but who was actually more faerie. You know that in mortals the bloodline weakens with passing generations, but in the faerie world it strengthens. Your great-grandmother, your father's grandmother, bore her faerie lover a son that was believed to be her husband's child. She kept the secret, but it was known in our world and set down in the Book of the Faerie Record. That son bore your father, and you were the third generation born of the line of Lord Rufus and his Hetarian lover, Thea. We had to wait. We had no chance if we did not. And it had to be a female child."

"Why?" Lara wanted to know.

"While the mortal world considers its females weak, we in the magic world know better," Kaliq said. "We did not choose to confront the Twilight Lord head-on. A woman has not only her intelligence but her sensuality with which to work. We wanted a female warrior who would be able to sow confusion in the Dark Lands, and you did. It was a great triumph, my love. Never believe your life has been worthless. You gave Hetar more than a century in which to correct itself. For a time after our battle with Ciarda and her false Hierarch, I thought we had turned the tide of Hetar's fate."

"But we did not," Lara said.

"Nay, we did not, and now it is too late."

"I cannot shake off the feeling that I have failed, Kaliq, and that if I just had a little more time I might turn the tide," Lara told him.

"That is your son's influence, Lara, attempting to deceive and beguile you into believing that if you stay just a little while longer you can change Hetar's fate. You cannot. Come, I would show you something, my love." Enfolding her within his cloak, he brought them to the oasis of Zeroun, which was one of Lara's favorite places. He flung back the cape so she might step forth.

Lara looked about her, puzzled. "Where are we, Kaliq?" she asked him. They stood in a desolate and sandy place. She saw the tumbled stone ruins of what looked to have been a well, and the rotting trunks of what had been palm trees. The sand beneath her sandaled feet, and for as far as her eye could see, was bloodred.

"This is Zeroun, Lara. A month ago, the desert sands turn crimson. The waters of the oasis dried up overnight, the well collapsed and the trees and other greenery that once flourished here died in a span of two days. Kolgrim destroyed it because he knows you love it, and he sent to me to tell me what he had done."

Lara's face mirrored astonishment. "To destroy such beauty," she said softly.

Kaliq nodded, and wrapping her again in his cloak, transported them back to Shunnar. "Look down into our valley," he said.

When she did Lara saw it was empty of the horse herds of the Shadow Princes. "Where are the animals? Where is Og?"

"They have gone to Belmair for safety. We opened a Golden tunnel to some fine meadows outside of Dillon's castle, and drove them through several days ago. Kolgrim wants your magic, Lara. He wants all the magic belonging to Hetar, and next to mine, yours is the most powerful. He is wickedly clever, this young Twilight Lord. He seeks to entrap you with Marzina, and me with you."

"Then we must leave very soon," Lara said.

"Aye, we must. But because Kolgrim has to believe we are still unaware of his plans for us, we must attend the wedding of Yamka and Vaclar."

"I don't want to go," Lara said.

"You must," he told her.

"I never want to see The City again," Lara said. "Besides that wedding is but for Grugyn Ahasferus. He would display this third granddaughter's great marriage to the other magnates and all of Hetar. If he were younger I would think he was planning a coup against Palben. Now I believe he simply wishes to be more powerful and important than Hetar's Lord High Ruler. He has no idea the beast he has invited into his house."

"Very well," Kaliq agreed. "It matters not if we offend Grugyn Ahasferus by not appearing at the Hetarian portion of this wedding. We will be at the Terahn one, and in evidence at the feasting afterward, my love."

"Have you heard from Marzina?" Lara wanted to know.

"I assume she is still at Fairevue."

"My mother was to speak with her," Lara said. "I hope she has. Oh, Kaliq, I must see her. I need to know she is safe from Kolgrim."

"Then call her, Lara," he told her quietly. He disliked seeing her so distressed.

Marzina! Marzina, hear my plea. Cease all else and come to me!
Lara said.

Almost immediately, and much to Kaliq's relief, Marzina
appeared.

"What is it, Mother? Are you all right?" the young faerie
woman asked anxiously.

"I had not heard from you…" Lara began. "I wondered if
you were going to your kinsman Vaclar's wedding to Yamka
Ahasferus."

"Aye, I am. Nyura cannot come for she is with child,"
Marzina began.

"You know? How do you know?" Lara asked, trying to keep
the irritation from her voice. "Have you been to the Dark
Lands of late?"

"Nay, nay, but Kolgrim came to me to tell me that I will soon
have a nephew," Marzina said with a smile. "It will be nice to
have a baby for a nephew for a change." She laughed. "All of
Taj's and Zagiri's children, and even their children, are long
grown."

Lara bit her lip so hard it began to bleed. "We may not be
here when the child is born," she said, unable to help herself,
and praying Marzina would not take offense.

"Oh," Marzina replied. "Aye, you are right, Mother. I had forgotten we must leave Hetar for good soon. I haven't told
Kolgrim."

"Don't!" Lara said.

"Of course not," Marzina replied. "I spoke with Grandmother yesterday. She wants me to come with her, Thanos and
my cousin Parvanah to Belmair. Dillon has offered them a wonderful refuge, and there is even a forested mountain where I may
rebuild Fairevue. My faerie servants have already gone in the
first group of Forest Faeries who left today. Grandmother

thought it best to send them a few at a time over several days so our exit causes no stirring in the air to attract Kolgrim."

"Your brother knows the good magic is departing Hetar," Lara said softly.

"Aye, he does, but no good can come from rubbing it in his handsome face," Marzina responded. "He believes he may entrap some of the magic before it can escape him. That's why I will go to the wedding as his companion since Nyura cannot. I even suggested it," she said, pleased with her own cleverness. "He was delighted."

"Oh, Marzina," Lara said. "You play a dangerous game. Your brother is evil incarnate for all his charm. You must beware of him. I cannot ever remember being afraid, although surely there was a time when I must have been. But now I am frightened for you, my daughter."

Marzina flung her arms about Lara. "Do not fear for me, Mother. I know the darkness that runs through my blood, but there is light, too, and I was raised in the light. I understand Kolgrim, and he is indeed evil. But I feel sorry for him, too, for he is so eager not just to conquer the world of Hetar, but to be loved, truly loved, as well. His blood is like mine, but that he was raised in the dark."

"Do not think you can change him, Marzina," Lara said, stroking her daughter's cheek. "You cannot. And do not believe you can trust him. You cannot. He killed his half sister without hesitation. He may kill Nyura one day. And if he believes you are in his way, or attempting to thwart him in any manner, he will kill you, too."

"I know," Marzina replied. "He is quite frightening, Mother, isn't he?"

"I do not understand you," Lara said low.

"I know you don't," Marzina laughed. "But is it not that way with all mothers and daughters? One day in the future we shall both come to understand one another. But now is not that time." She kissed Lara's cheek. "Will I see you at the wedding in a few days, Mother?"

"We will be there," Lara answered her. "Not in The City, but in Terah."

"Goodbye then," Marzina said, and she was gone in a puff of violet smoke.

"Are you satisfied now?" Kaliq asked Lara quietly.

"For now but I worry about her friendship with Kolgrim. Her lips say what she wants me to hear, but Marzina is fascinated by him. And he is fascinating, Kaliq."

"Be satisfied that she has agreed to go with her cousin and her grandparents to Belmair. I have told you before that Marzina has her own fate to follow. You cannot stop her, and you should not stop her. I understand you want to protect her, but you cannot and should not lest you alter the fate meant for her."

"What do you know of her fate?" Lara demanded of him.

"I know it is not yours to follow, my love. You have only begun to meet your destiny, Lara. There is more to come, and Marzina will not be a part of it. That is all I will say on the matter. You have always trusted me, my love. Trust me now."

She did trust him. He had always had her best interests at heart even when he wouldn't tell her. And he was right when he said that Kolgrim sought to snare her by taking Marzina, and trap Kaliq by taking her. And that could not happen. Her destiny was now tied to that of the Shadow Prince. Lara sensed whatever it was, it would be great, and it would be magical beyond anything either of them had ever done. Their powers combined would be unstoppable. And she wasn't going to allow her maternal fears to prevent them from doing whatever it was she had to do. "I think it is time," she said, "that my son be reminded of just who I am."

Kaliq began to chuckle. He had not heard Lara use that particular tone of voice in some time. "And by that," he said, "you mean to...?"

"I believe that rather than going to the wedding garbed in a beautiful gown I shall go as the faerie woman warrior that I have been in the past. None of these mortals now living have ever see me as such. Nor have they heard Andraste sing. I think that they should."

"You will frighten them," Kaliq told her.

"But perhaps they will take me and what I say more seriously. I know I cannot stop Kolgrim at this time, but let Hetar and Terah remember me as the warrior, not just a beautiful woman concerned for her family. That image fits what they would believe. My mistake was in letting the warrior hide behind that woman. I will do it no more."

"Aye," Kaliq said, agreeing with her. "Perhaps it is better that they remember you as the warrior who saved them several times in the past. The Hetarians and Terahns of today did not know that faerie woman. They only know a beautiful woman who does not age, and makes them uncomfortable. After the deaths of your children you sought to put them at ease by making yourself appear mortal, though you are not. They lost their belief in magic. Now they will suffer for it." He laughed again. "Aye, appear at the wedding in your leather trousers with Andraste, her jeweled eyes glaring, strapped upon your back."

"And you, my lord? How will you garb yourself?" Lara asked him.

"As I always do," he said. "I should not like to take away from the shock you will give the wedding guests." He grinned. He pulled her into his arms and kissed her passionately. "Soon, my beautiful faerie woman, we shall embark together upon a grand new adventure. We will not dally long in Belmair, Lara, for destiny awaits us, my love!"

"You make it sound so exciting, Kaliq!" Lara told him. She caressed his cheek.

His bright blue eyes looked down into her upturned face. "It will be," he promised her. Then his lips touched her again. "To spend forever with you is more than I could have ever hoped, Lara." His lips met hers again in a deep and potent kiss. Then he released her, smiling into her faerie green eyes.

"Why is it so quiet?" Lara asked him, suddenly aware of the deep silence.

"The Shadow Princes have gone from Hetar," Kaliq answered her. "We are the only ones left in Shunnar, my love."

"Where have they gone?" Lara wanted to know. "Will we ever see them again, Kaliq? Lothair did not say goodbye, nor Nasim, nor Coilen, nor any of the others."

"They have gone into the Cosmos to seek another home for us," Kaliq said. "We will not make a new home on Belmair. It is too small a world for us," he said. "We will rejoin them eventually, Lara, but not yet."

"How will we know how to find them?" she asked.

"We will know," he promised.

She nodded. "Does Kolgrim know?"

Kaliq shook his head. "Nay. My presence leads him to believe that everything is as it has always been in Shunnar. The High Council has not yet reconvened after its summer recess, and so our representatives are not yet missed."

"What of the faerie post? Surely we will not leave them behind," Lara said.

"They will disappear tomorrow when all of The City is involved in Yamka Ahasferus's wedding celebration. Remember we must use our magic to make it possible for the two worlds to move easily back and forth between Hetar and Terah," he reminded her. "'Twas a clever way to end the stalemate between the two sides over the wedding."

"It is not difficult," Lara said. "We simply open a short Golden tunnel between Hetar and Terah, but of course we will have to see it looks like a well-lit and beautifully decorated corridor so the wedding guests are not frightened by it. The bridal couple will be the first to pass through it, and the others will follow."

"Going from night to dawn will astound the Hetarians," Kaliq remarked. "They have no real concept of anyone or anything but themselves."

"The Terahns are little better," Lara agreed, "but few of them will go to the Hetarian ceremony. Vaclar's father and mother, of course. His uncle and great-uncle, perhaps. But simple Terahns are little interested in Hetar even today, although they have certainly embraced certain Hetarian customs and ways that the trading vessels and their sailors brought," Lara noted disapprovingly. "I remember Terah as I first saw it, and it was glorious, Kaliq. Now with that ridiculous imitation of The City on the plain before the castle..." She shook her head. "Dasras and I loved riding over that plain. But those times are gone, and they cannot be retrieved, more's the pity."

"Seeing something you love die is always difficult, my love, but we have a new life awaiting us in the Cosmos," Kaliq said.

"But first the wedding, a visit to Belmair, and then..."

"And then new adventures," he replied. "We will gallop together, you and I, upon Dasras's back amid the stars of the Cosmos, my darling. There are so many worlds out there, Lara, and new ones being born every day."

He sounded so happy, Lara thought. She had not heard that tone in his voice in years. It was boyish, excited. He was eager to move on now, and so was she. They had done their best for Hetar, but they were only magic, and magic could not correct all mortal ills. And sometimes it made them worse. Perhaps protecting Hetar from itself had been an error, and the magic should have left long ago.

As the servants had been sent from Shunnar, Lara fed them that night with faerie bread, and Kaliq conjured up a decanter of forest berry frine for them to drink. She did not know that he placed a strong protection spell about Shunnar that night, for he sensed the darkness reaching out with curious fingers. They must not be taken. He hoped that Kolgrim would keep the peace between them for the wedding, but he did not trust to it. Kaliq knew that, like a greedy child, Kolgrim was already tasting his victory, and was more than eager to have it all.

THE MORNING CAME. The bloodred sun rising into a dun-colored sky. They ate their final meal in their garden. Lara noticed that the flowers were drooping, and the sound of birdsong was gone. They hardly spoke, either with voice or in the silent language of their race. They ate, and then they bathed. The silence surrounding them had become almost eerie. Only the soft sound of the water soothed them.

Kaliq dressed himself in his white silk trousers and tunic. The tunic was simple, but its high collar and the cuffs of its sleeves were sewn with gold threads in a geometric design and tiny diamonds. On his feet were deep blue leather slippers. Atop his dark head he had a small turban centered with a large diamond. His long white silk cloak was lined with cloth-of-gold. He looked handsomer than Lara could ever remember. He was both powerful and impressive in appearance, and she told him so.

Lara, however, had done as she had promised him. She wore

fawn-colored fitted leather trousers, a forest-green silk vest over a full-sleeved cream-colored silk shirt, which was open to reveal her thin gold chain with its sparkling crystal star. Within the star her guardian spirit, Ethne, resided. Ethne had been silent of late, but suddenly she spoke.

Be careful today, my child.

Do you sense danger? Lara asked her.

The Twilight Lord will challenge you this day, Ethne answered.

I give him Hetar willingly, Lara replied.

Hetar is but part of his plan. He wants you, for he believes you are an important part of Hetar. He will try to strike you in your heart to gain his way. Be wary of all he says, and all he does, no matter how innocent he pretends to be. He will not keep the peace between you this day, my child. Ethne's light dimmed slightly, and she grew silent.

"Did you hear her?" Lara said to Kaliq as she drew on her well-worn boots.

"I did," he answered.

"Protect Marzina at all costs," Lara said to him. She strapped her singing sword, Andraste, onto her back. "I can protect myself."

I am Andraste, and I sense the blood of the wicked, the sword sang softly.

"It is time to go," Kaliq said. "Say your farewell to Shunnar, my love, for we shall not see it again." His bright blue eyes swept about his garden, and then he led her out to the wide corridor with its open balustrade. Looking down into the valley below, they saw the grassy meadow that had always been there but then, before their eyes, it disappeared, turning to bloodred sand. "Kolgrim's warning to us that he is now in charge," Kaliq said grimly. "The darkness has begun, but the light will come again one day."

Lara looked up into his face. She touched his sensuous lips with hers. "The light will always overcome the darkness, my lord. I will see you in Terah." And then she was gone in a puff of violet smoke that he noticed was suddenly tinged darker.

Wrapping his cloak about him, Kaliq transported himself to the beautiful rotunda of Grugyn Ahasferus's house, where the Hetarian wedding ceremony was just beginning. The auburn-haired bride garbed in cream-and-gold silk was weighed down with jewels. The groom was equally resplendent, and the guests were suitably impressed by the ceremony joining the heir to Terah with Grugyn Ahasferus's last granddaughter.

As it came to an end, Kaliq discreetly opened a Golden tunnel in a rear wall of the rotunda. To the mortal eye it appeared to be a grand corridor with a floor of gold and white marble squares down the center of which had been laid a dark red carpet. The walls of the corridor were lined with gold and crystal sconces burning scented candles that perfumed the air with the fragrance of late-summer lilies. The lights flickered and gleamed, but amazingly did not burn down. The ceiling of this grand passageway was glass that went from sunset to night and finally predawn. Terahns were wed at sunrise. Vaclar and his bride would reach the great gardens of his father's castle just in time.

Lara had already arrived. At first she was not recognized as the warrior she was. Lara smiled wickedly. "What, Cadarn? You do not know your own great-grandmother?"

He gaped at her.

"This is what you wear to a wedding?" Domina Paulina cried angrily. "Your garb was finer for your son's wedding. Is Terah to be less respected than Hetar, but then you are Hetarian," she sneered.

"I am faerie, Domina. Neither Hetarian nor Terahn. This is

my natural garb, and I honor you by reminding you of the faerie woman who, not once, but twice, saved Terah. By making a fresh blood tie between the children of Grugyn Ahasferus's grand-daughters I may have given you some respite from what is about to befall you." Reaching back, Lara drew her sword from its sheath.

Both Dominus Cadarn and his wife stepped back nervously.

Andraste opened her jeweled eyes, fixing them in her stern gaze. *I am Andraste, the sword of Justice. I greet you in peace great-grandson of Magnus Hauk,* she sang in her deep beautiful voice.

The Dominus and Domina stared openmouthed in surprise.

"How did you make the sword talk," Cadarn finally asked.

Lara laughed. "Andraste speaks for herself, my lord. I have nothing to do with it. She was forged for me by the great Shadow sword master, Prince Lothair."

"Magic is not welcome here," Cadarn said, and his wife nodded vigorously.

"Shall I depart then?" Lara taunted him. "Shall I close the Golden passageway that has just opened into your gardens so the bridal couple may easily emerge from Hetar in order that both you and the family Ahasferus may each have your day of boasting and celebration? Oh! I see your guests have already gathered." She smiled at the couple.

"Could you not at least dress as the widow of a Dominus should?" Cadarn said.

Lara fixed him with a hard look. "I am dressed as the faerie widow of Magnus Hauk would be dressed. You never knew that female. You only knew the quiet creature who tried so hard not to distress her son's wife, and her son's successors by being what she was not. *Mortal.* I am not mortal, Cadarn. I am *Faerie!* Be glad I have honored you on this day for after it I will be gone, and with me, all of the magic that once blessed this world. The only hope I can leave with you is that one day the light will come again, for the darkness cannot ever hope to prevail entirely. Now, Domina, go and greet the bridal couple for they are here, and must be properly prepared. It is almost dawn." Then Lara turned from them and went to greet Kaliq and her daughter, Marzina, who had come through the Golden tunnel together.

The Hetarian guests now coming through from what they believed was a Grand Corridor into the gardens of the Dominus's castle were both amazed and awed. Stepping into the broad passageway from the great rotunda of Grugyn Ahasferus's mansion, they had been unable to help looking up at the glass ceiling where the sky was ripe with the setting sun. As they strolled through the corridor's exquisitely decorated broad hall, admiring its elegance, their eyes kept gazing up. The skies above them grew darker until it was a night filled with myriad twinkling stars that faded into a false dawn and then the predawn sky. As they exited liveried servants hurried to escort them to their places. About them an autumn garden was in full bloom.

Certain of the guests were requested to follow the senior servants. The Ahasferus family, Palben, his wives, the Twilight Lord, Marzina, Kaliq and Lara were brought, not to their seats, but to the royal baths where they joined with the Terahn guests. Through an open portico they could see fingers of color—palest pinks, peaches, lavender and green, followed by potent reds, golds, oranges and purples—reaching forth to stain the sky. Then over the dark rimmed horizon the scarlet sun burst forth.

Vaclar and Yamka were divested of their bridal garments. They were displayed by the bath attendants to the gathered guests to show their bodies were healthy and fit to wed. Although they had been told of this custom the Hetarians present looked somewhat askance on the proceedings. But they stood silent with the Terahns as the young couple were thoroughly bathed before them. Then traditional Terahn wedding garments were brought forth. The Hetarians thought them rather plain and simple.

Yamka was garbed in a long sleeveless gown of white silk. The long skirt was pleated in rows of narrow pleats. The neckline was draped to rest upon her collarbone, and about her waist was a narrow gold chain. The bride's long dark auburn hair was braided with golden ribbons into a single thick plait, and she wore gold-bejeweled sandals upon her feet. Vaclar's garb matched his bride's. He wore a knee-length white silk tunic whose skirt fell in graceful folds rather than pleats. About his waist was a gold chain, and on his feet golden sandals. Around his neck was a heavy gold chain with a ruby pendant carved with the seal of Terah's heir.

Led back into the gardens that overlooked the fjord, the Domina Paulina placed a wreath of multicolored autumn flowers on the head of her son, the groom, and then on the head of his bride. She joined their hands, and the High Priest from the Temple of the Great Creator began the simple ceremony.

"Do you, Vaclar, son of Dominus Cadarn and Domina Paulina, grandson of Dominus Amhar, great-grandson of Dominus Taj, great-great-grandson of Dominus Magnus and great-great-great-grandson of Dominus Ejnar, of the Clan Hauk, and you, Yamka, daughter of Kavah and his wife, Ahana, granddaughter of Lord Grugyn Ahasferus and his wife, Camilla, pledge yourselves to each other as husband and wife?"

"Yes!" Vaclar said loudly.

"Yes!" Yamka echoed him.

"Then let it be so in the eyes of the Great Creator of us all. You are now wed, Prince Vaclar and Lady Yamka," the High Priest said. "The Great Creator blesses your union, and gives you many children and much happiness in the years to come. It is done. Now greet your guests!"

The bridal couple turned, and a great cheer went up from the assembled guests.

"So now you have united the world of Hetar as publicly as you did secretly once before," Kolgrim murmured in Lara's ear. "You have made it easier for me, dearest mother. Thank you for that."

"I have done what I could to save these mortals whom you will now drag into the darkness. Just remember, Kolgrim, the darkness will not prevail forever."

"So say you, but you cannot be certain this time that your words are not hollow," the Twilight Lord told his mother. "I will overcome the light. And when that day comes I will reach out to Belmair, and then I shall move out into the Cosmos, seeking new worlds to bring under my control."

"And will the son you have bred on Nyura wait patiently for his chance to rule while you play the conqueror, Kolgrim?" Lara taunted him. "Remember, this child's veins run doubly with Usi's blood. He will be stronger than you one day, especially if your beautiful Hetarian mate retains Ulla's gift," Lara said wickedly. "She has not given you her power yet, has she? Like all Hetarians, Nyura is acquisitive, my son."

"She does not know how to use her gift," Kolgrim shot back.

"But it makes no difference if you do not have it," Lara retorted. "Oh, dear."

Kolgrim laughed. "You may be faerie, Mother, but you have a tiny ribbon of cruelty in your heart that quite appeals to me."

"All faeries do, Kolgrim, and some faeries are quite naughty by nature," Lara told him as she took his arm, guiding him into a crowd of guests and away from Marzina.

"Then I hope the seeds I have planted in Divsha and Yamka that will one day bloom into two daughters will have that same cruelty," Kolgrim said to her.

"You seeded your wife's cousins?" Lara didn't know if she should be shocked or angry with him at this revelation.

"Do not fear, Mother. They will each bear their husbands a son first. Divsha is already with child. Do you not notice how cool the Lady Laureen is to her today, or how Palben is doting upon her, or how coyly Divsha is behaving. And tonight Vaclar will vigorously seed his bride, and it will be a son. Only then will I permit these females to bloom with my daughters. One day, Yamka's daughter will wed Divsha's son. And Divsha's daughter will wed Yamka's son. In this manner I will retain my hold on Hetar. Now am I not as clever as you, Mother? Have I not learned well from you?"

"Aye, you have learned from me," Lara agreed in pleasant tones. "But when will you accomplish something original, Kolgrim? So far all you have done is in imitation of your sire or me."

His face darkened with the insult, but he smiled, saying in a deadly soft voice, "I will soon have my sister's magic, Mother dear. Perhaps then we might discuss something unique and original."

Around them the wedding guests chattered as they moved into the Great Hall of the castle where a magnificent feast had been arranged. A battalion of servants dashed about with great bowls of shellfish boiled in wine or served raw, and enormous platters of roasted game and meats. There were large platters of poultry, and smaller ones of fish, broiled and lying upon beds of seaweed. There were huge bowls of salads, bread fresh from the ovens served upon polished cutting boards, big wheels of hard yellow cheese and smaller rounds of soft cheese. The guests hurried to take their seats as the silver goblets studded in green malachite were filled with rich wines. Each guest would be invited to take their goblet home as a souvenir, indicating to the Hetarians present that Terahns knew how to properly entertain on a great occasion.

You will never *have my daughter or her powers!* Lara hissed angrily at Kolgrim.

He laughed mockingly.

Lara fought back her rage, which was threatening to boil over. Unreasonable anger weakened one. Her ear caught the soft humming now coming from Andraste. She drew a deep breath to calm herself. Beside her Kolgrim sat eating enthusiastically as if he had not a care in the world. A servant bent to fill her cup. Lara stopped him with her hand. "Spring water," she said, and the servant nodded, snapping his fingers at an underling who, given the instruction, hurried to fill the silver goblet. Wine would fog her wits at a time when she needed them about her.

Kaliq, seated on the other side of her, reached out and squeezed her hand reassuringly. "Marzina is safe," he whispered in her ear. "It is but her image seated at this table. I spoke with her as we traversed the corridor between Hetar and Terah. Kolgrim was too busy speaking with the Lord High Ruler Palben to notice. She understood the danger today, and let me transport her to your mother in Belmair."

"The queen is there now?" They murmured softly to one another so Kolgrim could not hear them, as he would have heard had they spoken in the silent language.

"All the good magic has gone from Hetar now but for you and me," Kaliq said.

"Thank you for convincing Marzina to go," Lara said, relieved.

THE FEASTING HAD GONE ON the day long. There had been many entertainers to amuse the guests. Oiled wrestlers both male and female had battled before them. Lithe dancers in translucent silks had woven their way about the trestle tables in the Great Hall. A troupe of gaily costumed dwarfs had danced and turned somersaults atop six black-and-white ponies, half of whom had black manes, and half who had white. And then an ancient bard had come into the hall, which grew silent.

His name was Knud, and he was famous throughout Terah. He sang songs of Terah's past history. Then he concluded his entertainment by coming to stand before Lara while he sang of the beautiful faerie woman who had freed Terah from the curse of Usi the Sorcerer. Lara's eyes were filled with tears when he had finished, for this same lay had been sung at her wedding to Magnus Hauk in this very hall well over a hundred years ago. The last notes of his lyre dying, Knud took Lara's hand up in his and kissed it.

"Thank you," she told him, nodding. "That was as beautiful as the first time I heard it. Thank you!"

The bard nodded his head in return. "My father taught it to me, Domina. It was he who sang it at your wedding. After today I shall not sing it or any other song again for the darkness is even now falling, and I shall die tonight. I am one hundred years old." Then turning, Knud bowed to the Dominus and, walking slowly, left the hall, which was now wrapped in stunned silence.

The tension was broken with the entry of a magnificent cake of twelve tiers. It was covered in a purple sugar icing and gold leaf. This was a new innovation in Terah. Lara remembered her winter wedding to Magnus Hauk had concluded with baskets of winter fruits. Atop the cake were two naked sugar figures representing Vaclar and Yamka who stood facing one another. The male figure held a long rigid manhood in his hand that stuck straight out. The female stood, her hands pulling apart her nether lips, a coy smile upon her face. The cake was cut, and slices apportioned out to the guests, who devoured them eagerly. One fortunate among the guests would find a ruby in their slice. A shriek of delight erupted as a magnate's wife from Hetar was the lucky one.

Dominus Cadarn now arose from his place at the center of the High Board. "It is now time, having watched the sun come up together on this auspicious day of Vaclar and Yamka's wedding, to adjourn to the gardens to watch the sun set on the first day of their marriage. Please join us, my friends!" Then he and Domina Paulina led the guests from their Great Hall back outside.

The air was cooler now. The setting sun was every bit as beautiful as the rising sun had been. How many more days would it be? Lara wondered. And as the guests stood admiring the sunset sky Lara saw from the corner of her eye Vaclar and Yamka slipping off to their bridal chamber. Oddly they seemed well suited to each other, and were not unhappy with the dynastic match that had been made for them. Lara remembered how she and Magnus had remained with their guests for they were master and mistress of Terah then. And the entertainments had gone on long into the night. Finally Magnus had stood with Lara by his side. Together they had thanked their guests for coming, wishing them a safe journey home on the morrow.

How long ago had it been? One hundred and twenty or thirty years? Lara sighed with the memory. So much had happened since then. And yet little had changed. The sun still rose and set as it always had. She hoped that those Hetarians and Terahns who had come for this wedding would remember this day. Already some of them were beginning to return to The

City through the corridor the magic had made for them. She felt Kaliq's hand taking hers and, looking up at him, smiled, her faerie green eyes lighting with the deep and passionate love she felt for him.

"It is time to go," he said to her, and she nodded.

Hearing them, Kolgrim turned. "But Marzina remains with me," he said in a cold hard voice. His dark gray eyes danced with his triumph.

"Marzina is long gone, my lord," Kaliq said softly. "Did you think I would let you use her to break your mother's heart, to steal her magic?"

"Marzina stands there," Kolgrim said, pointing to the figure of the beautiful young faerie woman who stood looking at the last bit of color as the sun disappeared beneath the purple horizon.

"'Tis but a shade of your sister," Lara said, unable to keep the exultation from her voice. "Marzina is safe from you, Kolgrim. You will not have her magic or mine!" As she spoke the words she heard Andraste humming loudly within her scabbard.

"Curse you!" Kolgrim shouted angrily, and the remaining guests turned to look. Suddenly in the Twilight Lord's hand was a large broadsword. Its pommel was shaped in the head of an ugly male with onyx eyes that glowed red as it spoke in a dark voice.

I am Jasha, the Supplanter, the sword shouted.

Andraste was shrieking to be freed from her scabbard, and Lara obliged her weapon, who answered, *I am Andraste, and I will drink the blood of the supplanter!* She almost leaped from Lara's hand in her fury to do battle with Jasha. Lara's eyes glittered dangerously. "Sheathe your sword, Kolgrim," she told him, holding tight to her own weapon. "You do not want to do battle with me, boy."

"Do you think I am afraid of you, Mother?" he drawled. "You cannot kill me. My fate is to rule this world, to grind it beneath my heel, to bring it into the darkness."

"I killed before your coming was even written in the Book of Rule," Lara warned him softly. "Perhaps I cannot kill you, Kolgrim, but you will not win in combat with me. If you wish to maintain your status with these poor foolish mortals, do not challenge me. Remember that I have a destiny, and it is not to be spitted upon your sword."

"Can you be certain of that, Mother?" he demanded of her.

"Aye, I can," Lara replied.

"Domina!" Cadarn cried. "Put that weapon away before you hurt yourself. My lord Kolgrim, I beg you remember where you are."

Kolgrim turned to look briefly at Marzina. The shade faded away before his eyes. He turned back to Lara. "You cannot keep her from me," he said in a deadly voice. *Sister Marzina, hear my plea. Cease all else and come to me!*

But Marzina did not appear.

Lara shook her head. *You are pitiful, Kolgrim. Whatever you think you must do you will do without my daughter or her magic.*

She is my sister! he said angrily. *We share the same blood, a mother, a father. You have no right to keep her from me.*

Cadarn looked to Prince Kaliq. "Why are they just standing there, my lord?" he asked the Shadow Prince.

"They converse in the silent language of magic," Kaliq replied.

"Sheathe your weapon," Lara repeated aloud so that the witnesses to this scene would hear her and know it was she who was being provoked.

Instead he leaped forward, the blade of Jasha meeting Andraste as Lara moved to defend herself. The sound the two swords made was loud and ferocious. Kolgrim was almost weeping with his frustration.

"He will kill her!" Palben shouted, but he made no move to help.

"Neither of them will kill the other," Kaliq said quietly. "They cannot."

"Then why does she fight him?" Cadarn wanted to know. "She is but a delicate woman."

Kaliq laughed aloud. "She is a great swordswoman and a great warrior. If you had accepted your own history instead of rewriting it to suit your narrow ideology, my lord Dominus, you would know that. Now watch her, and learn that evil can be defeated."

The remaining wedding guests had unconsciously moved back to form an open space in which the two combatants now slowly circled each other. Lara's eyes never left her opponent as she waited for him to make his next move. Unnerved by her calm, Kolgrim flailed out with Jasha, his blow once again blocked by Andraste.

Kolgrim, walk away. You will lose to me, and then these mortals will know that you can be beaten despite your powerful magic, Lara taunted.

In reply the Twilight Lord began to rain blows with his sword upon his mother's sword, but she blocked him again and again. *If I could really be beaten, you and your kind would not be planning to flee Hetar. I will catch some of your magic before it goes,* he said to her stubbornly.

Lara deliberately kept her mind a blank. She was a consummate warrior, and always had been. She would give Kol's son a lesson he would not soon forget. Andraste was quivering within her grip to do battle. She raised the weapon, and began to fight him seriously, each blow deliberately and carefully planned, for it was she and not Kolgrim who was in charge of this game.

Metal clanged on metal as they fought. Kolgrim was soon winded as Lara parried and thrust, parried and thrust, wearing him down.

Then Andraste began to sing in her deep dark voice. *I am Andraste, slayer of evil!* And the great blade delivered a ferocious blow to Kolgrim's Jasha, severing it in two pieces, which fell to the earth. *And I taste the blood of the Twilight Lord,* she continued as she nicked Kolgrim's sword arm, and he cried out in pain.

THE CROWD OF HETARIANS AND TERAHNS HAD watched and howled excitedly during the match between the two combatants. Now they grew suddenly silent as Kolgrim dropped the damaged sword, and his hand reached out to touch the small wound that Lara had given him on his other arm. Seeing his fingers covered in his own blood, he looked horrified. He looked up at Lara. *You have blooded me, Mother.*

I warned you not to battle me, Kolgrim. Lothair, sword master of the Shadow Princes, was my teacher. If you intend picking quarrels with warriors in the future, I would suggest you get better instruction than you have had, Lara said drily.

"Kinsman, let me have my physician attend to your wound," Cadarn said.

"Nay, come back with me to Hetar, and my physician will see to it," Palben insisted while his two wives nodded vigorously in unison.

With a smothered curse Kolgrim bent to pick up the pommel of the now-destroyed Jasha. Then he disappeared from their sight in a clap of black thunder. The remaining guests were suddenly very silent.

"Those of you from Hetar," Lara said in a commanding voice, "go quickly through the corridor for we are going to close it up. Palben, remain. We will see you home safely. The rest of you go now!" She returned Andraste to her scabbard.

The Hetarians ran for the exit, and when the last of them had dashed through, Kaliq closed the Golden tunnel between Hetar and Terah. It would never open again.

"Send the rest of your guests home, Cadarn," Lara told him.

The Dominus did not question her. "I thank you all for coming this day," he said to those remaining, "but it is past time for you to return to your homes."

"Come with me now to Magnus Hauk's library," Lara said to the two rulers, and with Kaliq by her side she made her way back into the castle down familiar hallways to the chamber she sought. Entering it, she saw the room was exactly as it had been when her Terahn husband had been living. It was obvious that no one used the room. A memorial to Magnus but little more, she thought wryly. "Sit down," she told Cadarn and Palben and they did so without question. She could see the grudging respect in their eyes, and realized she should have never relinquished her control over her mortal family to mortals. They were but the weaker for it.

"Listen to me, and listen well," Lara began. "It is unlikely that after today you will ever see me again. All the magic that is good has departed your world. The darkness is upon you. You and your peoples are now in the hands of the Twilight Lord. You will find him a cruel master, but you have brought this upon yourselves by refusing to change your ways, by not learning from your history, but rather rewriting it to suit your own purposes and actions.

"You are a society totally involved with yourselves, your acquisitions, your pleasures, all of it to the detriment of others not as fortunate. Once Hetar offered opportunity to those who strived to better themselves. You no longer offer those chances to your citizens. You have made them weak by feeding, housing and entertaining them without asking anything in return. They have no education, no skills. They are no better than mindless slaves! And you have done this, not out of kindness, but to maintain your own positions, retain your ridiculous wealth and seek endless pleasures. May the Celestial Actuary help you now for the magic world will not.

"And you, Terah, once an idyllic land of farmers and artisans. A land with the kindness to offer refuge to a displaced people. There was a reason the ships of the Coastal Kings were not allowed within sight of your shores. It was to keep Terah safe and peaceful. But like the children you are, you were easily tempted, and now your coastal villages boast drunkards and cheap imitations of Hetar's Pleasure Women.

"I watched as my own son took away the small voice that Magnus Hauk had given to his people in the form of a High Council, and was shouted down when I protested it. I should have exerted my authority over Terah then, but I did not wish to undermine my son. Civil war, I believed, would have been worse. I was wrong. You have returned Terah to an age before Usi. Now you will be at the mercy of Usi's descendant, and the child he has sired on another of Usi's descendants will bring even greater misery upon you all."

Cadarn and Palben could barely comprehend what she was telling them. Why was she so angry, and yet so sad? There was nothing wrong at all with either Hetar or Terah.

"You don't believe me," Lara said, shaking her head wearily. "Then so be it, for I can do no more for you. But when the days ahead grow darker and darker, when the time comes when you think you can bear no more, and the darkness weighs upon you, remember this one thing. Even in the darkest night there is a light somewhere. And the knowledge of that light will give you hope." She walked over to Palben and kissed his cheek. "Farewell, son of Palben, and grandson of my beloved daughter Zagiri. Go home to Hetar now." And he disappeared from their sight.

Lara turned to Cadarn. "I will tell you this. Tonight Yamka will conceive a son for Terah. But her second child will be a daughter. Vaclar is not that girl's father. Kolgrim has seeded Yamka with a future seed that will not bloom until after your natural grandson is born. He has done the same thing to Divsha. Her first child will be Palben's son, but her second will be Kolgrim's daughter.

"Do not allow either of these grandchildren to be matched with Divsha's children. If you do, there is no hope for this world. Warn Vaclar of this, and tell him the day will come when he must resist his wife's demands for these marriages. Both Yamka and Divsha have been enchanted in order to serve Kolgrim's purposes. If you believe nothing else I have said to you, believe this, Cadarn." She bent and kissed his cheek. "Remember me, son of Amhar, grandson of Taj, great-grandson of Magnus Hauk and his faerie wife, Lara, daughter of Swiftsword."

Lara then reached out to take Kaliq's hand. He drew her to his side, flung his snowy white cloak about her, and they disappeared before the amazed eyes of Dominus Cadarn, who felt a sudden sadness, and worse, an emptiness. Standing up, he walked to the large windows of the chamber and looked out on the dark night sky. He could see the great star called Belmair blazing in the Cosmos. Some said it was another world, but of course that was ridiculous. Suddenly Belmair twinkled very distinctly not once, but twice. He had never seen such a thing but of course it had been a trick of his eyes for it had been a very long day, and he was extremely tired.

KALIQ HAD QUICKLY transported them away from Terah to Belmair. Kolgrim's anger was increasing his dark powers, and the Shadow Prince knew if they waited longer it would have been difficult for them to escape the pull of the darkness. He did not bring them immediately to the castle of King Dillon, their son. Instead, he had brought them to a meadow of horses. It was early evening. The air was soft with just a hint of rain in it although in the skies above, the stars were beginning to peep through. The great golden stallion raised his head and, seeing them, galloped over to where they stood.

Lara threw her arms about Dasras's neck. "You are safe," she said happily.

He nuzzled her shoulder and nickered softly. "You are safe," he replied in return. "I so feared your good heart would lead you into more difficulties than you should handle, mistress. Belmair is a fine resting spot for us before we must travel on. The king has been most gracious."

Lara stroked the stallion's coat. "It is a sad time for us, Dasras, but happy, too."

"More happy than sad, mistress," he responded. "It has been some time since we had any adventures to set out upon, and I am more than delighted at the surprises that lie ahead of us. Several of the princes have gone off to seek the perfect new world for us. The rest are temporarily residing in the Grand Dragon's castle. Your mother is visiting the king while her consort and the other Forest Faeries erect their dwellings in the new forest in which they have chosen to reside."

Lara turned to Kaliq. "Will we stay with my brother, or our son?"

"Let us decide while we walk," Kaliq said. "It is not far, and the two castles are separated, as you will recall, by a garden."

"Good night, dearest Dasras," Lara said, kissing his soft muzzle.

"Good night, beloved mistress," the stallion replied. Then he turned and trotted back to where a group of mares stood grazing.

"It is so peaceful here," Lara said as they walked across the green meadow. "I had forgotten what true peace was like." She bent and picked several yellow-and-white flowers. "In recent months even Shunnar seemed to hum with an underlying throbbing of some sort. What will happen to it, Kaliq?"

"Shunnar no longer exists," he told her. "It was our creation, and made possible by our magic. Our departure removed the last piece of magic holding it together. The realm of the Shadow Princes on Hetar is now all desert. No trace of us lives there any longer."

"How sad," Lara remarked.

"Aye, but we will rebuild Shunnar in our new world, and this time we will not dwell side by side with mortals, Lara. This world will be only for our magic, my love."

They had reached the edge of the meadow, and now stepped onto a pretty winding road that brought them to the king's castle. The guards at the gate were for a display of authority more than anything else. Belmair was a peaceful world. Recognizing the king's mother and her companion, the Shadow Prince, they straightened up and saluted as the couple strolled past them.

Dillon, son of Lara and Kaliq, had watched his parents as they walked toward the castle. He ran downstairs and into the courtyard as they entered to greet them. "Mother! My lord!" Catching Lara up, he swung her about, laughing. "You have come at last! Then Hetar is finished. I'm sorry for it." Born when his mother had been little more than a girl, his magic blood ensured that he remained youthful. He was a handsome man, whose dark hair held the sheen of a raven's wing. His bright blue eyes were those of a Shadow Prince. "Marzina is here with Grandmother. How lovely she is, Mother. We must find a husband for her sooner than later. It would sadden me to see her end like my sister, Anoush, alone and forgotten."

"Anoush chose to live with her father's people," Lara said quietly. "She was happy among them, and content with her life."

"She sublimated her gift of prophecy for them, Mother. It was wrong," Dillon said. Then he set her down, saying, "Let us go inside. Cinnia is waiting."

"And our grandchildren?" Lara asked him.

Dillon shrugged. "Out of doors probably, indoors... I can never keep track of them, but you will see them, Mother." He led his parents into the Great Hall of his castle, where his wife, the sorceress Cinnia, was waiting along with Lara's brother, Cirillo, and his wife, Nidhug, the beautiful Great Dragon of Belmair, who waved coquettishly at Kaliq.

He grinned and waved back.

"Do not encourage her, my lord," Lara whispered. "You know how it upsets my brother when she flirts with other men."

"Which is why she does it, my love. To this day Nidhug worries that Cirillo will leave her for another, although she would be horrified to learn that I know her secret. So she flirts with other men to make him jealous, and reassure herself that he loves her."

"But he does!" Lara said. "He adores her, and our mother

has never quite gotten over it. Only Parvanah's birth forced her to realize that Cirillo was not going to pick some faerie maid to get an heir upon."

Dillon's wife, Cinnia, the sorceress of Belmair, came forward to greet her in-laws. "Welcome to Belmair," she said, "although I could wish it were under happier circumstances. I am sorry about Hetar, Lara."

Lara shook her head. "It is over and done with," she answered, "though part of me would wish it otherwise. Thank you for sheltering Hetar's magic world, Cinnia. I know they are grateful to you and Dillon."

"Mother." Marzina was by Lara's side. "What is this Kaliq tells me? He says that you and Kolgrim fought when he found me gone. Poor Kolgrim."

Poor Kolgrim? Lara was astounded by her daughter's words.

"You didn't harm him, did you?" Marzina asked.

"I bloodied his arm to make my point after Andraste broke his weapon, a rather nasty blade named Jasha," Lara replied. Poor Kolgrim, indeed! But then to her surprise Marzina laughed softly.

"I'll bet he went off in a fine temper." She giggled. "Kolgrim is really a very bad loser, Mother. He had the sword known as Jasha especially forged to do battle with your Andraste. He knew of her and was jealous so he created Jasha to defeat her," Marzina responded. "He was, of course, once again seeking your attention."

"He gained it," Lara answered drily. "A pity I could not have killed him."

"*Mother!* What an unkind thing to say," Marzina cried.

"Your sister," Lara said to Dillon "is fascinated by her dark brother."

"He is fascinating," Dillon agreed, "but extremely dangerous. I think it is a good thing you are in Belmair now. Pretty little faerie girls can get eaten up by Twilight Lords." Dillon ruffled Marzina's dark hair affectionately.

Marzina stuck her tongue out at him. "Do not be so superior," she said to him.

Lara went to her mother, who was seated by one of the hall's large hearths. She sat next to her, taking Ilona's hand in hers. "I am sad, too," she told the Queen of the Forest Faeries.

"I am letting Thanos and the others rebuild before I join them," Ilona replied. "To have had to leave the forests of our faerie ancestors to Kolgrim breaks my heart, Lara."

"And yet you and the rest of our magic brethren let me bear him," she replied.

"There was no other choice," Ilona responded. "Even when you know that the darkness is going to come eventually, Lara, you think its time is distant. But with each day that passes it grows nearer, but it still seems distant until suddenly it is upon you. Had Hetar chosen a different path we could have held the darkness at bay perhaps forever."

"Never forever," Kaliq said, joining them. "There must be a balance, as you know, Ilona. The light will prevail in Hetar, but it will be centuries before it returns in force. You must not grieve, my dear friend."

Ilona smiled at her daughter and Kaliq. "I am weary," she admitted. "The last few months have been exhausting. How was the Terahn wedding?"

"Overly ostentatious with Hetar and Terah each trying to outdo the other in splendor. Lara and Kolgrim provided the final entertainment by battling before the guests," Kaliq said mischievously. "Andraste blooded him, and he was quite annoyed."

"How did such an incident occur?" Ilona exclaimed.

Lara shook her head. "For some reason he chose to challenge me to combat. I think he meant to impress his hosts, to make a point. Of course he did neither, and then stormed off in a temper. Ethne warned me of it this morning, and so I was not surprised."

"I cannot believe he did such a thing," Ilona said.

"It did not help that both Cadarn and Palben fell all over him offering him the services of their personal physicians." Lara smiled. "It but added to his embarrassment."

The evening meal was served, and Lara was delighted to see that Dillon and Cinnia's children had appeared to join them. There were six daughters. Maysun, Rima, Gormangabis, Abella, Jolan and Zeta. While they all possessed some magic, it was Rima and Abella who showed the greatest talent. Their brother, Biton, however, seemed to have the strongest magic of the seven. They were excited to reacquaint themselves with their Hetarian grandparents, great-grandmother and other relations. It was not long before Parvanah and Marzina were laughing and exchanging information with them.

"You must teach them what Cinnia and I cannot," Dillon said to his parents. "Especially Biton, who will one day inherit this throne."

"The purple sands in your life glass are still almost filled to the top," Lara noted.

"Oh, I shall reign for many decades to come, Mother," Dillon said. "I know that. It will give Biton time to learn all he can for one day the darkness may reach out to Belmair. Remember Kolgrim will soon have a son. He will not be satisfied to wait for my half brother to die so he may rule. He will want his own conquest."

"Before we leave you I shall cloak Belmair so you are protected from invaders," Kaliq said. "Such a near-perfect world should not be disturbed."

"And when will you go, Father?" Dillon asked. It was rare he addressed Kaliq in such a manner, usually calling him my lord.

"I am not certain yet," the great Shadow Prince said. "Your mother and I will know when it is time." He reached out to take Lara's hand in his.

"You know you are welcome to remain as long as you desire," Dillon responded. He was to his great dismay realizing that when Kaliq and Lara left it was unlikely he would ever see them again. Suddenly within what seemed a very short span of time everything was changing. Hetar as they had known it was no more. In a Cosmos that had always been friendly, his world would now have to be cloaked to keep it safe.

THE EVENING ENDED WITH LARA and Kaliq deciding to shelter with her brother, Cirillo, and Nidhug for a few days before staying with Dillon and Cinnia.

"Now that we are free of Mother you can tell me," Cirillo said to Kaliq and Lara as they walked across the large garden separating the two castles. The faeric prince was as handsome as he had ever been with his wavy golden hair, and faerie green eyes.

"Tell you what?" Lara asked her brother. "I think we said everything tonight."

"Where are you going?" Cirillo wanted to know.

"I don't know," Lara answered him honestly.

"Then how can you know you aren't meant to remain here?" he demanded.

Lara laughed and shook her head. "Belmair is not my destiny, little brother. I know now that my destiny is somewhere out in the Cosmos. And when I have found it, and fulfilled it, Kaliq and I will go to the new home that his brothers will find for us. We will not interact with the mortal races again, Cirillo. I know now that they must find their own path without our help."

"Is magic to end then?" he wondered.

"Nay, and here in Belmair it will live for thousands of years to come, but you will be protected from outside influences that might harm your world. In the time that our son has ruled, Belmairans have learned to live side by side again with magic. That is to the good, and your kingdom within a kingdom will be safe, Cirillo."

"I agree," Nidhug said. "Belmair is a good place to be, my love. And having given your mother our daughter, Parvanah, the Forest Faeries have an heiress after Queen Ilona. And our entire family will inhabit the same world. I am content."

"You don't mean to be mother's heir then?" Lara said to her brother.

"Nay," Cirillo responded. "I am more like my father in disposition, sister."

"And Thanos is gentle," Lara noted with a smile.

Cirillo smiled. "Aye, but gentle is not a particularly good trait in a faerie king," he chuckled. "Parvanah may have been created to look like a faerie, but she has dragon's blood in her veins. She will make an excellent queen one day."

"Can she shape-shift?" Kaliq asked curious.

"Of course!" Nidhug answered, "but do not tell Ilona. She would be horrified to learn her dainty faerie granddaughter can turn herself into an absolutely beautiful female dragon. Her scales are lavender and silver, and her wings gold and silver. She is exquisite, but she rarely indulges herself with that shape, more's the pity." Nidhug sniffed.

"My brother found a treasure in you, Nidhug," Lara said. "And while she will never admit to it, my mother did, too."

They had reached Nidhug's castle. Tavey, the dragon's personal servant, hurried forth to greet them all. "There is cake in the hall, mistress, and grape frine," he said.

"Well, perhaps just a small nibble before we retire, considering that Sarabeth went to the trouble," Nidhug agreed. Sarabeth was Nidhug's cook. She was famous throughout all of Belmair.

They all laughed knowing the dragon's predilection for sponge cakes soaked in sweet wine and covered with whipped cream. Sure enough they entered the hall to find two such cakes. One Tavey served to his mistress. The other he sliced for her husband and their two guests, setting aside what was left for he knew the dragon would eat it before retiring.

"They are never as good the second day." Nidhug excused herself as she finished the second cake, her forked tongue licking her chops as she did. Then she said, "I shall not see you again until your departure, my dear Lara and Kaliq. You know I must rest myself for the times when the king needs my help." Then fluttering her long heavy eyelashes at her husband, she said, "Do not be long, darling. Good night, all." And she departed the hall.

"She insisted I awaken her when you came," Cirillo said, "and she had already been sleeping for several weeks."

Lara shook her head. "I am yet astonished at how happy you are, brother."

Cirillo chuckled. "She is the perfect wife for me," he said. "I adore her."

"And what do you do with your time when your dragon wife slumbers?" Lara wanted to know of him.

"I have spent much of my time teaching your grandchildren the faerie magic they need to learn. I have spent time exploring Belmair, which is why I was able to advise my nephew, the king, the best sites to offer the refugees from Hetar. The descendants of the Yafir are delighted to have been able to provide

King Annan and his Water Faeries a new home on Belbuoy. They told me that they truly feel a part of Belmair now," Cirillo said. "But Kaliq, your grandson and two of your granddaughters could use your knowledge, and that of my sister's. I can teach them no more. The other four girls are content with what little I managed to pound into their frivolous little heads," he chuckled.

"There is a little time for us here," Kaliq agreed. "I shall be happy to teach Biton and his sisters what I can. Lara?"

She nodded. "I will help them," she agreed. "Marzina is talented, Cirillo. Why did you not ask her for aid?"

"Marzina is a light touched by the darkness," Cirillo said. "I didn't want her unleashing any of that darkness here in Belmair."

"She would not do that!" Lara defended her daughter.

"Not deliberately," Cirillo quickly agreed.

"You do not understand her," Lara said.

"And you love her too much," Cirillo replied.

"My lord, my lady," Tavey interrupted them cleverly. "Let me show you to your apartment. My mistress has arranged for you to have one with windows looking out over the gardens, and the countryside beyond. The entire southwest tower will be yours."

"Excellent!" Kaliq said, taking Lara's hand in his. "We will bid you good-night then, Cirillo, and thank you and Nidhug for your hospitality."

"I wasn't going to fight with him," Lara said as they followed Tavey.

"Aye, you were," Kaliq chuckled, "but I should rather you fight with me, and then we will take pleasures to make up for our bad tempers."

"You are incorrigible," Lara replied, smiling. "But I don't understand why Cirillo would say that Marzina has darkness within her."

"She does," Kaliq replied. "While she is not evil, Lara, her father's blood runs through her veins every bit as much as yours does. Do not fear for her, however, my love. There will come a time when it is an advantage to her to have Kol's blood."

"I don't think so at all," Lara said stubbornly. "I am relieved, however, that she has decided to stay with Mother. She cannot come with us, can she, Kaliq?"

"Nay." He shook his head.

"Here we are, my lord," Tavey said as they reached a large double oak door. He opened it to reveal a flight of stairs. "Your apartments are up in the tower. Shall I send Cadi to you, my lady?"

"Nay, not tonight," Lara replied. "But ask her to come to me in the morning."

"Very good," Tavey replied and, giving them a small bow, he hurried off.

They ascended the winding staircase finally reaching another smaller door. Opening it, they stepped into a lovely round day room. There was a hearth burning fragrant wood and through the windows they could see Delmair's twin silver and gold moons blazing down to light the gardens on one side, and the countryside beyond on another side. There was another door in the room, and, going to it, they discovered another smaller shorter staircase.

Climbing it, they found themselves in a beautiful bedchamber at the top of the tower. There was a small hearth burning the same scented wood as the day room, and an arch of windows that allowed the room to be flooded with moonlight. A door led to a small balcony, and before the hearth was a large circular stone. Kaliq looked carefully at this particular stone, and then he saw a little stone button next to the hearth's opening. He pressed it, and the circular stone slid back, revealing a round stone tub filled with water. The steam rising from the tub indicated the water was warmed.

"Ingenious!" he said, and immediately began stripping off his clothing. Naked, he stepped down several stone steps into the tub. As soon as he had settled himself comfortably in the water a small tray of soaps, oils and lotions appeared on the edge of the tub. "Your brother is a fine host," Kaliq remarked, smiling broadly.

Lara needed no invitation, and did not even bother to pull her garments off. She simply magicked them away, stepping into the tub to join Kaliq. "The water temperature is simply perfect," she noted, settling herself opposite him. "It feels wonderful after my little fray with Kolgrim. It has been a long time since I wielded Andraste." When she had divested herself of her garments she had sent the sword to hang over the hearth in the room below them. After a short time she said, "Come to me, my lord, and let me cleanse you free of the dust and the scent of Hetar."

"Then I will do the same for you, my love," he told her.

Lara took up a lovely sea sponge and filled it with liquid soap from the tray. She washed him thoroughly even his thick dark hair. And when she had finished he did the same for her. When he had finished, however, he drew her back against him, cupping her breasts in his palms, fondling them, pushing aside her wet hair, kissing the space between her neck and her shoulder. Lara sighed contentedly.

"For the first time in months," he murmured in her ear, "we are free to concentrate upon each other, and the pleasures we can obtain from our bodies." His kissed her ear, nibbling gently upon the tender lobe.

"I don't want to wait," Lara told him, turning in his arms, kissing his mouth.

"Neither do I," he said, his palms slipping beneath her buttocks to raise her up so he might fill her with his manhood.

Lara wrapped her legs about his torso, hooking her ankles together so she might grip him firmly. "You feel so good inside me," she said softly. "How wicked of Dillon to create this tub, for we could never have just bathed, and departed it. Surely he knew that, my lord." Her arms were now about his neck, and she pressed her full round breasts into his broad smooth chest.

Kaliq smiled into her eyes. "He is obviously his father's son," he whispered against her mouth. They kissed, tongues intertwining and dancing together as they did.

He put her back against the stone wall of the tub and began to piston her. As he did the tub suddenly emptied and instantly refilled with barely warm water that was scented with an aroma that filled them both with hot lust. It permeated the entire chamber. They instantly found pleasures that left them weak but still hungry with their need.

Together they stepped up from the tub. When they were clear of it the round stone cover slid back into place, and before the fire a towel rack filled with warm towels now appeared. They dried each other even as their need grew stronger and stronger. They fell upon the bed together, Kaliq burying his dark head between her soft white thighs as he peeled her nether lips apart, his tongue seeking for the jewel of her sex. Finding it, he used the tip of his tongue to tease and stroke it, drinking her juices which flowed copiously for him, and him alone.

Lara cried out with the pleasure he was offering her. "You are my love, my life, Kaliq of the Shadows," she gasped. Her fingers twined themselves in his damp dark hair.

He drew himself up lying half atop her, kissing her deeply so that she tasted herself on his foraging tongue. He stroked her face with one hand while his other caressed one of her breasts, bending to take the nipple into his mouth. Then he sucked upon it, and Lara cried out again. His teeth grazed the sensitive flesh until it burned. She pulled at him, forcing herself beneath him, catching his great cock in her hands, drawing it to her. *Faerie witch!* he murmured silently. *You are so greedy as always.*

Come into me, my lord, and take your pleasure of me. We have the whole night.

We have an eternity, he replied. *How is it I never tire of you, Lara, my love?* And then he slowly pushed himself into her. One hand smoothing back the hair from her face that he might watch as they shared of themselves with each other. He felt a jolt of pure passion as her faerie green eyes met his bright blue ones.

I love you, Kaliq, and I am never bored telling you so.

I love you, Lara, he replied. *And I never grow bored hearing you say it.*

He began to thrust back and forth within her, and soon they were both crying out with their pleasure. Finally they slept only to awaken in the predawn to make love again. They had been together for the majority of her life in one way or another. He had never interfered with her when she had wed, waiting patiently for the day when she would be his forever. He was not afraid of her independence or determination. Kaliq of the Shadows understood Lara better than she even understood herself. But he would not reveal that knowledge lest it interfere with her. They had been created for one another by a power far greater than all of their magic put together. He had had to wait for her. But he had done it with good grace.

OVER THE NEXT FEW MONTHS Kaliq and Lara tutored their grandson, Biton, and the two granddaughters who showed great promise for magic, Rima and Abella. Biton learned because he felt he should as his father's heir. He was the youngest of Dillon and Cinnia's children. Rima and Abella pursued their studies with great seriousness. They knew that their grandparents would eventually be leaving Belmair, and when they went the great magic would go with them. So they studied hard to learn all they could. If they were ever needed one day, Rima and Abella would be ready.

Ilona and her Forest Faeries settled into their new home in the Beltran province of Belmair. Thanos was delighted with the age of the forest, and the vast variety of trees there. He was already busily working at cataloging them.

And then one day as Spring arrived Ilona came to see her daughter. "We must talk," the queen of the Forest Faeries said to Lara. "It is Marzina."

"Is she all right?" Lara asked anxiously.

"Nay, I do not think she is," Ilona said. "She is restless, and seems to have no purpose here at all. She has reconstructed Fairevue on the side of a mountain, but she is bored, Lara. I cannot sugarcoat it. She misses Hetar."

"Hetar is lost," Lara said stonily. "Surely there is something for Marzina to do, Mother. What did she do in Hetar?"

"She visited The City regularly. She enjoyed pretending to be a Pleasure Woman now and again. She became friends with Maeve Scarlet's granddaughter," Ilona said.

"I did not know," Lara replied. "Marzina never told me."

"She did not tell you because she was afraid you would disapprove of her harmless little amusements," Ilona responded. Then she sighed. "She misses Kolgrim."

Lara shuddered. "That evil spawn I gave birth to has surely bewitched Marzina!" she cried angrily. "He wants her back, but I cannot let her go, Mother!"

"Do you mean to take her with you when you and Kaliq ride out into the Cosmos?" Ilona asked quietly.

"Nay! She was suppose to remain here on Belmair with you," Lara replied.

"She is not happy here," Ilona said.

"She is safe here!" Lara retorted.

"Let Kaliq speak with her," Ilona suggested. "She has always respected him."

Lara agreed. "Ask my daughter to come and visit me," she said. "I sense the time is drawing near for us to depart Belmair. While it has been a glorious interlude I feel the tug of my destiny as I have never before felt it, Mother."

Ilona nodded. "Aye, I am beginning to see it hovering around your head like a crown. I will tell Marzina to come and see you soon." The Queen of the Forest Faeries stood up and, bending down, kissed Lara's cheek. "Farewell, my daughter. I do not think I will see you again." She drew Lara up and hugged her hard. "You were crowned by destiny even before your conception, Lara. You have matured into an amazing, powerful faerie woman. More formidable than even your mother. I am proud of you. John Swiftsword would be proud of his daughter, too." Ilona kissed Lara on both cheeks this time. She tipped her daughter's face up smiling into the eyes so like her own. *Remember us, my darling. Goodbye!* And then she was gone in her burst of violet smoke.

Lara was crying when Kaliq found her. She told him what had brought her mother to see her, and of how Ilona had bid her a final farewell.

"Aye," Kaliq agreed. "It is time, but then you knew that."

"But you must speak with Marzina," Lara said.

"I will," he promised her, kissing away her tears.

Marzina came, and together she and Kaliq walked out into the spring gardens.

"You know what I must do, don't you?" Marzina said to him. Kaliq nodded. "I do."

"This is my fate. It is my destiny, Kaliq. I am not wrong, am I?" Marzina asked.

"Nay, you are not," the Shadow Prince told her. "You father conceived you on your mother through deception. He was angry, hurt and disappointed. Even a Twilight Lord has feelings, it seems, Marzina. When we manipulated the Book of Rule to make your mother the female with whom he would mate we did not consider those feelings or that he might actually fall in love with Lara. But he did. His actions were a desperate attempt to get her back. But Lara loved Magnus Hauk, and she was of the light. The Dark Lands could not contain her. When your birth followed immediately upon that of Taj Hauk, believed to be your twin brother, Lara, after some initial resistance, accepted you, and she has loved you ever since."

"She did not want me?" This was something Marzina had never known.

"She was shocked and startled by your birth," Kaliq explained, "and Lara realized immediately who your father must be. She was afraid at first that you would be evil as your sire was evil. She quickly understood that if you did not get all the love that a helpless infant should have you would be harmed. You have never disappointed her, Marzina. Your dark side reveals itself only in your recklessness. What you must do, however, is not reckless, though some will say it is. What you are going to do is brave, *my daughter.*"

His two words honored her. Her eyes moistened. "I cannot tell her," Marzina said.

He understood. "Just visit with her, and then bid her farewell. We go soon and shall not return to this part of the Cosmos again. I am cloaking Belmair to protect it."

"Aye, you should. My brother is a greedy creature, Kaliq," Marzina remarked.

Kaliq chuckled. Then he grew serious. "Never believe that you know him well, Marzina," he advised her.

Marzina shook her head. "Nay, my lord, I will not."

"Go and see your mother now. When she asks if we have spoken, say yes. Whatever else you say to her is your concern." He brushed the single tear from her cheek.

Marzina's violet eyes met those of the Shadow Prince in complete understanding. She stood when he did, and put her arms about him, standing on her toes to kiss his cheek. "Thank you, Kaliq of the Shadows, for your friendship and guidance." Then, turning, she went off to find her mother.

Seeing her daughter entering Nidhug's hall, Lara arose and went to greet her. "I am so glad you have come," she said. "Our time here grows short."

"So said Grandmother. I have come to say my farewells. Did I tell you, Mother? My new Fairevue has been magically constructed to exactly match my old home on Hetar. That way my servants and I had to change nothing. It is all as before, and the view is even lovelier than Hetar. The sky is a perfect shade of blue, and I see nothing but sky and trees from my house. Aren't Belmair's twin moons glorious?"

"Have you spoken with Kaliq, Marzina?" Lara asked her daughter, getting directly to the point. "His wisdom is great. I hope you heed it."

"I have always listened to Kaliq, and even heeded him when I thought I knew better, which of course I didn't," Marzina said with a smile.

"I know you are fond of Kolgrim," Lara said. "You are of a similar age. He is charming and fascinating. He is powerful. Your mortal siblings are gone, but Dillon is your older brother.

He is your kinsman, too. You have your grandmother, your uncle, Nidhug, Parvanah. You will not be lonely here. And they are of the light, Marzina. You need this light to overcome your father's blood."

Lara's voice was loving, but Marzina could hear the desperate edge in it. It saddened her, but she forced back the very unfaerie-like emotion. "Mother, I know I have everything I need here on Belmair," she said. "You must concentrate upon what lies ahead for you and Kaliq. Do not fear for me. I know what Kolgrim is. I always have, despite his charm and fascination." She laughed. "I believe that is why he actually likes me. I am the one creature who knows who he really is."

"If that is so then surely Kolgrim fears you, as well, Marzina, which makes him doubly dangerous toward you. Kaliq will wrap Belmair in a protective cloak shortly, and all here will be safe for eternity. Knowing you are here with your kinfolk is a relief."

Marzina kissed her mother's cheek. "It is the cloak of your love wrapped about me, Mother, from wherever you may be that will always keep me safe," she said. "It has always been there, and it will always be there for me. Now I must go, for if I remain I will become weepy." Marzina's image began to shimmer with light. *You will be in my heart forever, Mother. Farewell!* And then she was gone in her familiar haze of pale violet smoke, the tinkling of bells that had so often been associated with her sounding in Lara's ears as the youngest of her children disappeared from her sight.

Kaliq was by her side. *It is time, my love,* he said to her.

I know, Lara responded, and she did. *It was time.*

We will escort you for a short distance, Nidhug said to them.

They walked from the hall out into the garden that separated the two castles. There Dillon, Cinnia and their seven children, who had come to bid them their farewells, were assembled. Dasras stood patiently waiting for them.

"I leave Verica with you for good," Lara said of her staff of wisdom. "Your grandmother gave him to me long ago. Listen to his counsel for it is wise, Dillon, my firstborn." She kissed his cheeks, and he hugged her so hard Lara almost lost her breath. "Don't you dare cry!" she cautioned him for she herself was near tears. She had not thought it would be so hard to depart them all when her destiny called. Lara pulled quickly away from Dillon to kiss her daughter-in-law, Cinnia. Then she bade each of their seven children goodbye. But when she came to their third-born daughter, Gormangabis, she stopped, unbuckled her sword and scabbard and handed them to the surprised girl. "Did you think no one knew your talent for weaponry, especially swords, descendant of Swiftsword," Lara said with a smile. "Where I go I have no need for Andraste, but one day you will. You will venture forth and she will be your companion. Andraste, old friend and companion, greet your new mistress!"

I greet Gormangabis, daughter of Dillon, granddaughter of Lara, great-grandchild of Swiftsword as my new mistress, Andraste said in her deep singsong voice. But then the head of the sword turned back to Lara. *Farewell, Lara, daughter of Swiftsword and Ilona. We have fought well together. I will not ever forget you. Go always in the light!*

I will, Andraste, Lara said, realizing she would miss Andraste, too.

Dasras pawed the ground snorting impatiently. Laughing, Kaliq and Lara mounted him. She leaned forward, taking the stallion's reins firmly in her hands, Kaliq behind, a single arm about her. Then Dasras began to move, slowly at first, slipping into a canter and then a gallop as his beautiful wings unfolded and he rose into the blue skies of Belmair.

On either side of him for a brief time two dragons flew. The larger had iridescent scales of sea-blue and spring-green. Its crest was purple and gold. Its wings gold, its eyes dark with swirls of gold-and-silver edged with thick purple eyelashes. Its claws were painted a vivid shade of pink. Its companion was just slightly less showy as would befit the mate of the Great Dragon of Belmair, with scales of sky-blue and gold and silvery gold wings. And then the two dragons hovered for a long moment as Dasras climbed higher and higher into the skies of Belmair. Their dragon voices called out in unison *Go always in the light, Lara and Kaliq of the Shadows!* Then the two dragons dove back down from the skies to return to Belmair.

"Dasras, stop for a moment, and turn," Kaliq said. Certain that Nidhug and Cirillo had reached the blue of Belmair's skies once again, he spoke the spell that would keep Belmair safe from predators for all time. *Belmair from darkness shall be wary. Kept safe by Shadow and by Faerie. No eye, be it magic or mortal, shall see. For it is not where it should be. The memory of Belmair shall go to keep it safe from dark and foe.*

"'Tis a wonderful spell," Lara said as she looked to where the bright star that had been Belmair had been. There was nothing there now to her eye, but Lara knew Dillon's world still existed, and on it all that had been good in Hetar. She turned her head to look at Kaliq. "Are we ready now?" she asked him.

"Gallop on, Dasras!" Kaliq called to the stallion, who once again moved forward.

To their right Lara could see the world of Hetar now cloaked in a dun-colored atmosphere of gloom and darkness. "Look, Kaliq!" she said. "Our beautiful Hetar is truly gone now. The darkness has encompassed it, and Kolgrim rules." But then something caught Lara's eyes. A tiny pin spot of blinding, flickering light that darted across Hetar. She looked at it, and then with certainty gave a pained cry. *Marzina! Kaliq, it is Marzina! I am certain of it! She has returned to Hetar despite all that we said to her! This is surely the most reckless and foolish action she has ever taken!*

Nay, my love, he said in a calming voice. *From the moment she was born it was decided that when the day came that the darkness finally claimed Hetar, the daughter Kol forced upon you, a child of both the light and the dark, would remain behind to keep the hope alive that one day the light would return to Hetar. Marzina's destiny is less complicated than yours, Lara, but you can have faith that your daughter will not fail,* Kaliq said. *It will not be easy, and it will take time to accomplish. But Marzina is strong for she is your daughter. You, your mother and I have taught her well. She knows her brother better than any of us. Marzina made her choice to choose the light long ago.*

Lara was weeping. *She is so young a faerie, and Kolgrim so devious.*

Kolgrim is a creature of tradition. He cannot kill Marzina for he shares blood with her on both sides of their lineage. And he will never catch her. I have made certain of that. It was little enough, considering what she must do, Kaliq said. Reaching around her, he took the reins from her hands, his booted heels encouraging Dasras forward once again. *Marzina will survive, and the light will return again.*

Then Dasras leapt forward into the velvet dark Cosmos. Quickly Hetar disappeared from their sight. Around them were twinkling stars and great swirls of color in which there were stars now being born. They rode for what seemed hours, and suddenly Lara saw a smooth dark space ahead of them. She knew what she wanted to do, but she wasn't quite certain how.

Ah, Kaliq said, *you know you have arrived at the point of your destiny, my love.*

Aye, I do, but I don't know how to accomplish what I must, Kaliq, Lara said.

We must dismount, he said to her, and sliding off the horse's back, he helped her down. They now spoke only their silent language so as not to disturb the Cosmos.

It never occurred to Lara that they would fall. If the Cosmos would hold Dasras up it would certainly hold them. *It is for us both to do,* Lara said, smiling at him.

He nodded, and took her into his arms. *Think everything you would want it to be, and I shall do the same,* Kaliq told her.

Lara nodded. Her lips met his in a tender kiss, and she felt them beginning to spin faster and faster and faster. For a century or two they rotated like this in the Cosmos while about them a new world began to form. Its shape was round, and at first it was covered in water and mist. But then gradually it became more visible to the eye. Finally Lara and Kaliq emerged from the center of the sphere, sealing their exit carefully. They stepped out into the Cosmos again. A bright yellow star shone above them illuminating the new world, and there were several companion worlds revolving about the same star.

Those weren't here when we came, Lara noted.

They are creations of my fellow Shadow Princes, Kaliq told her. *They but awaited your decision as to where to place them. We call these worlds planets although only the one you and I have created is habitable for mortals right now. Eventually some of the others will be, but not for thousands of years.*

We have created no mortals for our world, Lara said.

They will come in their time, my love, he explained. *But not quite yet. There but remains one thing to do, and in this matter I shall defer to you, Lara, my love. You must name this world for us.*

Lara thought for a small time, and then she smiled. *Let us call it Earth,* she said.

And let us hope that the mortals who one day inhabit it will do better than those we left behind on Hetar, Kaliq responded.

Agreed! Lara replied.

How did you decide to name it Earth? Kaliq asked her curiously.

I simply used the same letters that make up Hetar and Terah, Lara answered.

'Tis clever, but then you were always the most clever faerie woman, Kaliq said as, mounting Dasras, he drew Lara up before him, kissing her mouth a deep and passionate kiss as he did so. *Are you ready, my love?* he asked her as faerie green eyes met bright blue ones.

Lara smiled a blinding smile of happiness at him. Her destiny had been met. A blue-and-green Earth now hung in the Cosmos spinning about the bright yellow star that would nurture and warm it forever. A new and hopefully safer refuge for a better race of mortals one day. An eternity lay ahead for her, and for Kaliq. Together, as it had always been meant to be. *I am ready!* she said.

And with a toss of his proud head Dasras, the great white stallion, galloped off through the stars and across the Cosmos toward Forever, a faerie woman and a Shadow Prince upon his back.